ACCLAIM FOR ANDY McNAB'S THRILLERS

FEATURING NICK STONE

FIREWALL

"A sweet one. . . . Throat-clutching, authentic scenarios, spectacular precision. . . . McNab writes like a dream. . . . Death zings its old sweet song as slugs sing off your Kevlar."

—*Kirkus Reviews*

"In many ways, Stone is the perfect thriller hero: someone strong enough to absorb punishment, smart enough to game-plan the details of the job and just enough of a line soldier not to ask too many questions. . . . In this genre, all plans are made to fail, except perhaps McNab's plan to take the thriller world by storm."

—*Publishers Weekly*

"Makes Clancy look like a Sunday-school teacher who moonlights as an adventure writer. . . . Explodes like a stun grenade. McNab . . . has used his exciting SAS background to spin a story that's as real a fiction can be. . . . *Firewall* has it all: suspense, high adventure, gripping story. . . . Couldn't put the sucker down."

—Col. David H. Hackworth,
New York Times bestselling author of *Brave Men*

CRISIS FOUR

"McNab adeptly puts the reader right in the thick of things, providing a wealth of detail about secret-service strategy and allowing us inside Stone's head as he plots every decision."

—*Booklist*

"Full of the kind of grit that gets under the fingernails . . . boasts the operational details of a *Rogue Warrior* escapade without the overdose of testosterone."

—*Publishers Weekly* (starred review)

"McNab's great asset is that the heart of his fiction is not fiction: other thriller writers do their research, but he has actually been there."

—*Sunday Times* (London)

"McNab is a terrific novelist. When it comes to thrills, he's Forsyth class."

—*Mail on Sunday* (London)

"Addictive. . . . Awash with wild action and spellbinding tradecraft."

—*Daily Telegraph* (London)

REMOTE CONTROL

"One of the most gripping reads of recent years."

—*Maxim*

"Superb."

—Stephen Coonts

"Bristles with authenticity."

—*The Times* (London)

"Action-packed and authentic in every detail, [he] gives us a hero who's at least as scary as the villains. Andy McNab is the real deal and a rare commodity— a hard guy who knows how to write."

—John Case, author of the *New York Times* bestseller *The Genesis Code*

"In thrillers, nothing beats a good chase and this one is fast and furious. A high-octane adventure."

—*Sunday Times* (London)

"The fiction is as pulse-racing as the reality."

—*Mail on Sunday* (London)

ALSO BY ANDY MCNAB

Nonfiction
Bravo Two Zero
Immediate Action

Fiction
Remote Control
Crisis Four
Firewall

Last Light

Andy McNab

POCKET BOOKS

New York   London   Toronto   Sydney   Singapore

POCKET BOOKS, a division of Simon & Schuster, Inc.
1230 Avenue of the Americas, New York, NY 10020

Copyright © 2001 by Andy McNab

Originally published in Great Britain in 2001 by Bantam Press

ISBN: 0-7434-0629-X

First Pocket Books paperback printing March 2003

10 9 8 7 6 5 4 3 2 1

POCKET and colophon are registered trademarks of
Simon & Schuster, Inc.

For information regarding special discounts for bulk
purchases, please contact Simon & Schuster Special Sales at
1-800-456-6798 or business@simonandschuster.com

Cover design by Carlos Beltran

Printed in the U.S.A.

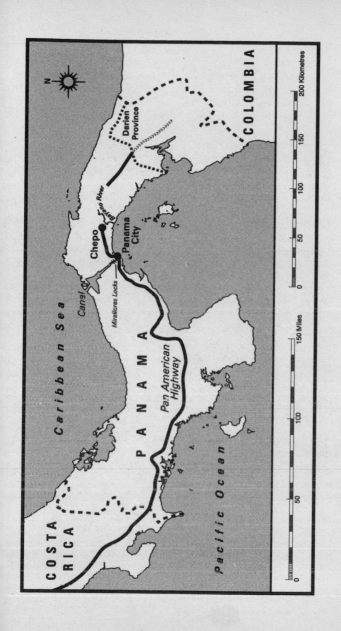

Last
Light

1

I didn't know who we were going to kill—just that he or she would be among the crowd munching canapés and sipping champagne on the terrace of the Houses of Parliament at three P.M., and that the Yes Man would identify the target by placing his hand on their left shoulder when he greeted them.

I'd done some weird stuff over the years, but this job was scaring me. In less than ninety minutes, I was going to be shitting on my own doorstep big-time. I only hoped the Firm knew what it was doing, because I wasn't too sure that I did.

As I looked down yet again at the clear plastic lunchbox on the desk in front of me, three flashlight bulbs sticking out of holes I'd burned in the lid stared back up. None of them was illuminated; the three snipers were still not in position.

Everything about this job was wrong. We'd been given the wrong weapons. We were in the wrong place. And there just hadn't been enough time to plan and prepare.

I stared through the net curtains across the boat-filled river. The Houses of Parliament were some 350 yards away to my half left. The office I'd broken into was on the top floor of County Hall, the former Greater London Council building. Now redeveloped into offices, hotels, and tourist attractions, it over-looked the Thames from the south side. I was feeling rather grand sitting behind a highly polished, dark wood desk, as I looked out at the killing ground.

Parliament's terrace spanned the whole of its river frontage. Two prefabricated pavilions with candy-striped roofs had been erected at the far left end, for use throughout the summer months. Part of the ter-race, I'd learned from their website, was for Mem-bers of the House of Lords, and part for the House of Commons. The public were not admitted unless they were with an MP or lord, so this was probably the nearest I was ever going to get.

The Department of Trade and Industry's guests today were a group of about thirty businessmen, plus staff and some family, from Central and South Amer-ica. Maybe the DTI was trying to curry a bit of favor and sell them a power station or two. Who cared? All I knew was that one of them would be getting dropped somewhere between the creampuffs and the éclairs.

Directly below me, and five stories down, Albert Embankment was thronged with hot-dog vendors and stalls selling plastic policemen's helmets and post-cards of Big Ben to people lining up for the Ferris wheel, or just enjoying a lazy Sunday afternoon. A sightseeing boat packed with tourists passed under Westminster Bridge. I could hear a bored voice telling the story of Guy Fawkes' plot to blow up Parliament over a crackly PA system.

It was the end of summer vacation and another news-starved week, so Rupert Murdoch and the tabloids were going to be ever so pleased with what I was about to do: the biggest explosion in London this year, and right in the heart of Westminster. With the added bonus of a major shooting incident, it would probably put their ratings right off the chart. Unfortunately, good news for them was bad for me. SB (Special Branch) were going to be working their asses off to find out who'd pressed the button, and they were the best in the world at this sort of thing. They'd been formed to stop the IRA carrying out exactly the kind of stunt I was about to pull.

Three lightbulbs were still unlit. I wasn't panicking, just concerned.

At either end of the row of lights was a white, rectangular bell-push from a door chime set, glued in position with the wires curling into the box. The one on the left was covered with the top from a can of shaving cream. It was the detonation pressel for the device that I'd set up as a diversion. The device was basically a black powder charge, designed to give off a big enough bang to grab London's attention but not to kill anyone. There would be some damage, there'd be the odd cut or bruise, but there shouldn't be any fatalities. The shaving cream top was there because I didn't want to detonate it by accident. The pressel on the right was exposed. This was the one that would initiate the shoot.

Next to the box I had a set of binos (binoculars) mounted on a mini-tripod and trained on the killing ground. I was going to need them to watch the Yes Man as he moved about the crowd and ID'd the target.

The lunchbox contained a big, green, square lithium battery, and a mess of wires and circuit boards. I'd never tried to make things look neat; I just wanted them to work. Two purple plastic-coated wire antennas stuck out of the rear of the box, trailed along the desk, over the windowsill I'd pushed it up against, then dangled down the outside wall. I had the window closed down on them to cut out as much noise as possible.

The loudest sound in the room was my breathing, which started to quicken as the witching hour got closer. It was only outdone by the occasional scream of delight from a tourist at ground level or a particularly loud PA system from the river.

All I could do was wait. I crossed my arms on the desk, rested my head on them, and stared at the bulbs that were now level with my eyes, willing them to start flashing.

I was shaken out of my trance as Big Ben struck two.

I knew the snipers wouldn't move into their fire positions until the last moment so that they didn't expose themselves longer than necessary, but I really wanted those lights to start flashing at me.

For about the millionth time in the past twenty minutes I pushed down on the uncovered pressel, resting the side of my head on my forearm to look inside the box, like a kid wondering what his mom had made him for lunch. A small bulb, nestled among the mass of wires, lit up with the current generated by my send pressel. I wished now that I'd burnt another hole in the lid for the bulb inside to join the others—but at the time I couldn't be bothered. I released it and pressed again. The same thing happened. The device was working. But what about the other three that I'd built for the snipers? I'd just have to wait and see.

The other thing I did for the millionth time was wonder why I couldn't just say no to this stuff. Apart from the fact that I was soft in the head, the answer was the same as always: it was the only thing I knew. I knew it, the Firm knew it. They also knew that I was desperate for cash again.

If I was truthful with myself, which I found pretty hard, there was another, much deeper reason. I got my eyes level with the bulbs once more and took a deep breath. I'd learned a few things since attending the clinic with Kelly.

Even at school there was desperation in me to be part of something—whether it was joining a wood-working group, or a gang that used to rob the Jewish kids of the dinner money they'd wrapped in hankies so we couldn't hear it rattle in their pockets as they walked past. But it never worked. That feeling of belonging only happened once I joined the Army. And now? I just couldn't seem to shake it off.

At last. The middle bulb, Sniper Two's, gave five deliberate, one-second pulses.

I put my thumb on the send pressel and, after a nanosecond to check I wasn't about to blow up London in my excitement, I depressed it three times in exactly the same rhythm, to say that I had received the signal, checking each time that the white circuit-test bulb inside the box lit up.

I got three flashes back immediately from the middle bulb. Good news. Sniper Two was in position, ready to fire, and we had comms (communications). All I needed now was One and Three, and I'd be cooking with gas.

I'd put everything these snipers needed to know—where to be, how to get there, what to do once in position, and, more importantly for them, how to get away afterward—with the weapons and equipment in their individual DLBs (dead letter boxes). All they had to do was read the orders, check the gear, and get on with the shoot. The three had different fire positions, each unknown to the others. None of them had met or even seen each other, and they hadn't met me. That's how these things are done: OPSEC (operational security). You only know what you need to.

I'd had an extremely busy ten nights of CTRs (close target reconnaissance, or recces) to find suitable fire positions in the hospital grounds on this side of the river and directly opposite the killing ground. Then, by day, I'd made the keys for the snipers to gain access to their positions, prepared the equipment they would need, then loaded the DLBs. Two hardware stores and a remote-control model shop in Camden Town had made a fortune out of me once I'd hit ATMs with my new Royal Bank of Scotland Visa card under my new cover for this job, Nick Somerhurst.

The only aspect of the business I was totally happy about was OPSEC. It was so tight that the Yes Man had briefed me personally.

Tucked in a very smart leather attaché case, he had a buff folder with black boxes stamped on the outside for people to sign and date as they authorized its contents. No one had signed any of them, and there was no yellow card attached to signify it was an accountable document. Things like that always worried me: I knew it meant a shitload of trouble.

As we drove along Chelsea Embankment toward Parliament in the back of a Previa MPV with darkened windows, the Yes Man had pulled two pages of printed legal-size paper from the folder and started to brief me. Annoyingly, I couldn't quite read his notes from where I was sitting.

I didn't like the condescending jerk one bit as he put on his best I-have-been-to-university-but-I'm-still-working-class voice to tell me I was "special" and "the only one capable." Things didn't improve when he stressed that no one in government knew of this job, and only two in the Firm: "C," the boss of SIS (Secret Intelligence Service), and the Director of Security and Public Affairs, effectively his number two.

"And, of course," he said with a smile, "the three of us."

The driver, whose thick blond side-parted hair made him look like Robert Redford when he was young enough to be the Sundance Kid, glanced in the rearview mirror and I caught his eye for a second before he concentrated once more on the traffic, fighting for position around Parliament Square. Both of them must have sensed I wasn't the happiest camper in town. The nicer people were to me, the more suspicious of their motives I became. But, the Yes Man said, I wasn't to worry. SIS could carry out assassinations at the express request of the Foreign Minister.

"But you just said only five of us know about this. And this is the U.K. It's not a Foreign Office matter."

His smile confirmed what I already knew. "Ah, Nick, we don't want to bother anyone with minor details. After all, they may not really want to know."

With an even bigger smile he added that should any part of the operation go wrong, no one would be held ultimately responsible. The Service would, as always, hide behind the Official Secrets Act or, if things got difficult, a Public Interest Immunity Certificate. So everything was quite all right, and I'd be protected. I mustn't forget, he said, that I was part of the team. And that was when I really started to worry.

It was blindingly obvious to me that the reason no one knew about this operation was because no one in their right mind would sanction it, and no one in their right mind would take the job on. Maybe that was why I'd been picked. Then, as now, I comforted myself with the thought that at least the money was good. Well, sort of. But I was desperate for the eighty grand on offer, forty now in two very large brown Jiffy envelopes, and the rest afterward. That was how

I justified saying yes to something I just knew was going to be a nightmare.

We were now on the approach road to Westminster Bridge with Big Ben and Parliament to my right. On the other side of the river I could see the County Hall building and to the left of that, the London Eye, the wheel turning so slowly it looked as if it wasn't moving at all.

"You should get out here, Stone. Have a look around."

With that, the Sundance Kid curbed the Previa, and irate motorists behind hit their horns as they tried to maneuver around us. I slid the door back and stepped out to the deafening sounds of jackhammers and revving engines. The Yes Man leaned forward in his seat and took the door handle. "Call in for what you need, and where you want the other three to collect their furnishings."

With that, the door slid shut and Sundance cut in front of a bus to get back in the traffic stream heading south across the river. A van driver gave me the finger as he put his foot down to make up that forty seconds he'd been delayed.

As I sat at the desk waiting for the other two bulbs to illuminate, I concentrated hard on that eighty grand. I didn't think I'd ever needed it so badly. The snipers were probably getting at least three times as much as I was but, then, I wasn't as good as they were at what they did. These people were as committed to their craft as Olympic athletes. I'd met one or two in the past when I, too, thought of going that route, but decided against it; professional snipers struck me as weird. They lived on a planet where everything was taken seriously, from politics to buying ice cream. They worshipped at the church of one round, one kill. No, sniping might pay well, but I didn't think I belonged there. And, besides, I now found bullet trajectory and the finer points of wind adjustment pretty boring after talking about them for half an hour, let alone my entire life.

From the moment the Yes Man dropped me off with my two Jiffy envelopes, I'd started protecting myself far more than I normally would. I knew that if I got caught by Special Branch the Firm would deny me, and that was part and parcel of being a K, or deniable operator. But there was more to it this time. The stuff I did normally didn't happen in the U.K., and no way would anyone in their right mind give this the go. Everything felt wrong, and the Yes Man would never want to be on the losing side. He'd knife his own grandmother if it meant promotion; in fact, since he took over the Ks Desk from Colonel Lynn, he was so far up C's ass he could have flossed his teeth. If things didn't go according to plan, and even if I did evade SB, he wouldn't hesitate to fuck me over if it meant he could take any credit and pass on any blame.

I needed a safety blanket, so I started by noting down the serial numbers of all three snipers' weapons before grinding them out. Then I took Polaroids of all the equipment, plus the three firing positions during the CTRs. I'd given the snipers photographs in their orders, and I kept a set myself. I had a full pictorial story of the job, together with photocopies of each set of sniper's orders. It all went into a bag in Left Luggage at Waterloo Station, along with everything else I owned: a pair of jeans, socks, underwear, toilet kit, and two fleece jackets.

After loading the three snipers' DLBs, I should have left them alone—but I didn't. Instead I put in an OP (observation post) on Sniper Two's dead letter box, which was just outside the market town of Thetford in Norfolk. There was no particular reason for picking Sniper Two's to OP, except that it was the nearest of the three to London.

The other two were both miles away: in the Peak District and on Bodmin Moor. All three had been chosen in uninhabited areas so that once they'd gotten the weapons, they could zero them to make sure that the optic sight was correctly aligned to the barrel so that a round hit the target precisely at a given distance. The rest—judging the wind, taking leads (aiming ahead of moving targets), and working out distance—is part of the sniper's art, but first the weapon sight and rounds need to be as one. How they did that, and where they did that within the area, was up to them. They were getting more than enough cash to make those decisions themselves.

Inside the DLB, a 45-gallon oil drum, was a large black Puma tennis bag that held everything needed for the shoot and was totally sterile of me: no fingerprints, certainly no DNA. Nothing from my body had made contact with this gear. Dressed like a technician in a chemical warfare lab, I had prepared, cleaned, and wiped everything down so many times it was a wonder there was any Parkerization (protective paint) left on the barrels.

Jammed into a Gore-Tex bivouac bag and dug in among the ferns in miserable drizzling rain, I had waited for Sniper Two to arrive. I knew that all three would be extremely cautious when they made their approach to lift the DLBs, carrying out their tradecraft to the letter to ensure they weren't followed or walking into a trap. That was why I had to keep my distance: sixty-nine yards to be exact, which in turn had meant choosing a telephoto lens on my Nikon for more photographic evidence of this job, wrapped in a sweatshirt to dampen the rewind noise, and shoved into a garbage bag so that just the lens and viewfinder were exposed to the drizzle.

I waited, tossing back Mars bars and water and just hoping Sniper Two didn't choose to unload it at night.

In the end it was just over thirty boring and very wet hours before Sniper Two started to move in on the DLB. At least it was daylight. I watched the hooded figure check the immediate area around a collection of old, rusty farm machinery and oil drums.

It edged forward like a wet and cautious cat. I brought up the telephoto lens. Tapered blue jeans, brown cross-trainers, three-quarter-length beige waterproof jacket. The hood had a sewn-in peak, and I could see the label on the left breast pocket: L.L. Bean. I'd never seen one of their shops outside the U.S.

What I'd also never seen outside the U.S. was a woman sniper. She was maybe early thirties, slim, average height, with brown hair poking out of the sides of the hood. She was neither attractive nor unattractive, just normal-looking, more like a young mother than a professional killer. She reached the oil drums, and carefully checked inside hers to make sure it wasn't booby-trapped. I couldn't help wondering why a woman would take up this line of work. What did her kids think she did for a living? Work at the cosmetics counter in Sears, and get dragged away a couple of times a year for week-long eyeliner seminars?

She'd been happy with what she saw inside the drum. Her arms went inside very quickly and lifted out the bag. She turned in my direction, taking the weight of it in both hands, and threw it over her right shoulder. I hit the shutter release and the camera whirred. Within seconds she'd melted once more into the trees and tall ferns; like a cat, she'd probably find a place to hide now and check out the spoils.

Sniping does not simply mean being a fantastic marksman. Just as important are the fieldcraft skills—stalking, judging distance, observation, camouflage and concealment—and judging by the way she lifted the DLB and got back into cover, I bet she'd won gold stars in all of those disciplines.

While in the Army I had spent two years as a sniper, in a Royal Green Jacket rifle company. I was as keen as anything: it had something to do with being left alone just to get on with it with your sniper partner. I learned a lot and was a good shot, but I didn't have the passion required to make it a life's vocation.

I was still staring at the three bulbs, waiting for One and Three to sign in. A helicopter clattered overhead, following the riverbank on the north side, and I had to look up to satisfy myself that it wasn't looking for me. My paranoia was working overtime. For a moment I thought that it had found the explosive device I'd placed on the roof of the Royal Horseguards Hotel in Whitehall the night before. The hotel was just out of sight, behind the MoD (Ministry of Defense) main building across the Thames to my half right. Seeing the three service flags fluttering on the roof of the massive light-colored stone cube prompted me to check something else for the millionth time.

Keeping the row of lightbulbs in my peripheral vision, I looked down at the river to check the wind indicators.

In urban areas the wind can move in different directions, at different levels, and in different strengths, depending on the buildings it has to get around. Sometimes streets become wind tunnels, redirecting and momentarily strengthening the gusts. Indicators were therefore needed at different levels around the killing area, so the snipers could compensate by adjusting their sights. The wind can make an immense difference to where a round hits because it simply blows it off course.

Flags are really useful, and there were more around here than at a UN summit. On the water there were plenty of boats moored with pennants at the stern. Higher up, on both ends of Westminster Bridge, there were the tourist stalls, selling plastic Union Jacks and Manchester United streamers. The snipers would use all of these, and they would know where to look because I'd keyed them onto the maps supplied in the DLB. The wind condition at river level was good, just a hint of a breeze.

My eyes caught movement in the killing ground. I felt my face flush and my heart rate quicken. Shit, this shouldn't be kicking off yet.

I had a grandstand view of the terrace, and the times-twelve magnification of the binos made me feel as if I were almost standing on it. I checked it out with one eye on the binos, the other ready to pick up any flashes from the bulbs.

A feeling of relief flooded through me. Catering staff. They were streaming in and out of the covered pavilions to the left of the killing ground, busy in their black-and-white uniforms, laying out ashtrays and placing bowls of nuts and nibbles on square wooden tables. A stressed-looking older guy in a gray, double-breasted suit stalked around behind them, waving his arms like a conductor at the symphony.

I followed the line of the terrace and spotted a photographer on one of the wooden benches. He had two cameras by his side and smoked contentedly as he watched the commotion, a big smile on his face.

I went back to the conductor. He looked up at Big Ben, checked his watch, then clapped his hands. He was as worried about the deadline as I was. At least the weather was on our side. Taking the shot through one of the pavilion windows would have made things even more difficult than they already were.

The three sniper positions were all on my side of the river; three trailers on the grounds of St. Thomas's Hospital, directly opposite the killing ground. Three different positions gave three different angles of fire, and therefore three different chances of getting a round into the target.

The distance between the first and third sniper was about ninety yards, and they'd be shooting over a distance of between 330 and 380 yards, depending on their position in the lineup. Being one floor up, the killing ground was below them, at an angle of about forty-five degrees. It would be just good enough to see the target from the stomach up if it was sitting down, and from about thigh up when standing, since a stone wall about a yard high ran the length of the terrace to stop MPs and lords falling into the Thames when they'd had a drink or two.

The riverbank in front of their positions was tree-lined, which provided some cover, but also obstructed their line of sight into the killing ground. These things are nearly always a matter of compromise; there is rarely a perfect option.

This would be the first time the snipers had ever been to the fire position, and it would also be the last. Soon after the shoot they'd be heading for Paris, Lille, or Brussels on Eurostar trains, which left from Waterloo Station just ten minutes' walk away. They'd be knocking back a celebratory glass of wine in the Channel tunnel well before the full extent of what they'd done had dawned on Special Branch and the news networks.

2

Once I'd satisfied myself that the only activity in the killing ground came from harassed catering staff, I got back to watching the three bulbs. Snipers One and Three should have signed on by now. I was well past concerned, and not too far short of worried.

I thought about Sniper Two. She would have moved cautiously into the fire position after clearing her route, employing the same tradecraft as at the DLB, and probably in a simple disguise. A wig, coat, and sunglasses do more than people think, even if Special Branch racked up hundreds of man-hours poring over footage from hospital security, traffic, and urban CCTV cameras.

Having first put on her surgical gloves, she would have made entry to her trailer with the key provided, closed the door, locked up, and shoved two gray rubber wedges a third of the way down and a third up the frame to prevent anyone's entering, even with a key. Then, before moving anywhere, she'd have opened the sports bag and begun to put on her work clothes, a set of light blue, hooded and footed coveralls for paint spraying. It was imperative that she didn't contaminate the area or the weapon and equipment that were going to be left behind with fibers of her clothing or other personal signs. Her mouth would now be covered by a protective mask to prevent leaving even a pinprick of saliva on the weapon as she took aim. I was pleased with the masks: they'd been on special.

The coveralls and gloves were also there to protect clothes and skin. If she was apprehended immediately after the shoot, residue from the round that she'd fired would be detectable on her skin and clothes. That's why suspects' hands are bagged in plastic. I was also wearing surgical gloves, but just as a normal precaution. I was determined to leave nothing, and disturb nothing too.

Once she'd gotten covered up, with just her eyes exposed, she would look like a forensic scientist at a crime scene. It would then have been time to prepare the fire position. Unlike me, she needed to be away from her window, so she'd have dragged the desk about three yards clear. Then she'd have pinned a net curtain into the wallboard ceiling, letting it fall in front of the desk before pinning it tight to the legs.

Next, she'd have pinned up the sheet of opaque black material behind her, letting it hang to the floor. As with the netting, I had cut it to size for each fire position after the CTR. The combination of a net curtain in front and a dark backdrop behind creates the illusion of a room in shadow. It meant that anyone looking through the window wouldn't see a fat rifle muzzle being pointed at them by a scarily dressed woman. Both sets of optics that she'd be using, the binos and the weapon sight, could easily penetrate the netting, so it wouldn't affect her ability to make the shot.

Some fifteen minutes after arriving, she'd be sitting in the green, padded swivel chair behind the desk. Her takedown weapon would be assembled and supported on the desk by the bipod attached to the forward stock. Her binos, mounted on a mini-tripod, would also be on the desk, and in front of her would be her plastic lunchbox. With the weapon butt in her shoulder, she would have confirmed the arcs of fire, making sure she could move the weapon on its bipod to cover all of the killing ground without being obstructed by the window frame or trees. She'd generally get herself organized and tune in to her environment, maybe even dry practice on one of the catering staff as they rushed around the terrace.

One of the most important things she would have done before signing on with me was check her muzzle clearance. A sniper's optic sight is mounted on top of the weapon. At very short ranges the muzzle may be three or four inches below the image the sniper can actually see through the sight. It would be a total fuckup if she fired a round after getting a good sight picture and it didn't even clear the room, hitting the wall or the bottom of the window frame instead.

To deaden the sound of the shot, each weapon was fitted with a suppressor. This had the drawback of making the front third of the barrel nearly twice the size of the rest of it, altering its natural balance by making it top heavy. The suppressor wouldn't stop the bullet's supersonic crack, but that didn't matter because the noise would be down-range and well away from the fire position, and covered anyway by the device going off; what it would stop was the weapon's signature being heard by hospital staff or Italian tourists eating their overpriced ice cream on the embankment just a few feet below.

The trailer's windows had to be slid open. Firing through glass would not only alert the tourists, but would also affect the bullet's accuracy. There was a risk that someone might think it unusual for the window to be open on a Sunday, but we had no choice. As it was, the suppressor alone would degrade the round's accuracy and power, which was why we needed supersonic rounds to make the distance. Subsonic ammunition, which would eliminate the crack, just wouldn't make it.

It would only be once she was happy with her fire position, and had checked that her commercial hearing aid was still in place under her hood, that she would sign on. Her box of tricks didn't have lights, just a green wire antenna that would probably be laid along the desk then run along the floor. A copper coil inside the box emitted three low touch tones; when I hit my send pressel, they picked that up through the hearing aid.

There was one other wire coming out of the box, leading to a flat, black plastic button; this would now be taped onto the weapon wherever she had her support hand in position to fire.

Hitting the pressel five times, once she was ready to go, was what lit up my number-two bulb five times.

There was nothing left for her to do now but sit perfectly still, weapon rested, naturally aligned toward the killing area, observe, wait, and maybe listen to the comings and goings just below her. With luck the other two were going to be doing the same very soon. If anyone from hospital security attempted to be the good guy and close her window, a woman dressed like an extra from the *X-Files* would be the last thing they ever saw as she dragged them inside.

It was only now that she was in position that her problems really began. Once she'd zeroed the weapon in Thetford Forest, it would have been carried as if it was fine china. The slightest knock could upset the optic sight and wreck the weapon's zero.

Even a tiny misalignment could affect the round by nearly an inch, and that would be bad news.

And it wasn't just the possibility of the optic being knocked, or the suppressor affecting the round's trajectory. The weapon itself, issued to me by the Yes Man, was "takedown." So, once she had zeroed it for that one, all-important shot, it had to be taken apart for concealment, before being reassembled at the firing point.

Thankfully this bolt-action model only had to be split in two at the barrel, and because they were brand-new, they wouldn't have suffered that much wear and tear on the bearing surfaces. But there only had to be a slight difference in the assembly from when it was zeroed, a knock to the optic sight in transit, for the weapon to be inches off where she was aiming.

This isn't a problem when an ordinary rifleman is firing at a body mass at close range, but these boys and girls were going for a catastrophic brain shot, one single round into the brain stem or neural motor strips. The target drops like liquid and there is no chance of survival. And that meant they had to aim at either of two specific spots—the tip of an earlobe, or the skin between the nostrils.

She and the other two would need to be the most boring and religious snipers on earth to do that with these weapons. The Yes Man hadn't listened. It annoyed me severely that he knew jack shit about how things worked on the ground, and yet had been the one who decided which gear to use.

I tried to calm down by making myself remember it wasn't entirely his fault. There had to be a trade-off between concealment and accuracy, because you can't just wander the streets with a fishing-rod case or the world's longest flowerbox. But hell, I'd despised him when he was running the support cell, and now it was worse.

I looked through the window at the distant black-and-white figures moving around the killing ground, and wondered if the Brit who'd first played about with a telescopic sight on a musket in the seventeenth century ever realized what drama he was bringing to the world.

I checked out the area with my binos, using just one eye so I didn't miss One or Three signing in. The binos were tripodded because twelve-times magnification at this distance was so strong that the slightest shudder would make it seem like I was watching *The Blair Witch Project*.

Things had moved on. The staff were still being hassled by the gray-suited catering bully. As guests came through the grand arched door onto the terrace, they'd now be greeted by trestle tables covered by brilliant white tablecloths. Silver trays of fluted glasses waited to be filled as corks were pulled from bottles of champagne.

Things would be kicking off soon, and all I had was one sniper. Not good; not good at all.

I refocused the binos on the arched doorway, then went back to watching the lights, willing them to spark up. There was nothing else I could do.

I tried—and failed—to reassure myself that the coordination plan for the shoot was so beautifully simple, it would work with only one sniper.

The snipers had the same binos as mine and would also have them focused on the door. They'd want to ID the Yes Man the moment he walked into the killing area, and they'd use binos first because they give a field of view of about ten yards, which would make it easier to follow him through the crowd until he made the target ID. Once that was done, they would switch to their weapon's optic sight, and I would concentrate on the lights.

The method I was going to use to control the snipers and tell them when to fire had been inspired by a wildlife documentary I'd seen on TV. Four Indian game wardens, working as a team in total silence, had managed to stalk and fire sedative darts into an albino tiger from very close range.

Whenever any of the snipers had a sight picture of the target and felt confident about taking the shot, they'd hit their pressel and keep it pressed. The corresponding bulb in front of me would stay lit for as long as they could take the shot. If they lost their sight picture, they released their pressel and the bulb would go out until they acquired it again.

Once I'd made the decision when to fire, I'd push my send pressel three times in a one-second rhythm.

The first press would tell the firer or firers to stop breathing so their body movement didn't affect the aim.

The second would tell them to take up the first pressure on the trigger, so as not to jerk the weapon when they fired.

As I hit the pressel the second time, I'd also trigger the detonation. The third time, the snipers would fire as the device exploded on the roof of the hotel. If all three were up and the target was sitting, that would be perfect—but it rarely happens that way.

The device would not only disguise the sonic cracks, but create a diversion on the north side of the river while we extracted. I just wished the Ministry of Defense building wasn't closed for the weekend: I'd have loved to see their faces as the blast took out a few of their windows. Never mind, with luck it would make the Life Guards' horses on Whitehall throw off their mounts.

None of the snipers would know if the others had the target. The first time they'd know the option was going ahead was when they heard the three tones in their ear. If they didn't have a sight picture themselves, they wouldn't take a shot.

After the explosion, whether they'd fired a round or not, they would all exit from their positions, stripping off their outer layer of coveralls and leaving the area casually and professionally with the protective clothing in their bag. The rest of the gear, and the weapons, would be discovered at some point by the police, but that wouldn't matter to me as I'd handed it over sterile. It shouldn't matter to these people either, as they ought to be professional enough to leave it in the same condition as they'd received it. If they didn't, that was their problem.

I rubbed my eyes.

Another light flashed.

Sniper One was in position, ready to go.

I hit the send pressel three times, and after a short pause Sniper One's bulb flashed three times in return.

I was feeling a little better now, with two snipers sitting perfectly still, watching and waiting as they continued to tune in to the killing ground. I could only hope that Sniper Three was close behind.

3

Big Ben struck half past two. Thirty minutes to go.

I continued to stare at the box, trying to transmit positive thoughts. The job was going to happen with or without Sniper Three, but what with the weapon problems, three chances of a hit were better than two.

My positive transmissions weren't working at all, and after ten minutes or so my eyes were drawn to the killing ground again. Things were happening. Different colors of clothing were moving among the black and white of the catering staff like fragments in a kaleidoscope. Shit, they were early.

I put one eye to the binos and checked them out, just as One and Two would be doing. The new arrivals seemed to be the advance party, maybe ten suited men, all of them white. I checked that the Yes Man wasn't among them and had messed up his own plan. He wasn't. He would have fit in nicely, though: they didn't really seem to know what to do with themselves, so they decided to mill around the door like sheep, drinking champagne and mumbling to each other, probably about how pissed they were to be working on a Sunday. Dark, double-breasted suits with a polyester mix seemed to be the order of the day. I could see the well-worn shine and creases up the backs of the jackets even from here. The jackets were mostly undone because of the weather or pot-bellies, revealing ties that hung either too high or too low. They had to be Brit politicians and civil servants.

The only exception was a woman in her early thir-ties with blond hair and rectangular glasses, who came into view alongside the catering bully. Dressed in an immaculate black pants suit, she seemed to be the only one of the new arrivals who knew what was what. With a cell phone in her left hand and a pen in her right, she seemed to be pointing out that every-thing his staff had done needed redoing.

The cameraman also wandered into my field of view, taking light readings, and clearly enjoying the last-minute flap. There was a flash as he took a test shot. Then there was another in my peripheral vision, and I looked down.

The third bulb. I nearly cheered.

I left the blond-haired PR guru to get on with it, and concentrated on the box as I replied to the flashes. Sniper Three duly acknowledged.

Big Ben chimed three times.

Relief washed over me. I'd known all along that these people would only get into position at the very last moment, but that didn't stop me worrying about it while I was waiting. Now I just wanted this thing over and done with, and to slip away on the Eurostar train to the Gare du Nord, then on to Charles de Gaulle Airport. I should make the check-in nicely for my nine P.M. American Airlines flight to Baltimore, to see Kelly and finish my business with Josh.

I got back on the binos and watched the PR guru tell the Brits, ever so nicely and with a great big smile, to get the hell away from the door and prepare to mingle. They cradled their champagne glasses and headed for the appetizers, drifting from my field of view. I kept my focus on the doorway.

Now that it was clear of bodies, I could just about penetrate the shadows inside. It looked like a cafeteria, the sort where you drag your tray along the counter and pay at the end. What a letdown: I'd been expecting something a bit more regal.

The door frame was soon filled again, by another woman with a cell phone stuck to her ear. This one had a clipboard in her free hand; she stepped onto the terrace, closed down her cell phone, and looked around.

The blond PR guru came into view. There was lots of nodding, talking, and pointing around the killing area, then they both went back where they'd come from. I felt a wave of apprehension. I wanted to get on with it and get aboard that Eurostar.

"One of the team," the Yes Man had said.

One of the team, my ass. The only things that would help me if this went wrong were my security blanket and a quick exit to the States.

Seconds later, human shapes began filling the area behind the door, and were soon pouring out into the killing area. The woman with the clipboard appeared behind them, shepherding them with a fixed, professional smile. She guided them to the glasses on the table by the door—as if they could have missed them. Then the catering staff were on top of them like flies on shit, with appetizers on trays, and a whole lot more champagne.

The South American contingent was easy to identify, not by brown or black skin but because they were far better dressed, in well-cut suits and expertly knotted ties. Even their body language had more style. The group was predominantly male, but none of the women with them would have looked out of place in a fashion magazine.

Obligingly, Clipboard coaxed the guests away from the doorway and into the killing area. They spread out and mingled with the advance party. It became clear that everybody was going to continue standing up rather than move over to the benches. I'd have preferred them to sit down like a line of ducks at a carnival, but it wasn't going to happen. We were going to have to settle for a moving target.

The Yes Man was due to arrive ten minutes after the main party. The plan was that he'd spend five minutes by the door, making a phone call, which would give all four of us time to ping him. From there he would move off and ID the target.

All three would now be taking slow, deep breaths so they were fully oxygenated. They would also be constantly checking the wind indicators until the last minute, in case they had to readjust their optics.

My heart pumped harder now. The snipers' hearts, however, would be unaffected. In fact, if they'd been linked to an ECG machine they'd probably have registered as clinically dead. When they were in their zone, all they could think about was taking that single, telling shot.

More people cut across my field of view, then the Yes Man appeared in the doorway. He was five foot six, and not letting me down by wearing the same sort of dark, badly fitting business suit as the rest of the Brits. Under it he had a white shirt and a scarlet tie. The tie was important because it was his main VDM (visual distinguishing mark). The rest of his outfit and his physical description had also been given to the snipers, but he was easy enough to identify from his permanently blushing complexion, and a neck that always seemed to have a big boil in the works. On any other forty-year-old it would have been unfortunate, but as far as I was concerned it couldn't have happened to a nicer guy.

On his left hand he wore a wedding ring. I'd never seen a picture of his wife in his office, and I didn't know if he had children. In fact, I really hoped he didn't—or if he did, that they looked like their mother.

Producing his cell phone, the Yes Man came off the threshold and moved to the right of the doorway as he finished dialing. He looked up and nodded hello to somebody out of my field of view, then gave a wave to them and pointed at the cell phone to show his intentions.

I watched him listen to the ringing tone, keeping his back against the wall so that we could check the tie. His hair was graying, or it would have been if he'd left it alone, but he'd been at the Grecian Formula, and I was catching more than a hint of copper. It complemented his complexion very well indeed. I felt myself grinning.

A young waiter came up to him with a tray of full glasses, but was waved away as he continued with his call. The Yes Man didn't drink or smoke. He was a born-again Christian, Scientologist, something like that, or one of the happy-clappy bands. I'd never really bothered to find out, in case he tried to recruit me and I found myself saying yes. And I didn't set much store by it. If the Yes Man discovered C was a Sikh, he'd turn up at work in a turban.

His conversation over, the phone got shut down, and he walked toward the Thames. As he wove and sidestepped through the crowd he bounced slightly on the balls of his feet, as if trying to give himself extra height. Watching his progress, I gently undid the tripod restraining clips so I could swivel the binos and continue to follow him if I needed to.

He passed the two PR women, who looked pretty pleased with themselves. Each had a phone and a cigarette in one hand and a glass of self-congratulatory champagne in the other. He passed the cameraman, who was now busy taking group shots with Big Ben in the background for the Latin folks back home. Little did he know that he was a couple of chimes short of a world exclusive.

The Yes Man sidestepped the photo session and continued to go left, still in the direction of the river. He stopped eventually by a group of maybe ten men, gathered in a wide, informal circle. I could see some of their faces, but not all, as they talked, drank, or waited for refills from the staff buzzing around them. Two were white-eyes, and I could see four or five Latino faces turned to the river.

The older of the two white-eyes smiled at the Yes Man and shook his hand warmly. He then began to introduce his new Latin friends.

This had to be it. One of these was the target. I looked at their well-fed faces as they smiled politely and shook the Yes Man's hand.

I could feel my forehead leaking sweat as I concentrated on who he was shaking hands with, knowing that I couldn't afford to miss the target ID, and at the same time not too sure if the Yes Man was up to the job.

I'd assumed they were all South Americans, but as one of their number turned I saw, in profile, that he was Chinese. He was talk-show-host neat, in his fifties, taller than the Yes Man, and with more hair. Why he was part of a South American delegation was a mystery to me, but I wasn't going to lose any sleep over it. I concentrated on how he was greeted. It was a non-event, just a normal handshake. The Chinaman, who obviously spoke English, then introduced a smaller guy to his right, who had his back to me. The Yes Man moved toward him, and then, as they shook, he placed his left hand on the small guy's shoulder.

I hated to admit it, but he was doing an excellent job. He even started to swing the target around so he faced the river, pointing out the London Eye and the bridges on either side of Parliament.

The target was also part Chinese—and I had to double-take because he couldn't have been more than sixteen or seventeen years old. He was wearing a smart blazer with a white shirt and blue tie, the sort of boy any parent would want their daughter to date. He looked happy, exuberant even, grinning at everyone and joining in the conversation as he turned back into the circle with the Yes Man.

I got a feeling that I was in worse trouble than I'd thought.

4

I forced myself to cut away. Forget it, I'd worry about all that on the flight to the States.

The conversation on the terrace carried on as the Yes Man said his good-byes to the group, waved at another, and moved out of my field of view. He wouldn't be leaving yet—that would be suspicious—he just didn't want to be near the boy when we dropped him.

Seconds later, I had three bulbs burning below me. The snipers were waiting for those three command tones to buzz gently in their ear.

It didn't feel right but reflexes took over. I flicked the shaving cream top from the box and positioned my thumbs over the two pressels.

I was about to press when all three lights went out within a split second of each other.

I got back on to the binos, just with my right eye, thumbs ready over the pressels. The group was moving en masse from left to right. I should have been concentrating on the bulbs but I wanted to see. The Chinaman's arm was around the boy's shoulders—it must have been his son—as they approached a smaller group of Latinos who were attacking a table laden with food.

A bulb lit up: Sniper Three was confident of taking the shot, aiming slightly ahead of his point of aim so that when he fired the boy would walk into the path of the round.

The bulb stayed lit as they stopped at the table with the other group of Latinos, getting stuck at the creampuffs. The boy was at the rear of the group and I could just ping glimpses of his navy blazer through the crowd.

Bulb three died.

I was having doubts, I didn't know why, and tried to get a grip. What did I care? If it was a straight choice between his life and mine there'd be no question. What was happening in my head was totally unprofessional, and totally ridiculous.

I gave myself a good mental slapping. Any more of this shit and I'd end up hugging trees and doing voluntary work for the Red Cross.

The only thing I should be doing was focusing on the box. What was happening on the terrace shouldn't matter to me anymore—but I couldn't seem to stop myself looking at the boy through the binos.

Number Two's bulb came up. She must have found his earlobe to aim at.

Then the boy moved toward the table, breaking through the crowd. He started to help himself to some food, looking back at his dad to check if he wanted anything.

All three lights now burned. How could they not?

I watched him pick at the stuff on the silver trays, sniffing one canapé and deciding to give it a miss. I studied his shiny young face as he wondered what would best complement his half-drunk glass of Coke.

All bulbs were still lit as I looked through the binos. He was exposed, tossing peanuts into his mouth.

Come on! Get on with the fucking thing!

I couldn't believe it. My thumbs just wouldn't move.

In that instant, my plan switched to screwing up the shoot and finding something to blame it on. I couldn't stop myself.

The snipers wouldn't know who else had a sight picture, and it wasn't as if we were all going to get together and have a debriefing over coffee the next morning. I'd take my chances with the Yes Man.

The boy moved back into the crowd, toward his dad. I could just about make out his shoulder through the crowd.

The three lights went out simultaneously. Then Two's came back on. This woman wasn't giving up on her target. I guessed she wasn't a mother after all.

Three seconds later it went out. Wrong or right, now was my time to act.

I pushed the send pressel once with my thumb, keeping my eyes glued on the boy. Then I pressed it again, and at the same time hit the detonation button. The third time, I pushed just on the send pressel.

The explosion on the other side of the Thames was like a massive, prolonged clap of thunder. I watched the boy and everyone around him react to the detonation instead of doing what I'd planned for him.

The shock wave crossed the river and rattled my window. As I listened to its last rumblings reverberate around the streets of Whitehall, the screams of the tourists below me took over. I concentrated on the boy as his father bustled him toward the door.

As panic broke out on the terrace, the photographer was in a frenzy to get the shots that would pay off his mortgage. Then the Yes Man came into view and stood beside the PR women, who were helping people back inside. He had a concerned look on his face, which had nothing to do with the explosion and everything to do with seeing the target alive and being dragged to safety. The boy disappeared though the door and others followed, but the Yes Man still didn't help. Instead he looked up and across the river at me. It was weird. He didn't know exactly where I was in the building, but I felt as if he were looking straight into my eyes.

I was going to be in a world of shit about this, and knew I had to have a really good story for him. But not today: it was time to head for Waterloo Station. My Eurostar left in an hour and five minutes. The snipers would now be standing at their crossover point—their exit door from a contaminated area to a decontaminated area—peeling off their outer layers of clothing, throwing them into their sports bags, but leaving their gloves on until totally clear of the trailer. The weapons, binos, and lunchboxes remained in place, as did the hide.

With speed but not haste, I leaned over to the window and opened it a fraction to retrieve the antennas. The clamor from people outside was now much louder than the explosion had been. There were shouts of fear and confusion from men, women, and children at embankment level. Vehicles on the bridge had braked to a halt and pedestrians were rooted to the spot as the cloud of black smoke billowed over the rooftop of the MoD building.

I closed the window and left them to it, taking down the tripod for the binos and packing away all my gear as quickly as I could. I needed to get that train.

Once all the equipment was back in the bag,

including the shaving-cream cap, I put the dirty coffee mug, Wayne's World coaster, and telephone back exactly where they'd been before I'd cleared the desktop to make room for the binos and lunchbox, using the Polaroid I'd taken as a reference. I checked the general area pictures I'd taken as soon as I broke in. Maybe the net curtain wasn't exactly as it should have been, or a chair had been moved a foot or so to the right. It wasn't superstition. Details like that are important. I'd known something as simple as a mouse pad out of place leading to an operator's being compromised.

My brain started to bang against my skull. There was something strange about what I had seen outside. I hadn't been clever enough to notice, but my unconscious had. I had learned the hard way that these feelings should never be ignored.

I looked back out of the window and it hit me in an instant. Instead of looking at the column of smoke to my right, the crowd's attention was on the hospital to my left. They were looking toward the sniper positions, listening to the dull thud of six or seven short, sharp, single shots. . . .

There were more screams below the window, mixed with the wail of fast-approaching police sirens.

I opened my window as far as it would go and pushed the net curtain aside, sticking out my head and looking left, toward the hospital. A fleet of police cars and vans with flashing lights had been abandoned along the embankment, just short of the sniper positions, their doors left open. At the same time I saw uniforms hastily organizing a cordon to block off the area.

This was wrong. This was very, very wrong. The event I was witnessing had been planned and prepared for. The frenzy of police activity down there was far too organized to be a spur-of-the-moment reaction to an explosion a few minutes earlier.

We had been set up.

Three more shots were fired, followed by a short pause, then another two. Then, from farther along the riverbank, I heard the heavy thuds of a flashbang going off inside a building. They were hitting Number Three's position.

Adrenaline jolted through my body. It'd be my turn soon.

I slammed the window down. My mind raced. Apart from me, the only person who knew the exact sniper positions was the Yes Man, because he needed to position the target well enough for it to be identified. But he didn't know precisely where I was going to be, because I hadn't known myself. Technically, I didn't even have to have eyes on target, I just needed to have comms with the snipers. But he knew enough. Messing up the shoot was the least of my worries now.

5

Helicopters were now rattling overhead and police sirens were going apeshit in the street as I closed the door gently behind me and moved out into the wide, brightly lit hallway.

My Timberlands squeaked on the highly polished stone floor as I headed toward the fire-exit door at the far end, maybe sixty yards away, forcing myself not to quicken my pace. I had to stay in control. I couldn't afford to make any more mistakes. There might be a time to run, but it wasn't yet.

There was a turning to the right about twenty yards farther down, which led to the stairwell that would take me to the ground floor. I reached it, turned, and froze. Between me and the stairwell was a wall of six-foot-high black ballistic shields. Behind them were maybe a dozen police in full black assault gear, weapon barrels pointing out at me through the gaps in the shields, blue assault helmets and visors glinting in the fluorescent lighting.

"STAND STILL! STAND STILL!"

It was time to run like the wind. I squeaked on my heels and lunged the couple of paces back into the main hallway, heading for the fire exit, just willing myself to hit that crossbar to freedom.

As I zeroed in on the exit door, the hallway ahead filled with more black shields and the noise of boots on stone. They held the line like Roman centurions. The last couple emerged from the offices on either side, their weapons pointing at me at far too close a range for my liking.

"STAND STILL! STAND STILL NOW!"

Coming to a halt, I dropped the bag to the floor and put my hands in the air. "Not armed!" I yelled. "I'm weapons free! Weapons free!"

There are times when it's an advantage just to admit to yourself that you're in the shit, and this was one of them. I just hoped these were real police. If I wasn't a threat, then in theory they shouldn't drop me.

I hoped, too, that my black cotton bomber jacket had ridden up enough to show them there wasn't a pistol attached to my belt or tucked into my jeans. "Not armed," I yelled. "Weapons free!"

Orders were screamed at me. I wasn't too sure what—it was all too loud and too close, a confusion of echoes along the hallway.

I pivoted slowly so they could see my back and check for themselves that I wasn't lying. As I faced the hallway intersection, I heard more boots thundering toward me from the stairwell, closing the trap.

A shield moved out of the corner then slammed into position on the floor at the hallway intersection. A muzzle of an MP5 came around the side of it, and I could see a sliver of the user's face as he took aim on me.

"Weapons free!" My voice was almost a scream. "I'm weapons free!"

Keeping my hands in the air I stared at the single,

unblinking eye behind the weapon. He was a left-handed firer, taking advantage of the left side of the shield for cover, and the eye didn't move from my chest.

I looked down as a red laser spot the size of a shirt button splashed on it dead center. It wasn't moving either. God knows how many splashes there were on my back from the fire-exit crew.

Frenzied shouts finished bouncing off the walls as a loud, South London accent took command and shouted orders that I could now understand. "Stand still! Stand still! Keep—your—hands—up . . . keep them up!"

No more turning, I did what he wanted.

"Down on your knees! Get down on your knees. Now!"

Keeping my hands up, I lowered myself slowly, no longer trying for any eye contact, just looking down. The left-handed firer in front of me followed my every move with the laser splash.

The voice shouted more orders from behind. "Lie down, with your arms spread out to your side. Do it now."

I did as I was told. There was total, scary silence. The cold of the stone floor seeped through my clothes. Minute pinpricks of grit pressed into my right cheek as I snorted up a lungful of freshly laid wax.

I found myself staring at the bottom of one of the stairwell group's ballistic shields. It was dirty with age and chipped on the corners, so that the layers of Kevlar that gave protection from even heavy-caliber ammunition were peeling back like the pages of a well-thumbed book.

The silence was broken by the shuffle and squeak of rubber-soled boots approaching me from behind.

My only thought was how lucky I was to be arrested.

The boots arrived at their destination, and heavy breathing from their owners filled the air around me. One old, black, creased-leather size ten landed by my face, and my hands were gripped and pulled up in front of me. I felt the cold, hard metal bite into my wrists as the handcuffs were ratcheted tight. I just let them get on with it; the more I struggled the more pain I would have to put up with. The handcuffs were the newer style, police issue: instead of a chain between them they had a solid metal spacer. Once these things are on, just one tap against the spacer with a baton is enough to have you screaming in agony as the metal finds your wrist bones.

I was in enough pain already as one man pulled at the cuffs to keep my arms straight, and someone else's knee was forced down between my shoulder blades. My nose got banged against the floor, making my eyes water, and all the oxygen was forced out of my lungs.

A pair of hands, their owner's boots on each side of me now that he'd removed his knee from my back, were making their way over my body. My wallet, containing my Eurostar ticket and my Nick Somerhurst passport, was taken from the inside pocket of my bomber jacket. I felt suddenly naked.

I turned my head, trying to get as comfortable as possible during the going-over, and rested my face on the cold stone. Through blurred vision I made out three pairs of jeans emerging from behind the shield at the intersection and heading my way. One pair of jeans moved out of vision as they passed me by, but the other two moved in close: a set of sneakers and a pair of light tan boots, their Caterpillar label now just inches from my nose.

I started to feel more depressed than worried

about what was coming next. Men in jeans just don't prance about during an armed arrest.

Behind me I heard the zip of my duffel bag being pulled back and the contents given a quick going-over. At the same time I felt my Leatherman being pulled out from its pouch.

There was still no talking as hands ran down my legs to check for concealed weapons. My face acted like a cushion for my cheekbone as I was hauled around like a sack of potatoes.

Hands forced themselves around the front of my stomach and into my waistband, then extracted the three or four dollars' worth of change in my jeans.

The same set of hands went under each armpit and hauled me up onto my knees, to the accompaniment of labored grunts and the squeak of leather belt-gear. My cuff-holder let go and my hands dropped down by my knees as if I was begging. The cold stone floor was hurting my knees, but I forgot about them instantly when I saw the face of the man wearing the Cats.

His hair wasn't looking so neat today: the Sundance Kid had been running about a bit. Above his jeans he was wearing a green bomber jacket and heavy blue body armor with a protective ceramic plate tucked into the pouch over his chest. He was taking no chances with me today.

There wasn't the slightest trace of emotion in his face as he stared down at me, probably trying to hide from the others that his part of the job hadn't gone too well. I was still alive; he hadn't been able to make entry into the office with the help of his new pals here and claim self-defense as he shot me.

My documents were handed to him and they went into his back pocket. He played with the coins in his cupped palms, chinking as they poured from one to the other. Sundance and his pal, Sneakers, were joined by the third pair of jeans, who had my bag over his right shoulder. I kept my eyes down at calf level now, not wishing to provoke him. It was pointless appealing to the uniforms for help. They'd have heard it all before from drunks claiming to be Jesus and people like me ranting that they'd been set up.

Sundance spoke for the first time. "Good result, Sarge." His thick Glasgow accent was directed to someone behind me, before he turned away with the other two. I watched them walk toward the stairwell, to the sound of Velcro being ripped apart as they started to peel off their body armor.

As they disappeared past the hallway intersection I was dragged up onto my feet by two policemen. With their strong grip under each of my armpits, I followed them toward the stairs. We passed the shields at the hallway intersection, as the armed teams started to break ranks, and made our way down the stone stairs. Sundance and the boys were about two floors below. I kept catching glimpses of them as they turned on the stone and iron-railed landings, and wondered why I hadn't been blindfolded. Maybe it was to make sure I didn't trip on the stairs. No, it would be because they didn't care if I saw their faces. I wasn't going to live long enough to see them again.

We exited the building via the glass and metal framed doors I'd made entry through earlier. At once the noise of boots on the stairs and the policemen's labored breathing from the effort of hauling me about was drowned out by the confusion on the street. Sweat-stained, white-shirted police officers were running about, their radios crackling, yelling at pedestrians to follow their directions and clear the area. Sirens blared. A helicopter chopped the air loudly overhead.

We were on the private entry road to the Marriott

Hotel, part of the County Hall building. To my left was its circular drive, bordered by a smart decorative hedge. Police were preventing guests from coming out of the main entrance as they tried to see what was happening or to run away, I wasn't sure which.

In front of me, at the curbside, was a white Mercedes station wagon, engine running, all doors open. One of the pairs of jeans was in the driver's seat ready to go. As a hand pushed down on top of my head and I was quickly bundled into the back, my feet connected with something in the footwell. It was my duffel bag, still unzipped.

The guy with the sneakers sat on my left and attached one end of a pair of handcuffs to the D ring of the center set of seat belts. He then flicked the free end around the pair that gripped my wrists. I wasn't going anywhere until these boys were good and ready.

Sundance appeared on the sidewalk and said his good-byes to the uniforms. "Thanks again, lads."

I kept trying to make eye contact with the guys who had dragged me down here, who were now standing by the entrance to the office block. Sundance got into the front passenger seat and closed his door, obviously aware of what I was doing. He bent down into his footwell. "That isn't going to help you, boy." Retrieving a blue light from the floor and slapping it onto the dashboard, he plugged the lead into the cigarette-lighter socket. The light started flashing as the car moved off.

We came out of the hotel's approach road and onto the main drag at the south end of the bridge, directly opposite the hospital buildings. The road was cordoned off and surrounded by every police vehicle in the Greater London area. The windows of the hospital were crammed with patients and nurses trying to get a grandstand view of the commotion.

We wove around the obstacles in the road and through the cordon. Once over the large traffic circle, we passed under the Eurostar track a hundred yards farther down. I could see the slick, aerodynamic trains waiting in the glass terminal above me, and felt sick that one of them should be leaving soon without me on it.

Sundance removed the flashing light from the dashboard. We were heading south toward Elephant and Castle and, no doubt, into a world of shit.

I looked at Sundance's face in the side mirror. He didn't return eye contact or acknowledge me in any way. Behind the stony face he was probably working out what he had to do next.

So was I, and I started to work on him straightaway. "This isn't going to work. I've got on tape the orders you drove for and I—"

There was an explosion of pain as Sneakers put all his force behind his elbow and rammed it into my thigh, deadlegging me.

Sundance turned in his seat. "Don't wind me up, boy."

I took a deep, deep breath and kept going for it. "I've got proof of everything that's happened. Everything."

He didn't even bother to look around this time. "Shut up."

Sneakers's hand chopped down on the spacer bar between the cuffs. The metal jarred agonizingly on my wrists, but I knew it was nothing compared with what would happen if I didn't buy myself some time. "Look," I gasped, "it's me set up today, it could be you guys next. No one gives a shit about people like us. That's why I keep records. For my own security."

We were approaching the Elephant and Castle traffic circle, passing the pink shopping center. I nodded to give Sneakers the message that I was going to shut up. I wasn't a fool, I knew when to shut up or talk. I wanted to make the little I knew go a long way. I wanted them to feel I was confident and secure, and that they would be making a big mistake if they didn't pay attention. I just hoped it wasn't me making the mistake.

I looked in the mirror again. It was impossible to tell whether this was having any effect on Sundance. I was just feeling that maybe I should get in another installment when he sparked up. "What do you know, then, boy?"

I shrugged. "Everything, including those three hits just now." Hell, I might as well go right to the top of the bullshit stakes.

Sneakers's brown, bloodshot eyes and broken nose faced me without emotion. It was impossible to tell whether he was going to hurt me or not. I decided to try to save my skin big-time before he made up his mind.

"I taped the briefing that you drove for." Which was a lie. "I've got pictures of the locations." Which was true. "And pictures and serial numbers of the weapons. I've got all the dates, all diaried, even pictures of the snipers."

We turned down toward the Old Kent Road, and as I shifted position slightly I glimpsed Sundance's face in the side mirror. He was looking dead ahead, his expression giving nothing away. "Show me."

That was easy enough. "Sniper Two is a woman, she's in her early thirties, and she has brown hair." I resisted the temptation to say more. I needed to show him I knew a lot, but without running out of information too early.

There was silence. I got the impression that Sundance had started to listen carefully, which I took as my chance to carry on. "You need to tell him," I said. "Just think about the shit you'll be in if you don't. Frampton won't be first in line for taking the blame. It'll be you guys who get that for sure." The message had at least gotten through to Sneakers. He was swapping glances with Sundance in the mirror: my cue not even to look up now, but let them get on with it.

We stopped at a set of lights, level with carloads of families swigging from cans of Coke and doing the bored-in-the-backseat stuff. The four of us just sat there as if we were on our way to a funeral. It was pointless my trying to raise the alarm with any of these people as they smoked or picked their noses waiting for the green. I just had to depend on Sundance to make a decision soon. If he didn't, I'd try again, and keep on until they silenced me. I'd been trying hard not to think about that too much.

We approached a large shopping mall, with signs for the Gap, McDonald's, and a hardware store. Sundance pointed at the entrance sign. "In there for five." The indicator immediately started clicking and we cut across the traffic.

I tried not to show my elation, and let my eyes concentrate hard on the lunchbox of tricks at the top of the sports bag as I felt the Merc lurch over a speed bump.

We stopped near a hot dog vendor, and Sundance immediately got out. Carts filled with potted plants, paint, and planks of wood trundled past on the pavement as he walked out of sight somewhere behind us, dialing into a phone that he'd pulled from his jacket.

The rest of us sat in silence. The driver just looked ahead through his sunglasses and Sneakers turned around in his seat to try to see what Sundance was up to, taking care to cover my handcuffs so the do-it-yourself-ers couldn't see that we weren't there for the kitchen sale.

I wasn't really thinking or worrying about anything, just idly watching a young sweat-suited couple load up their ancient XRi with boxes of wall tiles and grout. Maybe I was trying to avoid the fact that the call he was making meant life or death for me.

Sundance shook me out of my dreamlike state as he slumped back into the Merc and slammed the door. The other two looked at him expectantly, probably hoping to be told to drive me down to the waterfront and give me a helping hand in my tragic suicide.

There was nothing from him for twenty seconds or so while he put his seat belt on. It was like waiting for the doctor to tell me if I had cancer or not. He sat for a while and looked disturbed; I didn't know what to think but took it as a good sign, without really knowing why.

Eventually, after putting the StarTac away, he looked at the driver. "Kennington."

I knew where Kennington was, but didn't know what it meant to them. Not that it really mattered: I just felt a surge of relief about the change of plan. Whatever had been going to happen to me had been postponed.

At length Sundance muttered, "If you're fucking with me, things will get hurtful."

I nodded into the rearview mirror as he gave me the thousand-yard stare. There was no need for further conversation as we drove back up the Old Kent Road. I was going to save all that for later, for the Yes Man. Leaning against the window to rest my arms and ease the tension of the handcuffs on my wrists, I gazed like a child at the world passing by, the glass steaming around my face.

Somebody turned on the radio and the soothing sound of violins filled the Merc. It struck me as strange; I wouldn't have expected these boys to be into classical music any more than I was.

I knew the area we were driving through like the back of my hand. As a ten-year-old, I had played there while cutting school. In those days the place was one big mass of dingy housing projects, ripoff secondhand-car dealers, and old men in pubs drinking bottles of light ale. But now it looked as if every available square foot was being gentrified. The place was crawling with luxury developments and 911 Carreras, and all the pubs had been converted into wine bars. I wondered where all the old men went now to keep out of the cold.

We were approaching Elephant and Castle again. The music finished and a female voice came on with an update on the incident that had shaken London. There were unconfirmed reports, she said, that three people had been killed in a gun battle with police, and that the bomb blast in Whitehall had produced between ten and sixteen minor casualties, who were being treated at the hospital. Tony Blair had expressed his absolute outrage from his villa in Italy, and the emergency services were on full alert as further explosions could not be ruled out. No one as yet had claimed responsibility for the blast.

We rounded Elephant and Castle and headed toward Kennington, pulling over as two police vans sirened their way past.

Sundance turned to me and shook his head in mock disapproval. "Tut-tut-tut. See, you—you're a menace to society, you are."

As the news finished and the music returned I continued to look out of the window. I was a menace to myself, not society. Why couldn't I steer clear of shit for a change, instead of heading straight for it like a light-drunk moth?

We passed the Kennington subway station, then took a right into a quiet residential street. The street name had been ripped from its post and the wooden backing was covered in graffiti. We turned again and the driver had to brake as he came across six or seven kids in the middle of the road, kicking a ball against the gable end of a turn-of-the-century terrace. They stopped and let us through, then immediately got back to trying to demolish the wall.

We drove about forty yards farther, then stopped. Sundance hit his key fob and a graffiti-covered double garage door started to roll up. Left and right of it was a pitted brown brick wall; above was a rusty metal frame that had probably once held a neon sign. Empty drink cans littered the ground. Inside was completely empty. As we drove in, I saw that all around the old brick walls were tool boards with faded, red-painted shapes of what was supposed to be hanging there. Years ago it had probably been a one-man garage setup. A faded Chelsea football team poster was pinned to a door. Judging by the long hair-cuts, sideburns, and very tight shorts, it was seventies vintage.

The garage door rattled and squeaked its way down behind me, gradually cutting off the noise of the kids kicking the ball. The engine was cut and the three of them started to get out.

Sundance disappeared through the football poster door, leaving it open behind him, with luck for me to get dragged through. Anything to be out of the car and have the pressure off my wrists. Maybe I'd even be given a cup of tea. I hadn't eaten or drunk any-thing since the night before: there'd been too much to do and I'd simply forgotten. Just placing the bomb on the hotel roof had taken the best part of four hours, and an Egg McMuffin had been the last thing on my mind.

While I was watching the door swing back slowly to reveal the Chelsea mopheads again, Sneakers leaned down and undid the cuffs pinning me to the seat. Then he and the driver got hold of me and dragged me out. We headed toward the door; I was beginning to feel that maybe I'd get away with this after all. Then I gave myself a good mental slapping: every time I had this feeling I came unstuck. What was happening here meant nothing until I saw the Yes Man and told him my piece. I decided to try hard not to annoy these boys while we waited. They were doing their best to intimidate me; things are always more worrying when there is no verbal contact and no information, and it was working a little, that was for sure. Not a lot, but enough.

They dragged me through the door and into a windowless, rectangular space with pitted, dirty whitewashed brick walls. The room was airless, hot, and humid, and to add to the mix somebody had been smoking roll-up cigarettes. A harsh, double fluorescent unit in the ceiling gave the impression there was nowhere to hide.

On the floor in the left-hand corner was an ancient TV with a shiny new swordfish aerial hanging from a nail on the wall. It was the only thing in the room that looked as if it hadn't been purchased from a junk shop. Facing it was a worn-out brown velour three-piece suite of furniture. The arms were threadbare, and the seats sagged and were dotted with cigarette burns. Plugged into adaptors in the same outlet as the TV were a green upright plastic kettle, a toaster, and battery chargers for three cell phones. The place reminded me of a minicab office, with old newspapers and Burger King drink cups providing the finishing touches.

Sundance was standing by the TV, finishing another call on his cell phone. He looked at me and gestured toward the corner. "Keep it shut, boy."

The other two gave me a shove to help me on my way. As I slid down the wall I tried my hardest not to push against the cuffs and ratchet them up even tighter than they already were. I finally slumped onto the floor and ended up facing the TV.

6

I guessed this place had been just a temporary setup for the duration of the job—and the job, of course, was planning and preparing to kill me. No doubt there was a similar setup somewhere else in London where a whole lot of the boys and girls had prepared themselves for the hit on the snipers.

Sneakers went over to the TV as the other two headed back into the garage. I watched as he crouched down by the tea supplies, opening the kettle to check for water. His light brown nylon jacket had ridden up to expose part of a black leather pancake holster sitting on a leather belt, just behind his right hip, and a green T-shirt dark with sweat. Even the back of his belt was soaking, and had turned a much darker brown than the rest.

I could still hear the kids in the background, kicking their ball and yelling at each other. The pitch of their voices changed as one probably miskicked and was treated to squeals of derision. My hands, still stuck in the surgical gloves, were pruning up in the heat.

Sneakers lined up three not-too-healthy-looking

Simpsons mugs, Bart, Marge, and Homer, which pissed me off. Maggie was missing. There obviously wasn't going to be any tea for me. He threw a tea bag into each, splashed milk on top, then dug a spoon into a crumpled, half-empty bag of sugar, tipping heaps of it into two of the mugs.

A toilet flushed in the garage area, and the sound got louder then softer as a door opened and closed. I could hear Sundance and the driver mumbling to each other but couldn't make out what was said.

The Merc door slammed, the engine turned over, and there was more squeaking and grinding as the garage door shutter lifted. Thirty seconds later the car backed out into the road and drove away. Maybe one of the mugs was for me after all.

Sundance appeared at the office door, his back to us, checking that the shutter had fully closed. As the steel banged onto the floor, he walked to the couch and threw his green cotton bomber jacket onto the armrest of the nearest chair, revealing a wet maroon polo shirt and a chunky Sig 9mm, holstered just behind his right hip. On his left hip sat a light brown leather mag-carrier, with three thick pieces of elastic holding a magazine apiece. The first brass round of each glinted in the ceiling's white light. I almost laughed: three full mags, and just for little old me. I'd heard of overkill but this was something out of the last five minutes of *Butch Cassidy*. It was obvious where this boy had gotten his best ideas.

He stripped off his polo shirt and used it to wipe the sweat from his face, exposing a badly scarred back. Two indentations were clearly gunshot wounds: I recognized them because I had one myself. Someone had also given him the good news with a knife, some of the slashes running the whole length of his back, with stitch marks on either side. All in all, it looked quite a lot like an aerial photo of Clapham Junction train station.

Sneakers, who'd just finished squeezing and fishing out the tea bags, lifted up a brew for Sundance. "Still want one?" His accent was 100 percent Belfast.

"Right enough." Wiping his neck and shoulders, Sundance sat down in the chair nearest the TV, avoiding resting his wet, bare back against the velour by sitting upright on the edge. He took a tentative sip from Bart, the mug without sugar.

He had been hitting the weights, but didn't have the chiseled look of a bodybuilder. He had the physique of a con who'd been pumping iron: the diet in prisons is so bad that when the lads take to the weights they end up barrel-chested and bulked up, rather than well honed.

He glanced at me for the first time and caught me studying his back. "Belfast—when you was just a wee soldier-boy." He treated himself to a little giggle, then nodded at the third Simpsons mug still on the floor by Sneakers. "D'you want a tea, then, boy?"

Sneakers held up Marge.

I nodded. "Yeah, I would, thanks."

There was a pause for a couple of seconds while they exchanged a look, then both roared with laughter as Sneakers did a bad Cockney accent. "Gor blimey, guv, I would, fanks."

Sneakers sat himself down on the couch with Homer, still laughing as he messed with me. "Strike a light, guv'nor, yeah, I would, cheers. Luv a duck." At least someone was having fun.

Sneakers put his own brew on the cracked tiled floor and took off his jacket. He'd obviously had a tattoo removed by laser recently; there was the faintest red scar just visible on his forearm, but the outstretched Red Hand of Ulster was still plain to see. He had been, maybe still was, a member of the UDA (Ulster Defense Association). Maybe they'd both pumped their iron in one of the H blocks.

Sneakers's triceps rippled under his tanned, freckled skin as he felt behind the cushions and pulled out a packet of Drum tobacco. Resting it on his knees, he took out some Rizla papers and started to make himself a roll-up cigarette.

Sundance didn't like what he saw. "You know he hates that—just wait."

"Right enough." The Drum packet was folded and returned beneath the cushions.

It made me very happy indeed to hear that: the Yes Man must be on his way. Even though I'd never smoked I'd never been a tobacco Nazi, but Frampton certainly was.

My ass was getting numb on the hard floor so I shifted very slowly into another position, trying not to draw attention to myself. Sundance got up, mug in hand, walked the three paces to the TV, and hit the power button then each of the station buttons till he got a decent picture.

Sneakers sparked up, "I like this one. It's a laugh." Sundance shuffled backward to his chair, eyes glued to the box. Both were now ignoring me as they watched a woman, whose voice was straight off the BBC news, talk to the antique show's china expert about her collection of Pekingese dog teacups.

I couldn't hear the kids anymore over the TV as I waited for the Merc to return. On the screen, the woman tried not to show how pissed she was when the expert told her the china was only worth fifty pounds.

Whoever had christened Frampton the Yes Man was a genius: it was the only word he said to any of his superiors. In the past this had never worried me because I had nothing to do with him directly, but all that changed when he was promoted to run the U.K. Ks (deniable operators) Desk in SIS. The Firm used some ex–SAS people like me, in fact anyone, probably even my new friends here, as deniable operators. The Ks Desk had traditionally been run by an IB (member of Intelligence Branch), the senior branch of the service. In fact the whole service is run by IBs for IBs; these are the boys and girls we read about in the papers, recruited from university, working from embassies, and using mundane Foreign Office appointments as cover. Their real work, however, starts at six in the evening when the conventional diplomats begin their round of cocktail parties, and the IBs start gathering intelligence, spreading disinformation, and recruiting sources.

That's when the lowlifes like me come into the picture, carrying out, or in some cases cleaning up, the dirty work that they create while tossing the odd crabmeat sandwich and after-dinner mint down their throats. I envied them that, at times like this.

The Yes Man did, too. He had been to university, but not one of the right two. He had never been one of the elite, an IB, yet had probably always wanted to be. But he just wasn't made of the right stuff. His background was the Directorate of Special Support, a branch of wild-haired technicians and scientists working on electronics, signals, electronic surveillance, and explosive devices. He'd run the signals department of the U.K. Ks, but had never been in the field.

I didn't know why the Firm had suddenly changed the system and let a non-IB take command. Maybe with the recent change of government they thought they should look a bit more meritocratic, give a tweak or two to the system to make them look good and keep the politicians happy as they skipped back to Whitehall, instead of interfering too much with what really goes on. So, who better to run the Desk than someone who wasn't an IB, who kissed ass from breakfast to dinnertime, and who would do whatever he was told?

Whatever, I didn't like him and never would. He certainly wasn't on my speed dial, that was for sure. On the one occasion that I'd had direct contact with him, the job had fouled up because he'd supplied insufficient comms gear.

He'd only been in the job since Colonel Lynn had "taken early retirement" about seven months ago, but he'd already proved his incompetence more than once. The only thing he was good at was issuing threats; he had neither the personality nor the management skills to do it any other way. Lynn might have been just as much of an asshole, but at least you knew where you stood with him.

I was adjusting my position some more when the garage door rattled and I heard an engine rev outside.

They both stood up and put their wet shirts back on. Sundance walked over to turn off the TV. Neither of them bothered to look at me. It was still as if I weren't there.

The engine noise got louder. Doors slammed and the shutter came down again.

The Yes Man appeared at the door, still in his suit and looking severely pissed. Sneakers slipped dutifully out of the room, like the family Labrador.

I wouldn't have thought it possible but the Yes Man's face was an even brighter red than usual. He was under pressure. Yet again, C and his pals weren't too pleased with their non-IB experiment.

He stopped just three or four feet away from me, looking like an irate schoolteacher, legs apart, hands on hips. "What happened, Stone?" he shouted. "Can't you get anything right?"

What was he going on about? Only two hours ago he'd wanted me killed, and now he was telling me off like a naughty schoolboy. But it wasn't the moment to point this out. It was the moment to brown-nose big-time.

"I just don't know, Mr. Frampton. As soon as I had three lights up I sent the fire commands. I don't know what happened after that. It should have worked, all four of us had comms up until then but—"

"But nothing!" he exploded. "The task was a complete failure." His voice jumped an octave. "I'm holding you personally responsible, you do know that, don't you?"

I did now. But what was new?

He took a deep breath. "You don't understand the importance of this operation that you have completely botched, do you?"

Botched? I tried not to smile but couldn't help it. "Fucked up" was how Lynn would have put it.

The Yes Man was still playing the schoolteacher. "There's nothing to smile about, Stone. Who, in heaven's name, do you think you are?"

It was time for a bit of damage limitation. "Just someone trying to keep alive," I said. "That's why I taped our conversation, Mr. Frampton."

He was silent for a few seconds while that sank in, breathing heavily, eyes bulging. Ah, yes, the tape and pictures. He must have just remembered why I was still alive and he was here. But not for long; his brain switch was set to Transmit rather than Receive. "You've no idea of the damage you've done. The Americans were adamant that this had to be done today. I gave my word to them, and others, that it would." He was starting to feel sorry for himself.

"I can't believe I had so much confidence in you."

So it was an American job. No wonder he was panicking. The senior Brits had been trying to heal a number of rifts in their relationship with the U.S.A. for quite a while now—especially as some of the U.S. agencies just saw the U.K. as a route to extend its reach into Europe, and not as any sort of partner. The "special relationship" was, in effect, history.

But the big picture wasn't exactly on top of my agenda right now. I didn't care what had been botched. I didn't even care who had sponsored the job and why it had had to happen. I just wanted to get out of this room in one piece. "As I said, Mr. Frampton, the lights were up and I ordered the shoot. Maybe if the three snipers were debriefed they could . . ."

He looked at my lips but my words seemed not to register. "You have let a serious problem develop in Central America, Stone. Do you not realize the implications?"

"No, sir"—he always liked that. "I don't, sir."

His right hand came off his hip and he stared at the face of his watch. "No, sir, that's right, you don't, sir. Because of you, we, the Service, are not influencing events in a direction favorable to Britain."

He was starting to sound like a political broadcast. I couldn't have cared less what was happening in Central America. All I was worried about was now, here.

The Yes Man sighed as he loosened his scarlet tie and opened his collar. Some beads of sweat dribbled down the side of his flushed face. He thumbed behind him in the direction of Sundance. "Now, go with this man to collect the tape and all the other material that you claim to have on this operation, and I'll see about trying to save your tail."

"I can't do that, sir."

He stiffened. He was starting to lose it. "Can't do that, sir?"

I'd have thought it was perfectly obvious, but I didn't want to sound disrespectful. "I'm sorry, Mr. Frampton, but I need to make sure you don't have a change of heart about me." I chanced a smile. "I like being alive. I understand the reasons why the snipers were killed. I just don't want to join them."

The Yes Man crouched down so that his eyes were level with mine. He was struggling to control a rage that was threatening to burst out of his face.

"Let me tell you something, Stone. Things are changing in my department. A new permanent cadre is being installed, and very soon all the dead wood will be cleared away. People like you will cease to exist." He was nearly shaking with anger. He knew I had him by the balls, for now. Fighting his rage, he kept his voice very low. "You've always been nothing but trouble, haven't you?"

I was averting my gaze, trying to look frightened—and I was a bit. But unfortunately I caught sight of a large, freshly squeezed zit below his collar line. He didn't like that. He stood up abruptly, and stormed from the room. Sundance shot me a threatening glare and followed him.

I tried to listen to the mumbling going on between the four of them in the garage, but with no luck. A few seconds later car doors slammed, the shutter went up, and the car reversed out. The shutter hit the floor once more, and then everything went quiet.

Except in my head. One half was telling me everything was okay. No way would he chance the job's being exposed. The other was telling me that maybe he really didn't care what I was saying. I tried to make myself feel better by running through what had happened, convincing myself that I'd said the right things in the right way at the right time. Then I threw up my hands. It was too late now to worry about it. I'd just have to wait and see.

Sneakers and Sundance reappeared. I looked up, trying to read their expressions. They didn't look good.

The first kick was aimed at my chest. My body reflexed into a ball but Sundance's boot connected hard with my thigh. By now my chin was down, my teeth were clenched, and I'd closed my eyes. There was nothing I could do but accept the inevitable, curled up like a hedgehog, my hands still cuffed, trying to protect my face. I started to take it and just hoped that it wouldn't carry on for long.

They grabbed my feet and dragged me toward the center of the room. One of the mugs rattled over on the tiles. I kept my legs as bent as I could, fighting against their being stretched out to expose my stomach and balls. I opened one eye just in time to watch a Caterpillar boot connect with my ribs. I brought my head down farther, in an attempt to cover my chest. It must have worked, because another boot swung right into my ass this time, and it felt as if the inside of my sphincter had exploded. The pain was off the scale and to counteract it I tried to clench my cheek muscles together—but to do that I had to straighten my legs a little.

The inevitable boot flew into the pit of my stomach. Bile exploded from me. The acid taste in my mouth and nose was almost worse than the kicking.

It was past midnight and I was curled up back in my corner. At least they'd taken the cuffs off now. The lights were off and the TV flickered away with a Channel 5 soft-porn film. They'd had burgers and fries earlier and made me crawl over to wipe up my bile from the floor with the used wrappers as they drank more tea.

There was no more filling in, not even an acknowl- edgment of my being there. I had just been left to stew as Sundance lay half asleep on the couch. Sneakers was wide awake and on stag (watch), smok- ing his roll-up, draped across the two armchairs, making sure I didn't have any stupid ideas.

I slowly stretched out flat on my stomach to lessen the pain from the kicking, and rested my face on my hands, closing my eyes to try to get some sleep. It was never going to work: I could feel the blood pumping in my neck and couldn't stop thinking about what might happen to me next. My waterfront trip could still be in the cards with these two; it all depended on what the Yes Man had to say yes to, I supposed.

In the past, I'd always managed to get out of even the deepest shit with just the thinnest layer still stuck to me. I thought of my gunshot wound, sewn-back-on earlobe, and dog-bite scars, and knew how lucky I'd been on those jobs in the last few years. I thought of other jobs, of being blindfolded and lined up against the wall of an aircraft hangar, listening to the noise of weapons being cocked. I remembered hearing the men on each side of me, either quietly praying or openly crying and begging. I hadn't seen any reason to do either. It wasn't that I wanted to die; just that I'd always known that death was part of the deal.

But this did feel different. I thought of Kelly. I hadn't spoken to her since this job started. Not because there had been no opportunity—I had agreed times with Josh last month—it was just that I was too busy with preparations, or sometimes I just forgot.

Josh was right to give me hell when I did get through: she did need a routine and stability. I could see his half-Mexican, half-black shaved head, scowling at me on the phone. The skin on his jaw and cheekbone was a patchwork of pink, like a torn sponge that had been badly sewn back together. The scarring was due to me, which didn't help the situation much. He wouldn't be getting too many modeling offers from Old Spice, that was for sure. I tried to break the ice with him once by telling him that. He didn't exactly fall down with laughter.

I turned my head and rested my cheek on my hands, watching Sneakers suck on the last of his roll-up cigarette. I supposed I'd always known the day would come, sooner or later, but I didn't want this to be it. Stuff flashed through my mind as if I were a split second away from a massive car crash, all the sorts of things that must hit any parent when they know they're about to die. The stupid argument with the kids before leaving for work. Not building that tree house. Not getting around to filling out a will. The vacations not taken, the promises broken.

Josh was the only person apart from Kelly I cared for and who was still alive. Would he miss me? He'd just be pissed that we had unfinished business. And what about Kelly herself? She had a new start now—would she just forget all about her useless, incompetent guardian in a few years?

7

Sundance's StarTac phone's short, sharp tones cut the air after a long, painful night. It was just after eight. I didn't bother to move from the prone position because of my kicking, but tried instead to convince myself that the pain was just weakness leaving the body, something like that.

Sneakers jumped up to turn off the BBC breakfast news, showing the Houses of Parliament, as Sundance opened up his phone. He knew who it was. There was no preliminary waffle, just nods and grunts.

Sneakers hit the electric kettle button as the phone was closed down and Sundance rolled himself off the couch. He gave me a big grin as he brushed back his hair with spread fingers. "You have a visitor, and d'ye know what? He doesn't sound too pleased."

It was the witching hour.

I sat up and leaned into the corner of the brick walls as they pulled the armchairs apart and put their shirts on while waiting for the kettle to boil.

It wasn't long before I heard a vehicle and Sneakers went out to open the shutter. Sundance just stood there staring at me, trying to get me worked up.

The kettle cut out with a click just before the shutter opened; it looked like their tea was on hold for a while. I pulled myself up against the wall.

The slamming of car doors drowned out the sound of Kennington's morning commute. Before the shutter had come down, the Yes Man was striding into the room. Throwing a glance at Sundance, he walked toward me, screwing up his nose at the smell of cigarettes, fries, and early-morning farts.

He was dressed today in a light gray suit, and still in enraged-teacher mode. He stopped a couple of paces short of me, put his hands on his hips, and looked down at me in disgust. "You, Stone, are going to be given one chance, just one, to rectify matters. You don't know how very lucky you are." He checked his watch. "The target has just left the U.K. You will follow him tonight, to Panama, and you will kill this target by last light Friday."

I kept my head down and let my legs flop out straight, just inches from his highly polished black brogues, and raised my eyes to him.

Sundance made a move toward me. Should I be saying something? The Yes Man held up a hand to stop him, without taking his eyes off me. "FARC is waiting for the delivery of a missile launch control system—a computer guidance console, to you."

I looked down again, concentrating on the pattern of his shoes.

"Are you listening?"

Nodding slowly, I rubbed my sore eyes.

"One antiaircraft missile is already in their possession. It will be the first of many. The launch system has to be stopped—if FARC have a complete weapons system in their hands the implications for Plan

Colombia will be catastrophic. There are six hundred million dollars' worth of U.S. helicopters in Colombia, along with their crews and support. FARC must not get the capability to shoot them down. They must not get that launch control system. You don't need to know why, but the young man's death will stop that happening. Period."

He hunched down and thrust his face so close to mine I could smell menthol aftershave, probably for sensitive skin. There was a whiff of halitosis, too, as we had eye contact just inches apart. He breathed in slowly, to help me understand that what he was about to say was more in sorrow than in anger. "You will carry out this task in the time specified, with due diligence. If not? No matter when—next week, next month, or even next year—when the time is right, we will kill her. You know who I'm talking about, that Little Orphan Annie of yours. She will simply cease to exist and it will be your doing. Only you can stop that happening."

He burned with the kind of evangelical zeal I supposed he'd copied from whoever he'd heard in the pulpit last week, while Sundance smirked and moved back toward the couch.

The Yes Man hadn't finished with me yet. His tone shifted. "She must be about eleven now, eh? I've been told that she's settled in very well back in the States. It seems that Joshua is doing an absolutely sterling job. It must be hard for you now she lives there, eh? Missing her growing up, turning into a fine young woman . . ."

I kept my eyes down, concentrating on a minute crack in one of the tiles as he carried on with his sermon.

"That's the same age as my daughter. They're so funny at that age, don't you think? One minute wanting to be all grown up, the next needing to cuddle their teddies. I read her a story last night when I'd tucked her in. They look so wonderful, yet so vulnerable like that . . . Did you read to—Kelly, isn't it?"

I wouldn't give him the satisfaction of an acknowledgment, just concentrated hard on my tile, trying to show no reaction. He was really making a meal of this. He took another deep breath, his knees cracking as he straightened up and hovered above me once more.

"This is about power, Stone, who has it and who does not. You do not. Personally, I am not in favor of your being given a second chance, but there is the broader matter of policy to consider."

I didn't exactly understand what that meant, but it was a fair guess he'd been told to sort out this situation or he'd be severely in the shit. "Why kill the boy?" I said. "Why not the father? I presume he's the one moving this system."

He kicked my thigh with his shiny toecap. It was pure frustration. I was sure he'd meant it to be harder, but just didn't have it in him. "Clean yourself up—look at the state of you. Now go. These gentlemen will collect you from your residence at three."

He gave "residence" the full three syllables, enjoying every one. Sundance smiled like the village idiot as I hauled myself to my feet, the muscles in my stomach protesting badly.

"I need money." I looked down like a scolded schoolboy as I leaned against the wall, and that was exactly how I felt.

The Yes Man sighed with impatience and nodded at Sundance. He dug out his wallet from the back of his jeans, and counted out eighty-five pounds.

"You owe me, boy."

I just took it, not bothering to mention the six hundred U.S. dollars he'd liberated from my pocket, and

which had already been split between the two of
them.

Jamming it into my jeans, I started to walk, not
looking at either of them as I reached the door.
Sneakers saw me in the door frame and hit the shutter, but not before the Yes Man had the last word:
"You'd better make good use of that money, Stone.
There is no more. In fact, think yourself lucky you're
keeping what you already have. After all, Orphan
Annie will need new shoes from time to time, and her
treatment in the States will cost a great deal more
than it did at the Moorings."

Fifteen minutes later I was on the subway from
Kennington, heading north toward Camden Town.
The dilapidated old train was packed tight with
morning commuters, nearly every one radiating soap,
toothpaste, and designer smells. I was the exception,
which was bad luck for the people I was sandwiched
between: a massive black guy who'd turned his crisply
laundered, white-shirted back on me, and a young
white woman who didn't dare look up from the floor
in case our eyes met and she sparked off the madman
reeking of bile and cigarettes.

The front pages of the morning papers were covered with dramatic color pictures of the police attacking the sniper positions and the promise of a lot more
to come inside. I just held on to the handrail and
stared at the dot-com vacation ads, not wanting to
read them, instead letting my head jolt from side to side
as we trundled north. I was in a daze, trying to get
my head around what had happened, and getting
nowhere.

What could I do with Kelly? Nip over to Maryland,
pick her up, run away, and hide in the woods? Taking
her away from Josh was pure fantasy: it would only

screw her up even more than she was already. It would only be short-term, in any event: if the Firm wanted her dead, they'd make it happen eventually. What about telling Josh? No need: the Firm wouldn't do anything unless I failed. Besides, why stir him up any more than I had already?

I let my head drop and stared at my feet as we got to a station and people fought each other to get on and off all at the same time. I got shoved and jostled and gave an involuntary gasp of pain.

As the car repacked itself for the journey under the Thames, a pissed-off voice on the PA system told everybody to move right into the cars, and the doors eventually closed.

I didn't know if the Yes Man was bluffing—any more, probably, than he knew if I was. But it made no difference. Even if I did expose the job, that wouldn't stop Sundance and Sneakers taking their trip to Maryland. There were enough Serb families short of a kid or two because Dad hadn't gone along with the Firm's demands during the latest Balkan wars, and I knew it hadn't stopped there.

Try as I might, I couldn't stop myself picturing Kelly tucked up in bed, her hair spread in a mess over the pillow as she dreamed of being a pop star. The Yes Man was right, they did look both wonderful and vulnerable like that. My blood ran cold as I realized that the end of this job wouldn't put an end to the threats. She would be used against me time and again.

We stopped at another station and the crowd ebbed and flowed once more. I took a deep breath and exhaled slowly. I was starting to get pins and needles in my legs. No matter which way I looked at it, my only option was to kill the boy. No, not a boy, let's get this right, just as the Yes Man said, he was a young man—some of those weapons being cocked in the aircraft hangar all those years ago had been held by people younger than him.

I had screwed up big-time. I should have killed him yesterday when I had the chance. If I didn't do this job Kelly would die, simple as that—and I couldn't let that happen. I wouldn't fuck up again. I'd do what the Yes Man wanted, and I'd do it by last light Friday.

The train stopped again and most of the passengers left for their jobs in the City, London's financial center. I was exhausted and fell into a seat before my legs gave out. As I wiped the beads of sweat off my brow, my mind kept going back to Kelly, and the thought that I was going to Panama to kill someone just so that Josh could have her to look after. It was madness, but what was new about that?

Josh might not exactly be my pal, these days, but he was still the closest thing I had to one. He'd talk through gritted teeth, but at least he'd talk to me about Kelly. She'd been living with Josh and his kids since mid-August, just a couple of weeks after her therapy sessions had ended prematurely in London when the Yes Man handed me the sniper job.

She hadn't fully recovered from her PTSD (post-traumatic stress disorder), and I didn't know whether she ever would. Seeing your whole family butchered took some recovering from. She was a fighter, just like her dad had been, and had made dramatic strides this summer. She'd moved from being a curled-up bundle of nothing to being able to function outside the private care home in Hampstead where she'd spent the best part of the last ten months. She wasn't in mainstream schooling yet with Josh's kids, but that would happen soon. Or at least I hoped it would: she needed private tutoring and that didn't come cheap— and now the Yes Man had canceled the second half of the money. . . .

Since March I'd had to commit myself to being with her during the therapy sessions three times a week in Chelsea, and on all the other days had visited her at the place in Hampstead where she was being looked after. Kelly and I would subway down to the plush clinic, the Moorings. Sometimes we'd talk on the journey, mostly about kids' TV; sometimes we'd sit in silence. On occasion, she'd just cuddle into me and sleep.

Dr. Hughes was in her mid-fifties and looked more like an American TV anchor than a shrink in her leather armchair. I didn't particularly like it when Kelly said something that Hughes considered meaningful. She would tilt her elegant head and look at me over the top of her gold half-glasses. "How do you feel about that, Nick?"

My answer was always the same: "We're here for Kelly, not me." That was because I was an emotional dwarf. I must be—Josh told me so.

The train shuddered and squeaked to a halt at Camden Town. I joined a green-haired punk, a bunch of suits, and some early-start tourists as we all rode the up escalator. Camden High Street was teeming with traffic and pedestrians. We were greeted by a white Rastafarian guy juggling three beanbags for spare change and an old drunk with his can of Guinness waiting for Pizza Hut to open so that he could go and shout at its windows. The din of jackhammers on the building site opposite echoed all around us, making even people passing in their cars wince.

I diced with death as I crossed the road to get into Superdrug and pick up some washing and shaving things, then walked along the main street to get something to eat, hands in my pockets and eyes down at the sidewalk like a dejected teenager. I waded through KFC boxes, kebab wrappers, and smashed

Bacardi bottles that hadn't been cleaned up from the night before. As I'd discovered when I moved in, there was a disproportionate number of pubs and clubs around here.

Camden High Street and its markets seemed quite a tourist attraction. It was just before ten o'clock but most of the clothes shops already had an amazing array of gear hanging outside their shopfronts, from psychedelic bell-bottoms to leather bondage pants and multicolored Doc Martens. Shop workers tried ceaselessly to lure Norwegians or Americans, with packs on their backs and maps in their hands, inside with loud music and a smile.

I passed under the scaffold that covered the sidewalk on the corner of Inverness Street and got a nod from the Bosnian refugee who sold smuggled cigarettes out of a sports bag. He was holding out a couple of cartons to passersby—and in his imitation-leather bomber jacket and sweat pants he looked just like I felt, tired of life. We knew each other by sight and I nodded back before turning left into the market. My stomach was so empty it ached, adding to the pain from the kicking. I was really looking forward to breakfast.

The café was full of construction workers taking a break from building the new Gap and Starbucks. Their dirty yellow hardhats were lined up against the wall like helmets at a fire station, while they filled their faces with the three-pound all-day breakfast. The room was a noisy haze of fried food and cigarette smoke, probably courtesy of the Bosnian. I put in my order and listened to the radio behind the counter while I picked up my mug of instant coffee. The news gave only bullet-point headlines about yesterday's terrorist incident. It was already taking second place to Posh Spice's new hairdo.

I settled down at a four-seater wrought-iron-and-marble-effect garden table, moved the overflowing ashtray out of the way, and stared at the sugar bowl. The pins and needles had returned and I found that my elbows were on the table and my face was stuck in my hands. For some reason I was remembering being seven years old, tears running down my face, trying to explain to my stepfather that I was scared of the dark. Instead of a comforting cuddle and the bedroom light left on, I got a slapped face and was told not to be such a wimp or the night monster would come out from under the bed and eat me. He used to make me fret big-time, and I'd spend the whole night curled up under the blanket, petrified, thinking that as long as I didn't look out the night monster wouldn't get me. The same feeling of terror and helplessness was with me again after all these years.

I was jolted from my trance. "Breakfast special, extra egg?"

"That's me."

I sat back down and devoured bacon, sausage, and egg and started to think about my shopping list. At least I wouldn't need much clothing for my Central American trip. There now, maybe things weren't that bad: I was going somewhere warm.

I'd never been to Panama, but had operated on its border with Colombia against FARC (Revolutionary Armed Forces of Colombia) while in the Regiment (SAS). We were part of the U.K.'s first-strike policy in the eighties, an American-funded operation to hit drug manufacture at the source, which meant getting into the jungle for weeks on end, finding the DMPs (drug-manufacturing plants), and destroying them to slow the trafficking to the U.K. and U.S. We might as well not have bothered. Over 70 percent of the cocaine entering the States still originated from Colombia, and up to 75 percent of the heroin seized on the east coast of the U.S. was Colombian. FARC had their fingers in a substantial amount of that pie, and those kinds of numbers were also heading this way, to the U.K.

Having operated in the region for over a year, I still took an interest—especially as most of the Colombians I'd cared anything about had been killed in the war. To keep the peace with FARC, the Colombian government had given them control of an area the size of Switzerland, and they ran all their operations from there. It was hoped that things would change now that Plan Colombia was getting into full swing. Clinton had given the Colombian government a $1.3 billion military aid package to combat drug trafficking, including over sixty of the Yes Man's precious Huey and Black Hawk helicopters, along with other military assistance. But I wasn't holding my breath. It was going to be a long and dirty war.

I also knew that, for most of the twentieth century, the U.S.A. had paid for, run, and protected the Panama Canal and stationed SOUTHCOM (the U.S. Army's Southern Command) in-country. It was SOUTHCOM that had directed all military and intelligence operations from Mexico's southern border to Cape Horn during my time in Colombia. Thousands of U.S. troops and aircraft stationed in Panama had been responsible for all the antidrug operations in Central and South America, but that had stopped at midnight on December 31, 1999, when the U.S. handed back control of the canal to the locals, and SOUTHCOM and all American presence was withdrawn. It was now fragmented, spread around bases all over Central America and the Caribbean, and nowhere near as effective at fighting any kind of war as it once had been.

From what I'd read, the handover of the canal had sort of sneaked up on the American public. And when they discovered that a Chinese company, not American, had been awarded the contract to operate the ports at each end of the canal and take over some of the old U.S. military facilities, the right wing went apeshit. I couldn't see the problem myself: Chinese-owned companies ran ports all around the world, including Dover and others in this country. I hadn't thought of it at the time, but maybe that was why the Chinaman had been in the delegation, as part of the new order in Central America.

I felt a little better after some death-by-cholesterol, and left the café wiping egg yolk off my fingers and onto my jeans, where a fair amount of it had dribbled anyway.

A fifteen-minute shopping frenzy in the market bought me a new pair of knockoff Levi's for sixteen quid, a blue sweatshirt for seven, a pair of boxers and a pack of three pairs of socks for another five.

I carried on walking past fruit and vegetable stalls until I came to Arlington Road, and turned right by the Good Mixer pub, a 1960s monstrosity in need of a lick of paint. The usual suspects were sitting against the pub wall, three old men, unshaven and unwashed, tossing back cans of hard cider. All three held out their grime-ingrained palms for money without even looking up at the people they were begging from.

I was just a few minutes away from a hot shower. Maybe a hundred yards ahead, outside my impressive Victorian redbrick residence, I could see someone being trolleyed into the back of an ambulance. This was nothing unusual around here, and no one passing gave it a second look.

Walking past the graffiti-filled walls of the decaying, pollution-stained buildings, I approached the front entrance as the ambulance moved off. There was a white van behind it. Gathered around its open rear doors were a group of Eastern Europeans, all carrying sports bags or backpacks. Of course—it was Monday: the boys from Manchester were dishing out smuggled cigarettes and rolling tobacco for them to sell in the market and pubs.

Two worn stone steps took me to a set of large, glazed wooden doors, which I pushed my way through. I buzzed to be let through the second set of security doors, and pressed my head against the glass so whoever was on duty could check me out.

The door buzzed and I pushed through. I got a smile off Maureen at reception, a huge, fifty-year-old woman who had a liking for tent-sized flowery dresses, and a face like a bulldog with constipation. She took no nonsense from anybody. She looked me up and down with an arched eyebrow. "Hello, darling, what are you doing here?"

I put on my happy face. "I missed you."

She rolled her eyes and gave her usual loud bass laugh. "Yeah, right."

"Is there any chance of using a shower? It's just that the plumbing in my new place has broken down." I held up my bag of toiletries for her to see.

She rolled her eyes at my story and sucked her teeth, not believing a word of it. "Ten minutes, don't tell."

"Maureen, you're the best."

"Tell me something I don't know, darling. Remember, ten minutes, that's your lot."

I'd only said about a dozen words to her all the time I'd lived here. This was the closest we'd been to a conversation for months.

I walked up the steps to the second floor, where the

décor was easy-clean, thick-gloss walls, and a light gray industrial-linoleum staircase, then walked along the narrow hallway, heading for the showers at the end. To my left were rows of doors to bedrooms, and I could hear their occupants mumbling to themselves, coughing, snoring. The hallway smelled of beer and cigarettes, with stale bread slices and cigarette butts trodden into the threadbare carpet.

There was a bit of a racket on the floor above as some old guy babbled, having an argument with himself, and profanities bounced off the walls. It was sometimes difficult to work out if it was alcohol, drugs, or a mental condition with these guys. Either way, official policy seemed to mean leaving them to look after themselves.

The showers were three stained cubicles and I got into the center one, slowly peeling off my clothes as men wandered around the hallway and noises echoed. Once undressed, I turned on the water. I was in a daze again, just wanting my day to end, forcing myself to check the bruising on my legs and chest, even though I didn't care if it hurt.

Somebody in the hallway called out my name, and I recognized the voice. I didn't know his name, just that he was always drunk. As with the rest of them, it was the only way that he could escape his miserable life. In a slurred northern accent he shouted the same old thing, over and over again, about how God had fucked him over. He used to have a wife, kids, a house, a job. It had all gone wrong, he'd lost everything, and it was all God's fault.

I got under the water, trying my hardest to block out the noise as the others started to join in, telling him to shut the hell up.

The city-run "shelter" was what we used to call a flophouse when we were kids. Nowadays it was filled not only with homeless men of every age with uniformly sad lives, but also Bosnian, Serbian, and Kosovan refugees, who seemed to have brought their war to London as they fought among themselves in the hallways and bathrooms.

The noises outside the shower started to merge and magnify inside my head. My heartbeat went into overdrive and my legs felt numb with pins and needles again. I slumped down in the shower stall and covered my ears with my hands.

I just sat there covering my ears, squeezing my eyes shut, trying to block out the noise, plagued by the same childlike terror that had overwhelmed me in the café.

The image that the Yes Man had planted in my head, of Kelly in bed asleep, in the dark, was still with me. She'd be there now, this minute, in Maryland. She would be in her bunk bed, below Josh's eldest daughter. I knew exactly how she would look. I had woken up and tucked her back in so many times when it was cold, or when a memory of her murdered family had returned to haunt her. She would be half in, half out of her comforter, stretched out on her back, arms and legs out like a starfish, sucking her bottom lip, her eyes flickering under their lids as she dreamed.

Then I thought of her dead. No sucking of the lip, no REM, just a stiff, dead starfish. I tried to imagine how I would feel if that happened, knowing that I had the responsibility to make sure that it didn't. It didn't bear thinking about. I wasn't sure if it was in my head, or I was yelling it out loud, but I heard my own voice shout, "How the fuck did you end up like this?"

8

I was turning into one of those nutcases out there in the hall. I'd never had much difficulty understanding why they turned to drink and drugs to escape the shit of the real world.

I sat there for a few minutes longer, just feeling sorry for myself, looking at the only things I had to show for my progress through the real world: a pink dent in my stomach from a 9mm round, and the neat row of puncture holes on my right forearm from a North Carolina police dog.

I lifted my head out of my hands and gave myself a strict talking-to. "Pull yourself together, dickhead! Get a grip. Get yourself out of this . . ."

I had to cut away, just like I'd learned to do as a kid. No one was coming to help me deal with the night monster; I had to get on with it on my own.

I cleared my nostrils of mucus, and it was only then that I realized I must have been crying.

Hauling myself to my feet I pulled out the washing and shaving things and got to work. After I'd cleaned myself up I stayed in the cubicle for another ten minutes, using my old clothes to dry myself. I threw on my new jeans and sweatshirt; the only old things I put back on were my Timberlands, bomber jacket, and belt.

I left everything else in the shower—they could have that as my going-away present—and walked back along the hallway. Through his open door whatever-his-name-was had finished ranting about God and collapsed facedown on his urine-stained bed. A bit farther on, I passed the closed door to my old cell-like room. I'd only left the previous Saturday but it already had a new occupant; I could hear a radio being tuned in. He, too, probably had his carton of milk out on the sill of the narrow window. We all did—well, the ones who had a kettle.

I made my way down the stairs, brushing my hair back with my fingers and regaining some composure.

Down in the reception area, I picked up the wall-mounted phone, shoved in six and a half pounds' worth of coins, and started dialing Josh, trying desperately to think of an excuse for calling him so early. The east coast of the U.S. was five hours behind.

The distinctive tone rang just twice before I heard a sleepy American grunt. "Yeah?"

"Josh, it's me, Nick." I hoped he wouldn't notice the tremor in my voice.

"What do you want, Nick? It's just after six."

I covered the other ear to cut out some young guy who needed help up the stairs from an old drunk as he staggered about with glazed and drugged-out eyes. I'd seen them both before: the old guy was his father, who also lived here.

"I know, I'm sorry, mate. It's just that I can't make it until next Tuesday and I—"

There was a loud sigh. He'd heard my I-can't-make-it routine so many times before. He knew nothing of my situation, he knew nothing of what had been going on these last few months. All he'd seen of me was the money I sent.

"Look, I know, mate, I'm sorry, I really can't make it."

The earpiece barked: "Why can't you get your life in good order? We arranged *this* Tuesday—that's tomorrow, man. She's got her heart set on it. She loves you so much, man, so much—don't you get it? You can't just breeze in and—"

I knew what he was going to say and cut in, almost begging, "I know, I know. I'm sorry . . ." I knew where the conversation was going and also knew that he was right in taking it there. "Please, Josh—can I talk with her?"

He lost his cool for once and went ballistic. "No!"

"I—"

It was too late; he'd hung up.

I slumped down on a plastic stackable chair, staring at one of the notice boards telling people what and what not to do, and how to do it.

"You okay, darling?"

I looked across at Maureen, on the other side of the reception booth. She waved me over, sounding like an older sister, I supposed. "You look fed up. Come and have a chat, come on, darling."

My mind was elsewhere as I approached the hole in the wall that gave access of a kind to her desk. It was at head height. Anything bigger and lower and she wouldn't have had any protection from the drunks and the drugged-up who had a problem with the house rules.

"Been a bad call to that little girl of yours?"

"What?"

"You keep yourself to yourself, but I see things from this little cubbyhole, you know. I've heard you on the phone, coming off more depressed than when you went on. I don't just buzz the door open, you know!" She gave a loud roar as I smiled and acknowledged her attempt to cheer me up. "Was it a bad one, darling? You okay?"

"It was all right."

"That's good, I'm glad. You know, I've watched you come in and out of here, looking so sad. I reckoned it was a divorce—I can normally tell. It must be hard not seeing your little 'un. I was just worried about you, that's all, darling."

"No need, Maureen, things are okay, really."

She tutted in agreement. "Good . . . good, but, you know, things normally—"

Her attention was drawn momentarily to the staircase. Kosovans or whoever had started shouting angrily at each other on one of the upper landings. She shrugged at me and grinned. "Well, let's just say things have a way of sorting themselves out. I've seen that look of yours in here before. And I tell them all the same, and I'm always right. Things can only get better, you'll see."

At that moment a fight erupted above us somewhere and a Nike sports bag tumbled down the stairs, soon followed by its tobacco-selling owner in a brown V-neck sweater and white socks. Maureen reached for her two-way radio as a couple of guys jumped down after him and started giving the boy a good kicking. Maureen talked into her radio with a calm assurance that only comes from years of experience.

I leaned against the wall as a couple more tobacco-sellers appeared and tried to stop the fight.

Within minutes, sirens were wailing in the distance, and getting louder. Maureen hit the door buzzer and tobacco-sellers bomb-burst back into the hostel, bags in hand, thinking they were getting raided, running to their rooms to hide their stashes and leaving the boys from Manchester outside to fend for themselves. Close behind them, four police officers pushed their way in to sort out the commotion.

I checked Baby-G, a new black watch with purple illumination. Over three hours to go before pickup, and there was nothing I wanted to do. I didn't want to eat, didn't want to drink, didn't even want to just sit around, and I certainly didn't want Maureen gazing into my soul, no matter how helpful she was trying to be. She knew too much already. So I started heading out toward the street, nodding my thanks. Even in a time of crisis she gave me a second of her time. "You need to stop worrying, Nick. Worrying too much affects this, you know." She tapped the side of her forehead with her index finger. "I've seen enough of that in here to know, darling."

One of the phones rang behind her as the scuffle continued at the bottom of the stairs. "Got to go, luv. I hope things work out for you—they normally do, you know. Good luck, darling."

Once outside, the noise of the construction site drowned out the shouting. I slouched on the steps, staring at the paving slabs as the fighters were dragged away, their angry voices lost among the roar of jackhammers.

On the dot of three P.M. the Merc cruised past and found a space farther down the road. Sneakers was at the wheel and Sundance next to him. They left the engine running.

I unstuck my very numb ass from the steps and dragged myself toward them. They were dressed in the same clothes as this morning, and drinking coffee out of paper cups. I took my time—not to make them wait, but because my body couldn't move any quicker, just like my mind.

They gave me no acknowledgment as I got into the back and they put their seat belts back on.

Sundance threw a brown envelope over his shoulder at me as we drove off. "I've already taken five hundred out of the account, so don't bother trying again today. That covers the eighty-five sub—plus interest."

They grinned at each other. The job had its compensations.

My new passport and credit card were hot off the press but looking suitably aged, along with my new PIN number and open-return plane ticket, leaving Miami to Panama City, 7:05 A.M. tomorrow. How I got to Miami by then didn't bother me—I'd be told soon enough.

I flicked through my visas so I knew that I'd been on vacation for two weeks in Morocco in July. The stamps were all related to the truth—I had been there, just not as recently. But at least it meant I could bluff my way through a routine check at Immigration and Customs. The rest of my cover story would be the same as ever, just traveling after a boring life selling insurance; I had done most of Europe, now I wanted to see the rest of the world.

I still wasn't impressed by my cover name, though. Hoff—why Hoff? It didn't sound right. Nick Hoff, Nick Hoff. It didn't even start with the same letter as my real surname, so it was difficult not to get confused and hesitant when signing a signature. Hoff sounded unnatural: if you were called Hoff, you wouldn't name your son Nicholas unless you wanted to give him a tough time at school; it sounded like someone with a speech impediment saying "hiccough."

Sundance didn't ask for a signature, and that bothered me. I got pissed with bullshit when it was official, but even more so when it wasn't.

"What about my CA (cover address)?" I asked. "Can I call them?"

Sundance didn't bother to look around as we bumped along in the traffic. "It's already done." He dipped into his jeans and brought out a scrap of paper. "The new mini traffic circle has been built at last, but everyone is still waiting on the decision about the bypass. That comes through some time next month."

I nodded; it was an update on the local news from what the Yes Man had renamed the Cover Address. James and Rosemary had loved me like a son since I boarded with them years ago, or so the cover story went. I even had a bedroom there, and some clothes in the wardrobe.

These were the people who would both confirm my cover story and be part of it. They'd never take any action on my behalf, but would back me up if I needed them to. "That's where I live," I could tell whoever was questioning me. "Phone them, ask them."

I visited James and Rosemary whenever I could, so my cover had gotten stronger as time passed. They knew nothing about the ops and didn't want to; we would just talk about what was going on at the social club, and a bit of other local and personal stuff. I needed to know these things because I would if I lived there all the time. I hadn't wanted to use them for the sniper job, because that would have meant the Firm knowing the name I was traveling under, and where to. As things had turned out, it looked as if I'd been right.

Sundance started to tell me how I was going to make it to Miami in time for my flight to Panama. The Yes Man hadn't hung about. Within four hours I was going to be lying in a sleeping bag on top of some crates of military equipment stuffed into an RAF Tristar, leaving RAF Brize Norton, near Oxford, for Fort Campbell in Kentucky, where a Jock infantry battalion was having a joint exercise with the 101st Airborne Division "Screaming Eagles." They had given up their parachutes years ago and now screamed around in more helicopters than nearly all of the European armies put together. There were no commercial flights this time of day that would get me where I needed to be by tomorrow morning; this was the only way. I was getting kicked off in Florida, and a U.S. visa waiver would be stamped in my passport at the Marine base. I then had three hours in which to transfer to Miami airport and make the flight to Panama.

Sundance growled as he looked out at two women waiting for a bus. "Once you get there you are being sponsored by two doctors." He glanced at his notes again. "Carrie and Aaron Yanklewitz. Fucking stupid name."

He looked at Sneakers, who nodded in agreement before getting back to the scrap of paper.

"There will be no contact with Mr. Frampton or anyone here. Everything to, or from, is via their handler."

I wondered if there was just a faint chance the Yanklewitzes were Polish Americans. My head was pressed against the window as I gazed out at real life passing me by.

"Are you listening, fuckhead?"

I looked in the rearview mirror and could see him, waiting for a reply. I nodded.

"They'll be at the airport with a name card and a pass number of thirteen. You got that? Thirteen."

I nodded once more, this time not bothering to look at him.

"They'll show you the wee boy's house, and should have all the imagery and stuff by the time you get there. They don't know what your job is. But we do, don't we, boy?" He swiveled around to face me as I continued to gaze at nothing in particular, not feeling anything, just numb. "And that's to finish the job, isn't it?" He jabbed the air between us with his forefinger as he spoke. "You're going to finish what you were paid to do. And it's going to be done by Friday, last light. Do you understand, Stone? Finish it."

I felt more depressed and pissed off each time the job was mentioned. "I'd be lost without you."

Sundance's finger and thumb jabbed the air again as he made not too good a job of containing his rage. "Kill the fucking boy." He spat the words and flecks of saliva showered onto my face.

I got the feeling everyone was under pressure in this car, and I bet that was because the Yes Man was himself. I wondered if C had been told about my security blanket—or had the Yes Man decided to claim that the "botching" was down to bad comms? After all, that was what I'd told him, wasn't it? I couldn't remember now.

The Yes Man had probably told C that good old Stone—whom C wouldn't know if I fell out of the sky and landed on his head—was on the case, and everything was going to be just fine. But I had the sneaking suspicion I was only going to Panama instead of the waterfront because I was the only one on the books soft enough in the head to try to pull it off.

As we joined the A40 highway out of London and headed for Brize, I tried to focus on the job. I needed to fill my head with work instead of woe. At least that was the theory. But it was easier said than done. I was penniless. I'd sold the Ducati, the house in Norfolk, even the furniture, everything apart from what I could shove into a sports bag, to pay for Kelly's treatment. Twenty-four-hour private care in leafy Hampstead and regular trips to the Moorings had cleaned me out.

Walking away from the Norfolk house for the last time, I'd felt the same trepidation I had as a sixteen-year-old walking away from the projects to join the Army. Back then, I hadn't had a sports bag, but a pair of holed socks, a still-wrapped bar of Wright's Coal Tar soap, and one very old toothbrush in a drugstore plastic carrier. I planned to buy the toothpaste on my first payday, not knowing when exactly that was, or how much I was going to get. I hadn't really cared, because however bad the Army might be, it was getting me out of a life of correction facilities and a step-father who had graduated from slaps to punches.

Since March, the start of Kelly's therapy, I hadn't been able to work. And with no national ID card, no record of employment—not so much as a postcard to prove my existence after leaving the Regiment—I couldn't even claim welfare. The Firm wasn't going to help: I was deniable. And no one at headquarters wants to know you if you aren't able to work, or if there isn't any to give you.

For the first month or so of her sessions I'd done the bedsit shuffle around London—if I was lucky, being able to do a runner whenever the landlord was stupid enough not to ask for money up front. Then, with the help of Nick Somerhurst's national ID card bought in the Good Mixer, I was able to get a place in the hostel, lining up at mealtimes by the Hari Krishna van, just outside the Mecca bingo hall. It had also gotten me the Somerhurst passport and supporting documents. I didn't want to have the Yes Man tracking me with docs from the Firm.

I couldn't help smiling as I remembered one of the

Krishna gang, Peter, a young guy who always had a grin on his face. He had a shaved head and skin so pale he looked as if he should have been dead, but I soon discovered he was very much alive. Dressed in his red robes, hand-knitted blue sweater, and a multi-colored woolly hat, he used to run about inside the rusty white Mercedes van, pouring tea, dishing out great curries and bread, doing the Krishna rap. "Yo, Nick! Krishnaaa, Krishnaaaa, Krishnaaaa. Yo! Hari rammaaaaa." I never felt quite up to joining in, though some of the others did, especially the drunks. As he danced about inside the van the tea would spill and the odd slice of bread would fall off the paper plate, but it was still much appreciated.

I went on staring out of the window, cocooned in my own little rusty world while the other one passed me by on the street.

The A40 opened up into the expressway and Sundance decided it was time for a bit of a performance.

"You know what?" He looked over at Sneakers, making sure I could hear.

Sneakers swung into the outside lane, at the same time passing his tobacco to Sundance. "What's that, then?"

"I wouldn't mind a trip to Maryland. . . . We could go to Washington and do the sights first. . . ."

I knew what they were trying to do to me and I continued to stare at the hard shoulder of the road.

Sneakers was sounding enthusiastic. "It'd be good *craic*, I'm telling yer."

Sundance finished licking the cigarette paper before answering. "Aye, it would. I hear Laurel—" He turned to face me. "That's where she lives now, isn't it?"

I didn't answer. He knew very well it was. Sundance turned back to face the road. "Well, I hear it's very picturesque there—you know, trees and grass and all that shit. Anyway, after we finished up there in Laurel, you could take me to see that half-sister of yours in New York. . . ."

"No fucking way you're getting near her!"

I had a terrible feeling in the pit of my stomach and had to breathe out quickly as I thought about what might happen if I didn't get the job done. But I was fucked if I was going to play their game. Besides, I was just too tired to react.

Just over an hour later the Merc pulled up outside the military airport at Brize, and Sneakers got out to organize the next stage of my life.

Nothing was said in the car as I listened to the roar of RAF transport jets taking off and watched soldiers from the Argyll and Sutherland Highlanders wander past in camouflage gear, bergens on their backs and Walkmans clamped to their ears. It was like going back in time. I felt I'd spent half my military life at this airfield, because as well as loading up for flights on a regular basis, just like the Highlanders, I had learned to parachute here. I'd loved it: after being stationed in a garrison town with only three pubs—one of which was out of bounds to lowlifes like me—and a fish and chips shop, this place had been Disneyland. They even had a bowling alley.

I watched as a captain herded the grunts through the doors, ticking them off on a clipboard as they passed into the large 1960s glass building.

Sneakers came back with a nervous-looking Crab Air (Royal Air Force) movements corporal. He probably didn't have a clue what was going on, just that he had to escort some pissed-off-looking civilian onto one of his nice aircraft. He was told to wait short of the car as Sneakers came and opened the rear curb-side door. I could only see him from the chest down as his hand beckoned me out.

As I shuffled my ass across the seat, Sundance called out, "Oi!"

I waited, looking at the footwell.

"Don't fuck up, boy."

I nodded: after our little talk on the way here, and the Yes Man's lecture earlier, I'd gotten the message. I climbed out and nodded a greeting to the Crab corporal.

We'd only gone a few paces when Sundance called to me yet again. I went back and poked my head through the rear door, which Sneakers had kept open. The roar of a transport jet made him shout and me move back into the car, my knees on the seat. "I forgot to ask, how is that kid of yours? I hear you two were going to the shrink before she left. Little soft in the head as well, is she?"

I couldn't hold it any longer: my body started to tremble.

He grinned, having gotten from me at last what he'd been gunning for the whole trip. "Maybe if you fuck up it'd be a good thing for the wee one—you know, we'd be doing her a favor."

He was enjoying every moment of this. I tried to remain calm, but it wasn't working. He could see me boiling underneath.

"Hurts, eh?"

I did my best not to react.

"So, boy, just fuck off out of my face, and get it right this time."

Fuck it.

I launched myself forward off my knees and gripped his head with both hands. In one movement I put my head down and pulled his face hard toward the top of my crown. I made contact and it hurt, making me dizzy.

Once outside I threw both my arms up in surrender. "It's okay, it's okay . . ."

I opened my eyes fully and looked in at Sundance. He was sunk into the seat, hands covering his nose, blood running between his fingers. I started toward the Crab, feeling a lot better as another bunch of Highlanders walked past, trying not to take too much notice of what was going on.

Sneakers looked as if he was trying to decide whether to drop me or not. He still hadn't made up his mind as I virtually pushed the frightened Crab into the building with me.

Fuck 'em, what did I have to lose?

9

I ease the pistol into my waistband, my wet palms sliding over the pistol grip. If she's here I don't want her to see the weapon. Maybe she already knows what's happened. . . .

I put my mouth against a little gap between the boxes. "Kelly, you there? It's me, Nick. Don't be scared, I'm going to crawl toward you. You'll see my head in a minute and I want to see a big smile. . . ."

I move boxes and squeeze through the gap, inching toward the back wall.

"I'm going to put my head around the corner now, Kelly."

I take a deep breath and move my head around the back of the box, smiling away but ready for the worst as sweat pours down my face.

She is there, facing me, eyes wide with terror, sitting, curled up in a fetal position, rocking her body backward and forward, holding her hands over her ears, looking so vulnerable and helpless.

"Hello."

She recognizes me, but just carries on rocking, staring at me with wide, wet, scared eyes.

"Mummy and Daddy can't come and get you just now, but you can come with me. Daddy told me it would be okay. Are you going to come with me, Kelly? Are you?"

"Sir, sir?"

I opened my eyes to see a very concerned flight attendant. "You okay, sir? Can I get you some water or something?"

My sweaty palms slid on the armrests as I pushed myself upright in my seat. She poured from a liter bottle into a plastic glass.

"Could I take the bottle, please?"

It was handed to me with an anxious smile and I thanked her, taking it in a shaking, wet hand before drinking it rapidly down. I wiped my sweaty face with my spare hand. It had been part of the same bad dream I'd had on the Tristar. Shit, I must be really beat. I peeled the sweatshirt from my skin and pulled myself together.

We had just hit cruising altitude on the four-and-some-hour flight from Miami to Panama City, scheduled to land at about 11:40 A.M. local, which was the same time zone as the U.S. east coast and five hours behind the U.K. My window seat was next to Central America's most antisocial citizen, a mid-thirties Latino woman with big hair and lots of stiff lacquer to keep it that way. I doubted her skull could even touch the headrest, the stuff was on so thick. She was dressed in imitation-leather, spray-on jeans and a denim-style jacket patterned with black and silver tiger stripes, and stared at me in disgust, sucking her teeth, as I got myself organized and downed the last of the water.

It was her turn to crash out now as I read the tourist-guide pages in the inflight magazine. I always found them invaluable for getting an idea of wherever I was going on fastballs like this. Besides, it got me away from the other stuff in my head, and into thinking about the job, the mission, what I was here for. I'd tried to buy a proper guidebook to Panama in Miami airport, but it seemed there wasn't much call for that sort of thing.

The magazine showed wonderful pictures of exotic birds and smiling Indian children in canoes, and things I already knew but wouldn't have been able to put so eloquently. "Panama is the most southern of the Central American countries, making the long, narrow country the umbilical cord joining South and Central America. It is in the shape of an S bordered on the west by Costa Rica, on the east by Colombia, and has roughly the same land mass as Ireland."

It went on to say that most people, and that included myself until my days in Colombia, thought that Panama's land boundaries were north and south. That was wrong: the country runs west to east. Facts like that were important to me if I had to leave in a hurry. I wouldn't want to find myself heading for Colombia by mistake; out of the frying pan and into the fire. The only way to go was west, to Costa Rica, the land of cheap plastic surgery and diving vacations. I knew that, because I'd read it in the waiting room at the Moorings.

Tiger Lil had fallen asleep and was snoring big-time, twisting in her seat, and farting every minute or so. I opened both the air-conditioning vents above us and aimed them in her direction to try to divert the smell.

The three pages of blurb and pictures went on to tell me that Panama was best known internationally for its canal, joining the Caribbean and the Pacific, and its "vibrant banking services." Then just a few more pictures of colorful flowers, with captions reminding us what a wonderful place it was and how lucky we all were to be flying there today. Not surprisingly, they didn't say anything about Operation Just Cause—the U.S. invasion in '89 to oust General Noriega, or the drug trafficking that makes the banking system so vibrant.

All the wonderful places listed to visit were exclusively west of Panama City, which was called in here "the interior." There was no mention at all about what lay to the east, especially the Darien Gap, the jungle area bordering Colombia. I knew that Darien Province is like a low-intensity war zone. Narco traffickers and guerrillas—usually one and the same thing—move in big groups between the two countries, armed to the teeth. There are even a few DMPs as the locals try to cash in on the industry, and Panamanian border police buzz around the sky in helicopter gunships, locked in a conflict they will never win. Some adventurous types travel down there to birdwatch or hunt for rare orchids, and become hostages or dead after stumbling across things the traffickers would have preferred they hadn't.

I also knew that the narcos, especially FARC, had been getting more adventurous now that the U.S. had pulled out from Panama. They were making incursions farther west into the country, and with only about 150 miles between the Colombian border and Panama City, I bet everyone was stressed.

After flicking through the rest of the magazine and not finding anything of interest, just glossy ads, I used it to fan my face as Tiger Lil farted and grunted once more.

Looking down at the endless blue of the Caribbean

sea, I thought about yesterday's call to Josh. He'd been right to hang up on me; it was maybe the eighth or ninth time I'd done that to him. Kelly did need stability and an as-normal-as-possible upbringing. That was precisely why she was there with him, and the not-calling-when-I-should, calling-when-I-shouldn't thing wasn't helping her at all.

I should have been there today to sign over my guardianship of Kelly completely to him, to change the present arrangement of joint responsibility. In her father's will, Josh and I had both been named as guardians, but I was the one who'd ended up with her. I couldn't even remember how that had come about, it just sort of had.

Food was being served and I tried to extract my tray from the armrest. It was proving difficult as Tiger Lil had overflowed her own space. I shook her gently and she opened one blurry eye before turning over as if I was to blame.

My food turned up in its prepacked tray and made me think of Peter, getting all the flophouse boys rapping, "Krishna, yo! Krishna, yo! Krishna, yo! Hari rama." I peeled back the foil to see a breakfast of pasta. Wielding a fork and moving my arms very carefully so as not to stir up my new friend, I decided to make a donation to those Krishna boys if ever I got back alive. The thought of Peter surprised me; it had popped up out of nowhere—like a lot of other stuff lately. I wanted to get back in the comfort zone of work as quickly as possible, and cut away from that stuff before I found myself joining the Caravan Club.

As I finished the pasta, I got thinking about the job and the little information Sundance had given me. The pass number for the meet with Aaron and Carrie Yanklewitz was thirteen. The system is easy and works well. Numbers are far better than confirmation statements because they're easier to remember. I once had a confirmation statement that went, "The count is having sardines with your mother tonight," and I was supposed to reply, "The sardines are restless." Who the hell made that one up?

Pass numbers are also especially good for people who aren't trained in tradecraft or, like me, are crap at remembering confirmation statements. For all I knew, these people could be either. I didn't know if they were experienced operators who knew how to conduct themselves on the ground, just contacts who were going to help me out with bed and breakfast, or big-timers who couldn't keep their mouths shut.

I didn't like anyone else being involved in anything I did, but this time I had no choice. I didn't know where the target lived or the target's routine, and I didn't have a whole lot of time to find out.

After eating I sat back and pushed myself against the seat to relax my sore stomach muscles. Pain shot across my rib cage to give me further reminders of the strength and endurance of Caterpillar boots.

Trying to relieve the pain in my chest as I moved, I faced slowly away from Tiger Lil and lowered the window blind. Below me green jungle now stretched as far as the horizon, looking from this altitude like the world's biggest broccoli patch.

I pulled the blanket over my head to cut out the smell.

10

The flight touched down ten minutes early, at eleven-thirty local time. One of the first off, I followed the signs for Baggage Claim and Customs, past banks of chrome and brown leatherette seating.

After three hours of air-conditioning, the heat hit me like a wall. In my hand were the two forms we'd been given to fill in on the plane, one for Immigration, one for Customs. Mine said that Nick Hoff was staying at the Marriott—there is always a Marriott.

Apart from the clothes I stood up in—jeans, sweatshirt, and bomber jacket—the only items I had with me were my passport and wallet containing five hundred U.S. dollars. It had come from an ATM in Miami departures, courtesy of my new Royal Bank of Scotland Visa card in my crap cover name.

Feeling like one of the Camden boys, I'd looked at myself in a bathroom mirror: sleep creases all over my face and hair sticking up like the lead singer in an indie band.

I needn't have worried. Passing through Immigration turned out to be a breeze, even without any luggage. I just handed over my declaration form to a bored, middle-aged man and he waved me through: I guessed they'd hardly be on the lookout for anyone trying to smuggle drugs *into* Central America.

I also shot through Customs, because all I had was nothing. I should really have bought a piece of hand luggage in Miami to look normal, but my head must have been elsewhere. Not that it mattered; the Panamanian Customs boys were obviously in the same place.

I headed toward the exit, fitting my new Leatherman onto my belt. I'd bought it in Miami to replace the one Sundance had swiped from me, and airport security had taken it off me and packed it into a Jiffy envelope in case I tried to use it to hijack the plane. I'd had to collect it from the baggage service desk when we landed.

The small arrivals area was hosting the noise-and-crush Olympics. Spanish voices hollered, loudspeakers barked, babies cried, cell phones rang with every tune known to man. Steel barriers funneled me deeper into the hall. I walked on, scanning the faces of waiting families and taxi drivers, some holding up name cards. Women outnumbered men, either very skinny or very overweight but not much in between. Many held bunches of flowers, and screaming two-year-olds mountaineered all over them. Three or four deep against the barriers, they looked like fans at a Ricky Martin concert.

At last, among the surge of people, I spotted a square foot of white card with the name "Yanklewitz" in capitals in Magic Marker. The long-haired man holding it looked different from the clean-cut CIA operator I'd been expecting. He was slim, about my height, maybe five ten, and probably in his mid- to late-fifties. He was dressed in khaki shorts and a matching photographer's vest that looked as if it doubled as a hand rag at the local mechanic's. His salt-and-pepper hair was tied back in a ponytail, away from a tanned face that had a few days' silver growth. His face looked worn: life had obviously been chewing on it.

I walked straight past him to the end of the barrier, wanting to tune in to the place first, and watch this man for a while before I gave myself over to him. I carried on toward the glass wall and sliding exit doors about ten meters ahead. Beyond them was a parking lot, where blinding sunlight bounced off scores of windshields. The Flying Dogs hot dog and nacho stall to the left of the doors seemed as good a place as any to stop; I leaned against the glass and watched my contact getting pushed and shoved in the melee.

Aaron—I presumed it was him—was trying to check every new male arrival who emerged from Customs, while also checking every few seconds that the name card was the right way up before trying to thrust it above the crowd once more. The taxi drivers were old hands at this game and were able to stand their ground, but Aaron kept being buffeted by the surge of bodies. If this had been the holiday sales, he'd have come away with a pair of odd socks.

Now and again I caught sight of his tanned, hairless legs. They were muscular and scratched around the calves, and the soles of his feet were covered by old leather Jesus sandals, not the more usual sporty ones. This wasn't vacation attire, that was for sure. He looked more like a farmhand or hippie throwback than any kind of doctor.

As I watched and tuned in, Tiger Lil burst into the hall, heaving an enormous squeaky-wheeled suitcase behind her. She screamed in unison with two equally large black women as they jumped all over each other, kissing and cuddling.

The arrivals area was packed with food and drink stands, all producing their own smells that bounced off the low ceiling and had nowhere to escape to. Brightly dressed Latinos, blacks, whites, and Chinese all clamored to outdo each other in the loudest shout competition. My guess was that Aaron would lose that as well as the keep-your-place-in-the-crowd contest. He was still bobbing around like a cork on a stormy sea.

The air-conditioning might have been working, but not well enough to handle the heat of so many bodies. The stone floor was wet with condensation, as if it had just been mopped, and the bottom foot or so of the glass wall was fogged with moisture. The heat was already getting to me. I felt sweat leak from my greasy skin and my eyes were stinging. Taking off my jacket, I leaned against the glass once more, my clammy arm sticking to my sweatshirt.

A group of five stony-faced policemen hovered about in severely pressed khaki pants and badge-festooned, short-sleeved shirts. They looked very macho with their hands resting on their holstered pistols and feet tapping in black patent leather shoes. Apart from that, the only things moving were their peaked hats as they checked out three tight-jeaned and high-heeled Latino women passing by.

Sitting on a bench to the left of the policemen was the only person here who wasn't sweating and out of control. A thirtysomething white woman, she looked like G.I. Jane, with short hair, green fatigue cargo pants, and a baggy gray shirt that came high up to her neck. She still had her sunglasses on and her hands were wrapped around a can of Pepsi.

Two things struck me as I looked around the hall. The first was that virtually everybody seemed to have a cell phone on their belt or in their hand. The other was the men's shirts. Like the police uniforms, they were dramatically pressed and the arm crease went all the way over the shoulder and up to the collar. Maybe there was only one laundry in town.

After about a quarter of an hour the crowd was thinning as the last of the loved ones trickled through and the taxi fares got picked up. Calm descended, but probably only until the next flight arrived.

Aaron was now in my direct line of sight, standing with the remaining few still waiting at the barrier. Under his dirty vest he had a faded blue T-shirt with some barely readable Spanish on the front. I watched as he held up his card to the last few passengers, even leaning over the barrier, straining to read the flight numbers on their luggage tags.

It was now time to cut away from everything else going on in my head except work, the mission. I hated that word, it sounded far too Army, but I was going to use it to keep my head where it should be.

I had one last check around the hall for anything unusual, then realized that everything I saw fell into that category: the whole arrivals area looked like a shady-characters convention. I started my approach.

I must have been about three steps away from his back as he thrust his card under the nose of an American business suit pulling his bag on wheels behind him. "Mr. Yanklewitz?"

He spun around, holding the card against his chest like a schoolboy during show-and-tell. He had bloodshot but very blue eyes, sunk into deep crow's-feet.

I was supposed to let him initiate conversation with a story that involved a number, something like, "Oh, I hear you have ten bags with you?" to which I would say, "No, I have three," that sort of thing. But I really couldn't be bothered: I was hot, tired, and I wanted to get on.

"Seven."

"Oh, that would make me six then, I guess." He sounded a little disappointed. He'd probably been working on his story all morning.

I smiled. There was an expectant pause: I was waiting for him to tell me what to do next.

"Er, okay, shall we go, then?" His accent was soft, educated American. "Unless, of course, you want to—"

"I don't want to do anything, apart from go with you."

"Okay. Please, this way."

We started toward the exit and I fell into step on his left. He folded the card as he went, moving faster than I'd have liked. I didn't want us looking unnatural but, then, what was I worrying about in this madhouse?

On the other side of the automatic exit doors was the service road for drop-offs and pickups. Beyond that was the parking lot, and in the distance, under a brilliant blue sky, were lush green rugged mountains. Out there was virgin ground to me, and unless I had no choice, I never liked entering the unknown without having a look first.

"Where are we going?"

I was still checking out the parking lot. I didn't know if he was looking at me or not as he answered, in a very low voice, "That kinda depends on, er . . . my wife is—"

"That's Carrie, right?"

"Yes, Carrie."

I'd forgotten to introduce myself. "Do you know my name?"

Out of the corner of my eye, I saw his head turn toward me, so I turned as well. His blue eyes seemed jumpy, and focused slightly to one side of mine. "No, but if you don't want to tell me, that's fine. Whatever you feel safe with, whatever is best for you."

He didn't look scared, but was definitely ill-at-ease. Maybe he could smell the fuckup value on me.

I stopped and held out my hand. "Nick." Better to be friendly to the help rather than alienate them: you get better results that way. It was a small lesson the Yes Man could have benefited from taking on board.

There was an embarrassed smile from him, displaying a not-too-good set of teeth, discolored by too much coffee or tobacco. He held out his hand. "Aaron. Pleased to meet you, Nick."

It was a very large hand with hard skin, but the handshake was gentle. Small scars covered its surface; he was no paper-pusher. His nails were dirty and jagged, and there was a dull gold wedding band and a multicolored kids' Swatch on his left.

"Well, Aaron, as you can see, I haven't packed for a long stay. I'll just get my job done and be out of the way by Friday. I'll try not to be a pain in the ass while I'm here. How does that sound?"

His embarrassed grin gave me the feeling that it sounded good on both counts. Still, he was generous in his reply. "Hey, no problem. You did kinda throw me, you know. I wasn't expecting an English guy."

I smiled and leaned forward to tell him a secret. "Actually I'm American, it's a disguise."

There was a pause as he searched my eyes. "Joke, right?"

I nodded, hoping it would break the ice a bit. "I was expecting to see Carrie as well."

He pointed behind me. "She's right here."

I turned to see G.I. Jane approaching us. She greeted me with a smile and an out-thrust hand. "Hi, I'm Carrie."

Her hair was dark, cut into the nape of her neck. She was maybe mid- to late-thirties, just a few years younger than me. There were a few lines coming from behind the lenses of her dark glasses, and small creases in the side of her mouth as she spoke.

I shook her firm hand. "I'm Nick. Finished your Pepsi, then?" I didn't know if she'd seen me waiting, not that it really mattered.

"Sure, it was good." Her manner was brisk, sort of aggressive, and wouldn't have been out of place on Wall Street. Like Aaron's, her voice was educated—but then, anyone who pronounced their H's sounded educated to me.

She stood by Aaron and they certainly made an unusual pair. Maybe I'd gotten this wrong. Maybe they were father and daughter. He had a slight pot-belly and showed his age; she had a body that was well toned and looked after.

People poured in and out. The sound of planes and a gust of heat enveloped us each time the doors slid open.

Carrie shrugged. "What happens now?"

They were waiting for instructions.

"You haven't done this before, have you?"

Aaron shook his head. "First time. All we know is that we pick you up and you tell us the rest."

"Okay—do you have any imagery yet?"

She nodded. "It's satellite, I pulled it off the web last night. It's at the house."

"How far away is that?"

"If the rain holds off, four hours maybe. If not, anything over five. We're talking boondocks."

"How far to the other guy's house?"

"An hour and a half from here, maybe two. It's on the other side of the city—it's in the boonies, too."

"I'd like to see his place first, then back to yours. Will I be able to get close enough to have a good look?"

There wasn't enough time to spend maybe ten

hours on the road, or even prepare myself for a day under the rain forest canopy. I'd have to get on and do the CTR of the house first, since it was so close, and then, on the way back to their place, get planning what I was going to do next, and how.

She nodded, confirming with Aaron at the same time. "Sure, but like I said, it's in the forest." She turned to Aaron. "You know what? I'll go pick up Luce from the dentist and meet you two at home."

There was a pause as if there was more to say, as if she expected me to pick up on what she'd said. But I didn't care that much who Luce was. It wasn't important at the moment, and I was sure to be told soon anyway. "Ready when you are."

We headed outside and into the oppressive heat. I screwed up my eyes against the sun, which burned straight through the cheap polyester of my sweatshirt on my shoulders and the back of my neck.

She walked on the other side of Aaron. There was no wedding band, no watch or any other jewelry on either of her hands. Her hair was beyond dark, it was jet black, and her skin was only lightly tanned, not dark and leathery like Aaron's. Her armpits were shaved and, for some reason, I wouldn't have expected that. Maybe I'd been harboring images of New Age travelers from the moment I saw Aaron.

The service road was jammed with minibuses, taxis, and cars dropping off passengers, with porters hustling the drop-offs for business. The noise was just as loud out here as it had been in the hall, with vehicle horns sounding off and taxi drivers arguing over parking spaces.

The dazzling sunshine felt as if I had a searchlight pointed straight into my eyes. I squinted like a mole and looked down as they started to feel gritty. Aaron pulled a pair of John Lennon sunglasses from a pocket of his vest and put them on as he pointed to our right. "We're over here."

We crossed the road to what might have been a parking lot in any U.S. shopping mall. Japanese and American SUVs were lined up alongside sedans and vans, and none of them looked more than one or two years old. It surprised me: I'd been expecting worse.

Carrie broke away from us and headed toward the other side of the parking lot. "See you both later."

I nodded good-bye. Aaron didn't say a word, just nodded with me.

The ground was wet with rain and sunlight glinted off the pavement. My eyes were still half closed when we reached a blue, rusty, mud-covered Mazda pickup.

"This is us."

This was more what I'd been expecting. It had a double cab, with an equally old fiberglass Bac Pac cover over the rear that turned it into a van. The sheen of the paintwork had been burned off long ago by tropical heat. Aaron was already inside, leaning over to open my door.

It was like climbing into an oven. The sun had been beating down on the windshield and it was so hot inside it was hard to breathe. I was just pleased that there was an old blanket draped over the seats to protect us from the almost molten vinyl upholstery, though the heat was still doing the business.

A floating ball compass was stuck to the windshield, and fixed to the dash was a small open bottle half-filled with green liquid. Judging by the picture of flowers on the label, it had been air-freshener in a previous life.

"Will you excuse me, Nick? I need a moment. Won't be long."

I kept my door open, trying to let some air in as he closed his and disappeared behind the Mazda.

It had only been a hundred yards from the terminal building but I was already sweating. My jeans stuck to my thighs and a bead of sweat rolled down the bridge of my nose and added to the misery. At least the air-conditioning would kick in when he started the engine.

I caught sight of four Aarons and Carries in the broken side mirror, and standing next to her, four trucks. It was also a pickup, but a much older style than the Mazda, maybe an old Chevy, with a rounded hood and wings and a flatbed that had wooden slats up the sides, the sort of thing you'd transport livestock in. They were arguing as they stood by the opened driver's door. She waved her hands in the air and Aaron kept shaking his head at her.

I changed view and looked out at the green mountains in the distance and thought of the months I'd spent living in that stuff, and waited for them to finish as a jet-lagged headache started to brew.

A minute or two later he jumped into the cab as if nothing had happened. "Sorry about that, Nick, just some things I needed from the store."

By the way she'd reacted they must have been pretty expensive. I nodded as if I hadn't seen a thing, we closed our doors, and he started up.

Having kept my window closed to help the air-conditioner spark up, I saw Aaron frantically winding his down as he maneuvered out of the parking space, using just his fingertips to steer as the wheel must have been hot enough to peel skin. He sounded almost apologetic. "You need to belt up. They're pretty tough on that around here." Glancing at my closed window he added, "Sorry, no A.C."

I wound it down and both of us gingerly fastened belt buckles as hot as a tumble-dried coin. There was no sign of Carrie as we drove out of the lot; she must have driven away straight after being given her shopping list.

I lowered the sun visor as we passed a group of young black guys dressed in athletic shorts armed with large yellow buckets, sponges, and bottles of detergent. They seemed to be doing a roaring trade; their pools of soapy water on the pavement just lay there, not evaporating in the high humidity. The Mazda could have used their services, inside as well as out. Its worn rubber mats were covered in dried mud; candy wrappers were scattered all over, some stuffed into my door pocket along with used tissues and a half-eaten roll of mints. On the backseat lay yellowing copies of the *Miami Herald*. Everything looked and smelled tired; even the vinyl seat under the blanket was ripped.

Aaron was still looking nervous as we drove out of the airport and along a two-lane road. The exhaust rattled under the truck as we picked up speed, and the open windows made no difference to the heat. Billboards advertising everything from expensive perfumes to machined ball bearings and textile factories were banged into the ground at random, fighting to be seen above pampas grass nearly nine feet tall on each side of the road.

Less than two minutes later we had to stop at a toll booth and Aaron handed over a U.S. dollar bill to the operator. "It's the currency here," he told me. "It's called a Balboa."

I nodded as if I cared and watched the road become a newly paved two-lane road. The sunlight rebounded off the light-gray concrete big-time, making my headache worse.

Aaron could see my problem and rummaged in his door pocket. "Here, Nick, want these?"

The sunglasses must have been Carrie's, with large

oval lenses that Jackie Onassis would have been proud of. They covered half my face. I probably looked a nutcase, but they worked.

The jungle was soon trying to reclaim the land back from the pampas grass on either side of the roadway, at least on the areas that weren't covered with cinder block and tin shacks. King-size leaves and vines spread up utility poles and over fences like a green disease.

I decided to warm him up before I asked the important questions. "How long have you lived here?"

"Always have. I'm a Zonian."

It must have been obvious that I didn't have a clue what he was talking about.

"I was born here in the Zone, the U.S. Canal Zone. It's a ten-mile-wide strip that used to bracket the whole length of the canal. The U.S. controlled the Zone from the early nineteen hundreds, you know." There was pride in his voice.

"I didn't know that." I thought the U.S. just used to have bases there, not jurisdiction over a whole chunk of the country.

"My father was a canal pilot. Before him, my grandfather started as a tug captain and made it to tonnage surveyor—you know, assessing the ships' weights to determine their tolls. The Zone is home."

Now that we were moving at speed, the wind was hitting the right side of my face. It wasn't that cool, but at least it was a breeze. The downside was that we had to shout at each other over the wind rush and the flapping of newspaper and blanket corners against the vinyl.

"But you're an American, right?"

He gave a small, gentle laugh at my ignorance. "My grandfather was born in Minneapolis, but my father was also born here, in the Zone. The Americans have always been here, working for the canal authority or in the military. This used to be the headquarters of Southern Command—we've had up to sixty-five thousand troops stationed here. But now, of course, everything's gone."

The scenery was still very green, but now mostly grass. Much of the land had been cleared and the odd flea-bitten cow was grazing away. When the trees did come, they were the same size as European ones, not at all like the massive hundred-foot-tall buttress trees I'd seen in primary jungle farther south in Colombia or Southeast Asia. This low canopy of leaf and palm created secondary jungle conditions because sunlight could penetrate so vegetation could grow between the tree trunks. Tall grass, large palms, and creeping vines of all descriptions were trying their best to catch the rays.

"I read about that. It must be quite a shock after all those years."

Aaron nodded slowly as he watched the road. "Yes, sir, growing up here was just like small-town U.S.A.," he enthused, "apart from no A.C. in the house—there wasn't enough juice on the grid in those days. But what the hell? It didn't matter. I'd come home from school and wham! I'm right into the forest. Building forts, fishing for tarpon. We'd play basketball, football, baseball, just like up north. It was Utopia, everything we needed was in the Zone. You know what? I didn't even venture into Panama City until I was fourteen, can you believe that? For the Boy Scout jamboree." A smile of fondness for the good old days played across his face as his gray ponytail fluttered in the wind. "Of course I went north, to California, for my college years, came back with my degree to lecture at the university. I still lecture, but not so much now. That's where I met Carrie."

So she was his wife. I was pleased to have my curiosity satisfied, and got a sudden burst of hope for the future if I ever reached old age.

"What do you teach?"

As soon as he started to answer, I wished I hadn't bothered asking.

"Protecting the biodiversity of plants and wildlife. Forestry conservation and management, that sort of thing. We have a cathedral of nature here." He looked to his right, past me and up at the canopy and grass-covered mountains in the far distance. "You know what? Panama is still one of the richest ecological regions on earth, a motherlode of biodiversity. . . ."

He gazed out again at the mountains and had a tree-hugging moment.

I could only see red and white communication masts the size of the Eiffel Tower that seemed to have been positioned on every fourth peak.

"But you know what, Nick, we're losing it . . ."

Buildings started to come into view on both sides of the road. They ranged from tin shacks with rotting garbage piled up outside and the odd mangy dog picking at the waste, to neat lines of not-quite-finished brand-new houses. Each was about the size of a small garage, with a flat red tin roof over whitewashed cinder blocks. The construction workers were stretched out in the shade, hiding from the midday sun.

Ahead, in the far distance, I began to make out a high-rise skyline that looked like a mini Manhattan—something else I hadn't been expecting.

I tried to change the subject in case he turned into the Green version of Billy Graham. I didn't like the idea of losing trees to concrete, or anything else for that matter, but I didn't have enough commitment even to listen, let alone do anything about it. That was why people like him were needed, I supposed.

"Does Carrie lecture too?"

He shook his head slowly as he changed lanes to let a truck laden with bottled water scream past.

"No, we have a small research deal from the university. That's why I still have to lecture. We're not the Smithsonian Institution, you know. I wish we were, sure do wish we were."

He wanted to get off the subject. "You heard of FARC? The Fuerzas Armadas Revolucionarias Colombianas?"

I nodded and didn't mind talking about anything that let him feel at ease, apart from tree-hugging. "Yes, I hear they're crossing into Panama quite a lot now, with SOUTHCOM gone."

"Sure are. These are worrying times. It's not just the ecological problems. Panama couldn't handle FARC if they came in force. They're just too strong."

He told me that the bombings, murders, kidnappings, extortion, and hijackings had always gone on. But lately, now that the U.S. had withdrawn, they'd been getting more adventurous. A month before the last U.S. military left Panama completely, they'd even struck in the city. They'd hijacked two helicopters from an air base in the Zone, and flown them back home. Three weeks later, six or seven hundred FARC attacked a Colombian naval base near the Panamanian border, using the helicopters as fire support platforms.

There was a pause and I could see his face screw up as he worked out what he wanted to say. "Nick . . ." He paused again. Something was bugging him. "Nick, I want you to know, I'm not a spy, I'm not a revolutionary. I'm just a guy who wants to carry out his work and live here peacefully. That's all."

11

I nodded. "Like I said, I'll be out of here by Friday and try not to be a major pain in the ass." It was somehow good to know that someone else was unhappy with the situation.

He sort of smiled with me as we hit a causeway that cut across toward the city, about 150 yards from the land. It reminded me of one of the road links connecting the Florida Keys.

We passed a few rusty wriggly-tin shanty shacks built around concrete sewage outlets discharging into the sea. Directly ahead, the tall, slim tower blocks reared into the sky, their mirrored and colored glass glinting confidently in the sun.

Paying another Balboa to exit the causeway, we hit a wide boulevard with a tree-lined and manicured-grass meridian. Set into the curbs were large storm drains to take the tropical weather. The road was packed with manic cars, trucks, buses, and taxis. Everyone was driving as if they had just stolen the things. The air was filled with the smell of exhaust fumes and the sound of revving traffic and horns being leaned on. A helicopter flew low and fast somewhere above us. Aaron still had to shout to make himself heard, even at this lower speed. He jerked his head at mini-Manhattan. "Where the money is."

It looked like it. A lot of well-known banks from Europe and the U.S.A., as well as quite a few shady-sounding ones, had gleaming glass towers with their name stuck all over them. It was a dressy area: men walking the sidewalks were dressed smartly in pants, pressed shirts with creases up to the collar, and ties. The women wore businesslike skirts and blouses.

Aaron waved his hand out of the window as he avoided a beer delivery truck who wanted to be exactly where we were. "Panama is trying to be the new Singapore," he said, taking his eyes off the traffic, which worried me a bit. "You know, offshore banking, that kind of stuff."

As we passed trendy bars, Japanese restaurants, designer clothes shops, and a Porsche showroom, I smiled. "I've read it's already pretty vibrant."

He tried to avoid a horn-blowing pickup full of swaying rubber plants. "You could say that—there's a lot of drug money being rinsed here. They say the whole drug thing is worth more than ninety billion U.S. a year—that's like twenty billion more than the revenues of Microsoft, Kellogg's, and McDonald's put together."

He braked sharply as a motor scooter cut in front of us. I put out my arms to break the jolt and felt the hot plastic of the dashboard on my hands, as a woman with a small child in back diced with death. They were both protected only by cycle helmets and swimming goggles as she squeezed between us and a black Merc so she could turn off the main drag. Obviously an everyday thing: Aaron just carried on talking. "There's a big slice of that coming through here. Some of these banks, hey, they just say, 'Bring it on.'

Real crooks wear pinstripes, right?" He smiled rue-
fully. "Those traffickers are now the most influential
special-interest group in the world. Did you know
that?"

I shook my head. No, I didn't know that. When I
was in the jungle fighting them, it was the last thing
I needed to know. I also didn't know if I was going to
get out of this Mazda alive. If there were any driving
instructors in Panama, they obviously went hungry.

The traffic slowed a little then stopped completely,
but the horns kept going. Green-fatigued policemen
stood outside a department store in high-leg boots
and black body armor. The mirrored sunglasses under
the peaks of their baseball caps made them look like
Israeli soldiers, and all the more menacing for it.
Hanging around their necks were HK MP5s, and they
wore low-slung leg holsters. The Parkerization on the
9mm machine-guns had worn away with age, exposing the glinting steel underneath.

The traffic unchoked and we started to move. The
faces sticking out of the bus ahead of us got a grandstand view of my Jackie O's and a few started to smile
at the dickhead in the Mazda. "At least I've cheered
some people up today."

"Especially since you're a *rabiblanco*," Aaron
replied. "That's what they call the ruling elite—white
asses."

The boulevard emerged from little Manhattan and
hit the coastline, following the sweep of a few miles
of bay. On our left was a marina, its sea protection
built from rocks the size of Ford Fiestas. Million-
dollar motor boats were parked among million-dollar
yachts, all being lovingly cleaned and polished by uniformed crews. In the bay, a fleet of old wooden fishing boats was anchored around a sunken cargo ship,
its two rusty masts and bow jutting from the calm of

the Pacific. Farther out to sea, maybe two or three miles, a dozen or so large ships stood in line, pointing toward land, their decks loaded with containers. Aaron followed my gaze. "They're waiting to enter the canal."

We swerved sharply to avoid a battered old Nissan sedan as it decided to change lanes without telling anyone. I instinctively pushed down with my braking foot. This wasn't driving, this was a series of near-death experiences. There were a lot of brakes being hit in front of us and we followed suit, skidding slightly but coming to a halt without rear-ending the Nissan—unlike someone a few vehicles behind us. There was the tinkle of breaking glass and the sound of buckling metal, followed by some irate Spanish.

Aaron looked like a small child. "Sorry 'bout that."

The reason why we'd all stopped was now plain to see. A line of preteen schoolkids in pairs and holding hands was crossing the road, toward the promenade and the bay. The girls were all in white dresses, the boys in blue shorts and white shirts. One of the teachers was shouting at a taxi driver who complained at the delay, an old shaggy arm waving out of the window back at her. Now everyone seemed to be hitting their horns, as if that would change anything.

The kids' faces were two distinct shapes, the same as in Colombia. Those of Spanish descent had wild, curly black hair and olive skin, while the straight-black-haired Indians had more delicate features, slightly flatter faces, smaller eyes, and a browner complexion. Aaron grinned as he watched the children cross, chattering to each other as if nothing was happening around them. "You have kids, Nick?"

"No." I shook my head. I didn't want to start getting into that sort of conversation. The less he knew about me the better. A proper operator wouldn't have asked, and it was strange being with someone who didn't know the score. Besides, after next week I wouldn't have my child anyway—Josh would.

"Oh."

The kids were now being corralled by the teachers on the bay side of the road. Two girls, still holding hands, were staring at him, or my sunglasses, I couldn't make out which. Aaron stuck his thumb to his nose and made a face. They made cross-eyes and thumbed back, giggling together because they'd done it without the teachers seeing.

Aaron looked around at me. "We have a girl, Luce. She'll be fifteen this November."

"Oh, nice." I just hoped he wasn't going to start getting photos out of his wallet—then I'd have to say how pretty she was and all that stuff, even if she looked like she'd seen the flat end of a shovel.

The traffic started moving once more. He waved at the kids as they stuck their thumbs in their ears and flapped their fingers.

We fought our way through the traffic along the boulevard. To the right was a run of large, Spanish colonial–type buildings that just had to be government property. Fronted by tall, decorative wrought-iron fencing, they were all immaculately painted, set back in acres of grass, waterfalls, and flagpoles, all flying the red, white, and blue squares and stars of the Panamanian flag. Laid out between the buildings were well-manicured public parks with neat bushes and paths, and larger-than-life statues of sixteenth-century Spanish guys in oval helmets and pantaloons, pointing their swords heroically toward the sea.

Soon we were passing the equally impressive American and British embassies. Inside each compound, the Stars and Stripes or Union Jack fluttered above the trees and high perimeter railings. The thickness of the window glass indicated it wasn't just for show.

As well as knowing what direction you needed to head out of a country when in the shit, it's also good to check on where your embassy is. I always liked to know there was somewhere to run to if the wheels fell off. Ambassadors don't take too kindly to deniable operators begging for help. I'd have to jump the fence; they didn't let people like me in through the front door. But once I was inside, it would take more than the security to get me back onto the street.

We reached the end of the bay and what was obviously the rougher side of town. The buildings here had flaking, faded paint and some were derelict. Nonetheless, there was still a touch of civic pride. A three-foot-high wall ran the length of the bay, more to stop people falling onto the beach than as a sea defense. It was decorated with blue mosaic tiles, and a gang of about ten women in jeans and yellow T-shirts with "Municipad" stamped on the back were busy scrubbing it with broomheads dipped in large buckets of soapy water. They were also pulling up all the green stuff that was fighting its way between the paving slabs. A couple of them seemed to be on their break, leaning against the wall drinking the milk from a coconut or pink liquid from a plastic bag with a straw.

Sticking out to sea for about half a mile in front of me was the peninsula on which perched the old Spanish colonial town, a mishmash of ancient terracotta roofs huddled around the pristine white towers of a church. Aaron hung a right that took us away from the bay and into an even more rundown area. The road was bumpier and my headache worsened as the Mazda's suspension creaked and groaned. The buildings were low-level, flat-roofed, decaying tenement blocks. Their once multicolored façades had been bleached out by the sun, and the high humidity had given them dark stains. Big cracks in the plaster exposed the cinder blocks beneath.

The street narrowed and the traffic slowed. Pedestrians and motor scooters threaded their way between the vehicles, and Aaron seemed to need all his concentration to avoid hitting anyone. At least it shut him up for a while.

The sun was directly overhead now and seemed to push down on this part of town, keeping a lid on the heat and the exhaust fumes, which were much worse here than on the boulevard. Without circulating air I was sweating big-time and the back of my hair was soaking. The two of us were turning into the sweathog brothers.

I heard the roar of a bulldozer, and saw rusty metal gates covering every conceivable entry point into the ramshackle buildings. Washing hung from the windows and balconies, kids shouted at each other across the street.

The road became so narrow that vehicles were forced right up to the curb, their side mirrors occasionally scraping pedestrians. Nobody seemed to care; the crowds were too busy gossiping and snacking on fried bananas or drinking beer.

It wasn't long before the traffic flow congealed and every driver immediately leaned on his horn. I could smell strong, flowery perfume as women pushed past, and wafts of frying food from an open doorway. The whole place—walls, doors, even advertisements—was a riot of red and yellow.

We nudged our way forward a bit, then stopped by two old women flicking their hips to blaring Caribbean music. Beyond them was a dimly lit shop, selling gas cookers, washing machines, canned food, aluminum pots and pans. A Latin samba spilled onto the street. I liked it: mini-Manhattan did nothing for me; this was more my kind of town.

We passed through a street market and the traffic started to move a little more smoothly. "This is El Chorrillo. Do you remember Just Cause—you know, the invasion?"

I nodded.

"Well, this was ground zero when they—we—attacked the city. Noriega had his command center here. It's an open space now. Bombed flat."

"Oh, right." I looked out at a row of old women sitting behind flat card tables, with what looked like lottery tickets laid out neatly on display. A muscle-bound bodybuilder, a black guy in a very tight Golds Gym shirt and jeans, was buying some tickets from one of the tables, looking an absolute nutcase with a London gent–style umbrella in his hand to keep the sun off.

We eventually squeezed out of the market area, hit an intersection, and stopped. The road in front of us was a busy main drag. From the little I'd seen, the law here seemed to be that if you were bigger than the vehicle you were heading toward, you didn't have to stop: you just hit the horn and put your foot down. The Mazda wasn't exactly the biggest toy in the shop, but Aaron didn't seem to realize it was still big enough to get out there.

To my right was a wooden drink shack. Pepsi had won the cola wars hands down in Panama: every other billboard was covered with their ads, alongside stubble-chinned cowboys welcoming us to Marlboro Country. Next to the shack, in the shade of a tree and leaning against the tailgate of a highly polished Ford Explorer with sparkling chrome wheels and a Madonna hanging off the rearview mirror, were five

Latino guys, young men in their twenties. Shoe-horned into the rear of the Explorer was a massive pair of loudspeakers, banging out Latin rap. All the guys looked sharp, with their shaved heads and wrap-around mirror shades. They wouldn't have looked out of place in L.A. There was enough gold hanging around their necks and wrists to keep the old woman begging at the other side of the road in three-course dinners for the rest of her life. Lying all around them on the ground were mounds of cigarette ends and Pepsi bottle tops.

One of the boys caught a glimpse of my Jackie O specials. Aaron was still rocking the truck back and forth at the junction. The sun beat down on the static cab and turned up the oven temperature. A line of vehicles had developed behind us waiting to get out of the main. Horns were hit, and we were starting to attract some attention.

By now the news had spread about my fashion accessory. The Latino guys were getting to their feet to have a better look. One of them leaned against the tailgate again and I could clearly see the shape of a pistol grip under his shirt. Aaron was still tensed over the wheel. He saw it too, and got even more flustered, messing up getting out of the intersection to the point where there were now more cars hooting on the main for us to get back in than behind us telling us to get the fuck out.

The boys were laughing at my eyewear and obvi-ously making some very funny Spanish jokes as they high-fived and pointed. Aaron was staring straight ahead. Sweat poured down his head and beard, gath-ering under his chin and dripping. The steering wheel was slippery with it. He didn't like one bit what was happening with these guys only about five yards away.

I was sweating too. The sun was toasting the right side of my face.

All of a sudden we were in a scene from *Baywatch*. Two uniformed men with hip-holstered pistols had arrived on mountain bikes, clad in dark shorts and black sneakers, with *"Policia"* printed across the back of their beige polo shirts. Dismounting, they parked their bikes against a tree and calmly started sorting out the chaos. With their bike helmets and sunglasses still in place, they blew whistles hard and pointed at traffic. Miraculously, they managed to open up a space on the main drag, then pointed and whistled at Aaron, waving him on.

As we drew away from the intersection and turned left, the air was thick with angry shouts, mainly at the policemen. "Sorry about that. Crazoids like those shoot at the drop of a hat. It creeps me out."

Very soon we were out of the slums and moved into upscale residential. One house we passed was still under construction and the drills were going for it big-time. Men were digging, pipes were being laid. All the power was coming from a generator that belonged to the U.S. Army. I knew that because the camouflage pattern and the "U.S. Army" stenciling told me so.

Aaron obviously felt a lot better now. "See that?" He pointed at the generator. "What would you say? Four thousand dollars?" I nodded, not really having a clue. "Well"—there was undisguised outrage in his voice—"those guys probably laid out less than five hundred."

"Oh, interesting." Was it? But I was obviously going to get more.

"When SOUTHCOM couldn't clear out all the five remaining bases by the December deadline, they decided to abandon or simply give away any items valued at less than a thousand dollars. So what happened, to make life easier, nearly everything was valued at nine hundred and ninety-nine bucks. Technically it was supposed to have been given away to good causes, but everything was just marked down and sold on, vehicles, furniture, you name it."

As I looked around I realized it wasn't the only thing that had been offloaded. I spotted another gang of street cleaners in yellow T-shirts. They were digging up anything green that stuck out of the pavement and everybody seemed to be wearing brand-new U.S. Army desert-camouflage fatigues.

He started to sound like the village gossip. "I heard a story that a two-hundred-and-thirty-thousand-dollar Xerox machine got the nine ninety-nine tag because the paperwork to ship it back up north was just too much hassle."

I was looking around at a quiet residential area, nice bungalows with rubber plants outside, station wagons, and lots of big fences and gates. He pointed out nothing in particular as he continued. "Out there somewhere, there are guys repairing their vehicles with fifteen-thousand-dollar jet aircraft torque sets that cost them sixty bucks." He sighed. "I wish I could have laid my hands on some of that stuff. We just got odds and ends."

The houses were being replaced by parades of shops and neon signs for Blockbuster and Burger King. Rising into the sky about a couple of miles ahead, and looking like three towering metal Hs, were the stacks of container cranes. "Balboa docks," he said. "They're at the entrance to the canal. We'll be in the Zone," he corrected himself, "the old Canal Zone, real soon."

That was pretty evident just by looking at the road signs. There didn't seem to be many in this country, but I saw the odd U.S. military one now, hanging precariously from its post, telling us that U.S.A.F. Albrook wasn't far away. A large blue and white faded metal sign on the main drag gave us directions for the Servicemen's Christian Association, and soon afterward we hit a good-quality, gray concrete road that bent right around an airfield full of light aircraft and private and commercial helicopters. As we followed the airfield's perimeter road, Balboa docks were behind us and to our left. "That used to be Air Force Albrook. It's where FARC stole those choppers I told you about."

We passed a series of boarded-up barrack blocks, four floors high, with air conditioners poking out of virtually every window. Their immaculately clean cream walls and red-tiled roofs made them look very American, very military.

Skyscraping hundred-and-fifty-foot steel flagpoles that no doubt used to fly enormous Stars and Stripes were now flying the Panamanian flag.

Aaron sighed. "You know the saddest thing about it?"

I was looking at part of the air base that seemed to have become the bus terminal. A big sign saying "United States Air Force Albrook" was half pasted over with details of the bus routes, and lines of buses were being cleaned and swept out.

"What's that?"

"Because of the nine ninety-nine giveaway, the Air Force was in such dire need of forklifts they actually had to start renting some of their old ones back to get the final equipment loaded to the States."

As soon as we cleared the air base the road was flanked again on either side by pampas grass at least nine feet high. We hit another row of toll booths, paid our few cents, and moved through.

"Welcome to the Zone. This road parallels the

canal, which is about a quarter of a mile that way."
He pointed over to our left and it was as if we'd just
driven into a South Florida subdivision, with
American-style bungalows and houses, rows of telephone booths, stoplights, and road signs in English.
Even the street lighting was different. A golf course
farther up the road was advertised in English and
Spanish. Aaron pointed. "Used to be the officers'
club."

A deserted high school on the right looked like
something straight out of an American TV show.
Beside it squatted a massive white dome for all-
weather sports.

We were most definitely where the other half lived.

"How long till we get to the house?"

Aaron was looking from side to side of the virtually
deserted road, taking in the details of the Zone close-
down.

"Maybe another forty, fifty minutes. It was kinda
busy downtown."

It was time to talk shop now.

"Do you have any idea why I'm here, Aaron?"

Not much, I hoped.

He shrugged evasively and used his gentle voice
that was hard to hear above the wind. "We only got
told last night you were coming. We're to help you in
any way we can and show you where Charlie lives."

"Charlie?"

"Charlie Chan—you know, the guy from that old
black-and-white movie. That's not his real name, of
course, just what people call him here. Not to his
face, God forbid. His real name is Oscar Choi."

"I like Charlie Chan a lot better," I said. "Suits
him."

Aaron nodded. "For sure, he doesn't look like an
Oscar to me either."

"What do you know about him?"

"He's really well known here. He's a very generous guy, plays the all-around good citizen thing—patron of the arts, that kind of stuff. In fact, he funds the degree course I get to lecture in."

This wasn't sounding much like a teenager. "How old is he?"

"Maybe a bit younger than me. Say early fifties."

I started to get a little worried. "Does he have a family?"

"Oh, yeah, he's a big family man. Four sons and a daughter, I think."

"How old are the kids?"

"I don't know about the older ones, but I know the youngest son has just started college. Chose a good course—environmental stuff is cool right now. I think the others work for Charlie downtown."

My head was thumping big-time. I was finding it hard to concentrate. I got my fingers under the glasses and tried to get my eyes working.

Aaron obviously had views on the Chinaman. "It's strange that men like him spend all their lives slashing, burning, pillaging to get what they want. Then, once they've amassed all their wealth, they try to preserve everything they used to try to destroy, but underneath never change. Very Viking, don't you think, Nick?"

"What is he, a politician?"

"Nope, doesn't need to be, he owns most of them. His family has been here since the laborers started digging the canal in 1904, selling opium to keep the workers happy. He has his fingers in every pie, in every province—and in everything from construction to 'import and export.' " Aaron gave the quote sign with his right forefinger. "You know, keeping up the family tradition cocaine, heroin, even supplying arms to FARC or anyone else down south who has the money. He's one of the very few who are happy about the U.S. pullout. Business is so much easier to conduct now we've gone."

He lifted his left hand from the steering wheel and rubbed his forefinger and thumb together. "This has many friends, and he has plenty of it."

Drugs, guns, and legal business, it made sense: they usually go hand in hand.

"He's what my mother would have called 'someone's wicked son'—he's smart, real smart. It's a well-known story around here that he crucified sixteen men in Colombia. They were local-government people, policemen, that kind of thing, trying to cut him out of a deal he'd made with them for moving coke. He had them nailed up in the town square for everyone to see and let them die—someone's wicked son for sure."

A chain-link fence line started to appear on the right.

"This is"—he corrected himself once more—"*was* Fort Clayton."

The place was deserted. Through the fence was a line of impressive military buildings. The white flagpoles were empty, but still standing guard in front of them were perfect rows of tall, slim palm trees, the first four feet or so in need of another coat of whitewash.

As we drove farther on, I could see the same accommodation blocks that were at Albrook, all positioned in a neat line with concrete paths crisscrossing the uncut grass. Road signs were still visible telling troops not to drink and drive, and to remember they were ambassadors for their country.

We lapsed into silence for a few minutes, surveying the emptiness.

"Nick, do you mind if we stop for a Coke? I'm feeling pretty dry."

"How long is it going to take? How far until we get to Charlie's place?"

"Maybe another six, seven miles after the Coke stop. It's only a few minutes off the route."

Sounded good to me: I was going to be having a long day.

We passed the main gate of the camp and Aaron sighed. The bold brass letters that were secured to the entrance wall now just read "Layton." "I think they're going to turn it into a technology park, something like that."

"Oh, right." Who cared? Now he'd talked about it, all I wanted was a drink, and maybe an opportunity to find out more from him about the target house.

12

We stayed on the main drag for maybe another half mile before turning left onto a much narrower road. Ahead of us in the distance, on the high ground, I could just make out the superstructure and high load of a container ship, looking bizarre as it cut the green skyline.

"That's where we're heading, the Miraflores locks," Aaron said. "It's the only place around here to get a drink now—everyone moving along this road comes here, it's like a desert watering hole."

As we started to reach the higher ground of the lock a scene unfolded that made me wonder if Clinton was about to visit. The place was packed with vehicles and people. A line of brightly colored buses had brought an American-style marching band and eighteen-year-old baton twirlers. Red tunics, white pants, and silly hats with feathers sticking out were blowing into white enameled trombones and all sorts of horns as the baton girls, squeezed into red leotards and white knee-high boots, whirled their chrome sticks and streamers. It was a zoo up here: teams putting up bunting, unloading fold-up wooden chairs from trucks, lumbering around with scaffolding poles over their shoulders.

"Uh-oh," Aaron sighed, "I thought it was going to be on Saturday."

"What?"

"The *Ocaso*."

We drove into the large wired compound, jam-packed with private vehicles and tour company MPVs, around which were dotted some smart and well-maintained colonial-style buildings. The sounds of brass instruments tuning up and fast, excited Spanish poured into the cab.

"Not with you, mate. What's the *Ocaso*?"

"It's a cruise liner, one of the biggest. It means 'sunset' in English. Two thousand passengers plus. It's been coming through here for years, runs out of San Diego to the Caribbean."

While trying to find a parking space, he checked out some posters stuck up along a chain-link fence. "Yeah, it's this Saturday, the four-hundredth and final transit. It's going to be a big deal. TV stations, politicians, some of the cast of *The Bold and the Beautiful* will be on board—that show's a big deal here. This must be the dress rehearsal."

Just a few yards past the buses and chain-link, I caught my first glimpse of the enormous concrete locks, flanked by immaculately cut grass. None of it looked as breathtaking as I'd been expecting, more a hugely scaled-up version— about three hundred yards long and thirty wide— of any normal-sized set of canal locks.

Maneuvering into the first lock was the rust-streaked blue and white ship, five stories high and maybe six hundred feet long, powered by its own engines but being guided by six stubby-looking but obviously powerful aluminum electric trains on rails, three on each side. Six cables slung between the hull and the trains, four at the rear, the other two up front, helped guide it between the concrete walls without touching.

Aaron sounded off with the tour-guide bit as he squeezed between two cars. "You're looking at maybe six thousand automobiles in there, heading for the west coast of the States. Four percent of the world's trade and fourteen of the U.S.'s passes through here. It's an awesome amount of traffic." He gave a sweep of his hand to emphasize the scale of the waterway in front of us. "From the Bay of Panama here on the Pacific side up to the Caribbean, it only takes maybe eight to ten hours. Without the canal you could spend two weeks sailing around Cape Horn."

I was nodding with what I hoped was the required amount of awe when I saw where we'd be getting our Cokes. A truck-trailer had grown roots in the middle of the parking lot and become a café-and-tourist-shop. White plastic garden chairs were scattered around matching tables shaded by multicolored sun umbrellas. Hanging up for sale were enough souvenir T-shirts to clothe an army. We found a space and got out. It was sweltering, but at least I could peel my sweatshirt off my back.

Aaron headed toward the side window to join the line of tourists and two red tunics, each with a lump of brass under their arm, as they leered at a group of athletic-looking baton girls paying for their drinks. "I'll get us a couple of cold ones."

I stood under one of the parasols and watched the ship inch into the lock. I took off my Jackie O's and cleaned them: the glare made me regret it immediately.

The sun was merciless, but the lock workers seemed impervious to it, neatly dressed in overalls and hard hats as they went about their jobs. There was an air of brisk efficiency about the proceedings as a loudspeaker system sounded off quick, businesslike radio traffic in Spanish, just managing to make itself heard above the nightmare around the buses and the clatter of scaffolding poles. A four-tier grandstand was being erected on the grass facing the lock, supplementing the permanent one to the left of it, by the visitors' center, which was also covered in bunting. Saturday was going to be very busy indeed.

The ship was nearly into the lock, with just a couple of feet to spare on each side. Tourists watched from the permanent viewing platform, clicking away with their Nikons, as the band drifted onto the grass. Some of the girls practiced their splits, professional smiles, and top and bottom wiggles as they got into ranks.

The only person at ground level who seemed not to be looking at the girls was a white man in a fluorescent pink, flowery Hawaiian shirt. He was leaning against a large, dark blue GMC Suburban, watching the ship as he smoked with deep, long drags. The guy was using his free hand to wave the bottom of his shirt to circulate some air. His stomach had been badly burned, leaving a large scar the size of a pizza that looked like melted plastic. Shit, that must have been painful. I was glad my stomach pain was just from a session with Sundance's Caterpillars.

Apart from the windshield, all the GMC's windows had been blackened out with film. I could see it was a do-it-yourself job by a snag mark in one of the rear door windows. It made a clear triangle where the plastic had been ripped down three or four inches.

Then, as if he'd just realized he'd forgotten to lock his front door, Pizza Man jumped into the truck and drove out. Maybe the real reason was because he had a false plate on the GMC and he didn't want any of the police to scrutinize it. The truck had been cleaned, but not well enough to match the even cleaner plate. I'd always hit the car wash immediately before changing plates, then took a drive in the country to mess both the plate and the bodywork before using the vehicle for work. I bet there were a lot of people with false plates down here, keeping the banking sector vibrant.

A fragile-looking Jacob's ladder of wooden slats and knotted rope was dropped over the side of the ship and two men in pristine white shirts and pants climbed aboard from the grass below, just as Aaron came back with four cans of Minute Maid. "No Coke—they've been overrun today."

We sat in the shade and watched the hydraulic rams slowly push the gates shut, and the water— twenty-seven million gallons of it, according to Aaron—flooded into the lock. The ship rose into the sky before us as the scaffolders downed tools and took a seat in preparation for the girls' rehearsal.

Quiet contemplation obviously wasn't Aaron's thing and he was soon blathering on. "You see, the canal isn't as most people think, just a big ditch cut through the country, like the Suez. No, no, no. It's a very complicated piece of engineering—quite amazing to think it's more or less Victorian."

I had no doubt it was completely fascinating, but I had other, more depressing, things on my mind.

"The Miraflores, and the other two sets farther up, lift or drop these ships eighty feet. Once up there, they just sail on over the lake and then get lowered again to sea level on the other side. It's kind of like a bridge over the isthmus. Pure genius—the eighth wonder of the world."

I pulled the ring on my second orange juice and

nodded toward the lock. "Bit of a tight fit, isn't it?" That'd keep him babbling for a while.

He responded as if he'd designed the thing himself. "No problem—they're all built to Panamax specifications. Shipyards have been keeping the size of the locks in mind for decades now."

The vessel continued to rise like a skyscraper in front of me. Just then, the trumpets, drums, and whistles started up as the band broke into a quick-tempo samba and the girls did their stuff to the delight of the scaffolders.

Ten minutes later, when the water levels were equal, the front gate was opened and the process began all over again. It was like a giant staircase. The batons were still getting thrown into the air and the band was marching up and down the grass. Everyone seemed to be getting very Latin as some of the brass section chanced a few dance moves of their own as they strutted their stuff.

A black Lexus 4x4 with gold-mirrored side windows pulled up opposite the café. The windows slid down to reveal two shirt-and-tied white-eyes. The front-seat passenger, a muscular, well-tanned twentysomething, got out and went straight to the trailer window, ignoring the line. One of the new small, chrome-effect Nokias glinted from his belt along with a weapon holstered on his right hip. Just as with the GMC, however, I thought nothing of it—after all, this was Central America. I just tilted my head back to get the last of the drink down my throat, thinking of getting another couple for the journey.

A young American voice called out from the Lexus as the twentysomething went back with the drinks. "Hey, Mr. Y! What's happening, man?"

Aaron's head jerked around, his face breaking into

a smile. He waved. "Hey, Michael, and how are you? How was your break?"

I turned as well. My head was still back but I instantly recognized the grinning face leaning out of the rear passenger window.

Finishing the drink, I brought my head down as Aaron moved over to the car. My tiredness disappeared as adrenaline pumped. This was not good, not good at all. I looked at the floor, pretending to relax, and tried to listen above the music.

The boy held out a hand for Aaron to shake, but his eyes were on the girls. "I'm sorry, I can't get out of the car—my father says I have to stay in with Robert and Ross. I heard they'd be here today, thought I'd get a look on the way home, know what I mean, Mr. Y? Didn't you check out the pom-pom girls? I mean, before you got married . . ."

I could see that the two BG (bodyguards) weren't remotely distracted by the girls or the infectious Latin tempo; they were doing their job. Their faces were impassive behind tinted sunglasses as they drank from their cans. The engine was running and I could see the moisture drip from the air-conditioning reservoir onto the pavement.

The band stopped playing and now marched to the command of a bass drum. Michael jabbered on with excitement, and something he said made Aaron arch an eyebrow. "England?"

"Yes, I returned yesterday. There was a bomb and some terrorists were killed. My father and I were very close by, in the Houses of Parliament."

Aaron showed his surprise as Michael pulled back the ring on his can. "Hey, Nick, did you hear that?" He pointed me out to the target with a cock of his head. "Nick—he's British."

Shit, shit, Aaron—no!

Michael's eyes turned to me and he smiled, displaying perfect white teeth. The BG also moved their heads casually to give me the once-over. This wasn't good.

I smiled and studied the target. He had short black shining hair, side parted, and his eyes and nose looked slightly European. His smooth unblemished skin was darker than most Chinese. Maybe his mother was Panamanian, and he spent a lot of time in the sun.

Aaron had realized he had fucked up and stammered, "He kind of hitched a lift from me in the city to take a look at the locks—you know, and check out the chicks. . . ."

Michael nodded, not really that fussed. I turned back to the ship as it left the dock, wanting very much to walk right over and ram my can into Aaron's mouth.

After a minute or so of university stuff Michael got a nod from the BG and started to wind down the conversation. As he held out his hand again for a farewell he glanced over one more time at the leotards and pom-poms. A whistle sounded out commands and the drums sparked up once more. "I have to go now. Will I see you next week, Mr. Y?"

"Sure thing." Aaron gave him a high-five. "You get that project done?"

"I think you'll like it. Anyway, catch you later." Out of politeness he nodded to me over Aaron's shoulder, then the window powered up and the Lexus moved off, leaving behind a poodle-size piss puddle from the air-conditioning.

Aaron waved until they were out of sight, then spun toward me, his face abject as the brass section and girls joined in the fast drum rhythm. "Nick, I'm really sorry." He shook his head. "I just didn't think.

I'm not really cut out for this kind of thing. That's Charlie's son—did I tell you he's in the course I teach? I'm sorry, I just didn't think."

"It's okay, mate. No damage done." I was lying. The last thing I needed was to be introduced to the target and, even worse, have the BG knowing what I looked like. There was also the connection with Aaron. My heart was pounding. All in all, not a good day out.

"Those guys with him—Robert and Ross? They're the ones who hung up those Colombians. They're Charlie's special guys, I've heard stories about—" Aaron's expression suddenly changed. "Did you have something to do with that bomb in London? I mean, is this all about—"

I shook my head as I swallowed the last of the juice. I could feel the blood rushing around my head.

"I'm sorry, it's not any of my business. I don't really want to know."

I wasn't too sure if he'd believed me, but it didn't matter. "How far have we got left to Michael's house?"

"Like I said, five, maybe six miles. If the picture back at our place is anything to go by, it's some kind of palace."

I started to get my cash out as I walked toward the trailer window. "I think I'd better have a look at it, then, don't you? What about another drink while we wait for Michael to get home and settle down?"

The expression on his face still said guilty.

"Tell you what," I said, "you buy and then we're even."

At least that got a fleeting smile out of him as he delved into his grubby pockets for coins. "And see if they have anything for a headache, could you?"

Over on the other side of the parking lot was an ATM with the HSBC logo. I knew I wouldn't be able to withdraw any more money today, but within hours of my attempting to, the Yes Man would at least know I was in-country.

We spent the next forty minutes killing time at the plastic table with just the sound of the trains humming along their tracks as the entertainment took a break for lunch. I had the Jackie O's back on, trying to rest my eyes and head. It seemed no one ever got a headache around here.

Aaron took the opportunity to explain about the U.S. pullout the previous December. The fact that he could reel off all the dates and numbers so precisely emphasized his bitterness about what had happened.

In total, more than four hundred thousand acres of Canal Zone and bases, worth more than $10 billion, had been handed over—along with the canal itself, which had been built and paid for by the U.S. to the tune of a further $30 billion. And the only way they could come back was under the terms of the DeConcini Reservation, which allowed for military intervention if the canal was endangered.

It was all interesting stuff, but what was more important to me was confirming that Michael would be at the university this week.

"For sure." Aaron nodded. "They'll all be headed back. The fall semester started for most folks last week."

We headed for the house, driving into Clayton. Aaron explained that now the U.S. had gone, Charlie had gotten his hands on some of the Zone and built on it.

The only security these days at the guard house was an old guy sleeping on the porch of the guard room with half a glass of something resembling black tea by his side, looking quite annoyed to be woken up to lift the barrier.

Clayton might become a technology park one day,

but not yet. We passed deserted barrack blocks with tall grass growing between them. The U.S. Army's legacy was still very much in evidence. I could see stenciling on steel plates above every barrack door: *Building 127, HQ Theater Support Brigade, Fort Clayton, Panama, U.S. Army South*. I wondered if our SOUTHCOM bosses during my time in Colombia had sent us our satellite photography and orders from these very buildings.

The neighborhood looked as if it had been evacuated before a hurricane. The children's swings between the deserted bungalows and palm-fringed, two-floor apartment blocks were showing the first signs of rust through their blue paintwork, and the baseball field, which needed a good mowing, still had the results of the last game displayed on the scoreboard. U.S. road signs told us to travel at 15 m.p.h. because of children playing.

We reached the other side of the massive fort complex and headed into the mountains. The jungle closed in on both sides of the narrow, winding asphalt road. I could only see about five yards; after that everything blurred into a wall of green. I'd heard about a patrol in Borneo in the sixties who had a man down with a gunshot wound. It wasn't fatal, but he did need evacuation. Leaving him comfortable at the bottom of a high feature, all hands moved uphill to cut a winch point out of the jungle so the rescue helicopter could pull him out and med-evac him to a hospital. This was no big deal, and the wounded man would have been airborne by last light if only they hadn't made the fatal error of not leaving anyone with him or marking where he was lying. It took them over a week to find where they'd left him, even though it was less than a hundred yards away at the bottom of the hill. By then he was dead.

The sun beat down on the windshield, showing up all the bugs that had smashed against it and been smeared by the wipers. It couldn't have been easy for Aaron to see through.

This was secondary jungle; movement through it would be very, very difficult. I much preferred primary, where the canopy is much higher and the sun finds it difficult to penetrate to ground level so there's less vegetation. It's still a pain in the ass to travel through, because there's still all kinds of stuff on the ground.

Gray clouds were starting to cover the sky and make everything darker. I thought again about all the months I'd spent living in jungles while on operations. You'd come out twenty-five pounds lighter, and because of the lack of sunlight your skin became as white and clammy as an uncooked french fry, but I really liked it. I always had a fantastic sense of anticipation when I entered the jungle, because it's the most wonderful place to be; tactically, compared with any other terrain, it's a great environment to operate in. Everything you need is there: shelter, food, and, more importantly, water. All you really have to get used to is the rain, bites by mozzies (anything small that flies), and 95 percent humidity.

Aaron leaned forward and peered up through the windshield. "Here they are, look—right on time."

The gray clouds had disappeared, pushed out by blacker ones. I knew what that meant and, sure enough, the sky suddenly emptied on us. It was like sitting under an upturned bath. We hurriedly wound up our windows, but only about three-quarters of the way, because humidity was already misting up the inside of the windshield. Aaron hit the defroster, and its noise was drowned as the roof took a pounding.

Lightning cracked and sizzled, splashing the jungle

with brilliant blue light. An almighty clap of thunder boomed above us. It must have set off a few car alarms back at the locks.

Aaron slowed the car to walking pace as the wipers went into hyperdrive, slapping each side of the windshield and having no effect at all as rain dashed into the pavement and bounced back into the air. Water splattered through the top of the side window, spraying my shoulder and face.

I shouted at him, above the drumming on the roof. "Does this road go straight to Charlie's house?"

Aaron was leaning over the wheel, busy wiping the inside of the windshield. "No, no—this is a loop, just access to an electricity substation. The new private road to the house leads off from it. I thought maybe I could drop you off where the two join, otherwise I'd have nowhere to go."

That seemed perfectly reasonable to me. "How far to the house from the junction?"

"If the scale on the imagery is right, maybe a mile, a mile and then some. All you've got to do is follow the road."

The deluge continued as we crawled uphill. I leaned down and felt under my seat, trying to find something to protect my documents. I wasn't going to leave them with Aaron: they were going everywhere with me, like communication codes, to be kept on the body at all times.

Aaron looked at me. "What do you need?" He was still strained forward against the wheel, as if that were going to help him see any better through the solid sheet of rain as we crawled along at about 10 m.p.h.

I explained.

"You'll find something in the back, for sure. Won't be long now, maybe two or three miles."

That was fine by me. I sat back and let myself be mesmerized by the rain bouncing around us.

We followed the road as it curved to the right, then Aaron moved over to the edge of the road and stopped. He pointed just ahead of us. "That's the road that goes to the house. Like I said, maybe a mile, a mile and a half. They say from up there Chan can see the sun rise over the Caribbean and set in the Pacific. What do you want me to do now?"

"First, just stay here and let me get into the back."

I got out and put my jacket back on. Visibility was down to maybe twenty yards. Rain hammered on the top of my head and shoulders.

I went to the rear of the truck and opened the tailgate. I was soaked to the skin before I got halfway. I was just pleased not to be in a country where being wet also meant freezing my balls off.

I rummaged around in the back. Four five-gallon U.S. Army fuel cans were fixed with bungee cords to the far end of the flatbed, adjacent to the cab. At least we wouldn't be running out of fuel. Scattered around them were more yellowing newspapers, a tire jack, a nylon towrope, and all the associated crap that would be needed for a wreck like this. Among it, I found what I was looking for, two small plastic bags. One contained a pair of greasy old jump-leads, the other was empty, apart from a few bits of dried mud and vegetable leaves. I shook them both out, tucked my passport, plane ticket, and wallet into the first and wrapped them up. I put that into the second, gave it a twist, and placed it in an inside pocket of my jacket.

I had another look around, but found nothing else that could be of any use to me on the recce. Slamming the tailgate, I went around to Aaron's door and put my face up against the gap in the window. "Can you give me that compass, mate?" I had to shout to be heard.

He leaned across, unstuck it from the windshield, and passed it through. "Sorry, I didn't think about it. I should have brought a good one, and a map."

I couldn't be bothered to say it wasn't a problem. My head was banging big-time and I wanted to get on. Water cascaded down my face and off my nose and chin as I pressed the illumination button on Baby-G.

"When's last light?"

"Six-thirty, or thereabouts."

"It's just past three-thirty. Drive well away from here, all the way back to the city, whatever. Then come back to this exact spot at three A.M."

He nodded without even thinking about it.

"Okay, park here, and wait ten minutes. Keep the passenger door unlocked and just sit in the car with the engine running." On a job, the engine must always be kept running: if you switch it off, Murphy's law dictates that it's not going to start up again. "You also need to think of a story in case you're stopped. Say you're looking for some rare plant or something."

He stared vacantly through the windshield. "Yes, that's a good idea. In fact the barrigon tree is common in disturbed areas and along roads and—"

"That's good, mate, good, whatever works, but make sure the story's in your head by the time you pick me up, so it sounds convincing."

"Okay." He nodded sharply, still looking out of the window and thinking trees.

"If I'm not here by ten past three, drive off. Then come back around again and do exactly the same every hour until it gets light, okay?"

His eyes were still fixed on the windshield as he nodded sharply. "Okay."

"Then, at first light, I want you to quit. Stop doing the circuit. Come back for me at midday, but not here—wait at the locks, by the trailer. Wait for an hour, okay?"

He nodded some more.

"Got any questions?"

He hadn't. I figured I'd given myself enough time, but if there was a mess-up and I didn't make this RV (rendezvous), all was not lost. I could get to a river, clean all the jungle shit off, and, with luck, dry myself off if the sun was shining tomorrow morning. Then I wouldn't stand out too much once I got among the real people at the locks.

"Now, worst-case scenario, Aaron—and this is very, very important." I was still shouting above the noise of the rain. Rivulets of water ran down my face and into my mouth. "If I don't appear at the locks by midday tomorrow, then you'd better call your handler and explain exactly what I wanted you to do, all right?"

"Why's that?"

"Because I'll probably be dead."

There was a pause. He was obviously shaken: maybe he hadn't realized what game we were playing here; maybe he'd thought we really were here for the tree hugging. "Have you got that?"

"Sure. I'll just tell them, word for word." He was still looking through the windshield, frowning and nodding.

I tapped on his window and he turned his head. "Hey, don't worry about it, mate. I'm just planning for the worst. I'll see you here at three."

He smiled quite nervously. "I'll fill up beforehand, yeah?"

I tapped once more on the glass. "Good idea. See you later, mate."

Aaron drove off. The engine noise was drowned by the rain. I walked off the road into the murky, twilight world of the jungle. At once I was pushing against palm leaves and bushes. Rainwater that had been trapped on them sluiced all over me.

I moved in about five yards to get out of sight while I waited for Aaron to get well away from the area, and plonked down in the mud and leaf litter, resting my back against a tree trunk as yet more thunder erupted across the sky. Water still found me as it cascaded from the canopy.

Pushing back my soaked hair with my hands I brought up my knees and rested my forehead against them as the rain found its way from the back of my neck and dripped away over my chin. Underneath my jacket, my left arm was being chewed. I gave the material a good rub and attempted to squeeze to death whatever had gotten up there, quietly welcoming myself to Aaron's "cathedral of nature." I should have looked out for some mozzie repellent in the Miami departures lounge instead of a guidebook.

My jeans were wet and heavy, hugging my legs as I stood up. I wasn't exactly dressed for crawling around in the jungle, but tough, I'd just have to get on with it. If I was going to hunt, I had to get my ass over to where the ducks were, so I headed back to the loop. For all I knew, it might have stopped raining out there by now. Inside the canopy you'd never know because the water still falls for ages as it makes its way down leaf by leaf.

I turned right onto the single-track paved road: it was pointless moving through the jungle from this distance. The downpour had eased a little, now only bouncing an inch or two off the pavement, but it was still enough to mean that a vehicle wouldn't see me until it was right on top of me.

As I started to walk up the road I checked the ball compass. I was heading uphill and west, as we had been all the way from Clayton in the Mazda. I kept to one side so I could make a quick entry into cover, and didn't move too fast so I'd be able to hear any approaching vehicles above the rasping of my soaked jeans.

I still had no idea how I was going to do this job, but at least I was in an environment I understood. I wished Dr. Hughes could see me now: then she'd know there was something I was good at.

I stopped and scratched the skin at the base of my spine to discourage whatever was munching at it, then moved on up the road.

13

For the best part of a mile of uphill trek I was deluged with rain and drenched in my own sweat, hair plastered to my face and clothes clinging to my body like long-lost friends.

At last, the rain subsided, and the sun emerged between the gaps in the clouds, burning onto my face and making me squint as it reflected off the mirror of wet pavement. The Jackie O's went back on. I looked at the compass—I was heading west with a touch of north in it—and also checked my plastic bags. They'd done their job well: at least I had dry documents.

Humidity oozed from the jungle. Birds began to call once more from high up in the canopy. One in particular stood out, sounding like a slowed-down heart-rate monitor. Other forms of wildlife rustled in the foliage as I walked past and, as ever, there was the blanket noise of crickets, cicadas, whatever they were called. They seemed to be everywhere, in every jungle, though I'd never seen one.

I wasn't fooled by the sunshine or the animals rustling in the foliage. I knew there was more rain to come. The dark clouds hadn't completely dispersed, and thunder still rumbled in the distance.

I rounded a gentle bend and a pair of iron gates came into view, blocking the road about four hundred yards ahead. They were set into a high, whitewashed wall that disappeared into the jungle on each side. Once I'd confirmed that I was still heading westerly, it was time to get back into cover. I eased my way in, moving branches and fronds aside carefully rather than just crashing through. I didn't want to mark my entry point with top sign—sign that is made above ground level and which in this case might be seen from the road. A large rubber leaf or a fern, for example, doesn't naturally expose its lighter underside; that only happens if it's disturbed by someone or something brushing past. The leaf will eventually turn back to its darker side so it can gather light, but to the trained eye in the meantime it's as good as dropping your business card. I had no idea if these people would be tuned-in enough to notice such things as they drove past, but I wasn't going to leave that to chance.

Once under the canopy, I felt like I was in a pressure cooker; the humidity has nowhere to go, and it gives your lungs a serious workout. Rainwater still fell in bursts as unseen birds took flight from the branches above.

Having moved maybe thirty yards in a direct line away from the road, I stopped to check the compass. My aim now was to head west again and see if I hit the perimeter wall. If I encountered nothing after an hour I'd stop, move back, and try again. It would be very easy to become "geographically embarrassed," as officers call it: in the jungle the golden rule is to trust your compass, no matter what your instincts are telling you. The wall of green was maybe seven yards away, and that was where I would focus my attention as I moved, to detect any hostiles and find the house.

As I headed off, I felt a tug on my sleeve and realized I'd encountered my first batch of wait-a-while. It's a thin, twinelike vine, studded with tiny barbs that dig into clothing and skin, much like a bramble. Every jungle I'd been in was infested with the stuff. Once it's caught you, the only way to get clear is to tear yourself free. If you try to extricate yourself barb by barb, you'll be there forever.

I pushed on. I had to get to the house before last light so I could carry out a decent recce with some degree of visibility. Besides, I didn't want to be stuck in here once it was dark: I'd never make the morning RVs, and would then waste time waiting for midday, instead of preparing for the job I was here to do.

For the next half hour or so I headed uphill and west, frequently untangling myself from batches of wait-a-while. At last I stopped and leaned against a tree to catch my breath and check the compass. I didn't know what sort of tree it was; for some strange reason I could recognize a mahogany, and this wasn't one. My hands were covered with small cuts and scratches now, which hurt like wasp stings.

I moved off once more, thinking about the CTR. Under ideal conditions, I'd take time to find out the target's routine, so that I could take him on in a killing ground of my choosing; that way, I had the advantage. But I didn't have time, and the only thing I'd learned from Aaron about Michael's movements was that he would be going in to college at some point this week.

It's easy enough to kill someone; the hard part is getting away with it. I needed to find the easiest way of dropping him so there was as little risk to me as possible. I could get all Rambo'd up and storm the place, but that wasn't part of my plan, not yet anyway.

I saw open space about six or seven yards ahead, just beyond the wall of green, flooded with brilliant sunlight and awash with mud. I moved slowly back into the jungle until it disappeared from sight, and stood against a tree.

Standing still and doing nothing but take deep breaths and wipe the sweat from my face, I started to hear the world above me once more.

I was hot, sticky, out of breath, and gagging for a drink, but I found myself captivated by the amazing sound of a howler monkey in the treetops, busy living up to its name. Then I slapped my face yet again to zap whatever it was that had landed to say hello.

Moisture seeped out of my leather belt as I squeezed it open, tucked in my sweatshirt, and generally got myself organized. I knew that my jeans would soon be hanging off my ass again, but it didn't matter, this just made me feel better. I felt the first of what I knew was going to be a whole colony of itchy bumps on my neck, and quite a big one coming up on my left eyelid.

My basic plan for the recce was to simulate one of those electric toys that motor around the floor until they bump into a wall, then rebound, turn around, move off, turn around again, and bounce back onto the wall somewhere else.

A lot of questions needed answering. Was there physical security, and if so, were they young or old? Did they look tuned-in and/or armed? If so, what with? If there was technical security, where were the devices, and were they powered up?

The best way of finding answers was just to observe the target for as long as possible. Some questions can be answered on site, but many only pop up once you're tucked up with a cup of cocoa and trying to come up with a plan. The longer I stayed there, the more information would sink into my unconscious for me to drag out later if I needed it.

The big question—would I have to do a Rambo?— remained, but I'd answer that on target. My mind drifted back to the Yes Man and Sundance, and I knew I might have to if there was no other way. But then I cut away from that stuff; what I needed to do now was get my ass up to that mud a few yards away and have a look at what was out there before I got lost inside my head.

Concentrating on the green wall, I moved carefully forward.

I saw the sunlight reflecting off the puddles maybe six yards in front of me and dropped slowly onto my stomach in the mud and rotting leaves. Stretching out my arms, I put pressure on my elbows and pushed myself forward on the tips of my toes, lifting my body just clear of the jungle floor, sliding about six inches at a time, trying to avoid crushing dead, pale yellow palm leaves as I moved. They always make a brittle, crunching noise, even when they're wet.

It felt like I was back in Colombia, closing in on the DMP to carry out a CTR so an attack could be planned with the information we brought back. I never thought that I'd still be doing this shit nearly ten years later.

I stopped every couple of bounds, lifted my head from the dirt, looked, and listened, while slowly pulling out thorns from my hands and neck as the mozzies got busy again. I was starting to have second thoughts about my little love affair with the jungle. I realized I only liked it when I was standing up.

My alligator impression was hard work in this humidity, and I was starting to pant, with every sound magnified tenfold so close to the ground; even the leaves seemed to crackle more than they normally would. The sharp pain in my ribs didn't help much, but I knew all the discomfort would disappear once I was on top of the target house.

I inched closer to the wall of sunlight as leaf litter and other shit from the jungle floor worked its way inside my jacket sleeves and down the front of my sweatshirt. The plastic bag rustled gently inside my jacket. Now that my jeans had worked their way back down my ass, bits of twig and broken leaf were also finding their way onto my stomach. I was not having a good day out.

Another bound, then I stopped, looked, and listened. Slowly wiping away the sweat that was running into my eyes and wishing that they weren't so tired, I squashed some airborne monster that was munching away at my cheek. I still couldn't see anything in front of me apart from sunlight and mud, and knew I was so low down that I'd have to wait until I was right up on the canopy's edge to get a good view of whatever was out there.

The first thing I spotted of any significance was wire fencing along the edge of the tree line. I moved carefully toward the most prickly and uninviting bush at the edge of the clearing and wormed my way into it, cutting my hands on the barbs that covered its branches. They were so sharp that the pain of being cut wasn't instant; it came a few seconds later, like getting sliced with a Stanley knife.

Lying on my stomach, I rested my chin on my hands, looked up and listened, trying to take in every detail. As soon as I'd stopped moving, the mozzies formed into stacks above me, like 747s waiting to land at JFK.

I found myself looking through a four-inch chain-link fence, designed more to keep out wildlife than humans. The house was obviously very new, and by the look of things Charlie Chan had been so keen to move in he hadn't waited for proper security.

The open space in front of me was a gently undulating plateau covering maybe twenty acres. Tree stumps stuck out here and there like rotten teeth, waiting to be dragged out or blasted before a lawn was laid. I couldn't see any oceans from where I lay, just trees and sky. Caterpillar-tracked plant was scattered about the area, lying idle, but business at Choi and Co. was obviously booming in every other respect, now that the U.S. had gone. The house looked more like a luxury hotel than a family hideaway. The main building was sited no more than three hundred yards to my left. I wasn't face-on to the target, along the line of the gate and wall; I must have clipped a corner because I'd come onto the right-hand perimeter. I had a clear view of the front and right-hand elevation. It was a massive, three-floor, Spanish-style villa with brilliant whitewashed walls, wrought-iron balconies, and a pristine terracotta roof. Standing proud of this was a belvedere tower, constructed completely of glass. That was where you'd see the oceans from.

Other pitched roofs at different heights radiated out in all directions from the main building, covering a network of porches and archways. A swimming pool sparkled to the right of the main house, surrounded by a raised patio; distressed, Roman-style stone pillars were dotted about, to give it that *Gladiator* look. The only things missing were a few statues of sixteenth-century Spaniards with swords and baggy pants.

A set of four tennis courts stood behind a line of fencing. Nearby, three large satellite dishes were set into the ground. Maybe Charlie liked to watch American football, or check the Nasdaq to see how his money-laundering activities were shaping up.

Including the Lexus, there were six shiny SUVs and pickups parked outside a large circular drive that bordered a very ornate stone fountain, then led down to the front gates, maybe three hundred yards to my left. I looked back at the vehicles. One in particular had caught my eye. A dark blue GMC with blacked-out windows.

Most impressively, there was a white and yellow Jet Ranger helicopter using some of the driveway in front of the house as a pad. Just the thing to beat the morning commute.

I lay still and watched, but there was no movement, nothing going on. I opened my jaw a little to close off my swallowing sounds, trying to pick up any noise from the house, but I was too far away and they were too sensible: they kept indoors in the conditioned air.

My head was getting covered with lumps as I watched thousands of large dark red ants start to trundle past just inches from my nose, carrying scraps of leaf sometimes twice their own size. The leading few hundred were blazing the path maybe thirty abreast, the rest behind so closely packed I could hear them rustling.

I got back to looking at the target and became aware of a pretty unpleasant smell. It didn't take long to work out that it was me. I was wet, covered in mud, bits of twig and brush, itching all over and desperate to rub at the mozzie bites. I was sure I could feel something new munching at the small of my exposed back. I just had to let it munch: the only things I could risk moving were my eyes. Maybe I'd get back to loving the jungle tomorrow, but at the moment I wanted a divorce. After nearly twenty years of this stuff I really did need to get a life.

There was certainly no need to become an electric toy and do a 360-degree tour of the target: I could see everything I needed from here. Getting close to the house in daylight would be impossible—there was far too much open ground to cover. It might be just as difficult at night; I didn't yet know if they had any night-viewing facility, or closed-circuit TV with white light or an IR (infrared) capability covering the area, so I had to assume they did.

My problems didn't end there. Even if I did get to the house, where would I find Michael? Only Errol Flynn can walk into the front hall and pop behind a big curtain while squads of armed guards march past.

Swapping my hands over and adjusting the position of my chin, I started to take in the scene in front of me. I had to squeeze my gritty eyes shut constantly, then refocus. The ant columns were doing just fine as an enormous black butterfly landed an inch or two from my nose. Again I was back in Colombia. Anything that was colorful and flew, we caught for Bernard. He was over six foot four, weighed two-sixty, and looked as if he ate babies for breakfast. He sort of let everyone down by collecting butterflies and moths for his mother instead. We would come back into base camp from a patrol and the fridge would be filled with sealed jars full of things with wings instead of cold drinks and peanut butter. But no one was ever going to say anything to his face in case he decided to pin us to the wall instead.

In the distance there was the slow, low rumble of thunder as the heat haze shimmered over the open ground in front of me, and steam rose gently from the mud.

It would have been wonderful to get out there and stretch out in the sun, away from this world of gloom and mozzies. The shrill buzzing as they attacked the side of my head sounded like a demonic dentist's drill and I had definitely been bitten by something psychopathic on my lower back.

There was movement from the house.

Two white, short-sleeved shirts-and-ties came out of the main door with a man in a shocking pink Hawaiian shirt who climbed into the GMC. My friend the Pizza Man. The other two got into one of the pickups, and a fourth, running from the main door, jumped onto the back. Standing up, leaning forward against the cab, he looked like he was leading a wagon train as the pickup rounded the fountain and headed for the gates with the GMC following. He wasn't dressed as smartly as the other two: he was in black rubber boots and carried a wide-brimmed straw hat and a bundle of something or other under his arm.

Both trucks stopped for maybe thirty seconds as the gates swung open, then drove out of sight as they closed again behind them.

A gust of wind made the trees sway at the edge of the canopy. It wouldn't be long before the next batch of rain was heading this way. I'd have to get going if I wanted to be out of the jungle by last light. I started to shift backward on my elbows and toes, got onto my hands and knees for a while, and finally to my feet once I was safely behind the wall of green. I gave myself a frenzied scratch and shake, tucked everything back in, ran my fingers through my hair, and rubbed my back against a tree. A rash of some sort was developing at the base of my spine and the temptation to scratch it more was unbearable. My face probably looked like Darth Maul's by now. My left eyelid had swollen up big-time, and was starting to close.

Baby-G told me it was just after five: maybe an hour and a bit before last light, as it gets dark under the canopy before it does outside. I was dying for a drink but I'd have to wait until it rained again.

My plan now was to move south toward the road, turn right, and parallel it under the canopy until I hit the edge of the cleared area again nearer the gate, then sit and watch the target under cover of darkness. That way, as soon as I'd finished, I could jump onto the road to meet Aaron down at the loop at three A.M. instead of being stuck in here for the night.

I headed off through the thick wall of humidity. Wet pavement and a dark, moody sky soon came into sight through the foliage, just as the BUBs (basha-up beetles) started to go for it all around me with their high-pitched screams. They sounded like crickets with megaphones. They were telling me that God was about to switch off the light in here and go to bed.

A distant rumble of thunder resonated across the treetops, and then there was silence, as if the jungle was holding its breath. Thirty seconds later, I felt the first splashes of rain. The noise of it hitting the leaves even drowned out the BUBs, then the thunder roared directly overhead. Another thirty seconds and the water had worked its way down from the canopy and back onto my head and shoulders.

I turned right and picked my way toward the fence line, paralleling the road about seven or eight yards in. Mentally I was preparing myself for a miserable few hours in the dark. However, it was better to kill time watching the target while I waited for Aaron than doing nothing down at the loop. Time in reconnaissance is seldom wasted. And at least I knew there was no need to crawl into position: the house was too far away for them to spot me.

I moved forward, trying to make a record in my

head of everything I'd seen so far at the target. Every twenty paces or so I stopped to check the compass as thunder detonated high above the canopy and rain beat a tattoo on the leaves and the top of my head. I was displaying a builder's crack where my jeans should have been, but it didn't matter, I'd get myself organized again later on. I started to slip and slide on the mud beneath the leaf litter. I just wanted to get up to the fence before it got dark.

I fell onto my knees at one stage and discovered some rocks concealed beneath the mud. I sat there for a while in the dirt, rain running into my eyes and ears and down my neck, waiting for the pain to ease. At least it was warm.

I got up, still resisting the temptation to scratch my back rash to death. A few more yards and a large rotted tree trunk blocked my way. I couldn't be both ered working around it then back onto my compass bearing, so I just lay across it on my stomach and twisted myself over. The bark came away from the rotting wood like the skin on a blister and my chest throbbed from the beating Sundance and his pal had treated me to in the garage.

As I got to my feet, looking down, brushing off bark, I caught a glimpse to my right of something unnatural, something that shouldn't have been there.

In the jungle there are no straight lines and nothing is perfectly flat; everything's random. Everything except this.

The man was looking straight at me, rooted to the spot five or six yards away.

14

He was wearing a green U.S. Army poncho with the hood over his head. Rain dripped from the wide-brimmed straw hat perched on top of that.

He was a small guy, about five-five, his body perfectly still, and if I could have seen his eyes they would probably have been wide and dancing around, full of indecision. Fight or flight? He must have been panicking. I knew I was.

My eyes shot toward the first six inches or so of a gollock (machete) that his right hand was resting on and which protruded from the green nylon of his poncho. I could hear the rain pounding on the taut nylon, like a drumroll, before it dripped down to his black boots.

I kept my eyes fixed on the exposed part of what was probably two feet of gollock blade. When he moved, so would that thing.

Nothing was happening, no talking, no movement, but I knew that one of us was going to get hurt.

We stood there. Fifteen seconds felt like fifteen minutes. Something had to be done to break the standoff. I didn't know what he was going to do—I didn't think he did yet—but I certainly wasn't going to be this close to a gollock and not do something to protect myself, even if it was with just a pair of pointed pliers. The knife on my Leatherman would take too long to find and pull out.

I reached around with my right hand, and felt for the soaking, slimy leather pouch. My fingers fumbled to undo the retaining stud then closed around the hard steel of the Leatherman. And all the time, my eyes never left that still static gollock.

He made his decision, screaming at the top of his voice as he ran at me.

I made mine, turning and bolting in the direction of the road. He probably thought my hand was going for a pistol. I wished it had been.

I was still fumbling to get the Leatherman out of its pouch as I ran, folding the two handles back on themselves, exposing the pliers as he followed in my wake.

He was shouting stuff. What? Shouting for help? Telling me to stop? It didn't matter, the jungle swallowed it.

I got caught on wait-a-while, but it might have been tissue paper to me right then. I could hear the nylon poncho flapping behind me and the adrenaline pumped big-time.

I could see pavement . . . once on that he wouldn't be able to catch me in those boots. I lost my footing, falling onto my ass but gripping the Leatherman as if my life depended on it. *It did*.

I looked up at him. He veered left and stopped, eyes wide as saucers as the gollock rose into the air. My hands went down into the mud and I slipped and slithered, moving backward, trying to get back onto my feet. His screams got higher in pitch as the blade flashed through the air.

It must have been a cheap buy: the blade hit a sapling and made a thin tinny sound. He spun around, exposing his back to me in his frenzy, still screaming and shouting as he, too, slipped on the mud and onto his ass.

As he fell, the rear of the poncho caught on some wait-a-while and was yanked vertically. With the Leatherman still in my right hand I grabbed the flailing material with my left and pulled back on it as hard as I could, not knowing what I was going to do next. All I knew was that the gollock had to be stopped. This was one of Chan's men, those boys who crucified and killed their victims. I wasn't going to join the lineup.

I pulled again as he landed on his knees, yanking him completely backward onto the ground. I grabbed another handful of cape and pulled, constricting his neck by bunching the nylon of the hood as I got up. I could hear the rain hitting the pavement beyond as he kicked out and I dragged him—and our noise— back into the jungle, still not too sure what I was doing.

He had his left hand around the hood of his poncho, trying to protect his neck as the nylon squeezed against it. The gollock was in his right. He couldn't see me behind him, but still he hit out, swirling around in desperation. The blade slashed the poncho.

Still screaming at the top of his lungs in fear and anger, he kicked out as if he was having an epileptic fit.

I bobbed and weaved like a boxer, not knowing why—it just seemed a natural reaction to having sharp steel waved in my face. His ass bulldozed through leaves and palm branches. The struggle must have looked like a park ranger trying to drag a pissed-off crocodile out of the water by its tail. I was just concentrating on getting him back into the jungle and making sure the whirling blade didn't connect with me.

But then it did—big-time—sinking into my right calf.

I screamed with pain as I held on, still dragging him backward. I had no choice: if I stopped moving he'd be able to get up. Forget if anyone heard us, I was fighting for my life.

The crocodile thrashed and twisted around on the floor as there was another almighty clap of thunder, a deep resonant rumbling that seemed to go on forever. Forked lightning crackled high above, its noise drowning out his shouts and the clatter of rain.

The sharp pain of the cut spread out from my leg, but there was nothing I could do but go on dragging him into the jungle.

I didn't see the log. My legs hit it and buckled and I fell backward, keeping my grip on the poncho as I crashed into a palm. Rainwater came down in a torrent.

The pain in my leg was gone in an instant. It was more important to fill my head with other things, like living.

The guy felt the material around his neck relax, and instantly turned around. As he scrambled onto his knees, the gollock was up. I crabbed backward on my hands and feet, trying to get myself upright again, trying to keep clear of his reach.

Cursing and screaming in Spanish, he lunged forward in a wild frenzy. I saw two wild dark eyes as the gollock blade swung at me. I thrashed backward and managed to get myself onto my feet. It was time to run again.

I felt the gollock whoosh through the air behind me. This was getting outrageous—I was going to die.

Fuck it, I had to take a chance.

I turned and charged straight at him, face down, bending forward so that only my back was exposed. My whole focus was on the area of the poncho where his stomach should have been.

I screamed at the top of my voice, more for my own benefit than his. If I wasn't quick enough, I'd soon know because I'd feel the blade slice down between my shoulders.

The Leatherman pliers were still in my right hand. I got into him and felt his body buckle with the impact as I wrapped my left arm around him and tried to pinion his gollock arm.

Then I rammed the pointed tips against his stomach.

Both of us moved backward. The pliers hadn't penetrated his skin yet: they were held by the poncho and whatever was underneath. He screamed, too, probably feeling the steel trying to pierce him.

We hit a tree. His back was against it and I lifted my head and body, using my weight to force the pliers to penetrate his clothing and flesh.

He gave an agonized howl, and I felt his stomach tighten. It must have looked as if I was trying to have sex with him as I kept on pushing and bucking my body against him, using my weight against him with the pliers between us. At last I felt his stomach give way. It was like pushing into a sheet of rubber; and once they were in, there was no way they were coming out again.

I churned my hand up and down and around in circles, any way that I could to maximize the damage. My head was over his left shoulder and I was breathing through clenched teeth as he screamed just inches from the side of my face. I saw his bared teeth as they tried to bite me, and head-butted him to keep him away. Then he screamed so loudly into my face I could feel the force of his breath.

By now I wasn't even sure if the gollock was still in his hands or not. I smelled cologne and felt his smooth skin against my neck as he thrashed his face around, his body bucking and writhing.

The stab wound must have enlarged, as he was leaking over me. Blood had gotten past the hole in the poncho and I could feel the warmth of it on my hands. I continued to push in, keeping my body up against his, using my legs to keep him trapped between me and the tree.

His noises were getting softer and I could feel his warm slobber on my neck. My hand was virtually inside his stomach now, taking the poncho with it. I could smell the contents of his intestinal tract.

He collapsed forward onto me and took me down with him onto my knees. Only then did I withdraw my hand. As the Leatherman emerged and I kicked him off, he fell into the fetal position. He might have been crying; I couldn't really tell.

I moved away quickly, picked up the gollock from where he'd dropped it, and went and sat against a tree, fighting for breath, unbelievably relieved it was all over. As my body calmed down, the pain came back to my leg and chest. I pulled up my slashed jeans on my right leg and inspected the damage. It was to the rear of the calf; the gash was only about four inches long and not very deep, but bad enough to be leaking quite badly.

My hand, clenched around the Leatherman, looked much worse than it was as the rain diluted his blood. I tried to fold out the knife blade but it was difficult; my hand was shaking, now that I'd released my tight grip, and probably through shock as well. In the end I had to use my teeth, and when the blade was finally open I used it to cut my sweatshirt sleeves into wet strips. With these I improvised a bandage, wrapping it around my leg to apply pressure on the wound.

I sat there in the mud for a good five minutes, rain-water streaming down my face and into my eyes and mouth, dripping off my nose. I stared at the man, still lying in a fetal position, covered in mud and leaf litter.

The poncho was up around his chest like a pulled-up dress, and the rain still beat on it like a drumskin. Both his hands clutched his stomach; blood glistened as it seeped through the gaps between his fingers. His legs made small circular movements as if he was trying to run.

I felt sorry for him, but I'd had no choice. Once that length of razor-sharp steel started flying around it was either him or me.

I wasn't feeling too proud of myself, but had placed that feeling in my mental garbage can with the lid back on when I began to see that this wasn't exactly the local woodcutter I'd stumbled across. His nails were clean and well manicured, and though his hair was a mess of mud and leaves, I could see it was well cut, with a square neck and neatly trimmed sideburns. He was maybe early thirties, Spanish, good-looking and clean-shaven. He had one unusual feature: instead of two distinct eyebrows, he had just one big one.

This guy wasn't a farmhand, he was a city boy, the one who'd been standing in the back of the pickup. As Aaron had said, these people didn't fuck about and he would have sliced me up without a second thought. But what had he been doing in here?

I sat and stared at him as it got darker and the rain and thunder did its thing above the canopy. This episode spelled the end of the recce, and both of us were going to have to disappear. For sure he was going to be missed. Maybe he had been already. They would come looking for him, and if they knew where he had been, it wouldn't take them long to find him if I left him here.

I folded down my bloodstained Leatherman and put it back in its pouch, wondering if Jim Leatherman had ever imagined his invention would be used like this.

I guessed that the fence must be closer than the road now: if I headed for that, at least I'd have something to guide me out of the jungle in the darkness.

Unibrow's breathing was shallow and quick, and he was still gripping his stomach with both hands, his face screwed up in pain as he mumbled weakly to himself. I forced his eyes open. Even in this low light there should have been a better reaction in his pupils; they should have closed a lot quicker. He was definitely on his way out.

I went in search of his hat, gollock in hand. The machete was a bottom-of-the-line thing, with a plastic handle riveted on each side of very thin, rust-spotted steel.

What to do with him once we were out of here? If he was still alive I couldn't take him to a hospital because he'd talk about me, which would alert Charlie and compromise the job. I certainly couldn't take him back to Aaron and Carrie's place because that would compromise them. All I knew was that I had to get him away from the immediate vicinity. I'd think of something later.

Hat retrieved, I went back to Unibrow, got hold of his right arm, and hoisted him in a fireman's lift over my back and shoulder. There were moans and groans from him and he tried in a pathetic way to kick out at me.

I grabbed his right arm and leg and held them together, jumping gently up and down to get him comfy around my shoulders. The small amounts of oxygen that his injuries allowed him to take in were knocked out of him again, no doubt making him feel even worse, but I couldn't help that. The poncho flapped over my face and I had to push it away. I grabbed his hat, and then, gollock back in hand, I checked the compass and headed for the fence line.

It was getting much darker; I could only just make out where my feet were going. I felt something warm and wet on my neck, warmer than the rain, and guessed it was his blood.

Pushing myself hard I limped on, stopping occasionally to check the compass. Nothing else mattered but getting to the road and making the RV. Within minutes I came to the fence line. The BUBs were reaching a crescendo. In another quarter of an hour it was going to be pitch black.

Ahead of me, in the open, semidark space, was a solid wall of rain, thumping into the mud with such force it was creating mini craters. Lights were already on in the house, and in one area, probably a hallway, an enormous chandelier shone through a high window. The fountain was illuminated but I couldn't see the statue. That was good, because it meant they couldn't see me.

I followed the fence for a few minutes, my passenger's head and poncho constantly snagging on branches of wait-a-while so that I had to stop and backtrack to free him. All the time I kept my eyes glued on the house. I came across what looked like a small mammal track, paralleling the fence and about two feet in. I followed it, past caring about leaving sign in the churned-up mud. The rain would sort that out.

I'd gone no more than a dozen steps when my limping right leg was whipped away from under me and both of us went crashing into the undergrowth.

I lashed out in a frenzy: it was as if an invisible hand had grabbed hold of my ankle and thrown me to one side. I tried to kick out but my right foot was stuck fast. I tried to crawl away but couldn't. Next to me on the ground, Unibrow gave a loud groan of pain.

I looked down and saw a faint glimmer of metal. It was wire: I was caught in a snare; the more I struggled, the more it was gripping me.

I turned around to make sure where Unibrow was. He was rolled up in his own little world, oblivious to the thunder and forked lightning rattling across the night sky.

It was simple enough to ease open the loop. I got to my feet and went over and heaved him back up onto my shoulders, then set off along the track.

Just another five minutes of stumbling brought us to the start of the whitewashed rough-stone wall and, ten yards or so later, the tall iron gates. It was good to feel pavement under my feet. I turned left and moved as quickly as I could to get away from the area. If a vehicle came I'd just have to plunge back into the undergrowth and hope for the best.

As I shuffled forward with the weight of the man over my shoulder, I became much more aware of the pain in my right calf. It hurt too much to raise my foot, so I kept my legs as straight as possible, pumping forward with my free arm. Rain ricocheted a good six inches off the pavement, making a horrendous racket. I realized I'd never be able to hear a vehicle coming up behind us, so I had to keep stopping and turning around. Thunder and lightning roared and crackled behind me and I kept moving as though I was running away from it.

It took over an hour but I finally got us both into the canopy at the loop. The rain had eased off but Unibrow's pain hadn't, and neither had mine. The jungle was so dark now I couldn't see my hand in front of my face, only the small luminous specks on the jungle floor, maybe phosphorescent spores or nighttime beasties on the move.

For an hour or so I sat, rubbed my leg, and waited for Aaron, listening to Unibrow's whimpers, and the sound of his legs moving about in the leaf litter. His groans faded, and eventually disappeared. I crawled over to him on my hands and knees, feeling for his body. Then, following his legs up to his face, all I could hear was weak, wheezy breath trying to force itself through his mucus-filled nostrils and mouth. I pulled out the Leatherman and jabbed his tongue with the blade. There was no reaction, it was just a matter of time.

Rolling him onto his back, I lay on top of him and jammed my right forearm into his throat, pushing down with all my weight, my left hand on my right wrist. There was little resistance. His legs kicked out weakly, moving us about a bit, a hand floundered about my arm and another came up weakly to scratch at my face. I simply moved my head out of the way and listened to the insects and his low whimpers as I cut off the blood supply to his head, and oxygen to his lungs.

15

*I*t's Kev, Kelly's dad. He's lying on the living room floor, eyes glazed and vacant, his head battered, an aluminum baseball bat lying beside him.

There's blood on the glass coffee table and the thick shag-pile carpet, some even splattered on the patio windows.

I put my foot on the bottom stair. The shag pile helps keep the noise down, but still it's like treading on ice, testing each step gently for creaks, always placing my feet to the inside edge, slowly and precisely. Sweat pours off my face, I worry if anyone is hiding up there, ready to attack.

I get level with the landing, I point my pistol up above my head, using the wall as support, move up the stairs backward, step by step. . . .

The washing machine is on its final thundering spin downstairs, still the soft rock plays on the radio.

As I get nearer to Kev and Marsha's room I can see that the door is slightly ajar, there's a faint, metallic tang . . . I can also smell shit, I feel sick, I know I have to go in.

Marsha: she's kneeling by the bed, her top half spreadeagled on the mattress, the bedspread covered with blood.

Forcing myself to ignore her I move to the bathroom. Aida is lying on the floor, her five-year-old head nearly severed from her shoulders; I can see the vertebrae just holding on.

Bang, I go back against the wall and slump onto the floor, blood is everywhere, I get it all over my shirt, my hands, I sit in a pool of it, soaking the seat of my pants. There is a loud creak of wood splitting above me. . . . I drop my weapon, curl up, and cover my head with my hands. Where's Kelly? Where the fuck is Kelly?

"Shit! shit! shit!"

There was the crash of branches, followed swiftly by the thud on the jungle floor, close enough that I felt the vibration in the ground—as it does when two tons of dead tree have just given up the will to stay upright.

The crash spooked not only me but also the birds lazing on branches high above. There was screeching and the heavy, slow flap of large wings getting their owners the hell out of there.

A few gallons of canopy-held rain had followed the deadfall. I wiped the water from my face and stood up. *Shit, it's getting bad. I've never had them on a job and never had them about Kev and his gang. It must be because I'm so beat, I just feel totally drained. . . .*

I pushed hair off my forehead and got a grip on myself. *Beat? So what? Just get on with it. Work is work; cut away from that shit. You know where she is, she's safe, just do the job and try to keep her that way.*

Deadfall was a constant problem in the jungle, and checking to see if there were any dead trees or branches nearby or overhead when basha'ing up (rigging up a shelter) for the night was an SOP (Standard Operating Procedure) that was taken seriously. I marked time, trying to do something with my legs. I could feel pins and needles. *Please, not here, not now*.

According to Baby-G it was 2:23, not long to pickup.

The rain had held off while I'd been here, but now and again a bucketful still fell after being dislodged, bouncing off the foliage on its way down with the sound of a finger tapping on a side drum, as if to accompany my static marching.

I'd been here among the leaf litter for nearly six hours. It was like having a night out on belt-kit—not having the comfort of being off the ground in a hammock and under a poncho, instead having to rough it with just the equipment that you have on your belt: ammunition, twenty-four hours of food, water, and medical supplies. Only I didn't even have that. Just guaranteed misery as I became part of the jungle floor.

I finished with marking time: the sensation had gone away. I'd fought off jet lag, but my body still wanted desperately to curl into a ball and sink into a deep sleep. I felt my way back down against the hard rough bark of a tree and was surrounded by invisible crickets. As I stretched out my legs to ease the cramp in the good one and the pain in the other, I felt around to make sure the sweatshirt dressing was still tight around the wound; it didn't feel as if it was bleeding anymore, but it was painful and, I imagined, messy down there. I could feel the pulse throbbing against the edge of the wound.

As I moved to relieve the numbness in my ass once more, the soles of my Timberlands pushed against Unibrow. I'd searched him before we went into the tree line, and found a wallet and several yard lengths of copper wire tucked into a canvas pouch on his belt. He'd been setting traps. Maybe he was into that sort of stuff for fun: it wasn't as if the bunch up at the house would be in need of the odd wild turkey.

I thought back over some of the stuff I'd done over the years, and right now I hated all the jobs I'd ever been on. I hated Unibrow for making me kill him. I hated me. I was sitting in shit, getting attacked by everything that moved, and I'd still had to kill someone else. One way or another that was the way it had always been.

Until midnight I'd heard only three vehicles moving along the road, and it was hard to tell if they were heading toward the house or away from it. After that, the only new sounds were the buzzing of insects. At one point a troop of howler monkeys passed us by, using the top of the canopy so they had some starlight to help them see what they were doing. Their booming barks and groans reverberated through the jungle, so loud they seemed to shake the trees. As they swung screeching and bellowing from tree to tree they disturbed the water caught in the giant leaves, and we were rained on again.

I sat gently rubbing around the cut on my leg as more buzzes circled my head, stopping just before I felt something bite into my skin. I slapped my face just as I heard movement high above me in the canopy, sending another downpour. Whatever it was up there sounded like it was moving on rather than coming down to investigate, which was fine by me.

At 2:58 I heard the low rumble of a vehicle. This time the noise didn't fade. The engine note took over gradually from the chirping of the crickets, passing my position until I could clearly hear the tires splashing in puddled-up potholes. It stopped just past me, with a gentle squeak of not-too-good brakes. The engine turned over erratically. It had to be the Mazda.

Leaning on the gollock to help me get to my feet, I stretched my legs and tried to get them warmed up as I checked to make sure I still had my docs. The wound felt even more tender now that I was standing again, and my clothing was sodden and heavy. Having given in to temptation hours ago, I scratched my lumpy back.

I felt around for Unibrow, got hold of an arm and a leg, and heaved him over my shoulder. His body was slightly stiff, but far from rigid. The heat and humidity probably had something to do with that. His free arm and foot flopped around as I jiggled him into position.

With the gollock and hat in my right hand I made my way slowly toward the edge of the tree line, my head and eyes at an angle of about forty-five degrees to the ground and half closed to protect them from the unseen wait-a-while. I might as well have closed them completely: I couldn't see a thing.

The moment I emerged from the forest, I saw the silhouette of the Mazda, bathed in a glow of white and red reflecting off the wet pavement. I laid down Unibrow with his hat in the mud and tall grass at the jungle's edge, and squelched toward the passenger side, gollock in hand, checking to make sure there was only one body shape in the cab.

Aaron was sitting with both hands gripping the wheel, and in the dull glow of the instruments I could see him staring rigidly ahead like some sort of robot. Even with the window down, he didn't seem to register I was there.

I said quietly, "Seen any of those barry-whatever trees yet?"

He jumped forward in his seat as if he'd just seen a ghost.

"Is the back unlocked, mate?"

"Yes." He nodded frantically, his voice shaking.

"Good, won't be long."

I walked to the rear, opened the tailgate, then went back to fetch Unibrow. Lifting him in my arms and leaning back to take the weight, I carried him across to the vehicle, not knowing whether Aaron could see what was happening. The suspension sank a little as I dumped the body on the crap-strewn floor. His hat followed, and in the dim glow from the taillights I covered him with his own poncho, then lowered the tailgate before gently clicking it shut. The back window was a small oval, covered in grime. Nobody would be able to see through.

I went around to the passenger door and jumped in. Water oozed from my jeans and soaked into the blanket covering the seat. Aaron was still in the same position. "Let's go then, mate. Not too fast, just drive normally."

He pushed the shift into Drive and we moved off. A cool draft of air from the open window hit my lumpy face, and as we splashed through potholes I leaned down and placed the gollock under my feet.

Aaron at last found the courage to speak. "What's in the back?"

There was no point beating about the bush. "A body."

"God forbid." His hands ran through his hair as he stared through the windshield, before attacking his beard once more. "God forbid . . . What happened?"

I didn't answer, but listened to the rasping of stubble as his left hand wiped imaginary demons from his face.

"What are we going to do, Nick?"

"I'll explain later—it's okay, it isn't a drama." I tried to keep my voice slow and calm. "All we need to worry about is getting away from the area, and then I'll sort the problem out, okay?"

Switching on the cab light, I fumbled for Unibrow's wallet in my jeans and pulled it apart. He had a few dollars, and a picture ID that called him Diego Paredes and said he had been born in November 1976—two months after I'd joined the Army. There was a cropped photograph of him and what looked like his parents and maybe some brothers and sisters, all dressed up, sitting at a table, glasses raised at the camera.

Aaron had obviously seen it. "Someone's son," he said.

Weren't they all? I put everything back in the leather compartments.

His head was obviously full of a million and one things he wanted to say. "Can't we take him to the hospital? We can't just keep him in the back, for God's sake."

I tried to sound relaxed. "Basically, we have to— but only for now." I looked across at him. He didn't return my glance, just stared at the headlights hitting the road. He was in a world of his own, and a frightening one it was.

I kept my gaze on the side of his face, but he couldn't bring himself to make eye contact. "He belongs to Charlie. If they find his body, it could put *all* of us in danger—all of us. Why take that risk?" I let that sink in for a bit. He knew what I was talking about. When a threat's extended to a man's wife and children, it invariably focuses his way of thinking.

I needed to instill confidence in this character, not anxiety. "I know what I'm doing and he's just got to come with us for now. Once we're out of the area we'll make sure we dump him so he's never found."

Or at least, as far as I was concerned, not before Saturday morning.

There was a long, awkward silence as we drove along the jungle-lined road and eventually hit the ghost town of Clayton. The headlights picked out the shadows of empty houses, barracks, and deserted streets and children's play areas. It looked even more deserted at night, as if the last American soldier had turned off the lights before he went home for good.

We turned a corner and I could see the high-mounted floodlights of the locks a few miles in the distance, shimmering like a big island of white light. The superstructure of a heavily laden container ship was facing to the right, half hidden as it waited in the lock for the water to surge in and raise its massive bulk.

16

I was just too done in to worry about anything, but Aaron was in deep panic mode. His left hand couldn't stop touching or rubbing his face. His eyes kept checking through the rear window, trying to see the body in the back, even though it was in pitch darkness.

We were driving alongside a very wide, deep, U-shaped concrete storm trench. I got Aaron to stop and turn off his lights, and he faced me for the first time, probably hoping that we were going to do something about Unibrow.

I nodded toward the lights. "I've got to clean myself up before we hit all that." I wanted to look at least a bit normal, in case we were seen or stopped as we went through the city. Being wet wasn't unusual here, it rained a lot. I could have told him it was time for my daily prayers and he would probably have replied the same way.

"Oh, okay."

Once I forced my aching body out of the Mazda I could see what was going on under the floodlights. The stumpy electric trains were moving up and down the tracks beside the ship, looking like little toys from this distance and too far away to be heard properly. Only a muffled version of the radio traffic from the speakers reached us. The glow from the powerful arc-lights got to us, though, giving just enough light to see what was going on about us, and cast a very weak shadow on the Mazda as I went to the rear and lifted the tailgate to check Unibrow. He had been sliding about and he was pushed hard against the side body-work, his nose and lips compressed, his arms thrown behind him as if they couldn't catch up. The stench of blood and guts was so strong I had to move my head away. It smelled like a freezer after a power outage.

Leaving the tailgate up, I scrambled two or three yards down the side of the concrete ditch and into the surging storm water. Bits of tree and vegetation raced past my legs as I pulled the plastic bag from under my jacket and wedged it above the waterline in the gap between two of the concrete sections. Even if I had to run naked from this spot I would still be armed with my documents.

I squatted in the edge of the flow and washed off all the mud, blood, and leaf litter that covered me, as if I was having a bath with my clothes on. I didn't bother to check the wound; I'd clean it up later, and in the meantime all I'd do was keep the cut-up sweat-shirt wrapped around it and just sit in the water and rest for a second.

I hadn't really noticed it up till now, but the sky was very clear and full of stars, sparkling like the phosphorescence on the jungle floor as I slowly took off my jacket.

I heard Aaron's door creak open and looked up to see him silhouetted against the glow from the canal. By now I was nearly naked, rinsing my jeans in the trench before wringing them out and throwing them up onto the grass, then checking out my back rash and face.

I watched as he stuck his head slowly into the back of the wagon. He recoiled and turned away, vomit already exploding from his mouth. I heard it splatter against the side of the vehicle and pavement above me, then the sounds of him retching up those last bits that stay in your throat and nose.

I scrambled up onto the grass and hurriedly dressed in my wet clothes. Aaron had his last cough and snort and walked back to the cab, wiping his beard with a handkerchief. Sidestepping the pool of vomit on the pavement, I covered Unibrow again with the poncho, lowered the tailgate, and climbed in next to Aaron, ignoring what had just happened even though I could smell it on his breath. "That's better, wet but clean-ish." I grinned, trying to lighten the tone.

Aaron didn't respond. He looked terrible, even in this low light. His eyes were glistening with tears and his breathing was sharp and quick as he swallowed hard, maybe to stop himself throwing up again. His large hairy Adam's apple bobbed up and down like a fishing float with a bite. He was having a moment with his thoughts, not even realizing I'd spoken as he rubbed his stubble with shaking hands.

"Back to your place, then—how far is it again, mate?"

I patted him on the shoulder and he nodded, turning the ignition with another little cough. He gave a quiet, resigned, "Sure." His voice trembled as he added, "It's about four hours, maybe more. We've had some very heavy rain."

I made the effort and kept my happy voice on, not really knowing what else to do or say. "We'd better get a move on, then, hadn't we?"

We got through Fort Clayton and hit the main drag; the barrier was up, it seemed the old security guy didn't play at night. I'd been wrong, the street lighting wasn't used now that there wasn't much traffic on it anymore.

We turned left, leaving the lock and Clayton behind us, traveling in silence. A distant arc of light in the night sky indicated the city, along with flashing red lights from the top of a profusion of communication towers. Aaron just stared straight ahead, swallowing hard.

Before long we approached the floodlit tollbooths by the old Albrook air force base. The noise of the bus terminal blasted all around us as power hoses washed the buses. A surprisingly large number of workers were waiting for transport, most holding small coolers and smoking.

Aaron spent the best part of a minute fumbling in his pockets and the glove compartment at the tollbooth. A bored, middle-aged woman just stared into space with her hand out, no doubt dreaming about getting onto one of those buses at the end of her shift.

I let my head bob about as we bounced along the potholed road and into the sleeping city via El Chorrillo. A few lights were on here and there in the apartment blocks, and the odd scabby mongrel skulked along a sidewalk, then a black BMW screamed past us at warp speed. Five or six heads with cigarettes glowing in their mouths jutted backward and forward to the beat of some loud Latin music as it roared down the street. The BMW had violet-colored headlights, and a powerful fluorescent glow beneath the bodywork made it look like it was hovering. My eyes followed it into the distance as it hung a right, tires squealing like something out of *NYPD Blue*.

I looked over at Aaron. He probably wouldn't even have reacted if we'd been overtaken by the U.S.S. *Enterprise*. He screwed up his face and deep lines cut into his skin. He looked as if he was going to be sick again as we bounced along, turning right at the junction the BMW had taken. Once more we drove past the Pepsi stand, barred up for the night, and into the market area.

I thought I needed to say something to fill the silence, but I didn't know what. I just looked out at the garbage overflowing from the piles of soaked cardboard boxes that fringed the square, and cats fighting over the scraps.

In the end it was Aaron who broke the deadlock, wiping his nose into his hand before he spoke. "Nick . . . ?"

"What's that, mate?" I was almost too tired to speak.

"Is that what you do—kill people? I mean, I know it happens, it's just that—"

I pointed down at the gollock in the footwell. "I nearly lost my leg with that thing, and if he'd had his way, it would have been my head. I'm sorry, mate, there was no other way. Once we're on the other side of the city, I'll dump him."

He didn't reply, just stared intently through the windshield, nodding slowly to himself.

We hit the bay once more, and I saw a line of ships' navigation lights flickering out at sea. Then I realized Aaron had started to shake. He'd spotted a police car at the roadside ahead, with two rather bored-looking officers smoking and reading the papers. I gave myself a mental slapping, but not enough for him to see.

I kept my voice calm. "Don't worry, just drive normally, everything's okay."

It wasn't, of course: they might stop a beaten-up Mazda just to relieve the boredom.

As we passed, the driver glanced up from his newspaper, and turned to say something to his pal. I kept my eyes on the cracked side mirror, watching the four multiplied police cars as I spoke. "It's okay, mate, there's no movement from behind. They're still static. Just keep to the limit and smile."

I didn't know if he responded. My eyes were glued to the vehicles in the mirror until they dropped out of sight. I caught a glimpse of my face for the first time. It was a pleasant surprise. My left eye was half closed but not as swollen as it felt.

I looked over again to see how Aaron was doing—and the answer was, not good. He wasn't enjoying his visit to my planet one little bit. I wondered why and how he'd gotten involved in this shit. Maybe he'd had no choice. Maybe he was just like me and Diego, in the wrong place at the wrong time.

We splashed our way through mini-Manhattan, where large neon signs flashed down from the tops of buildings onto the wet pavement below. It was a completely different world from El Chorrillo, and a whole galaxy away from what had just been happening in the old Zone.

Aaron gave a small cough. "You know what you're going to do with that guy yet, Nick?"

"We need to hide him somewhere on the way to your place, once we're out of the city. Any ideas?"

Aaron shook his head slowly from side to side. I couldn't tell whether he was answering or if it had just come loose.

"We can't leave him to rot . . . God forbid. He's a human being, for God's sake." There was resignation in his voice. "Look, I'll bury him for you. There's an old tribal site near the house. No one will find him there. It's the right thing to do—he's someone's son, Nick. Maybe even someone's father. The family in the picture, they don't deserve this."

"No one goes there?"

He shook his head. "Not in a few hundred years."

I wasn't going to argue with that. If he wanted to dig a hole, that was fine by me.

I got back to looking at the neon as he drove, and hoped that someone like him found my body one day.

We came to the airport road tollbooth on the other side of the financial district, and this time I got out a dollar of my own money. I didn't want us standing still any longer than we had to. Diego would take quite a bit of explaining.

He paid the woman with a sad *"Gracias"* and a thanks to me for giving him the money. This wasn't a good night out for him at all.

The lights faded behind us as we hit the road out of town. I dug out the wallet again, hit the cab light, and looked at Diego's family picture. I thought of Kelly, and the way her life would be if I died without sorting out the mess I'd created. I thought of all the things I'd wanted to say to her, and hadn't ever managed to.

I wondered if his mom had wanted to say those things to her son, to tell him how much she loved him, or to say sorry about the stupid argument they'd had. Maybe that had been the stuff that had flashed through Diego's head in the moments before he died, things he wanted to say to these people raising their glasses at the camera as I killed him.

The wind through my window got stronger as we gathered speed. I wound it up only halfway to keep me awake, and I tried to concentrate on what I'd seen on the CTR and then get back to work. Instead, I found myself wanting to curl up like a seven-year-old, desperate to keep the night monster at bay.

* * *

"Nick! The police! Nick, what do we do? Wake up! Please!"

Before I'd even fully opened my eyes I was trying to calm him down. "It's all right, don't worry, it'll be okay." I managed to focus on the VCP (vehicle checkpoint) ahead, set up in the middle of nowhere: two police vehicles, sideways, blocking the road, both facing left. I could see silhouettes moving across the two sets of headlights that cut through the darkness. It felt as though we were heading straight into the Twilight Zone. Aaron's foot had frozen on the accelerator pedal.

"Slow down, for God's sake. Calm down."

He came out of his trance and hit the brakes.

We'd gotten close enough to the checkpoint for me to see the side windows of the four-wheel-drives reflecting our headlights back at us. Aaron dabbed at the brakes to bring us to a stop. There was a torrent of shouts in Spanish, and the muzzles of half a dozen M-16s came up. I placed my hands on the dash so they were in clear view.

Aaron killed the lights and turned off the engine as three flashlight beams headed our way. The shouting had stopped, and all I could hear now was the thump of boots on pavement.

17

The three men who approached with M-16s at the ready were dressed in olive green fatigues. They split up, two going left, to Aaron, the others toward me. Aaron started to wind down the remaining half of his window. His breathing was becoming increasingly rapid.

There was an abrupt command in Spanish as the nearest man shouldered his assault rifle. Aaron lifted his ass from the seat and searched around in his back pocket. I saw the red glow of cigarettes beyond the 4x4's headlights as figures moved about in the shadows.

A green baseball cap and bushy black mustache shoved its way through Aaron's window and demanded something from me. I didn't respond. I didn't have a clue what he was asking and just couldn't dig deep enough for the energy to look interested. His M-16 swung around from his back and banged against the door. I saw sergeant's stripes and *"Policia"* badges on his sleeve.

"He wants your ID, Nick."

Aaron presented his own. It was snatched away by

the sergeant, who stopped shouting and stood back from the window, using his mini-Maglite to inspect the docs.

"Nick? Your ID, please don't vex these people."

I pulled out my plastic bag lethargically from under my jacket and rummaged in it like a schoolboy in his lunchbox, just wanting this to go away.

The other policeman on Aaron's side had been standing behind the sergeant, his assault rifle shouldered. I heard boots behind the truck, but couldn't see anything in the mirror.

I gripped myself: *What the fuck am I doing? Switch on! Switch on!*

My heart-rate pumped up a few more revs per minute, and at the same time as I looked in my bag I made a mental note of where the door handle was, and checked that the door-lock knob was up. Lethargic or not, if I heard the squeak of rusty hinges from the tailgate I'd be out and running. Handing my passport over to Aaron for the sergeant, I knew I was reacting too slowly to all of this.

There's a body in the back, for fuck's sake!

The sergeant was jabbering about me as he looked at my passport with his Maglite. I only understood the odd word of Aaron's replies. *"Britanico . . . amigo . . . vacaciones . . ."* He nodded away like a lunatic, as if he had some sort of nervous disease.

The sergeant now had both our IDs in his hands, which would be a problem if I needed to do a runner. Without a passport, my only option was west, or the embassy.

Straining my ears, I waited for the tailgate to open. I ran my hands through my hair, keeping my eyes on the door handle and visualizing my escape route, which wasn't exactly difficult: three steps into the darkness to my right. From there, I'd just have to take my chances.

I was brought back to the real world by the sergeant bending down once more and pointing at my clothes as he rattled off something to Aaron. He replied with something funny, and forced a laugh, as he turned to me. "You're a friend and I picked you up from the airport. You wanted so much to see the rain forest so I took you in at the edge of the city. Now you never want to go in again. It was so funny, please just smile."

The sergeant had joined in the laughter and told the other guy behind him about the dickhead *britanico* as he handed back the IDs. Then he banged the roof of the Mazda and followed the others toward the blocking wagons. There was a lot of pointing and shouting, followed by the roar of wagons being revved and maneuvered clear of the road.

Aaron was shaking like a leaf as he turned the ignition, but managed to appear relaxed and confident from the neck up for the police's benefit. He even waved as we passed. Our headlights caught four or five bodies lined up on their backs on the side of the road. Their clothes glistened with blood. One of the kids was still open-mouthed, arms flung out and eyes wide, staring up at the sky. I looked away and tried to focus on the darkness beyond the headlights.

Aaron said nothing for the next ten minutes as we bounced along the potholed road, headlights lurching. Then he braked suddenly, pushed the shift into Park, and jumped out as if a bomb was about to go off. I could hear him retching and straining as he leaned against the Bac Pac, but not the sound of anything coming up. He'd left it all at Clayton.

I just let him get on with it. I'd done the same myself, when I first started: sheer terror engulfs you and there's nothing you can do but fight it until the drama is over. It's later, when there's time to think, not only about what's happened but, worse, what the consequences might have been if things had gone wrong—that's when you part company with your last meal. What he was doing was normal. The way I had behaved back there wasn't, not for me.

The suspension creaked as he closed the door, wiping his waterlogged eyes. He was plainly embarrassed, and couldn't bring himself to look at me. "I'm sorry, Nick, you must think I'm a real pussy. Guys like you can handle this stuff, but me, I'm just not made for it."

I knew that wasn't exactly true, but I didn't know how to say so. I never did at times like this.

"I saw a couple of guys blown away a few years ago. I had nightmares about it. Then, seeing Diego's body and those kids back there hacked to death, it just . . ."

"Did he tell you what had happened?"

"It was a robbery. FARC. They cut them up with those things." He pointed down at the gollock. "It doesn't really make sense—they normally don't bother folks here. No money." He sighed, both hands on the steering wheel, and leaned forward a bit. "You see what they'd done to those kids? Oh, God, how can people behave like that?"

I wanted to change the subject. "Look, mate, I think we'd better get rid of Diego. As soon as there's a bit of light we'll find somewhere to hide him. We can't go through that shit again."

He lowered his head onto the wheel and nodded slowly. "Sure, sure, you're right."

"It'll be okay, he'll be found sooner or later and buried properly. . . ."

We drove on. Neither of us wanted to talk about Diego or bodies anymore.

"What road are we on?"

"The Pan-American Highway."

It didn't feel like one. We were bouncing around in ruts and potholes.

"Runs all the way from Alaska to Chile, apart from a ninety-three-mile break in the Darien Gap. There's been talk about joining it up, but with all the trouble in Colombia and the destruction of the forest, I guess we prefer it how it is."

I knew about the southern part of the highway; I'd been on it enough times. But I wanted us to keep talking. It stopped my having to think. I leaned down and rubbed the sweatshirt wrapped around my now very painful leg. "Oh, why's that?"

"It's one of the most important stretches of rain forest still left in the Americas. If there are no roads, that means no loggers and farmers, and it's kind of like a buffer zone with Colombia. Folks call it Bosnia West down there. . . ."

The headlights were sweeping across each side of the road, illuminating nothing. "Is that where we're going, to the Gap?"

He shook his head. "Even if we were, this eventually becomes not much more than a track, and with this rain it's just darned impassable. We're heading off the road at Chepo, maybe another ten minutes or so."

First light was starting to edge its way past the corners of the sky. We bounced along for a while in silence. My headache was killing me. The headlights exposed nothing but tufts of grass and pools of mud and water. This place was as barren as a moonscape. Not much good for hiding a body. "There's not a whole lot of forest here, mate, is there?"

"Hey, what can I say? Where there's a road, there's loggers. They keep on going until everything's leveled. And it's not just about money: the folk around here believe it's manly to cut down trees. I reckon less than twenty percent of Panama's forest will survive the next five years. That's including the Zone."

I thought of Charlie and his new estate. It wasn't just the loggers who were tearing chunks out of Aaron's jungle.

We drove on as daylight spread its way gloomily across the sky. A primeval mist blanketed the ground. A flock of maybe a hundred big black birds with long necks took off ahead of us; they looked suspiciously like pterodactyls.

Ahead and to our left I could see the dark shadows of trees, and I pointed. "What about there?"

Aaron thought for a few seconds as we got closer, clearly disturbed again, as if he'd managed for a moment to forget what we had in the back. "I guess so, but it's not that far to where I could do it properly."

"No, mate, no. Let's do it now." I tried to keep my voice level.

We pulled onto the side of the road and under the trees. There wasn't going to be time for ceremony. "Want to help?" I asked, as I retrieved the gollock from under my feet.

He thought hard. "I just don't want the picture of him in there, you know, in my head. Can you understand that?"

I could: there were a whole lot of pictures in my own head I wished weren't there. The most recent was a blood-soaked child staring open-mouthed at the sky.

As I climbed out the birds were in full song: daylight was nearly here. I held my breath, opened the back, and pulled Diego out by his armpits, dragging him into the tree line. I concentrated on not looking at his face and keeping his blood off me.

About ten yards inside the gloom of the canopy I rolled both him and the wiped-clean gollock under a rotted deadfall, covering the gaps with leaves and debris. I only needed to hide him until Saturday. When I'd gone, maybe Aaron would come back and do what he'd wanted to in the first place. It shouldn't be hard to find him; by then there'd be so many flies they'd sound like a radio signal.

Having closed down the tailgate I got back into the cab and slammed the door. I waited for him to move off, but instead he turned. "You know what? I think maybe Carrie shouldn't know about this, Nick. Don't you think? I mean—"

"Mate," I said, "you took the words right out of my mouth." I tried to give him a smile, but the muscles in my cheek weren't working.

He nodded and steered back onto the road as I tried to curl up once more, closing my eyes, trying to kill the headache, but not daring to sleep.

Maybe fifteen minutes later we hit a cluster of huts. An oil lamp swung in one of them, splashing light across a roomful of faded, multicolored clothes hung up to dry. The huts were made of cinder block, with doors of rough planks nailed to a frame and corrugated tin thrown over the top. There was no glass in the windows, nothing to hold back the smoke from small fires that smoldered near the entrances. Scrawny chickens ran for cover as the Mazda approached. It wasn't at all the sort of thing I'd been shown in the inflight magazine.

Aaron jerked his thumb over his shoulder as we drove past. "When the loggers leave, these guys turn up—subsistence farmers, thousands of them, just poor people trying to grow themselves something to eat. The only problem is, with the trees gone, the topsoil gets washed away, and within two years they can't grow anything except grass. So guess who comes in next—the ranchers."

I could see a few mangy-looking cows with their heads down, grazing. He jerked his thumb again. "Next week's burger."

Without warning, Aaron spun the wheel to the right, and that was our quitting the Pan-American Highway. There were no signs on the gravel road, just like in the city. Maybe they liked to keep the population confused.

I saw a huddle of corrugated roofs. "Chepo?"

"Yep, the bad and sad side."

The compacted-gravel road took us past a scattering of more basic farmers' huts on stilts. Beneath them, chickens and a few old cats mooched around rusty lumps of metal and piles of old tin cans. Some of the shacks had smoke spilling from a clay or rusty metal chimney. One was made out of six or seven catering-size cans, opened on both ends and knocked together. Apart from that there was no sign of human life. The bad and sad side of Chepo was in no hurry to greet the dawn. I couldn't say I blamed them.

The odd rooster did its early-morning bit as the huts gradually gave way to larger one-story buildings, which also seemed to have been plonked randomly on any available patch of ground. Boardwalks, instead of pavements, led here and there, supported on rocks that were half submerged in mud. Garbage had been collected in piles that had then collapsed, the contents strewn. A terrible stink wafted through the Mazda's cab. This place made the flophouse in Camden look like the Waldorf.

Eventually we passed a gas station, which was closed. The pumps were old and rusty, 1970s vintage, with an oval top. So much diesel had been spilled on the ground over the years that it looked like a layer of slippery tar. Water lay in dark, oil-stained puddles. The Pepsi logo and some faded bunting hung from the roof of the gas station itself, along with a sign advertising Firestones.

We passed a rectangular building made from more unpainted cinder blocks. The mortar that oozed between the blocks hadn't been pointed, and the builder certainly hadn't believed in plumblines. A sinewy old Indian guy wearing green athletic shorts, a string undershirt, and rubber flip-flops was crouched down by the door, with a rolled cigarette the size of a Rastafarian Old Holborn hanging from his mouth. Through the windows I could see shelves of canned food.

Farther up the road was a large wooden shack, up on stilts like some of the huts. It had been painted blue at one stage in its life, and a sign said that it was a restaurant. As we drew level I saw four leopardskins stretched out and nailed to the wall of the porch. Below them, chained up in a cage, was the scrawniest big cat I'd ever seen. There was only enough space for it to turn around, and it just stood, looking incredibly pissed—as I would be, if I had to stare at my best pals pinned to the wall all day. I'd never felt so sorry for an animal in all my life.

Aaron shook his head. There was obviously some history to this. "Shit, they've still got her in there!" For the first time I was hearing anger in his voice. "I know for a fact that they sell turtle too, and it's protected. They can't do that. You're not even allowed to have a parrot in a cage, man, it's the law. . . . But the police? Shit, they just spend their whole time worrying about narcos."

He pointed a little ahead of us and up to the left. We were driving toward what reminded me of an army security base in Northern Ireland. High, corrugated-iron fencing protected whatever buildings were inside. Sandbags were piled on top of each other to make bunkers, and the barrel and high-profile sight of an American M-60 machine gun jutted from the one covering the large double gates. A big sign with a military motif declared this was the police station.

Four enormous trucks were parked up on the other side of the station with equally massive trailers filled with stripped tree trunks. Aaron's voice was now thick with anger. "Just look at that—first they cut down every tree they can get their hands on. Then, before they float the logs downstream for these guys to pick up, they saturate them in chemicals. It kills the aquatic life. There's no subsistence farming, no fishing, nothing, just cattle."

We left the depression of Chepo behind us and drove through rough grassland cratered with pools of rusty-colored water. My clothes were still damp in places, quite wet in others where my body heat wasn't doing a good enough job. My leg had started to feel okay until I stretched it out and broke the delicate scabbing. At least Aaron's getting sparked up about what was happening in Chepo had diverted his mind from Diego.

The road got progressively worse, until finally we turned off it and hit a rutted track that worked its way to some high ground about three or four miles away. No wonder the Mazda was in a shit state.

Aaron pointed ahead as the truck bucked and yawed and the suspension groaned. "We're just over that hill."

All I wanted to do was get to the house and clean myself up—though from the way Aaron had rattled on in his eco-warrior Billy Graham voice, I half expected them to live in a wigwam.

18

The Mazda rolled from side to side, the suspension creaking like an old brigantine as the engine revs rose and fell. To my surprise, Aaron was actually driving the thing with considerable skill. It seemed we had at least another hour and a half of this still to go—so much for "just over that hill."

We plowed on through the mist, finally cresting the steep, rugged hill. The scene confronting us was a total contrast to the rough grassland we'd been traveling through. A valley lay below us, with high, rolling hills left and right, and as far as the eye could see the landscape was strewn with felled, decaying wood. The trunks nearest us were almost gray with age. It was as if somebody had tipped an enormous box of matchsticks all over a desert of rust-colored mud. The low mist within the valley made it eerier still. Then, at the far end of the valley, where the ground flattened out, maybe five or six miles away, was lush green jungle. I couldn't work it out.

We started our descent and Aaron must have sensed my confusion. "They just got fed up with this side of the hills," he shouted above the truck's creaks and groans. "There wasn't enough hardwood to take, and it wasn't macho enough for the *hombres* to take these little things away. But hey, at least there are no farmers, they can't clear all this on their own. Besides, there's not enough water down here—not that they could drink it if there was."

We reached the valley floor, following the track through the downed trees. It looked as if a tornado had torn through the valley then left it for dead. The morning sun was trying its hardest to penetrate a thin layer of cloud. Somehow it seemed much worse than if the sun had been completely out; at least then it would have come from one direction. As it was, the sun's rays had hit the clouds and scattered. It was definitely time for the Jackie O look again. Aaron followed my lead and threw his shades on too.

We carried on through the tree graveyard until we were rescued by the lush canopy at the far end of the valley. "Won't be long now," Aaron declared. "Maybe forty-five, fifty minutes."

Twenty would have been better; I didn't think the truck could take much more, and neither could my head. I thought it was going to explode.

We were back in secondary jungle. The trees were engulfed in vines reaching up into the canopy. All sorts of stuff was growing between them and above the track. It felt like we were driving through a long gray tunnel. I took off my Jackie O's and everything became a dazzling green.

Baby-G told me it was 7:37, which meant we'd been on the road for over four hours. My eyes were stinging and my head still pounding, but there wouldn't be any time for relaxing just yet. I could do all that on Sunday maybe, or whenever it was that I finally got to the safety of Maryland. First, I needed to concentrate on how I was going to carry out the hit. I needed to grip myself and get on with the job. But try as I might to think about what I'd seen during the CTR, I just couldn't concentrate.

Aaron had been exactly right. Forty-five minutes later we emerged into a large clearing, most of it lying behind a building that was sideways and directly in front of us, maybe two hundred yards away. It looked like the house that Jack built.

The clouds had evaporated, to reveal sun and blue sky. "This is us." Aaron didn't sound too enthusiastic. He put his glasses back on, but there was no way I was wearing the Jackie O's again—not if I was about to see their owner.

To my left, and facing the front of the house, was a hill with a steep gradient covered with more fallen trees and rotten stumps, with tufty grass growing between them. The rest of the clearing was rough, but fairly flat.

We followed the track toward the large building, which was more or less on one level. The main section was a one-story, terracotta-roofed villa, with dirty green plastered walls. There was a covered porch out front, facing the high ground. Behind the main building, and attached to it, was a corrugated-iron extension maybe twice as big as the house itself and with a much higher roof.

On my right were row upon row of white plastic five-gallon tubs, hundreds of them, about two feet high and the same in diameter. Their lids were sealed, but sprays of different colored plants of all shapes and sizes shot from a circular hole cut out of the middle of each. It looked like Aaron and Carrie were running the area's first garden-center megastore.

Dotted around us were corrugated-iron outbuilding, with piles of wooden barrels and boxes, and the occasional rotting wooden wheelbarrow. To my right, past the tubs, was a generator under a corrugated-iron roof with no side walls, and at least ten forty-five-gallon oil drums.

As we got closer I could make out drainpipes leading from the gutters into green plastic water barrels that ran at intervals along the length of the building. Above the roof, supported on scaffolding, was a large blue plastic water tank; beneath it was an old metallic one, with all sorts of pipes coming out of it. A pair of satellite dishes were mounted nearby, one pointing west, one east. Maybe they liked to watch both Colombian and Panamanian TV. Despite the technology, this was definitely Planet Tree-Hug; all I needed to complete the picture was a couple of milking cows named Yin and Yang.

Now that we were nearer the house, I could see the other pickup truck, parked on the far side of the porch. Aaron hit the Mazda's horn a few times, and looked worried as Carrie emerged from the porch, putting on her wraparound sunglasses. She was dressed the same as when I'd met her, but had gelled her hair.

"Please, Nick—not a word."

The truck stopped and he jumped out as she stepped down from the porch. "Hi."

I got out, ready to greet, squinting to fight both the glare and my headache.

I took a few steps toward them, then stopped to give them some space. But there weren't any greetings, kisses, or touches, just a strained exchange.

Not thinking much, just feeling hot and bothered, I moved toward them.

I put on my nice-and-cheery-to-the-host voice. "Hello."

It wasn't gel that was holding back her hair; she'd just had a shower.

She noticed my hobble and ripped jeans. "What happened? You okay?"

I didn't look at Aaron. Eyes give so much away. "I walked into some sort of animal trap or something. I'm—"

"You'd better come and get cleaned up. I've got some porridge fixed."

"That sounds wonderful." It sounded like shit.

She turned to walk back to the house, but Aaron had other ideas. "You know what? I'm going to clean the truck out—there's been a fuel spillage in the back and, well, you know, I'd better clean it out."

Carrie turned. "Oh, okay."

I followed her toward the house as Aaron's sunglassed eyes gave me one last look and nod before going back to the truck.

We were just short of the porch when she stopped and turned once more. As Aaron moved the Mazda over toward the tubs, I could see my bitten, lumpy face and scary sticking-up hair reflecting back at me in her slightly mirrored glasses. The lenses were too opaque for me to see anything of her eyes.

"Luce, our daughter, thinks you're part of a U.K. study group, and you're here for a few days to see how we work. Okay?"

"Sure, that's not a problem." I was going to have to do my best to look like a tree-hugging academic. I wished I could see her eyes. I hated talking to mirrored glass.

"She knows nothing about why you're really here. Nor do we, when it comes to that. She's asleep, you'll see her soon."

She tapped her left lens and pointed at my swollen eye.

"Don't worry about that. It'll be fine in a few days."

19

I was so tired I could hardly keep my eyes open as we stepped across cracked, faded terracotta tiles, past two darkwood Victorian rocking chairs and an old rope hammock scattered with coffee- and dribble-stained pillows. The front door was open, and Carrie pulled open a screen door with a creak of hinges. To the left, and set above a screened window, was a wall light, its bowl full of dried insects, fatally attracted to its glow. I caught the screen before it sprang back, and followed her inside.

We were in near darkness after the blinding brilliance outside, and there was a strong smell of wood. It was like being in a garden shed. I stifled a yawn; my eyes were trying to close, but I had to fight them. This was virgin territory and I had to take note of every detail.

The room was large, with a high ceiling. Hefty tree trunks supporting the building were set into plastered walls, which had once been painted cream but were now scuffed and discolored. It was furnished like a vacation rental, basic stuff, a bit rough, and not a lot of it.

Carrie was heading straight to another door, painted a faded yellow, about ten yards dead ahead. I followed as she took off her glasses and let them fall around her neck. To our left were four armchairs built out of logs, covered with dirty cushions with flowery patterns that didn't match. The chairs were evenly arranged around a circular coffee table, which was made from a slice of dark wood more than three feet in diameter. Trained over the coffee table and chairs were two 1950s-style, freestanding electric fans with protective wire covers. The chrome had seen better days, and it was a shame there was no ribbon hanging from the wire to give them that authentic look.

The wall to the left had two more doors, also painted yellow and set into flaking brown frames. The farthest one was partly open and led into what I presumed was their bedroom. A large natural wood headboard held one end of a once-white mosquito net; the other was suspended from the ceiling. The bed was unmade and I saw purple sheets. Men's and women's clothes were thrown over a chair. The wooden butt of a rifle hung on the wall to the right of the bed. I thought I'd keep it a little closer, living out here.

Farther along, in the corner, was the kitchen area, with a small table and chairs. An array of different patterned mugs hung from hooks in the wall.

On my right, the whole wall, as far as the door we were heading for, was covered by bookshelves. The only break was another window, also covered with protective screening, which seemed to be the only other source of natural light.

I began to smell porridge. Steam rose from a large pot sitting on one of the kitchen units to the side of the stove. Next to it lay a big bunch of bananas and a bowl of oranges.

Carrie disappeared through the door, and I followed her into the larger, corrugated-iron extension. The walls were lined with plywood, and there was a rough concrete floor. Hanging down from the high ceiling on the end of steel rods were two old and very dirty old-fashioned ceiling fans, both stationary. The room was a lot hotter than the one we'd just left, but lighter, with large sheets of clear corrugated plastic high up in the walls serving as windows.

The extension might be cheap and low-tech, but what it housed wasn't. Running the length of the wall in front of me and continuing after a right angle down the left-hand side was one continuous desk unit, formed out of trestle tables. On it, and facing me, were two PCs with webcams attached to the top of the monitors; in front of each was a canvas director's chair, the green backrests well sagged with use. The screen of the PC on the right was displaying an image of the Miraflores lock. It must have been a webcam online, because the screen was just at the point of refreshing itself to show a cargo ship halfway out of one of the locks. Going by the bright reflection in the puddles on the grass, we weren't the only part of Panama with sun.

The PC to the left was closed down, and had a set of headphones with the mike attached hanging over the camera. Both machines were surrounded by paper and general office clutter, as was the area underneath, with wires running everywhere and packs of office supplies. The desk against the wall to the left, facing me, housed a third PC, also with a webcam with headphones hanging, and was surrounded by schoolbooks. This had to be Luce's Land.

Carrie turned immediately to the right through the only other door and I followed. We entered what looked like a quartermaster's store, a lot smaller than the other two areas and a lot hotter. It smelled like the local deli. Rows of gray angle-iron shelving lined the walls to the left and right of me, turning the middle into a hallway. Stacked on each side of us were all sorts of things, boxes of canned food, hurricane lamps, flashlights, packs of batteries. On pallets on the floor were bags of rice, porridge oats, and milk powder the size of coal sacks. Enough supplies, in fact, to keep *Survivor* going for a year. Laid out in the hallway was a U.S. Army cot and a blanket, a dark green U.S. Army lightweight still in its thin, clear plastic wrapping. "That's for you."

She nodded toward a corrugated-iron door facing us as she quickly closed the one to the computer room behind us, plunging this area into near darkness. "That'll take you outside. You'll be able to see better out there. I'll bring out the first-aid kit."

I walked past her, dropped my jacket on the cot, then turned back to see her climbing up the shelves. "Could I see the imagery, please?"

She didn't look down at me. "Sure."

I went outside. The sun was casting a shadow on this side of the building, which was good as my head was thumping big-time and being in the full glare wouldn't help at all. The crickets were still out doing their stuff; they're not great for headaches, either.

In front of me, two hundred yards away, lay the massed ranks of white tubs with their greenery sticking out of the top and the sunlight bouncing off puddles around them as the generator chugged rhythmically. Aaron was in the distance, where the tubs met the track, a hose in his hands, flushing out the back of the truck. A flock of large black and white birds lifted from the tree line beyond the tubs and whooshed overhead just above the rooftop.

I slumped down on the concrete foundation that protruded along the wall, my back against one of the green water barrels, and closed my eyes for a second, trying to relieve the pain. It wasn't happening so I opened the hole in my jeans to inspect the wound. The sweatshirt was still wet and muddy in the creases and knots, even after the cleanup in the drainage ditch. It had done the job of stopping the blood flow pretty well, though I couldn't be sure about infection. I'd had tetanus boosters, but probably only Aaron knew what kind of weird and wonderful microbes lurked in the Panama jungle.

I checked out the clotting between the material and flesh: the two had been trying their hardest to dry together and become one, and the swollen bruising around the wound felt kind of numb. I knew from experience that this sort of injury would be a major drama if you were stuck out in the jungle for any length of time, becoming a pus-filled mound within days, but at least here I could clean it up.

Carrie appeared from the storeroom with an old-fashioned, brown-checkered suitcase and a sheet of legal-size paper. She placed both on the concrete and lifted the suitcase lid to reveal what looked like quite a good basic medical pack. She came close in to look at the sweatshirt around my leg, and for the first time I caught a glimpse of her eyes. They were big, and very green. Her wet hair had fallen from behind her ears, and I was close enough to smell apple shampoo.

She didn't look up at me, just carried on digging around in the case. Her voice was clear, concise. "So, what is it you're here for?"

She started to pull stuff out; I wasn't too sure if she was going to dress the wound herself or just show me what was available. She didn't look up at me as she continued. "I was told nothing except that you'd be coming and we were to help."

By now there were rolls of bandages in crunchy cellophane, packages of pills, and half-used bottles of medicine on the concrete as she continued to rummage.

"There's something we need Charlie to do. I'm here to give him a reminder."

She didn't look up or otherwise acknowledge my answer. I looked at her hands as she bent over the suitcase and laid out different-colored tubes of cream. They were working hands, not those of a lady who lunched. There were a few little scars here and there, but her fingernails weren't ingrained with dirt like Aaron's. They were short and functional, no hint of polish, but all the same they looked cared for.

"Don't you know what you're here to remind him about? I mean, don't they tell you these things when you're sent out, or whatever the word is?"

I shrugged. "I thought maybe you might know."

"No, I know nothing." She sounded almost sad about it.

There was another pause. I certainly didn't know what else to say, so I pointed to the bits and pieces spread about on the concrete. "I need to clean myself up before I dress the wound. I'm afraid I don't have any other clothes."

She stood up slowly, looking over at the truck. "You can use some of Aaron's. The shower is out in back." She pointed behind her. "I'll get a towel."

Before reaching the door she half turned to me. "We have a two-minute rule here. First minute for soaking, then turn off the hose and soap yourself down. The second minute is to rinse. We get a lot of rain but seem to have trouble capturing it." She gripped the handle. "Oh, and in case you're tempted, don't drink from the shower. Only drink from the hoses marked with a D—that's the only treated water." There was a smile as she disappeared. "Otherwise it'll be giving you a pretty big reminder of why it needs to be treated."

I took a look at the printout of the satellite imagery. Its grainy reproduction covered the whole page and was zoomed right into the target, giving me a plan view of the house, the more or less rectangular tree line, and the broccoli patch surrounding it. I tried to get to work, but I couldn't do it—even knowing how important this was to me, I just couldn't get my head to work.

Instead, my eye caught one of the dark brown bottles of pills. The label said dihydrocodeine, an excellent painkiller, especially when taken with aspirin, which boosts its effect. I shook one out and dry swallowed as I rummaged in the case for an aspirin. Eventually, pushing one out of its package, I got that down as well.

I placed one of the cloth bandages on top of the paper to hold it down, got up, and started limping around to the back in the direction of the shower. Maybe it was the light, or just that I was beat, but I was feeling very woozy.

Hobbling past the storeroom entrance, I looked in and saw that the computer-room door was still closed. I stopped and looked at the cot. It was old-style, canvas rather than nylon, on a collapsible alloy frame. I had good memories of these things: they were easy to put up, comfortable, and kept you about two feet off the ground—not like the Brit ones, where you needed a physics degree to assemble them, and ended up only about six inches off the ground. If you got a saggy one, you could spend your night lying on cold concrete or with your ass in the mud.

Some bird or other warbled and chirped in the distance, and the humid air was heavy with pungent aromas. I sat down on the cot, dragged Diego's wallet from my jeans, and looked at the picture once more. Another nightmare for later, I supposed. It'd just have to join the lineup.

Aaron had finished and was driving back to the house. I got up and closed out the daylight, then stumbled back to the cot, still in my damp clothes, and lay down on my back, my heart pumping faster as my head filled with Kelly, bodies, Diego, more bodies, the Yes Man, even Josh. And hell, why had I told Carrie I was here to give Charlie a reminder? Why had I told her anything about the job at all?

Shit, shit, shit . . .

The pins and needles returned. I had no control as they moved up my legs and my skin tingled. I turned over and curled up, my arms holding my shins, not wanting to think anymore, not wanting to see anymore.

20

I walk into the bedroom, Buffy and Britney posters, bunk beds, and the smell of sleep. The top bunk is empty as I move toward them in the dark, kicking into shoes and teen-girl magazines. She is asleep, half in, half out of her comforter, stretched out on her back, stretched out like a starfish, her hair spread in a mess over the pillow. I put her dangling leg and arm gently back under the comforter.

Something is wrong . . . my hands are wet . . . she is limp . . . she isn't sucking her bottom lip, she isn't dreaming of being a pop star. The lights go on and I see the blood dripping from my hands onto her mutilated face. Her mouth is wide open, her eyes staring at the ceiling.

Sundance is lying on the top bunk, the blood-stained baseball bat in his hands, his eyes black and nose broken, looking down at me, smiling. "I wouldn't mind a trip to Maryland . . . we could go to Washington and do the sights first . . . I wouldn't mind a trip to Maryland . . . we could go to Washington and do the sights first. . . ."

I cry, fall to my knees, pins and needles.
I pull her from the bed, trying to take her with me.

"It's okay, Nick, it's okay. It's just a dream. . . ."

I opened my eyes. I was kneeling on the concrete, pulling Carrie toward me.

"It's okay," she said again. "Relax, you're in my house, relax."

I focused on what was happening, and quickly released my grip, jumping back onto the cot.

She stayed down on the floor. The half-light from the living room illuminated a concerned face.

"Here, have some."

I took the half-empty bottle of water from her and started to unscrew the top, feeling embarrassed, my legs stinging with pins and needles.

I cleared my throat. "Thanks, thank you."

"Maybe you have a fever—picked up something in the forest yesterday. See what it's like in the morning and we'll take you to the clinic in Chepo."

I nodded as I drank, pushing back my soaked hair before stopping to take a breath.

"There's some medication in the kit if you need it."

"No, that's fine, thanks. How long have you been here?"

"You just woke us, we were worried." She reached out and put the back of her hand to my forehead. "These fevers out here can make you maniacal."

"I was having a nightmare. I can't even remember what it was about."

She started to get up as I pulled the wet sweatshirt away from my skin. "It happens. You okay now?"

I shook my head to try to clear it. "I'm fine, thanks."

"I'll see you in the morning, then. Good night."

"Yeah, um . . . thanks for the drink."

She walked back into the dark computer room, closing the door behind her. "You're welcome."

I checked my watch. 12:46 A.M. I had been out for over fourteen hours. Getting slowly to my feet, I squatted up and down, trying to get my legs back to normal while I had some more water. Then I ripped the plastic from the blanket, lay down, and covered myself, blaming the drug cocktail for my doziness. Dihydrocodeine does that to you.

I tossed and turned, eventually rolling up my jacket as a replacement pillow, but it didn't work. My body was telling me I still needed sleep, but I really didn't want to close my eyes again.

Half an hour later I checked Baby-G and it was 3:18 A.M. So much for not closing my eyes. I lay there, rubbing my legs. The pain had gone, and I didn't feel as groggy as before. I felt around below the cot for the water bottle. Blinking my eyes open, I drank to the noise of the crickets.

I didn't want to lie and think too much, so decided to have a walkabout to keep my head busy. Besides, I was nosy.

Pushing myself upright, I sat on the edge of the cot for a while, rubbing my face back to life before standing up and reaching for the light switch. I couldn't find it, so felt for the door handle instead and bumbled into the computer room, water in hand. The switch in here was easy to find. As the fluorescent lighting flickered I saw that the living-room door was closed. I checked the darkness on the other side.

The plywood behind the two blank screens nearest to me was covered with pinned-up printouts in Spanish, and handwritten messages on university letterhead, alongside Post-Its with everyday stuff like "need more glue." This was how modern tree-hugging must be: out shoveling shit all day, then back to the PC to work out leaf tonnages or whatever.

To the left of that was a cork board with a montage of photographs. All of them seemed to be of the extension being built, and of the clearing behind. A few showed Aaron up a ladder hammering nails into sheets of corrugated tin, some of him with what looked like a local, standing next to craters in the ground with half blown-up trees around them.

Taking a swig of the water I walked over to what I assumed was Luce's PC. The school textbooks were American, with titles like *Math Is Cool*, and there was a Tower of Pisa of music CDs ready to play in the drive. The plywood behind was covered with world maps, best-effort drawings, and pictures of Ricky Martin torn from magazines, along with a Latin band with permed hair and frilly shirts. I looked down at the desk and noticed her name scribbled on exercise books as kids do when they are bored—mine were always covered. Her name was spelled *Luz*. I remembered from my Colombia days that their *Z* is pronounced as *S*. So her name was the Spanish for "light"—it wasn't short for Lucy at all.

I could feel the layer of greasy sweat over me as I headed for the living room, checking their bedroom once more before hitting the brass light switch on the other side of the door.

The room was lit by three bare bulbs, hanging on thin white cord that was taped to the supports. The stove was a chipped white enamel thing with an eye-level broiler and gas-ring burners. There was an old-style steel coffee percolator on the stove, and various family-hug photos fixed to the fridge with magnets. Near it was a white Formica dining-room set, with four chairs, that could have come straight out of a

1960s household and looked out of place in a world of dark hardwoods.

I pulled a couple of bananas from a bunch lying next to the oranges, and looked idly at the photographs while my back reminded me I'd been bitten big-time. The pictures were of the family having fun about the house, and some of an older guy in a white polo shirt, holding hands with Luz on the porch.

I peeled the skin off the second banana as my eye fell on a faded black-and-white picture of five men. One of them was most certainly the older guy with Luz. All five were in swim trunks on the beach, holding up babies in saggy diapers and sunhats for the camera. The man on the far left had a badly scarred stomach.

I leaned forward to get a closer look. His hair had been darker then, but there was no doubt about it. The long features and wiry body belonged to Pizza Man.

Taking another couple of bananas off the bunch, I wandered over to the coffee table and sat down, resisting the temptation to give my back a good hard scratch, and trying not to make a noise.

I put down the water and munched away. The slab of dark wood looked a good six inches thick, and though the top was polished, the bark around the edge had been left untouched. Strewn across it were tired-looking copies of *Time* magazine and the *Miami Herald* among glossy Spanish titles I didn't recognize, and a teen mag with some boy band posing on the cover.

I sat, finishing off the bananas, while I ran my eye along the shelves. There was a selection of hardbacks, paperbacks, large coffee-table books, and carefully folded maps. The well-worn spines covered everything from natural history to Mark Twain, quite a lot of American political history, and even a Harry Potter. But most seemed to be stern-looking textbooks on rain forests, global warming, and flora and fauna. I looked closer. Two were by Aaron.

One of the shelves was given over to four hurricane lamps with already blackened wicks, and as many boxes of matches, lined up like soldiers on standby for the next power outage. Below that, two silver candlesticks and a silver goblet sat alongside a selection of leatherbound books with Hebrew script on the spine.

Finishing off the water, I got up and dumped the banana skins into the plastic garbage bag under the sink and headed for the cot. I'd had a long rest but I still felt like more.

I opened my eyes to the sound of the generator and a vehicle engine. I stumbled over the medical case as I made my way to the outside door.

Blinding sunlight hit me, and I was just in time to see the Mazda heading into the tree line. As I held up my hand to shield my eyes, I saw Carrie at the front of the house. She turned to me, and I couldn't tell from her expression if she was smiling, embarrassed, or what.

"Morning."

I nodded a reply as I watched the truck disappear.

"Aaron's gone to Chepo. There's a jaguar that's been caged up for months. I'll get you those clothes and a towel. You okay?"

"Yes, thanks. I don't think I need to go to the clinic. The fever's gone, I think."

"I'm fixing breakfast. You want some?"

"Thanks, I'll have a shower first if that's okay."

She moved back toward the porch. "Sure."

The hard flooring at the rear of the extension was

covered by an open-walled lean-to roof. It was obviously the washing area. In front of me was the shower, three sides formed out of corrugated tin, and an old plastic curtain across the front. A black rubber hose snaked down from a hole in the roof. Beyond it was an old stainless-steel double sink unit supported by angle-iron, fed by two other hoses, with the wastepipes disappearing into the ground. Farther back was the toilet cubicle.

Above the sinks were three toothbrushes, each in a glass, with toothpaste and hairbrushes alongside a huge box of soap powder. An empty rope clothesline was also suspended under the corrugated-iron awning, with wooden clothespins clamped all along it, ready and waiting. A few of the white tubs were stacked up in the corner, one of them full of soaking clothes.

The ground to the rear of the house sloped gently away so that I could just see the treetops maybe three hundred yards in the distance. Birds flew over the trees and a few puffy white clouds were scattered across the bright blue sky.

I pulled back the plastic shower curtain, took off all my stuff and dropped it on the hard flooring, but left the sweatshirt bandage in place around my leg. I stepped into the cubicle, a rough concrete platform with a drainage hole in the middle, and a shelf holding a bottle of shampoo, a half-worn bar of soap streaked with hairs, and a blue disposable razor—not Aaron's, that was for sure. Soapsuds were still dripping down the tin walls.

I twisted myself to inspect the rash on my lower back, which was now incredibly sore. It was livid and lumpy, and about the size of my outspread hand. I'd probably been visited by a family of chiggers while lying in the leaf litter. The tiny mites would have burrowed into my skin as I lay there watching the house, and there wasn't a thing I could do about it except play host for the next few days until they got bored with me and died. I scratched gently around the edge of the rash, knowing I shouldn't but I couldn't stop myself.

The bruising on the left side of my chest had come on nicely since Sunday afternoon, and my ribs burned even when I reached out to undo the hose sprinkler.

I soaked the sweatshirt material with lukewarm water to try to soften up the clotting, then, holding the hose over my head, I counted off my sixty seconds.

Closing off the flow, I lathered myself down with the flowery-smelling soap and rubbed shampoo into my hair. When the water had had enough time to do its stuff with the bandage, I bent down and untied the sweatshirt, trying to peel it away gently.

My vision blurred. I was feeling dizzy again. What the hell was happening to me? I sat down on the rough concrete and rested my back against the cool metal. I'd been making excuses by telling myself that all this shit was because I was beat. But I had been beat all my life. No, this was going on in my head. I'd been so busy feeling sorry for myself, I hadn't even given serious thought to how I was going to get the job done yet, and had lost a whole day of preparation. I could have been on the ground by now.

I gave myself a good talking to: *Get a grip . . . The mission, the mission, nothing matters except the mission, I must get mission-oriented, nothing else matters.*

21

The flesh refused point-blank to unstick itself from the material. They'd been buddies for too many hours now and just didn't want to be parted. I ripped it away like a sticking Band-Aid, and immediately wished that I hadn't: the pain was outrageous, and that was before the soapy lather started running into the raw, red, messy wound.

"Fuck, fuck, fuck!" I couldn't help myself.

As I gritted my teeth and rubbed soap into the gash to clear out the crap, there was a noise from the sink area. I poked my newly switched-on head out to say thanks to Carrie for the clothes and towel, but it wasn't her, it was Luz—at least, I presumed it was. She was dressed in a blue, rather worn-looking long T-shirt style nightgown, and had the wildest black curly hair I'd ever seen, like Scary Spice plugged into the circuits. Near her on the drainer was a pile of khaki-colored clothes and a blue striped towel. She stood there, staring at me with big dark eyes above high, pronounced Latin cheekbones and not a teenage zit in sight. She was going to be a very beautiful woman one day, but not just yet. Sticking out of her nightgown was a pair of lanky legs, skinny as shaved pencils, the shins covered with tomboy bruises.

She looked at me, not scared or embarrassed, just interested at the sight of a soapy version of Darth Maul sticking out from behind the shower curtain.

"*Hola.*"

That sort of Spanish I understood. "Oh, *hola.* You're Luz?"

She nodded, trying to figure me out, or maybe she just found the accent strange. "My mom told me to bring you these." She spoke American, tinged with a hint of Spanish.

"Thank you very much. I'm Nick—nice to meet you, Luz."

She nodded—"See you"—and left, going the long way around so as not to pass the shower.

I got back to business. The wound was about four inches long and maybe an inch deep, but at least it was a clean cut.

The soap and shampoo were starting to cake on me now as I stood and came to grips with the mission, and myself. Letting loose with the hose, I rinsed off for my allotted sixty seconds, having a piss at the same time, and the smell was bad. My urine was a horrible dark yellow, which meant I was very dehydrated. I supposed that might account for the dizziness.

I toweled myself dry in the open air, then got dressed in Aaron's clothes, khaki cotton pants with two map pockets on either side, and a very old, long-sleeved, faded gray T-shirt, telling the world, "Just do it." The pants were a few inches too big around the waist, but a couple of turns of the waistband tightened them up. The pants pockets had good Velcro seals, so I put my wallet, passport, and plane ticket, still in their plastic bags, in the righthand one.

After slicking back my hair I attacked the drinkable D hose, sucking at the bitter-tasting water, then stopped for a while to catch my breath as I felt my stomach swell with the much-needed warm fluid.

The next thing I did was take my Leatherman out of its case to wash off Diego's blood, then put it into my pocket. After another big water-sucking session, I hung the wet towel on the line like a good boy. With my old clothes rolled in a ball in my left hand and my Timberlands in the right, I walked back around to the storeroom, picked up the medical kit and satellite picture, then, after crawling about under the cot, Diego's wallet, and sat outside on the foundations again.

Looking at the satellite image I could clearly see the road from Charlie's house down to the gate, trucks parked, diesel fumes belching from a bulldozer as it dragged a tree stump out of the ground, bodies lazing by the pool. This was good stuff, but told me nothing I didn't already know. I'd been hoping for maybe a covered approach route from the rear or something that would spark off an idea.

I found antibiotic powder in a little puff bottle and gave my wound a good dousing, then applied a gauze dressing and secured it with a cloth bandage, realizing, as I saw the dihydrocodeine bottle, that my headache had gone.

Carrie hadn't provided any socks or underpants, so I just had to let my boys hang free and put my own socks back on. They were the consistency of cardboard, but at least they were dry now. I pulled on my boots, rubbed antihistamine cream over the small of my back and the lumps on my face, then packed everything back into the case. I found two safety pins to secure the map pocket, and took the case back to the storeroom. I dumped all my old gear under the

cot and rummaged about for matches, then gouged a
hole in the earth with the heel of my Timberland, and
emptied the contents of Diego's wallet into it, less the
$38. I watched his picture ID and family photo curl
and turn black as I thought about what I was going to
do with Michael.

I didn't have that many options to consider. It was
going to have to be a shoot. Nothing else would work
with such little time, information, and equipment: at
three hundred–ish yards and with even a half-decent
weapon, I should be able to drop him. No fancy tip-
of-an-ear stuff, just going for the center mass of his
trunk. Once he was down and static I could get
another few rounds into him to make sure. If my only
chance at dropping him presented itself as he got into
a vehicle leaving for or returning from college, then I
was going to have to take the shot pretty sharpish.

Afterward, I'd stay in the jungle until Sunday, keeping out of the way before popping out and getting
myself to the airport. Even if I didn't find an opportunity until last light tomorrow, I could still be at Josh's
by Tuesday. As for the possibility of not seeing the target at all, I didn't want to go there.

After pushing mud over the little pile of ash, I
headed for the kitchen, keeping the antihistamine
with me. I threw the wallet onto the back of a shelf as
I passed through the storeroom.

The fans in the living area were turning noisily,
whipping up a bit of a breeze. Carrie was at the stove
with her back turned; Luz was sitting at the table, eating porridge and peeling an orange. She was dressed
like her mother now, in green cargo pants and T-shirt.

I put on my cheerful voice again and gave a general, "Hello, hello."

Carrie turned and smiled. "Oh, hello." She didn't
look at all embarrassed about last night as she

pointed at me with a porridge-covered spoon, but said to Luz, "This is Nick."

Luz's voice was confident and polite: "Hi, Nick."

"Thanks again for bringing me the clothes," was answered with a routine, "You're welcome."

Carrie ladled porridge into a white bowl and I hoped it was for me. "Sit down. Coffee?"

I did as I was told. "Please." By the time I'd pulled up my chair, the porridge and a spoon were on the table in front of me. A bunch of four bananas was next, and she tapped the top of a green jug in the center of the table. "Milk. Powdered, but you get used to it."

Carrie turned her back to me and made coffee. Luz and I sat facing each other, eating.

"Luz, why don't you tell Nick how we do things? After all, that's what he's here to find out. Tell him about the new power system."

Her face lit up with a smile that revealed a row of crooked white teeth in braces. "We have a generator, of course," she said earnestly, looking me in the one and a half eyes she could see. "It gives power to the house, and also charges two new banks of batteries linked together in parallel. That's for emergencies and to keep the generator noise down at night." She giggled. "Mom goes totally postal if the generator is left on late."

I laughed, though not as much as Luz as she tried to drink some milk. Carrie joined us with two steaming mugs of coffee. "It's not that funny."

"Then why has milk come through my nose?"

"Luz! We have a guest!" As she poured milk into her mug and passed the jug over to me, her eyes were fixed on Luz with a look of such love and indulgence that it made me feel uncomfortable.

I nodded at the stove. "So you have gas as well?"

"For sure." Luz carried on with her lecture. "It's bottled. It comes by helicopter with the other stuff, every fifth Thursday." She looked at her mother for confirmation. Carrie nodded. "The university hires a helicopter for deliveries to the six research stations in-country."

I looked as interested as I could, given that what I really wanted to discuss was how to get my hands on the rifle I'd seen on the wall, and to see if it was any good for what I had in mind. I peeled a banana, wishing that I'd had a resupply every fifth week during my stays in the jungle over the years.

Luz was just finishing her food as Carrie checked the clock by the sink. "You know what? Just leave your plate on the side and go and log on. You don't want to keep Grandpa waiting." Luz nodded with delight, got up with her plate, and put it down next to the sink before disappearing into the computer room.

Carrie took another sip of coffee, then called out, "Tell Grandpa I'll say hello in a minute."

A voice drifted back from inside the computer room. "Sure."

Carrie pointed at the hug pictures on the fridge door and one in particular, the guy in a polo shirt with gray-sided black hair, holding hands with Luz on the porch. "My father, George—he teaches her math."

"Who are the ones holding the babies?"

She turned back and looked at the fading picture. "Oh, that's also my father, he's holding me—we're on the far right. It's my favorite."

"Who are the ones with you?"

Luz stuck her head around the corner, looking and sounding worried. "Mom, the locks picture has closed down."

"That's okay, darling, I know."

"But, Mom, you said it must always be—"

Carrie was sharp with her. "I know, baby, I've just changed my mind, okay?"

"Oh, okay." Luz retreated, looking confused.

"We home-school everything else here. This keeps her in contact with her grandfather, they're real close."

I shrugged. "Sounds good," I said, really not that fussed that she hadn't answered my question. There were more important things on my mind. It was time to cut to the last page. "Is that rifle in the bedroom in working order?"

"You don't miss much, do you, fever man? Of course . . . why?"

"For protection. We can call your handler for one, it's not a problem. It's just that I haven't got much time and I want to get going as soon as I can."

She rested her arms on the table. "Do you people never feel secure without a weapon?"

Those intense green eyes burned into me, demanding an answer. Problem was, I reckoned her question was more complicated than it seemed.

"It's always better to be safe than sorry—that's why you have it, isn't it? Besides, Charlie's no Mr. Nice."

She stood up and walked toward her bedroom. "For sure, like death—but if he catches you doing whatever it is you're going to do, you'll need more than an old rifle."

She disappeared behind the door. From this side of the room I could see the foot of the bed and the opposite wall. It was covered with photographs, both old and new, smiling adults and children doing more family love-fest stuff. I could hear working parts moving back and forth, and the chink of brass rounds as they fell onto each other. I supposed you'd have it loaded and ready to go, otherwise why have it on the bedroom wall?

She reappeared with a bolt-action rifle in one hand, and a metal box with webbing handles in the other. It didn't have a lid, and I could see cardboard boxes of ammunition.

My eyes were drawn to the weapon. It was a very old-style piece of equipment indeed, with the furniture (the wood that shapes the weapon) stretching from the butt all the way along the quite lengthy barrel to just short of the muzzle.

She put it down on the table. "It's a Mosin Nagant. My father took it from the body of a North Vietnamese sniper during the war."

I knew about this weapon: it was a classic.

Before passing it across, she turned it to present the opened bolt and show me that the chamber and magazine were clear. I was impressed, which must have been plain to see. "My father—what's the use of having one if you don't know how to use it?"

I checked chamber—clear—and took the weapon from her. "What service was he in?"

She sat down and picked up her coffee cup. "Army. He made general before retiring." She nodded over at the fridge pictures. "The beach? Those are his Army buddies."

"What did he do?"

"Technical stuff, intelligence. At least there's one good thing that can be said about George—he's got smarts. He's at the Defense Intelligence Agency now." She allowed herself a smile of pride as she gazed at the picture. "There's a senior White House adviser and two other generals, one still serving, in that photograph."

"That's some bad-looking scar on the end. Is he one of the generals?"

"No, he left the service in the eighties, just before the Iran-Contra hearings. They were all involved in one way or another, though Ollie North took all the heat. I never did know what happened to him."

If he was part of the Iran-Contra affair, George would know all about jobs like this one. Black-ops jobs that no one wanted to know about, and people like him wouldn't tell anyway.

The connection between these two, George and the Pizza Man, was starting to make me feel uncomfortable. But I was a small player and didn't want to get myself involved with whatever was going on down here. I just had to be careful not to bump into it, that was all. I needed to get to Maryland next week.

Luz called from the other room, "Mom, Grandpa needs to talk with you."

Carrie got up with a polite, "Won't be long," and disappeared into the next room.

I took the opportunity to have a double-take at the tall, square-jawed, muscular George smiling with Luz on the porch. It was easy to see where she got her big green eyes from. I checked out the digital display on the bottom right of the picture. It was taken in 4-99, only eighteen months ago. He still looked like the all-American boy with his short hair and side part, and, what was weird, he looked younger than Aaron. The Pizza Man, on the other hand, looked like death warmed over compared with his black-and-white former life. He was skinnier, grayer, and probably had lungs like an oil slick, going by the way I'd seen him take down that nicotine.

22

I got back to the real world and examined the weapon, which looked basic and unsophisticated compared with the sort of thing around nowadays. Not that the basics had changed for centuries: trigger, on and off switch, sights, and barrel. I wasn't a weapons buff, but I was familiar enough with the Russian weapon's history to know that, regardless of how it looked, these things had sent thousands of Germans to their graves on the eastern front in the forties. The arsenal marks stamped into the steel of the chamber showed it had been made in 1938. Maybe this was one of them. It probably had quite a history, including zapping American targets in Vietnam.

The one I had in my hands had been beautifully maintained. The wooden furniture was varnished, and the bolt action had been lightly oiled and was rust-free. I got it into the aim and looked through the quite unconventional optic sight, unsure if it was the original. It was a straight black and worn tube about eight inches long and about an inch in diameter mounted on top of the weapon.

It had to be a fixed power sight as there was no

zoom ring to adjust the magnification, just two dials halfway along the sight—the top one to adjust for elevation (up and down), and the one on the right-hand side for windage (left and right). The dials had no graduation marks anymore—the top discs were missing—just some scratch marks where it had been zeroed.

Looking into the sight and aiming at a fuzzy book spine at this short distance, I could see I had a post sight to aim with. A thick black bar came up from the bottom of the sight and finished in a point in the center of the sight picture. Just below the point was a horizontal line that crossed the whole width of the sight.

I'd never liked post sights: the post itself blocked out the target below the point of aim, and the farther away the target was, the smaller it became and the more the post blocked it out. But beggars can't be choosers, and as long as it went bang when I pulled the trigger, I'd be halfway happy. There were also conventional iron sights on the weapon—a rear sight that was set just forward of the bolt, about where my left hand would go on the stock. The sight could be set between 400 and 1200 meters. It was set at the all-around "battle sight" setting of 400. The foresight was protected by a cylindrical guard on the muzzle.

I placed the weapon on the table and went and helped myself to more coffee from the stove. Thinking about this rifle's possible history reminded me that, years earlier, in the early eighties, when I was an infantry squaddie in BAOR (British Army of the Rhine), I'd owned a Second World War bayonet that an old German had given me. He told me he'd killed over thirty Russians with it on the eastern front, and I wondered whether he was bullshitting me, since most Germans of that generation said they fought the Russians during the war, not the Allies. I'd put it away in a cabinet at the house in Norfolk and forgotten about it; then, along with everything else, it had been sold to pay for Kelly's treatment. A skinhead with a stall in Camden Market gave me twenty quid for it.

I'd nearly finished pouring when Carrie returned. "Do you know how to adjust the sights?"

"No." It would save me a lot of time if I didn't have to experiment.

"It's got a PBZ at three hundred and fifty yards," she said, walking to the table. "Do you know what that is?" I nodded as she picked up the weapon and turned the dials. Point blank zero. "Stupid, I'm sure you do."

I could hear the clicks even above the noise of the fans before she handed it to me. "There, the notches are in line." She showed me the score marks leveled off against the sight on both dials to indicate the correct position for the sight to be zeroed.

I put down my coffee, took it from her, and checked out the dull score marks. "Anywhere I can go to check zero?"

She waved her arms. "Take your pick. There's nothing but space out there."

I picked up the ammunition box. "Can I have some of your printer paper and a marker?"

She knew exactly what I needed it for. "Tell you what," she said, "I'll even throw in some tacks for free. See you outside."

She went into the computer room and I went out through the squeaking screen door and onto the porch. The sky was still brilliant blue. The crickets were going at it like there was no tomorrow, and a monkey or something was making a happy noise somewhere in the canopy. But I wasn't fooled. No matter: after a shower and some cream on my back, the love affair with the jungle was back on.

Even in the shade of the porch, it was already much hotter out here. I was glad I was beginning to feel better, because it was an oppressive heat.

My dizziness had all but disappeared, and it was time to stop feeling sorry for myself and get a grip on what I was here to do. The screen door squeaked open and chopped off my train of thought as Carrie came out carrying a crunched-up paper bag. She handed it over. "I've told Luz you might go hunting later, so you want to try out the rifle."

"I'll be over there." I indicated the tree line about two hundred yards away, to the right of the house. It was on the opposite side to the track, so if Aaron came back early from rescuing jaguars he wouldn't get a 7.62 in his ear. "See you in a bit."

As soon as I left the shelter of the porch, the sun's fierce glare blinded me. I screwed up my eyes and looked down. Most of the moisture had evaporated off the grass, but the heavy humidity meant the puddles were still intact apart from a muddy crust around the edges.

I could feel my shoulders and the back of my neck burning as I kept my eyes on the rough, thick-bladed grass. I knew that once I got to the tree line things would improve. It would be just as hot and sticky, but at least this *rabiblanco* wouldn't be getting blow-torched.

I had a quick check of Baby-G. Unbelievably, it was only 10:56. The sun could only get hotter.

Carrie called out from behind me, still on the porch. "Look after it." She pointed to the weapon. "It's very precious to me." I had to squint to see her, but I was sure there was a smile.

"By the way, only load up four rounds. You can place five in the magazine okay, but can't close the bolt without stripping off the second round—got it?"

I lifted the weapon as I walked. I'd keep the PBZ (point blank zero), if it still existed. Why mess with something that might already be right? I might mess it up by trying to improve it.

I let my hand drop with the weapon and carried on toward the tree line, thinking of how the three snipers in London would have reacted to the idea of using a PBZ to drop a target, on top of ammunition that could have been made by the local blacksmith. To ensure consistency, they'd have pulled apart every one of the rounds I supplied them with to check there was exactly the same amount of propellant in each cartridge case.

PBZ is just a way of averaging out the averages to ensure the round at least hits the target somewhere in the vital area. Hunters use it; for them, the vital area is about seven inches centered on the animal's heart. The way it works is quite simple. As a round leaves the barrel, it rises, then begins to fall because of gravity. The trajectory is relatively flat with a large 7.62mm round like these: over a range of 350 meters the round won't rise or fall more than seven inches. As long as the hunter isn't farther away than 350 meters, he just aims at the center of the killing area, and the round should drop the bear or whatever else is charging toward him. My shoot should be from a maximum of 300 meters, so if I aimed at the center of the target's sternum, he should take a round somewhere in the chest cavity—what is known in the sniper world as a target-rich environment: heart, kidneys, arteries, anything that will make him suffer immediate and catastrophic loss of blood. It was not as sophisticated as the London snipers' catastrophic brain shot, because the weapon and rounds weren't exactly state-of-the-art, and I hadn't had enough practice.

A heart shot would probably make the target unconscious, and kill him in ten or fifteen seconds. The same went for the liver, because the tissue is so soft; even a near miss can sometimes have the same effect. As the round travels through the body, crushing, compressing, and tearing away the flesh, a shock wave comes with it, causing a massive temporary inflation of neighboring tissues that messes them up big-time.

A hit to the lungs would incapacitate, but it might not kill him, especially if he was treated quickly enough. The ideal would be for the round to hit the target's spine high up, above his shoulder blades, as it exited, or entered if I took him from the back. This would have very much the effect the three snipers had been trying to achieve: instant death, dropping him like liquid.

This was all very fine in theory, but there was a host of other factors to contend with. I might be trying to hit a moving target, there might be a wind. I might only have one part of a body to aim at, or only one weird angle to take the shot from.

Trying not to think about the boy smiling out of the Lexus, I wandered the two hundred or so yards to the tree line, put down the ammunition box, and stood for a while in the shade, looking toward the hill, the target area. Then I set off toward the rising ground.

I found a suitable tree and pinned a sheet of paper to the bottom third of the trunk with one of the tacks. With a marker I drew a circle about the size of a two-pound coin and inked it in. It was a bit of a lumpy circle with uneven edges because I was pushing it against the bark, but it would do.

I then pinned a sheet above and another below the first, then, making the best of the shade, turned and walked back with the weapon and rounds, counting out a hundred one-yard paces. At that range, even if the sight was wildly inaccurate, with luck I would cut paper to see how bad it was. If the zero was off by, say, two inches at a hundred yards, then at two hundred yards it would be four inches, and so on. So if I lay down initially at three hundred, I could be six inches off, either up, down, left, or right, possibly missing the paper altogether. Trying to see my strike as I fired would waste time, of which I didn't have much.

A hundred paces later and still in the shade of the tree line, I checked for beasties, sat against a tree, and slowly closed the bolt action. It was extremely well made: the action was soft, almost buttery, as the oil-bearing surfaces moved over each other without resistance. I pushed the bolt handle down toward the furniture, and there was a gentle click as it fell into its locked position.

Before I fired this weapon I needed to find out what the trigger pressures were. Correct trigger control will release the firing pin without moving the weapon. All trigger pressures are different, and nearly all sniper weapons can be adjusted for the individual firer. I wasn't going to do that because I didn't know how to on a Mosin Nagant, and I wasn't that particular anyway—I usually adjusted myself to whatever the pressures were.

I placed the center of the top pad of my right index finger gently against the trigger. There was just a few millimeters of give as I squeezed backward until I felt resistance. This was the first pressure. The resistance was the second pressure; I gently squeezed again, and instantly heard the click as the firing pin pushed itself out of the head of the bolt. That was fine for me: some snipers prefer no first pressure at all, but I quite liked having that looseness before firing.

Pulling the bolt back once more, I took one of the twenty-round boxes of large brass 7.62 rounds out of the ammunition box, and fed in four, one at a time, from the top of the breech, into what should have been a fixed five-round mag. Then I slid home the bolt once more, watching as it pushed the top round into the chamber. There was a slight resistance only as I pushed the cocking handle down toward the furniture and the bolt locked into place, securing the round so it could be fired. The on/off switch was at the back of the cocking piece, a flat circle of metal at the rear of the bolt about the size of a fifty-pence piece, and turning it to the left I applied Safe. It was a pain in the ass to do, but I supposed there wasn't much call for them when this thing was made—it was too busy killing Germans.

I looked for a small mound in the rough ground to double as a sandbag, and after a beastie check, lay down behind it in the prone position. The steel plate of the weapon butt was in the soft tissue of my right shoulder and my trigger finger ran over the trigger guard. My left forearm was resting against the mound and I let my hand find its natural position along the stock of the weapon, just forward of the rear sight. There were grooves cut into the furniture on each side to give a better grip.

Your bones are the foundation for holding a weapon; your muscles are the cushioning that holds it tightly in position. I had to make a tripod of my elbows and the left side of my ribcage. I had the added benefit of resting my forearm against the mound. I needed to ensure that the position and hold were firm enough to support the weapon, and that I was also comfortable.

I looked through the sight, making sure there was no shadowing around the edges of the optic. There was no problem about closing my left eye: half the job had already been done for me yesterday. The biggest mistake made by novice firers using a post sight is that they think the point to aim at is where the horizontal line crosses the post. It's not, it's the top of the post, right where the point is. The horizontal line is so you can check there's no canting (weapon tilting).

I took aim at the center of the not-too-circular black circle, then closed my eyes and stopped breathing. I relaxed my muscles slightly as I emptied my lungs. Three seconds later, I opened my eyes, started to breathe normally, and looked through the sight once more. I found that my point of aim had shifted to the left-hand edge of the sheet of paper, so I swiveled my body around to the right, then did the same thing twice more until I was naturally aligned to the target. It was pointless trying to force my body into a position that it didn't want to be in: that would affect the round when I fired. I was now ready to take the first shot.

I took three deep breaths to oxygenate my body. If you're not oxygenated you can't see correctly; even if you're not firing a weapon, if you just stand and gaze at something in the far distance and stop breathing, you will see it go blurry very quickly.

The weapon sight moved up and down with my body as I sucked in air, and settled to a gentler movement as I started to breathe normally. It was only then that I took off the safety, by pulling back and turning it to the right. Acquiring a good sight picture once more, I aimed before taking up the first pressure. At the same time I stopped breathing, in order to steady the weapon.

One second, two seconds . . . I gently squeezed the second pressure.

I didn't even hear the crack, I was so busy maintaining concentration and nonreaction while the weapon jumped up and back into my shoulder. All the time I kept my right eye open and followed through the shot, watching as the point of aim came back to settle on the center of the target. That was good: it meant my body was correctly aligned. If not, the point of aim would have moved to where my body was naturally pointing.

The round needed to be followed through because although there might only be less than a second between my taking the second pressure, sending the firing pin forward and striking the round, and the bullet heading up the barrel as the gases forced it out toward the target, the slightest movement would mean the point of aim not being the same at the instant the bullet exited the muzzle as when I fired. Not good news if you're trying to kill somebody with a single round.

That was the end of the firing sequence. I became aware of the different colors and sizes of the flocks of birds lifting from the trees. The canopy rustled as they screamed and flapped their wings to make their getaway.

In real time there are many occasions when these drills can't be used. But as long as you understand them, and have used them to zero the weapon, there's a good chance you can take on an opportunity target and drop it.

I looked through the sight to check where my round had fallen. I'd hit the top of the main sheet of paper: about five inches high. That was okay, it should be high at this close range: the optic was set at 350. The main thing was that it wasn't higher than seven inches.

The problem was that, although the round was at more or less the correct height for the range, it had gone to the left of the center line by maybe as much as three inches. At 300 yards that would become nine inches. I would have missed the chest, and maybe hit an arm if he was static and I was lucky. That wasn't good enough.

I lay back and watched the birds coming back to their nests. I waited maybe three minutes before reloading because I needed this to be a cold barrel zero: when I took the next shot, the barrel had to be as cold as the last. Variations in the barrel's temperature will warp the metal. Taking into account the inconsistency in the ammunition, it would be stupid to zero with a hot, or even warm barrel, since it would be cold when I took the shot.

That got the little sniper in my head ticking away. It reminded me that damp, humid air is thicker than dry, causing the bullet to drop faster. Hot air has the reverse effect because it is thinner, so offers less resistance and sends the bullet higher. What was I supposed to do on a very hot day in a very humid jungle? Forget it, I'd leave it alone, I'd only just gotten rid of my headache, I didn't want it back. Five inches should be okay. I'd be confirming back at 300 anyway.

I took another shot and followed through, my point of aim staying on the circle. My round still cut paper to the left, less than a quarter of an inch in from the first. The shots were well grouped, so I knew that the first round wasn't just a wild crazy one; the sight did need adjusting.

The birds were very pissed-off at being disturbed a second time, and I sat up and watched them as I waited for the barrel to cool. It was then that I saw Carrie making her way toward me from the rear of the house.

23

She was about 150 yards away, swinging a two-liter bottle of water in her right hand. I waved. As she looked at me and waved back, I got a flare of sunlight from her sunglasses. I sat back against the tree and watched her get nearer. She looked as if she were floating above the heat haze.

When she got closer I could see her hair flick back and forth with each stride. "How's the zero going?"

"Fine, just off a bit to the left."

She held out the bottle with a smile. The condensation glistened on the plastic: it had come straight out of the fridge. I nodded my thanks and stood up, catching my own reflection again in those fly's-eye glasses of hers.

I sat back down against the tree, unscrewing the top.

She looked down, fingering her hair behind her ears. "It's a real hot one today."

"Sure is." It was routine, the bullshit stuff that people exchange when they don't know each other, plus I was trying to keep her well away from any mention of last night. I got the bottle to my lips and took some long, hard swallows. The plastic started to collapse in my fingers; I wasn't letting any air past the tight seal of my lips.

She stayed above me, hands on hips, in the same position the Yes Man had taken a few days earlier, but without the attitude.

"The sight might've taken some knocks over the months. I use the iron sights, they're never off—anyone out here in the open is within their range."

I stopped drinking. There was a pop and a gurgle as air rushed into the vacuum and the plastic resumed its normal shape.

"Ever had to?"

Her glasses hid any clues her eyes might be giving away. "Once, a few years back. These things can happen out here, you know." She put out her hand for the water.

I watched as she threw her head back and took five or six gulps above me, her throat moving with each swallow. I could hear the fluid going down, and see the muscles in her right arm tauten as she tilted the bottle. Her skin had a light sheen of moisture; on me it would just have looked like sweat.

She wiped her mouth with the back of her hand. "Question. If it's just for protection, how come you're checking the scope?" She pointed into the jungle. "No good in there, is it?"

I gave her my most disarming smile. "As I said, I just like to be prepared, that's all."

"And is that according to your training, or according to you?" She hesitated. I wished I could see her eyes. "How do you get to do this sort of thing?"

I wasn't sure I could explain. "Want to help me?"

She caught my tone and went with it. "Sure."

We took the few paces over to the grassy mound.

"Is silence your way of dealing with it, Nick? I

mean, is silence the way you protect yourself from the things you need to do for your work?"

I saw my reflection as I tried to look through her lenses: she was smiling, almost taunting me. "All I want you to do is aim dead center into the black circle. I just want to adjust the sights."

"One shot zero, right?"

"Right."

"Okay, tell you what—you aim, you're stronger. I'll adjust."

I opened the bolt, ejecting the empty case, reloaded, and applied Safe as we reached the mound. "I want the same elevation."

She raised an eyebrow like she thought I was born yesterday. "Sure."

Instead of supporting it with my left hand, I started to push the stock into the mud. Her sandals were inches from my face. "Tell me when."

I looked up. Her sunglasses were now on the back of her neck with the arms facing forward and the black nylon retaining necklace dangling down onto her shirt. Her huge green eyes were blinking to adjust to the light.

I started to pack mud around the stock: the weapon needed to be locked tight into position for this to work. Once that was done, I checked that the score marks were still in line on the sight, and aimed at dead center of the black circle. "Okay."

There was an "Affirmative" from above as she pushed down on the mound with her sandaled foot, compacting the earth around the stock as I held it firmly in position. My arms strained as I tried to keep the weapon in a viselike grip to ensure the post sight stayed dead center. I could have done this on my own but it would have taken a whole lot longer.

She had finished packing the soil over the weapon

and I still had a good sight picture, so I told her this—
"On"—and moved my head to the left so she could
lean over and see the target through the sight. Our
heads touched as her right hand moved onto the
windage dial on the left side of the optic, and started
to turn it. I heard a series of metallic clicks as she
moved the post left until the point of aim was directly
below the two rounds that I had fired, while remaining in line with the center of the black circle.

It only took her fifteen seconds, but it was time
enough for me to smell the soap on her skin, and feel
the gentle movement of air as she controlled her
breathing.

My breath stank after not brushing since Saturday,
so I moved my lips to divert the smell away from us
both as she clicked away. She moved her head back
more quickly than I wanted her to and squatted on
her knees. "Okay, done." I could feel the warmth of
her leg against me.

I had to move my arm out of the way to drag my
Leatherman out of my pocket and passed it up to her,
glad that I'd cleaned it. "Score it for me, will you?"

She opened out the knife blade and leaned over to
scrape a line from the dial onto the metal housing of
the optic, so I'd be able to tell if the dial had been
inadvertently moved, knocking the zero off.

Her shirt was gaping in front of me as she worked
and I couldn't stop myself looking. She must have
seen me: I couldn't move the focus of my gaze quickly
enough as she returned to her kneeling position.

"Who sprinkled you with horny dust?" There was a
smile to go with her question, and she kept her big
green eyes on mine, but her expression couldn't have
given me a bigger no. "Are you going to confirm?"

Pulling the weapon from the mud, I cleared my
throat. "Yeah, I suppose I'll annoy the birds again."

She stood up to get out of the way. "Ooookay . . ."

I recocked and went through the firing sequence, aiming at the center of the circle and, sure enough, I pissed off the birds again big-time.

The zero was good; the round went in directly above the point of aim, roughly in line with the other two rounds to the left. At 300 the round should cut paper slightly above the circle, but I'd soon find out.

I was still looking through the sight when I felt Carrie's knees against my arm again. "Is it okay?" I kept my eye on my shot, still checking. "Yeah, it's fine. Dead on."

I ejected the round and moved my head away from the sight as she leaned over to pick up the empty cases.

We stood up together and she walked back into the shade as I cleaned the mud off the rifle's furniture.

"If that wasn't a window to your mind, I don't know what is."

Maybe I should have worn her Jackie O's.

"Your eyes aren't as silent as your mouth, are they?"

I heard the metallic clink of the empty cases as she threw them into the ammo box. She sat down under a tree, crossing her legs.

I worked hard to think of something to say as I walked over to her. "How did the house come to be here? I mean, it's a bit off the beaten track, isn't it?"

She picked up the bottle and took a swig as I settled down a few feet away. We faced each other and I took the water when she offered it to me. "A rich hippie guy built it in the sixties. He came down here to escape the draft." The fly's eyes looked at me, and the smile stayed on her face as she fished out a tobacco tin and Zippo from her cargo pants. "He swapped the forests of Vietnam for the forests of Panama. Apparently he was a real character, kept the dealers and bars in Chepo in business for over twenty years. He died maybe eight or nine years ago."

There was a pop as the tin opened, and she picked out one of the three or four already-prepared roll-up cigarettes. She giggled to herself, showing a set of brilliant white teeth as she checked the cigarette was still intact. The lenses turned on me again and my reflection moved up and down with her shoulders as she started to laugh. "Got killed by a logger's truck after a night hitting the bars. He staggered out into the road, trying to stop the truck from leaving, claiming that the wood belonged to the forest and it had spirit. Strangely enough, the truck seemed not to hear him, and that was that. Sawdust."

I laughed with her, seeing in my mind's eye the absurd contest of man versus truck. She flicked the Zippo deftly and lit up. The twisted end of the roll-up flared as she took a deep breath, held it, then slowly exhaled. An unmistakable smell filled the air between us. She chuckled to herself before finishing off the story. "He was the one who had spirit, but unfortunately for him that night it was all in his bloodstream."

I took in more water as she turned her gaze once more to the building, picking bits of wacky backy from her lips. "He'd left the house and the land to the university, for research. We've been here nearly six years now. Cleared the land out back for the helicopter. Even put up the extension ourselves."

She turned back and offered me the joint.

I shook my head. If other people wanted to, that was up to them, but it was something I'd never even thought of trying.

She shrugged and took another drag. "We can only do it out of the house so Luz doesn't catch us. She'd freak if she knew what Mommy was doing right now. Talk about role reversal." She inhaled deeply, her face screwing up as the smoke blew from her mouth. "I suppose someone like you wouldn't do this, would you? Maybe you're worried you'll drop that guard of yours. What do you think?"

"Aaron told me you met at the university. . . ."

She nodded as I started to fill the magazine with more rounds. " 'Eighty-six. Without him I'd never have had the stamina to get my Ph.D. I was one of his students."

She looked at me and smiled expectantly, obviously well used to the reaction to her announcement. I probably fell in with the one she anticipated.

Her tone challenged me. "Oh, come on, Nick, have you never been attracted to an older woman?"

"Yeah, Wonder Woman, but that was when I was the same age as Luz."

I'd made her laugh, though maybe the giggleweed had a little to do with it.

"Half the university staff ended up marrying a student. Sometimes they had to divorce one student to set up with another—but, hey, why should the course of true love run smoother in a faculty building than any other place?"

I sensed it was a well-rehearsed explanation of their relationship. "Staying here to study while the folks went back up north and got divorced was great," she went on. "You know, straitlaced Catholic family gone wrong—the rebellious teenage years, father not understanding—that sort of stuff." Her glasses pointed my way and she smiled, maybe thinking about those good times as she took another drag. "There's even a kind of convention about sleeping with your teacher, you know. Not exactly as a rite of passage, more a visa stamp, proof you've been there.

Someone like you would understand that, no?"

I shrugged, never having known anything about what went on at those places, but now wishing I did.

She picked up the fully loaded rifle that lay between us. The bolt was back and she checked the chamber before laying the weapon across her knees, then slowly moved the bolt forward to pick the top round out of the magazine, feeding it into the chamber. But instead of locking down the bolt as you would to fire, she pulled it back so the brass round was ejected from the chamber with a clink and into the grass. Then she pushed the bolt home again to repeat the action.

"How does Luz fit in here?" Even as I started to speak I knew I'd fucked up, but it was too late to stop the flow. "She isn't your natural child, is she?"

She might have been: she could have had her with somebody else. I was crashing and burning here. I tried to recover. "I didn't mean that, what I mean is, she isn't—"

She laughed and cut in to save me. "No, no, you're right, she isn't. She's kind of fostered."

She took a long, reflective drag and looked down, concentrating on the slow ejection of another round as it flew out of the chamber onto the rough grass. I couldn't help but think of Kelly and what my version of fostering had added up to these past three or four years.

"She was my dearest and only friend, really, Lulu. . . . Luz is her daughter. . . . Just Cause." She looked up sharply. "You know what that is?"

I nodded. Not that she could see me: she was already looking down again. "The invasion. December 'eighty-nine. Were you and Aaron here?"

She pulled back the bolt on the third round and shook her head slowly and sadly from side to side.

"No one can imagine what a war is like unless they witness one. But I guess I don't need to tell *you* that."

"Mostly in places I can't even pronounce, but they're all the same wherever they are—shit and confusion, a nightmare."

The fourth round tumbled out of the weapon. "Yep, you're right there. Shit and confusion . . ." She picked one up and played with it between her fingers, then took another puff of the spliff, making it glow gently.

Her head was up now but I couldn't tell if she was looking at me or not as she blew out smoke. "Months before the invasion things were getting really tense. There were riots, curfews, people getting killed. It was a bad, bad situation—only a matter of time before the U.S. intervened, but nobody knew when.

"My father kept wanting us to move north, but Aaron wouldn't have any of it—this is his home. Besides, the Zone was only a few miles away, and whatever happened out here, in there we'd be safe. So we stayed."

She dropped the round onto the ground, picked up the water, and took a long swig, as if she was trying to wash away a bad taste. "On the morning of the nineteenth, I got called by my father telling us to get into the Zone because it was going down that night. He was still in the military then, working out of D.C."

She had a moment to herself and gave a fleeting smile. "Knowing George, he was probably planning it. God knows what he gets up to. Anyways, he'd arranged accommodation for us in Clayton." She took another swig, and I waited for the rest of the story.

She put down the bottle and got the last out of her herbal roll-up before stubbing it out into the ground, then picking up another round to fiddle with. "So we moved into the Zone and, sure enough, we saw enough troops, tanks, helicopters, you name it, to take on Washington State." She shook her head slowly. "That night we lay in bed, we couldn't sleep—you know what it's like. Then just past midnight the first bombs hit the city. We ran out onto the deck and saw bright sheets of light filling the sky, then the sound of the explosions just seconds behind. They were taking out Noriega's headquarters, just a few miles from where we were standing. It was terrible—they were bombing El Chorrillo, where Lulu and Luz lived."

24

Her voice was devoid of emotion now, her body suddenly still. "We went back inside and turned on the radio for news. Pan National had music, and about a minute later there was an announcement saying that Panama was being invaded, and alerting the Dingbats."

"Dingbats?"

"The Dignity Battalions—Noriega's private army. The station was calling them to arms, calling for everybody else to go on the streets and defend their country against the invaders, all that kind of crap. It was a joke—nearly everybody wanted this to happen, you know, get Noriega out.

"We left the radio on, and turned on the TV to the Southern Command station. I couldn't believe it, they hadn't even interrupted the movie! Aaron got totally freaked out. We could still hear the bombing outside."

I was listening intently, taking the occasional sip of water.

"The Defense Department seal soon filled the screen on all the Pan channels, and a voice came on telling everybody in Spanish to stay indoors and keep tuned in. And that's exactly what we did. Not that they told us much apart from 'Everything's fine, just stay calm.' Soooo, eventually we went back out on the deck, and watched more explosions. They were coming from all parts of the city now. There were jets zooming around in the dark, sometimes coming so low we could see their afterburners.

"This carried on until maybe about four, and then it all went quiet, apart from the jets and helicopters. We really didn't know what to do or think—I was worried for Lulu and Luz.

"At dawn, the sky just seemed to be filled with helicopters, and smoke coming out from the city. And there was this huge plane, constantly circling. In the end, it was there for weeks."

The way she described it, it was probably a Specter gunship: those things can operate day or night, it doesn't matter; it's always a clear day for them. They would be up there, in support of the ground troops, acting like airborne artillery. They have infrared and thermal imaging cameras that can pick out a running man or a square inch of reflective tape from thousands of feet up. They have onboard computers, controlled by operators who are protected inside a titanium cell, to help them decide whether to use their 40mm and 20mm cannons or machine guns, or if the shit was really hitting the fan below, a 105mm howitzer artillery piece sticking out the side.

Carrie continued talking, telling me about the Dingbats looting, raping, destroying everything in their path as they tried to escape the Americans. For her and Aaron it wasn't until the day after Christmas that they went back to their house near the university. "It was fine. . . ." She smiled fleetingly again. "It wasn't even looted, though some of the locals had been out making the most of the opportunities elsewhere. Somebody had stolen a whole lot of Stetsons from a store—suddenly there were about thirty guys in the neighborhood thinking they were John Wayne."

I smiled at the image, but her face was soon serious again.

"The place was an occupation zone, checkpoints, troops, they were everywhere. We were so worried about Lulu and Luz, we went to El Chorrillo to check them out. It looked like a newsreel of Bosnia. There were bombed-out buildings, troops with machine guns cruising around in armored vehicles with loudspeakers." She mimicked their words: " 'Merry Christmas, we're soldiers from the United States of America. We're going to be searching your houses very soon, please leave your doors open and sit in the front part of your home. You will not be harmed. Merry Christmas.' It was so surreal, like a movie or something."

Her face was suddenly drained. "We got to Lulu's walk-up and it was just a heap of rubble. Her neighbors told us she'd been inside. Luz had been sleeping over at Lulu's sister's place in the next block. That was bombed, too, and the sister had been killed, but there was no trace of Luz. It was terrible, looking for Luz after that. I had that feeling, you know, that frantic feeling like when you think you've maybe lost a child in a crowd. The idea of her walking around the streets without anyone to protect her, you know, look after her. Do you know that feeling?"

I thought of last night's dream. I knew that feeling all right.

"We found her eventually in one of the reception camps, in a nursery area with all the other parentless kids. The rest is kind of history. From that day till this, we've looked after her." She sighed. "We loved Lulu so much."

I'd been slowly nodding ever since her question, listening, but troubled by my own thoughts. "I have lost friends," I said. "All of them, really. I miss them too."

"Lonely without them, isn't it?" She picked up the last of the water and offered me a share, waiting for me to continue. I shook my head and let her finish it. I wasn't going to let that happen.

"Do you think the U.S. did the right thing?" I asked.

The bottle was back in her mouth for a couple of sips. "It should have come earlier. How could we just sit and watch Noriega—the deaths, torture, corruption? We should have done something sooner. When the word was out that he had turned himself over to the U.S., there were horns sounding all over the city. There was a lot of partying that night." An edge of bitterness crept into her voice. "Not that it's done any good. With the pullout from the Zone, we've given everything away." She retreated into her own thoughts for a second or two and I just watched her face get sadder. At length she looked up. "You know what, Nick? Back then, something happened that I'll never forget. It changed my life."

I carried on looking at her and waiting as she finished the water.

"We were back in our house and it was New Year's Day, nearly two weeks after the invasion. I was watching TV with Luz in my arms. Barbara Bush was in the audience of some show and a group on stage started to sing 'God Bless America.' The whole audience stood up and joined in. Just at that moment, a helicopter flew low over us, right over the house, and I could still hear the giant plane circling overhead—and I started to cry. For the first time it made me feel so proud to be American."

A tear ran down her cheek from behind her sunglasses. She made no attempt to wipe it away as another followed.

"But you know what? I feel so sad for us now—that we could just give away everything down here that people died for back then. Can you understand that, Nick?"

Yes, I understood, but I never went there. If I did, I wasn't sure that I could navigate my way out again.

"I met a guy called Johnny Applejack, a Delta Force captain, in 'ninety-three. Well, that's what we called him . . ." I told her about his patrol going into a Panamanian government office during the first night, and finding three million dollars there, in cash. The only reason all six of the team weren't now driving Porsches was that Johnny radioed it in without thinking about what he was doing. "It was only after he got off the air that he understood he'd just kissed goodbye to the patrol retirement fund. I don't know what he's like now, but back in 'ninety-three he looked as if his lottery numbers had come up and he'd just realized he'd forgotten to buy a ticket."

She smiled.

There was a pause I was aching to fill as I watched her place her index fingers under her glasses and give each eye a wipe. But I'd done the damage I'd wanted to: I'd broken the spell.

I pointed at the weapon still across her lap as I got to my feet. "Coming back to three hundred?"

"Why not?"

I waited as she got up. Her dark lenses zeroed in on me again. "The other stuff getting too close for you, Nick?"

I turned and started counting off another two hundred paces in my head, with her at my side. *Twenty-six, twenty-seven, twenty-eight.*

I filled the space with business. "I've been thinking. I need to be back at Charlie's by four tomorrow morning, so I'll have to leave here at ten tonight—and we're going to need to work out how I can return this." I held up the weapon. "I presume you'll want it back?"

Thirty-nine, forty, forty-one.

"Sure do, it's the only present my father ever gave me that had any use. We'll work it out."

I realized I'd lost the count. I started at forty-five as Carrie's sunglasses turned to me. "Do you know how you're going to do it yet—you know, give him a reminder?"

Fifty-two, fifty-three, fifty-four.

"I've had one or two thoughts. . . ."

Fifty-six, fifty-seven, fifty-eight.

I looked out at the clearing, then had another. "You got any explosives left? I saw the pictures, on the corkboard."

Seventy-three, seventy-four, seventy-five.

"You *are* nosy, aren't you?"

She pointed toward the far tree line that faced the rear of the house. "There's a stash of the stuff down there in the shack."

I was amazed. "You mean you've just left it there? In a shed?"

"Hey, come on. Where are we? There's more to worry about around here than a few boxes of explosives. What do you want it for, anyway?"

"I need to make a lot of noise—to remind him."

I couldn't see any outbuildings, just greenery: because of the downhill slope the bottom third of the tree line was in dead ground.

"Do you know how to use it? Oh, of course—stupid."

"What kind is it?"

She pulled a face. "It goes bang and blows up trees, that kind. George and some of the local guys played with it."

I'd lost count again. I was guessing eighty-nine, ninety, ninety-one, then Carrie stopped to announce: "First one hundred."

She pointed toward the dead ground. "I'll take you down there after we've—"

"Mom! Mom! Grandpa wants to talk!" Luz was yelling for her from the rear of the house.

Carrie put her hands to her mouth. "Okay, baby." She sounded quite concerned as she put down the bottle and ammo box. "I've got to go."

She emptied her pockets of the tobacco tin and Zippo then threw them into the ammo box. She turned to me and smiled. "She'd ground me."

Jogging out into the sun to cover the two hundred yards or so to the house, she pointed once more toward the invisible hut in the tree line. "You can't miss it. Later."

I left everything where it was and headed for the trees at the bottom of the cleared patch, keeping in the shade of the ones I was under. The hut didn't come into view for a while, and even when it did I couldn't face walking out into the sun to cut the corner. The heat haze that shimmered above the ground wasn't exactly inviting: I was a sweaty mess already.

I scratched away at my back and followed the shade of the tree line around two sides of the square, eventually getting to what looked like a wooden outdoor privy. The door hung precariously on the lower rusty hinge and grass grew high right up against the door. Spiderwebs were spun all over the hut as if forming a protective screen. I looked through the gap in the broken door, but didn't see a toilet. Instead I saw two square, dull metal boxes with red and black stenciling.

This was a gift from heaven: four tin boxes, eight kilos in each. I couldn't understand the Spanish, but made out what was important: it contained 55 percent nitroglycerin, a high proportion. The higher the amount of nitro, the more sensitive it is; a high-velocity round would easily detonate this stuff as it passed through, which wouldn't have been the case with military standard high explosive, which is shock-proof.

I wrenched open the door and stepped inside. Pulling off the opening key from the side of the top box, I saw the date on the pasted-on label, 01/99, which I presumed was its Best Blown-up-by date. This stuff must be old enough to have been used when Noriega was in diapers.

I got to work, peeling the sealing strip of metal just below the lid exactly as if I was opening a giant tin of corned beef.

A plan was already forming in my mind to leave a device by Charlie's gates. If I couldn't drop the target as he moved outside the house, I could take him out while his vehicle waited for the gates to open by getting a round into this shit, instead of him. My fire position would have to be in the same area I'd been in yesterday to ensure a good view of the pool and the front of the house, as well as the road going down toward the gate. I'd have to rig the device so it was in line of sight of the fire position, but I couldn't see that as a problem.

Sweat was gathering on my eyebrows. I wiped it as it was about to drip into my eyes and pulled back the lid of the tin container to reveal the inner wooden box liner. I cut the string banding with my Leatherman and lifted that too. I found five sticks of commercial dynamite, wrapped in dark yellow waxed paper, some stained by the nitro, which had been sweating in this heat for years. A heavy smell of marzipan filled the air and I was glad I was going to work with this stuff outdoors. Nitroglycerin can damage your health, and not just when it's detonated. It won't kill you when you handle it, but you're guaranteed the mother of all fearsome headaches if you work with it in a confined space, or if you get it into a cut or it's otherwise absorbed into the bloodstream.

I took three of the eight-inch sticks and wandered back to the firing point, following the shade of the tree line once more, pulling back the waxed paper as I walked to reveal sticks of light green Plasticine-type material. Minute gray crystals of dried-out nitro coated the surface. Passing the weapon and ammo box, I continued the other two hundred paces to the target area, where I placed them side by side at the trunk of the thickest tree I could find near my paper targets. Then, back at the two-hundred point, I got into my firing position and took a slow, deliberate shot at the black circle.

The zero was good: it went in directly above the one-shot zero round I'd fired—just as it should.

Now came the acid test, both for the zero and HE (high explosive). Picking up the ammo, weapon, and bottle, I took another hundred paces to roughly the 300-yard mark, lay down, checked the area to make sure Carrie or Luz hadn't decided to take a stroll from the house toward the target area, then aimed at the sternum-sized target of green dynamite.

When I was sure my position and hold were correct, I had one last check around the area. "Firing, firing!" The warning shout wasn't necessary, since no one else was about, but it had become a deeply ingrained habit from years of playing with this stuff.

Aiming center of the sternum, I took a slow, controlled shot.

The crack of the round and the roar of the explosion seemed to be as one. The earth surrounding it was dried instantly by the incredible heat of rapid combustion, turned into dust by the shock wave, and sent up in a thirty-foot plume. Slivers of wood were falling all around the high ground like rain. The tree was still standing, and so it should be considering the size of it, but it was badly damaged. Lighter-colored wood showed like flesh beneath the bark.

"NIIICK! NIIICK!"

I jumped up and waved at Carrie as she ran from the back of the house. "It's okay! Okay! Just testing."

She stopped at the sight of me and screamed at the top of her voice, easily covering the ground between us. "YOU IDIOT! I THOUGHT—I THOUGHT—"

Cutting abruptly from her screams, she turned and stormed back inside.

Luckily there was no need to do anything more: the zero was on for all ranges, and the dynamite worked. All I had to do now was make a charge that'd take out a vehicle.

Clearing the weapon, I picked up all the other bits and pieces and headed back to the house.

25

The screen door slammed shut behind me and I felt the sweat start to cool on my skin in the breeze from the two fans by the coffee table.

I headed straight for the fridge, dumping the weapon and ammo box on the way. The light didn't come on when I opened the door, maybe some tree-hugging measure to save power, but I could still see what I was looking for—another couple of two-liter plastic water bottles like the one we'd emptied. The long gulps of chilled water tugged at my throat and gave me an instant headache but it was worth it. I refilled the bottle I'd brought in from the garden-hose tap marked D and put it back in the fridge.

My T-shirt and pants were still sticking to me, and the rash on my back was itching big-time. I got the cream out of my pocket and gave it a good smear all over. There was no point toweling myself off in this humidity.

After washing my gooey hands and face and devouring a couple of bananas, it was time to start thinking about the device I was going to make with the HE. With the half-empty water bottle in my hand,

and Carrie's giggleweed and Zippo in my pockets, I knocked on the door of the computer room as I entered.

Carrie was sitting in the director's chair on the left with her back to me, bent over some papers. The sound of the two overhead fans filled the room, a loud, methodical *thud-thud-thud* as they spun on their ceiling mounts. The room was much cooler than the living area.

The PC with the webcam was switched off; the other in front of Carrie showed a spreadsheet full of numbers, and she was comparing the data on her papers with what was on the screen.

It was Luz who saw me first, seated at her desk farther down the room. Swiveling in her chair to face me, she gave a *"Booom!"* with a big smile spread over her face and an apple in her hand. At least she thought it was funny. I shrugged sheepishly, as I had so many times to Kelly when I'd messed up. "Yeah, sorry about that."

Carrie turned in her seat to face me. I gave her an apologetic shrug too. She nodded in return and raised an eyebrow at Luz, who just couldn't stop smiling. I pointed at the storeroom. "I'm going to need some help."

"Gimme a minute."

She raised her voice to primary-school level and wagged a finger. "As for you, young lady, back to work."

Luz got back down to it, using her thumb and forefinger to tap the pencil on the table in four-four time. She reminded me so much of Kelly.

Carrie hit a final few keys on the PC and stood up, instructing Luz as she did so, still in schoolmistress mode, "I want to see that math sheet completed by lunchtime, young lady, or no food for you again!"

There was a smile and a resigned "Oh, Mooom, pleeeease . . ." in return, and she took a bite from her apple as we headed for the storeroom.

Carrie closed the door behind her. The outside entrance was open, and I could see the light fading on the rows of white tubs. The sky was no longer an unrelenting blue; clouds were gathering, casting shadows as they moved across the sun.

I passed over the tobacco tin and the Zippo and received a smile and a "Thanks" as she placed a foot on a bottom shelf and climbed up to hide them under some battery packs.

I'd already spotted something I needed and was picking up a cardboard box that told me it should be holding twenty-four cans of Campbell's tomato soup, but in fact had only two. Wanting just the box, I took out the cans and stacked them on the shelf.

It was Little America up on these shelves, everything from blankets and shovels to eco-friendly dish liquid, oversize packs of Oreos and decaf coffee.

"This is like WalMart," I said. "I was expecting more of a wigwam and incense sticks."

I got a laugh from her as she jumped off the shelf and walked toward the outside door.

I looked at her framed in the doorway as she gazed out at the lines of white tubs, then I walked over to join her, carrying the water bottle and soup box. We stood together in the doorway for a few moments, in silence but for the generator humming gently in the background.

"What exactly do you do here?"

She pointed to the tubs and ran her hand along their regimented lines. "We're searching for new species of endemic flora—ferns, flowering trees, that sort of thing. We catalog and propagate them before they disappear forever." She stared at nowhere in particular, just into the far tree line, as if she was expecting to find some more.

"That's very interesting."

She faced me and smiled, her voice heavy with sarcasm. "Yeah, right."

I actually was interested. Well, a bit.

"I don't believe you, but it's very kind of you to pretend. And actually, it is very interesting . . ." She waved her arms toward the tubs and the sky above them, now dark with clouds. "Believe it or not, you're standing at the front line of the battle to save biodiversity."

I gave her a grin. "Us against the world, eh?"

"Better believe it," she said.

We looked at each other for less than a second, but for me it was half a second longer than it should have been. Our eyes might have been locked, but there was no way of telling behind her glasses.

"A hundred years from now, half the world's flora and fauna will be extinct. And that, my friend, will affect everything: fish, birds, insects, plants, mammals, you name it, simply because the food chain will be disrupted. It's not just the big charismatic mammals that we seem to fixate on"—she rolled her eyes and held her hands up in mock horror—"save the whales, save the tiger . . . It's not just those guys, it's everything." Her earnest expression suddenly relaxed and her face lit up. "Including the sandfly your eye has already gotten acquainted with." The smile didn't last. "Without the habitat, we're going to lose this forever, you know."

I moved outside and sat on the concrete, putting the soup box down beside me and untwisting the water bottle top. As I took a swig she came and sat beside me, putting her glasses back on. As we both stared at the rows of tubs, her knee just touched mine as she spoke. "This rate of extinction has only happened five times since complex life began. And all caused by a natural disaster." She held out a hand for the bottle. "Take dinosaurs. They became history because of a meteorite crashing into the planet about sixty-five million years ago, right?"

I nodded as if I knew. The Natural History Museum hadn't been where I spent my days as a kid.

"Right, but this sixth extinction is not happening because of some external force, it's happening because of us—the exterminator species. And there ain't no Jurassic Park, we can't just magic them back once they're gone. We've got to save them now."

I didn't say anything, just looked into the distance as she drank and a million crickets did their bit.

"I know, you're thinking we're some kind of crazy save-the-world geeks or whatever, but—"

I turned my head. "I don't think anything like that—"

"Whatever," she cut in, her free hand up, a smile on her face as she passed the bottle. "Anyway, here's the news: all the plant life on the planet hasn't been identified yet, right?"

"If you say so."

We grinned at each other.

"I do say so. And we're losing them faster than we can catalog them, right?"

"If you say so."

"I do. And that's why we're here, to find the species that we don't know of yet. We go into the forest for specimens, cultivate them, and send samples to the university. So many of our medicines come from those things out there in the tubs. Every time we lose a species, we lose an option for the future, we lose a potential cure for HIV, Alzheimer's, chronic fatigue syndrome, whatever. Now, here's the cool part. You ready?"

I rubbed the bandage on my calf, knowing it was coming regardless.

"The drug companies provide grants for the university to find and test new species for them. So, hey, go figure, we have a form of conservation that makes business sense." She nodded in self-approval and got busy polishing her nails. "But despite all that, they're closing us down next year. Like I said, we're doing great work, but they want quick results for their buck. So maybe we're not the crazy ones, eh?"

She turned once more to gaze out toward the tubs, her face no longer happy or serious, just sad. I was quite enjoying the silence with her.

I'd never had the tree-hugging case put to me like that before. Maybe it was because it came from her, maybe it was because she wasn't wearing a windbreaker and trying to ram it down my throat.

"How do you reconcile what you do here with what you're doing for me? I mean, the two don't exactly stand together, do they?"

She didn't turn to face me, just kept looking out at the tubs. "Oh, I wouldn't say that. Apart from anything else, it's helped me with Luz."

"How's that?"

"Aaron's too old to adopt, and it's so complicated trying to get things done here." I thought for a moment that she was going to blush. "Soooo, my father came up with the offer of a U.S. passport for her, in exchange for our help—that's the deal. Sometimes we do wrong things for right reasons—isn't that true, Nick whatever-your-name-is?" She turned to me and took a deep breath.

Whatever was about to be said, it changed, and she gazed back out over at the tree line as a swarm of sparrow-sized birds took flight and chirped in frantic unison.

"Aaron doesn't approve of our doing this. We fight. He wanted to keep hassling for an adoption. But there's no time, we need to head back to Boston. My mother went to live there again after the divorce. George stayed on in D.C., doing what he's always done." She paused, before going off on a tangent. "You know, it was only after the divorce that I discovered how powerful my father is. You know, even the Clintons call him George. Shame he didn't use some of it to save his personal life. It's ironic, really. Aaron's like him in so many ways. . . ."

"Why go after so long—because you're being closed down?"

"Not only that. The situation is getting worse down here. And then there's Luz to think about. Soon it'll be high school, then college. She's got to start having a normal life. Boyfriends who double-date, girlfriends who talk about you behind your back, that kind of stuff. . . ." She smiled. "Hey, she wants to go, like yesterday."

The smile soon died but her voice wasn't sorrowful, just practical. "But Aaron . . . Aaron hates change—just like my father. He's just hoping all the troubles will go away." Her head tilted up and back as the flock of birds screeched by, inches above the house. I looked up as well, and tracked them across the sky. She sighed. "I'll miss this place."

I knew I was supposed to say something, but I didn't know what. I felt that the mess I'd made of my own life didn't exactly qualify me to help sort out hers.

"I love him very much," she said. "It's just that I've gradually realized I'm not *in* love with the man, I guess. . . . Oldest cliché in the book, I know. But it's so difficult to explain. I can't talk to him about it. It's . . . I don't know, it's just time to go. . . ." She paused for a moment. I could feel the blood pumping through my head. "There are times when I feel so terribly lonely."

She used both hands to put her hair behind her ears then turned toward me. There was a silence between us again as the pulse in my neck quickened, and I found it difficult to breathe. "What about you, Nick?" she said. "Do you ever get lonely?"

She already knew the answer, but I couldn't help myself. . . .

I told her that I lived in a flophouse in London, that I had no money, had to line up to get free food from a Hari Krishna soup wagon. I told her that all my friends were dead apart from one, and he despised me. Apart from the clothes I was wearing when I arrived at their house, my only other possessions were in a bag stuck in Left Luggage at a railway station in London.

I told her all this and it felt good. I also told her the only reason I was in Panama was that it would stop a child being killed by my boss. I wanted to tell her more, but managed to force the lid back on before it all came flooding out.

When I'd finished, I sat, arms folded, feeling uncertain, not wanting to look at her, so I just stared out at the tubs again.

She cleared her throat. "The child . . . is that Marsha or Kelly?"

I spun my head around and she mistook my shock for anger.

"I'm sorry, sorry . . . I shouldn't have asked, I know. It's just I was there, I was with you all night, I hadn't just appeared . . . I was going to tell you this morning, but we both got embarrassed, I guess. . . ."

Fuck, what had I said?

She tried to soften the blow. "I had to stay, otherwise you would have been halfway to Chepo by now.

Don't you remember? You kept on waking up shouting, trying to get outside to look for Kelly. And then you were calling out for Marsha. Somebody had to be there for you. Aaron had been up all night and he was out of it. I was worried about you."

The pulse was stronger now and I felt very hot. "What else did I say?"

"Well—Kev. I thought it was your real name until just now and—"

"Nick Stone."

It must have sounded like a quiz-show quickfire answer. She looked at me a moment, a smile returning to her face. "That's your real name?"

I nodded.

"Why did you do that?"

I shrugged, not too sure. It had just felt right.

When I spoke next, it was as if I was in a trance. As if someone else was doing the talking, and I was just hearing them from a distance. "The girl's name is Kelly. Her mother was Marsha, married to my friend, Kev. Aida was her little sister. They were all murdered, in their house. Kelly's the only one left. I was just minutes too late to save them. She's why I'm here—she's all I have left."

She nodded slowly, taking it all in. I was vaguely aware that the sweat was now leaking more heavily down my face, and I tried to wipe it away.

"Why don't you tell me about her?" she said quietly. "I'd love to hear about her."

I felt the pins and needles return to my legs, felt the lid forcing itself open, and I had nothing left to control it.

"It's okay—it's okay, Nick. Let it out." Her voice was cool, soothing.

And then I knew I couldn't stop it. The lid burst open and words crashed out of my mouth, hardly giving me time to breathe. I told her about being Kelly's guardian, being totally inconsistent, going to Maryland to see Josh, the only sort of friend I had left, people I liked always fucking me over, signing Kelly over permanently to Josh's care, Kelly's therapy, the loneliness . . . everything. By the end, I felt exhausted and just sat there with my hands covering my face.

I felt a hand gently touch my shoulder. "You've never told anybody that before, have you?"

I shook my head, letting my hands fall, and tried to smile. "I've never sat still long enough," I said. "I had to give the therapist a few details about the way Kev and Marsha died, but I did my best to keep the rest of it pretty well hidden."

She could have been looking right through me. It certainly felt that way. "She might have helped, you know."

"Hughes? She just made me feel like a—like a—like an emotional dwarf." I felt my jaw clench. "You know, my world may look like a pile of shit, but at least I sometimes get to sit on top of it."

She gave me a sad smile. "But what's the view like from your pile of shit?"

"Not a match for yours but, then, I like jungles."

"Mmm." Her smile widened. "Great for hiding in."

I nodded, and managed a real smile this time.

"Are you going to keep hiding for the rest of your life, Nick Stone?"

Good question. What the fuck was the answer?

I stared at the tubs for a long while as the pins and needles disappeared, and eventually she gave a theatrical sigh. "What are we going to do with you?"

We looked at each other before she got to her feet. I joined her, feeling awkward as I tried to think of something, anything, to say that would prolong the moment.

She smiled again, then clipped me playfully across the ear. "Well, then, recess over, back to work. I have some math to check."

"Yes, right. I need one of your tubs—I think I saw some empties near the sinks."

"Sure, we're maxed out. They won't be needed soon, anyway." The smile was still there, but it had become rueful.

I held up the box. "I'm going to play with that explosive down in the shack for a while, and I promise, no more bangs."

She nodded. "That's a relief," she said. "I think we've both had quite enough excitement for one day." She turned toward the storeroom but then paused. "Don't worry, Nick Stone, no one will know about this. No one."

I nodded a thank-you, not just for keeping quiet, as she headed for the storeroom. "Carrie?"

She stopped and half turned once more. "Okay if I have a look around in the stores and take some stuff with me? You know, food and equipment for tonight."

"For sure, but just tell me what you've got so we can replace it, okay? And, of course, nothing that can identify us, like that." She pointed at the soup box, which had a white sticky label saying "Yanklewitz 08/14/00," probably the helicopter delivery date.

"No worries."

She gave that rueful smile again. "As if, Nick Stone."

I watched her disappear into the store before heading around the corner toward the sinks, then got to work. I peeled off the label in three stubborn bits, which went into one of the glasses. Then, after getting a drink from the D hose and refilling my bottle, I wandered across the open ground to the shack, swinging the tub I'd just collected in one hand, the box and water bottle in the other, trying to think about nothing except the job. It was hard. She was right, I did have worries, but at least I hadn't jabbered about who the real target was.

The clouds were gathering big-time. I'd been right not to be fooled by the sun this morning. Just as I reached the gentle incline and started to see the roof of the hut, I heard a succession of short bursts from a vehicle's horn and looked back. The Mazda was bumping along the track, and Luz was running out to greet her dad. I stood watching for a while as he jumped out of the truck to be hugged and talked to as they walked onto the porch.

Sitting in the still humid shade of the hut, I tore off the top and bottom flaps of the Campbell's box, scrunched them up in the bottom of the tub, and was left with the main carcass, a four-sided cube, which I ripped apart at a seam and opened out so that I had one long, flat section of cardboard. I started fitting it into the tub, running it around the edges then twisting it until I'd made a cone with its apex about a third of the way up from the bottom, with all the scrunched-up flaps beneath. If I let it go now the cone shape would spring apart, so I started to pack HE, still in its wrappers, around the base to keep it in place. Then, with the cone held fast, I peeled open the other boxes, unwrapped more HE, and played with the puttylike substance, packing it into the tub and around the cone.

I was trying to make a copy of the French off-route mine. These are the same shape as the tub, but a little smaller, and designed so that, unlike a conventional mine, they don't have to be directly beneath the target when detonated to destroy it. It can be concealed off to one side of a road or track, hidden in the bushes or, as I was planning, up a tree. It's a handy device if you're trying to mine a paved road, say, without having your goodies laid out for everyone to see.

One version of the mine is initiated by a cable as thin as a strand of silk that's laid over the pavement and crushed. I was going to detonate it with a round from the Mosin Nagant.

Once triggered, the manufactured ones instantly turn a cone of copper into a hot, molten slug, the shaped charge, propelling it at such speed and power that it penetrates the target's armor and rips its insides apart. I didn't have any copper; in its place, and shaped very much the same way, was the cardboard cone, but there should be enough force in the HE alone to do the job required of it.

I continued squashing down the HE, trying to make it one solid mass over the cone. My hands stung as the glycerin got into my cuts, and my headache was back, really giving it to me.

Thinking about the old German guy who'd given me the bayonet gave me the idea of using the explosive this way. He'd told me a story about the Second World War. German Paras had taken a bridge, stopping the Brits from demolishing it as they withdrew. The charges were still in position, but the Germans disconnected the detonators so that a Panzer column could cross and kick the shit out of the Brits. A young British squaddie took one shot with his standard Lee Enfield .303 rifle at the placed charges. Because it was old-style explosive, just like this stuff, it detonated, and set off all the other charges that were connected by the det (detonation) cord. The whole bridge dropped, stopping the Panzers ever getting through.

As I packed the last of the HE, I was hoping that the squaddie had at least gotten a couple of weeks' leave as a reward, but I very much doubted it. Proba-

bly just a tap on the helmet with a riding crop and a
"Jolly well done, that man," before getting killed a few
weeks later.

When I'd finished, I sealed the top on the tub, left
the device in the shed, and started back to the house,
thinking about what else I had to prepare for a possible four nights on the ground.

The sky had turned metallic, the clouds every
shade of gray. A gentle breeze was the only consola-
tion.

There was a loud rumble of thunder in the distance
as I crested the slope. Aaron and Carrie were standing by the sinks, and I could see they were arguing
again. Carrie's arms were flying about and Aaron
was standing with his head jutting forward like a
rooster's.

I couldn't just stop and go back: I was in no-man's-
land here. Besides, my hands were stinging badly with
the nitro and I needed to wash it off, and to get some
aspirin down my throat. Dihydrocodeine would do the
job better, but I needed to be awake later tonight.

I slowed down, lowered my head, and hoped they'd
see me soon.

They must have spotted me out here in the open
ground, looking everywhere and anywhere apart from
the washing area, because the arms stopped wind-
milling. Carrie went to the storeroom door and disappeared as Aaron dried himself.

I got to him as he retied his hair, clearly embarrassed.

"Sorry you had to see that."

"None of my business," I said. "Besides, I'll be gone
tonight."

"Carrie told me you'll need dropping off—ten,
right?"

Nodding, I released the water pressure and soaked

my hands before cutting the supply and soaping up to get all the nitro off me. "You said you had a map? Is it on the bookshelf?"

"Help yourself, and I'll get you a real compass."

He passed me to hang the green towel next to mine on the line. "You feeling better now? We were worried."

I started to rinse off. "Fine, fine, must have picked something up yesterday. How's the jaguar?"

"They promised they're going to do something this time, maybe the zoo, but I'll believe it when I see it." He hovered awkwardly for a moment, then said, "Well, Nick, I'm heading to go catch up on some work here. It's been sort of backing up on me this week."

"See you later, mate."

I pulled my towel off the line as he headed for the storeroom door.

26

Now that the sky had grayed over completely the storeroom was almost dark. I eventually found the string-pull for the light and a single fluorescent strip flickered on, dangling precariously from wires about six feet from the high ceiling.

The first thing I saw was that the weapon and ammunition had been placed on a shelf for me, along with a Silva compass and map.

I needed to make some "ready rounds," so I ripped about six inches off a roll of one-inch duct tape, placed a round of ammo on the sticky side, and rolled. As soon as the round was covered I placed another, rolled a little, then another, until four rounds were in a noiseless bundle, easy to fit into my pocket. I folded over the last two inches of tape to make it easier to pull apart, then started on another. A box of twenty was still going into the bergen; you never know how these jobs are going to end up.

I rummaged around in the medical case for the aspirin and swallowed two. They were helped on their way with a liter bottle of Evian I broke out from a new case of twelve, and I lobbed three onto the cot for later.

My leg was starting to hurt again but I really couldn't be bothered to change the dressing. I'd be wet and covered with mud later tonight anyway, and the aspirin would help.

I had to prepare for as much as four nights in the field—up to two on target and two in the jungle before popping out once the dust had settled and making my own way to the airport. Come what may, I needed to make Josh's by Tuesday.

I found an old A-frame bergen in the storeroom, its green canvas patchy with white haze after years of exposure to the elements. Joining the bergen and water on the cot went nine cans of tuna and an assortment of honey sesame bars that looked as if they'd get me through daylight hours.

Judging by what was on the shelves, they had certainly gotten their hands on enough of that military giveaway. I grabbed a poncho and some dark green mosquito nets. I could make a shelter from a poncho with the hood tied up and a couple of yards of string through the holes at each corner, and the mozzie nets would not only keep the beasties off me at night, but also act as camouflage netting. I took three—one for protection, and the other two for camouflaging me and the tub once we were in position. A large white plastic cylinder in a tree, tilted down at the road on the other side of the gate, just might arouse suspicion.

Most importantly, I found a gollock, an absolute necessity for the jungle because it can provide protection, food, and shelter. No one worth their salt is ever without one attached to their body once under the canopy. This one was U.S. Army issue and much sturdier than the one Diego had been swinging at me. It was maybe six inches shorter, with a solid wooden handle and a canvas sheath with a light alloy lip.

I climbed up the angle-iron framework of the shelves and, holding on to one of the struts, checked out the goodies higher up. Next door, Luz suddenly sounded very pleased with herself. "Yesss!" Baby-G told me it was 3:46—probably her schoolwork ending for the day. I wondered if she was aware of the arguments Aaron and Carrie had had about her. What did she know about what was happening now? If they thought she didn't know what was going on, they were probably kidding themselves—if she was anything like Kelly she never missed a trick.

For a second or two my thoughts wandered to Maryland: we were in the same time zone, and right now Kelly would probably be doing the same as Luz, packing up her books. It was private, individual, and expensive, but the only way forward until she had adapted between the one-on-one attention she'd been receiving in the clinic and the push and shove of mainstream education alongside Josh's kids. I had a flash of worry about what would happen now that I wasn't going to make the second half of the money—then remembered that that was the last thing to be concerned about.

I realized what I was doing and made the cut. I had to force myself to get on with the job—wrong, the mission.

I knew what gear I wanted, which wasn't very much. I'd learned the lesson the hard way, just like so many vacationers who take five suitcases with them, only to discover they only use the contents of one. Besides food and water, all I needed was the wet clothes I'd be standing up in, plus a dry set, mozzie net, lightweight blanket, and hammock. All this would be kept scrupulously dry in plastic in the bergen, and by the poncho at night. I already had my eye on the string hammock on the porch if I didn't find anything better.

None of these things was absolutely essential, but it's madness to choose to go without. I'd spent enough time in the jungle on hard routine in places like Colombia, so close to the DMP that no hammock or poncho could be put up, sitting all night in the shit, back to back with the rest of the patrol, getting eaten alive by whatever's flying around or mooching over you from out of the leaf litter, not eating hot food or drink for fear of compromise due to flame and smell, while waiting for the right day to attack. It doesn't help if you're spending night after night like that with all your new insect pals, snatching no more than a few minutes' sleep at a time. Come first light, bitten to death and exhausted, the patrol still has to get on with its task of watching and waiting.

Some patrols lasted for weeks like that, until trucks or helicopters eventually arrived to pick up the cocaine and we hit them. It's a fact that these conditions degrade the effectiveness of a patrol as time goes on. It isn't soft to sleep under shelter, a few inches above the shit rather than rolling around in it, it's pure common sense. I wanted to be alert and capable of taking that shot as easily on the second day as on the first, not with my eyes swollen up even more because I'd been trying to hardcore it in the shit the night before. Sometimes that has to happen, but not this time.

I carried on rooting around, climbing up and down the shelves like a howler monkey, and was so happy to find the one thing I was desperate for, its clear thick liquid contained in rows of baby-oil–style plastic bottles. I felt like the thirsty Arlington Road winos must feel when they find a half-full bottle in the garbage, especially when the label said it was 95 percent proof. Diethyltoluamide—I just knew it as deet—was magical stuff that would keep the little mozzies and creepy-crawlies away from me. Some commercial stuff contains only 15 percent, and is crap. The more deet the better, but the problem is it can melt some plastics—hence the thickness of these bottles. If you get it into your eyes it hurts; I'd known people have their contact lenses melt when it had been brought into contact with them by sweat. I threw three bottles onto the cot.

After another ten minutes of digging in boxes and bags, I started to pack the bergen. Having removed the noisy wrappers from the sesame bars and put them all into a plastic bag, they got stuffed into the large left-hand side pouch for easy access during the day. I shoved a bottle of Evian into the right-hand one for the same reason. The rest of the water and the tuna went into the bottom of the pack, wrapped in dish-cloths to muffle any noise. I'd only pull that food out at night when I wasn't in my fire position.

I put a large plastic garbage bag into the long center pouch at the front of the bergen. It would be taking any dumps I did while I was in the jungle: I'd have preferred individual bags, but couldn't find any, so one big one would have to take it all. It was important not to have any smell or waste around me because that would attract animals and might compromise my position, and I didn't want to leave anything behind that could be DNA'd.

Into a similar clear plastic bag went the mozzie net I was going to use for protection at night, and one of the blankets that was out of its wrapping. The hammock would join the contents of this bag once I'd swiped it from the porch later on. All the stuff in this bag needed to be dry at all times. Into it also would go my dry clothes for sleeping in, the same ones I'd wear once out of the canopy and heading for the airport. I'd get those from Aaron at the same time I got the hammock.

I laid the other two mozzie nets beside the bergen, together with some four-inch-wide, multicolored nylon luggage straps. Black, brown, in fact any color but this collection would have been better to blend into a world of green. I placed them inside the top flap, ready to make a sniper seat. The design originated in India during the days of the Raj, when the old sahibs could sit up in a tree in them for days with their Lee Enfields, waiting for tigers below. It was a simple device, but effective. The two straps were fixed between two branches to form a seat and you rested your back against the trunk. A high viewpoint looking down onto the killing area makes for a great field of view because you can look over the top of any obstructions, and it would also be good for concealment—as long as I tucked the mozzie net under it, to hide the rainbow holding up my ass.

I sat on the cot, and thought about other stuff I might need. First up was a shade for the front of the optic sight, so that sunlight didn't reflect off the objective (front) lens and give away my position.

I got a container of antifungal powder, again U.S. Army issue, in a small olive-green plastic cylinder. Emptying the contents, I cut off the top and bottom, then split it down the side. After wiping away all the powder on the inside, I put it over the front of the sight. It naturally hugged the metal cylinder as I moved it back and forth until the section protruding in front of the lens was just slightly longer than the lens's width. The sunlight would now only reflect off the lens if the sun itself was visible within my field of view.

Next I needed to protect the muzzle and working parts from the rain, and that was going to be just as easy. I fed a plastic bag over the muzzle and taped it to the furniture, then loaded up with rounds, pushed the bolt action forward to make ready the weapon, and applied the safety.

I ripped open the bottom of one of the clear plastic bags that had held the blankets, so only the two sides were still sealed, then worked it over the weapon like a hand muff until it was covering the sight, magazine, and working parts, using the duct tape to fix each open end to the furniture. Then, making a small slit in the plastic above the sight, I pushed it down so that the sight was now clear, and duct-taped the plastic together underneath to keep the seal. Everything in that area, bar the sight, was now encased in plastic. The weapon looked stupid, but that didn't matter, so did I. The safety could still be taken off, and when the time came I could still get my finger into the trigger by breaking the plastic. If I needed to fire more than one round, I'd just quickly rip the bag to reload. This had to be done because wet ammunition and a wet barrel will affect the round's trajectory—not a lot, but it all counts. I'd zeroed this weapon with a dry, cold barrel and dry ammunition, so it had to stay like that to optimize my chances of a one-round kill.

Next, I used the clear plastic from the last of the blankets on the shelf to protect the map, which said it had been compiled by the U.S. Army's 551st Engineer Company for the Panamanian government in 1964. A lot would have changed on the ground since then— Charlie's house and the loop road being just two of them. That didn't concern me too much; I was interested in the topographical features, the high ground and water features. That was the stuff that would get me out of there when I needed to head toward the city.

The compass still had its neck cord on, so I could just put it over my head and under the T-shirt. What it didn't have was any of its roamers for measuring off scale: mosquito repellent had already been on this one and the plastic base was just a frosted mess. I didn't care, as long as the red needle pointed north.

The map, compass, gollock, and docs would stay on my body at all times once under the canopy. I couldn't afford to lose them.

The last thing I did before laying my head down was thread the end of a ball of twine through the slit drilled into the rifle butt designed to take a webbing or leather sling, and wrap about four feet of it around the butt, cut it, and tie it secure. The weapon would never be over my shoulder unless I was climbing a tree. Only then would I tie the string into the slit in the stock and sling it.

I pushed everything that was left off the bed, and gave the light string a tug. I didn't want to see the others; it wasn't that I was feeling antisocial, just that when there's a lull before the battle, you lay your head down.

Lying on my back, my hands behind my head, I thought about what had happened with Carrie today. I shouldn't have done it. It was unprofessional and stupid, but at the same time, it felt okay. Dr. Hughes had never managed to make me feel like that.

I was woken suddenly. I snapped my wrist in front of my face to check Baby-G, and calmed down: it was just after a quarter past eight. I didn't need to get up until about nine.

The rain played a low, constant drumroll that accompanied the low thud of the fans next door as I rubbed my greasy, clammy head and face, pleased that there hadn't been any more dreams.

The canvas and alloy frame of the cot squeaked and groaned as I turned gently onto my stomach, running through my bergen list. It was then, just now and again above the sound of the rain and fans, that I heard some conspiratorial-sounding murmurs—I should know, I'd done enough of that stuff.

The cot creaked as I slowly swung my feet over the side and stood up. The sound was coming from the computer room, and I felt my way toward the door. A sliver of light from beneath it guided me.

I put my ear to the wood and listened.

It was Carrie. In a whisper she was answering a question I hadn't heard: "They can't come now . . . What if he sees them? . . . No, he knows nothing, but how am I going to keep them apart? . . . No, I can't . . . He'll wake up. . . ."

My hand reached for the door handle. Gripping it tightly, I opened the door slowly but deliberately no more than half an inch to see who she was talking to.

The six-inches-by-six, black-and-white image was a little jittery and fuzzed around the edges, but I could clearly see whose head and shoulders were filling the webcam. Wearing a checked jacket and dark tie, George was looking straight into his camera.

Carrie was listening via the headphones as his mouth moved silently. "But it wouldn't work, he won't buy that. . . . What do you want me to do with him? . . . He's next door asleep. . . . No, it was just a fever. . . . Christ, Dad, you said this wouldn't happen. . . ."

George was having none of it and pointed at her through the screen.

She answered angrily. "Of course I was . . . He likes me."

In that instant I felt as if a giant wave had engulfed me. My face began to smart and burn as I rested my head on the door frame. It was a long time since I'd felt so massively betrayed.

I knew I shouldn't have opened up to her, I just knew it.

You've screwed up big-time . . . Why can you never see when you're getting fucked over?

"No, I've got to go get ready, he's only next door. . . ."

I didn't have the answer to this, but I knew what I had to do.

When I pulled the door open Carrie was clicking away at the keyboard. She jumped out of her seat with shock, the headset wire jerking tight as the headset pulled down around her neck and the screen closed down.

She recovered, bending forward to take them off. "Oh, Nick—sleep better?"

She knew, I could see it in her eyes.

Why didn't you see the lying in them before?

I'd thought she was different. For once, I'd thought . . . Fuck it, I didn't know what I'd thought. I checked that the living-room door was closed and took three paces toward her. She thought she was about to die as I slapped my hand hard over her mouth, grabbed a fistful of hair at the back of her head, and lifted. She let out a whimper. Her eyes were bigger than I'd ever thought eyes could be. Her nostrils snorted in an attempt to get some air into her lungs. Both her hands were hanging onto my wrists, trying to release some of the pressure from her face.

I dragged her into the darkness of the storeroom, her feet scarcely touching the ground. Kicking the door shut so that we both became instantly blind, I put my mouth right up to her left ear. "I'm going to ask questions. Then I'm going to let go of your mouth and you'll answer. Do not scream, just answer."

Her nostrils were working overtime and I made sure I pressed my fingers even harder into her cheeks to make me seem more scary. "Nod if you understand."

Her hair no longer smelled of shampoo: I could only smell coffee breath as she gave a succession of jerky nods into my hands.

Taking a slow, deep breath, I calmed down and whispered into her ear once more. "Why are you talking to your dad about me? Who is coming?"

I released my grip from her mouth a little so she could suck in air, but still gripped her hair. I felt her damp breath between my fingers. "I can explain, please, just let me breathe—"

Both of us heard the noise of a truck approaching as it labored up the muddy track.

"Oh, God, oh, please, Nick, please just stay in here. It's dangerous, I'll explain later, please."

I hit the light and it started to flicker above us as I grabbed the weapon from the shelf, ripped the plastic from the bolt, and rammed the two bundles of ready rounds into my pockets.

She was still begging as the engine got louder. "Please stay here, don't leave the room—I'll handle this."

I moved to the exit door. "Fuck you—turn the light off, now!"

The roar of the engine was right on top of the house. I stood at the door with my ear pressed against the corrugated iron.

"Lights!"

She pulled the switch.

27

I eased the door open a couple of inches. With one eye pressed against the gap, I looked to the right, toward the front of the house. I couldn't see a truck, just the glow of headlights bouncing off the porch through the rain.

I slipped through the door and closed it gently behind me, leaving Carrie in the darkness. Turning left, I made for the washing area just as two vehicle doors slammed in quick succession, accompanied by a few overlapping shouts—not aggressive, just communicating. I guessed the language was Spanish, though I couldn't tell from this distance, and didn't really care.

As soon as I'd rounded the corner I set off in a straight line toward the shack in the dead ground, using the house as cover. I didn't look back. With the weapon gripped tightly in my right hand and my left holding down the ready rounds, I just went for it, crouched low, doing my best to keep my footing in the mud and tree stumps in the darkness.

I moved for maybe two hundred wet and muddy yards before risking a glance back. The house was silhouetted in the glow of headlights, and the engine noise had faded. I turned and moved on; another twenty paces and the lights, too, slowly disappeared as I gradually dropped down into the dead ground, heading toward the hut.

Turning right, I ran for the other tree line. The back of my throat was dry and I swallowed constantly, trying to moisten it as I fought to get my breath back. At least I was out of the immediate danger area.

Once I'd gotten about halfway toward the trees I turned right again and started moving up the crest, back toward the house, my Timberlands squelching in the mud and pools of water. I'd been concentrating so hard on what I was doing that I hadn't realized the rain had stopped: it was the racket of the crickets that made me aware.

I slowed when I was maybe a hundred and fifty yards behind the house, and started to move more cautiously, now with the butt of the rifle in my shoulder, placing each foot carefully, keeping my body as low as possible. There was still complete cloud cover, and I felt confident I could get closer.

My angle of view gradually changed. I could see the glow coming from the side bookcase window, not strong enough to reach the ground, and then the area in front of the porch, caught in the headlights of a large 4x4 parked next to the Mazda. On the roof, upside down and strapped on tight, I could see a Gemini, an inflatable rubber boat.

I knew there were tubs in front of me somewhere and I'd be bumping into them soon. Slowing even more, I crouched as low as my legs could bend. The low revs of the engine became audible as I finally reached the rows of white plastic. I got onto my knees and right hand and, with the weapon balanced in my left, moved like a gorilla between the rows. I made three or four movements, then stopped to observe. A small animal rustled nearby and scuttled away between the tubs, which were less than an inch apart. I could hear frenzied scratching on plastic as it ran for its life.

Making sure I didn't get tangled in the irrigation tubes trailing along the ground, I carried on feeling my way through the grass and mud. The noise of the crickets was horrendous, but with luck drowned out any sound I made.

I was starting to get sticky again from a combination of tension and sheer physical effort as I inched forward. The scene on the porch slowly came into focus: I was about eighty yards away and could see two male figures with Carrie. All three were bathed in light and shadow. One man was quite a bit shorter than the other, and all I could see of him was his dark-checked shoulders, on each side of a supporting pillar. He looked as though he had skipped a good few sessions with his personal trainer.

There seemed to be no weapons involved, and I couldn't hear their voices.

Keeping the gun in my left hand and out of the mud, I eased myself down into a firing position between the tubs, making my movements as slow and deliberate as possible. Gloop immediately began to soak into my front.

The safety catch clicked gently as I twisted it to the right and got a blurred sight picture owing to the rain on the lenses.

Carrie's head filled half the optic through a haze of cigarette smoke, with moths fluttering around the light on the wall behind her. I focused on her face, trying to read it. She didn't look scared as she spoke, just serious.

More smoke blew into my sight picture from the left. I panned and picked up the taller of the two men taking another drag of his cigarette before speaking. He was Latino, round-faced, with a crew-cut and rough-looking beard, and wearing a black collarless shirt. I panned down to see muddy green fatigue pants tucked into equally dirty boots. He was quite animated, pointing first at Carrie, then at the shorter man. Something was wrong: I didn't need to lip-read Spanish to know that.

The movements stopped and he looked at Carrie again, expecting some sort of answer. I panned right, onto her. She nodded slowly, as if not too happy with what she was agreeing to, and I followed her as she pulled open the screen door and shouted into the house, "Aaron! Aaron!"

I looked over at the vehicle. Moths, and anything else airborne, were jiggering about in the headlights. It was a GMC, its block shape high off the ground and its bodywork splattered with mud. All the doors were closed and the engine was still running, probably for the air.

The screen door squeaked and slammed shut. I aimed back toward the porch and saw Aaron. There weren't any greetings for him: Carrie just spoke to him for less than a minute, then with a nod he went back into the house, a worried-looking man. Carrie and the other two followed. Black Shirt threw his finished cigarette onto the porch decking. The check-shirted guy carried an aluminum briefcase that I hadn't seen until then. He, too, was looking rough, with a patchy beard over his chubby face. I watched as they passed the bookshelf window, heading toward the computer room. There was nothing else to do now but wait.

All of a sudden, to my left, there was a flash in my peripheral vision. I turned to see the last of a match burning in the dark of the GMC's interior, its yellow light illuminating the two dirt-free semicircles on the windshield.

I brought the weapon back into the aim, and saw a bright red glow from the rear seat. Some long, hard drags were being taken in there. I ran the optic down the side windows of the GMC, but couldn't tell whether or not they were blacked out until another drag was taken. That wasn't long in coming; I couldn't see anything from the side apart from a gentle red triangular glow in the rear door window. It had to be the GMC from the locks. What was the chance of the same VDM? Another long, deep drag illuminated the triangle.

I watched as the cigarette was sucked to death, and the glow disappeared, then I slowly brought my weapon out of the aim, resting it on my forearms to keep it out of the mud. At that moment, the rear door of the GMC farthest from the porch opened and a body stepped out. I slowly lifted the weapon back into the aim, at the top half of a man taking a piss. I recognized the long features and nose, even without the GMC.

This wasn't good, not good at all. The Pizza Man had been at the locks; the locks were on the webcam here. He had been at Charlie's; I was on my way there now. He knew George; George knew about me. No, this definitely wasn't good.

The screen door squeaked, followed immediately by the two guys stepping down from the porch as he jumped back into the truck midflow. The little fat one was still clutching his briefcase. Carrie followed them out but stayed on the porch, hands on hips, and watched as Black Shirt threw what was left of a cigarette into the mud before they both climbed in.

The engine revved and headlights flooded the area

around me as the truck turned. I hugged the ground, waiting for the light to wash over me, then got onto my knees and watched and listened as the engine noise and taillights faded back into the jungle.

Pulling myself out of the mud, I applied Safe and moved toward the house. As I let the screen door slam back into position, I could see Aaron and Carrie both in Luz's room, comforting her in bed. Neither looked around as I went to the fridge and pulled off the black-and-white beach picture of the Pizza Man. The round magnet keeping it in place dropped and rolled across the wooden floor. I stopped, had second thoughts. There had to be a reason for his not wanting to be seen. Could I make the situation worse for myself if I told them, and they told George? Maybe even jeopardize the job altogether?

I found the magnet and replaced the photograph. I took a deep breath, calmed down, and thought business as I headed for the storeroom. The light was on now, and I placed the weapon gently on the cot as Carrie came into the computer room, sat at the PCs, and buried her head in her hands. I closed the door behind her. "Tell me."

She just held her face as if in another time and place as the fans thudded above us. She looked very scared as her face came up to look at me, pointing out toward the porch. "This whole thing is creeping me out—have you any idea how crazy those people are? I hate it when they come, I hate it."

"I can see that, but who are they?"

"They work for my father. They're doing some sort of operation against FARC, on the Bayano somewhere. It's part of Plan Colombia."

She wasn't just scared but physically shocked. Her hands trembled as she brushed her hair back behind her ears. "It's a drugs-surveillance thing . . .

we have the relay board for their communications. It's secure, so it comes through us, then to George. He said to keep it from you for operational security."

"So why did they break OPSEC by coming when I was here?"

"The webcam . . . they're monitoring ships suspected of drug-trafficking on the canal. I was told to close it down before you arrived, but I forgot. Good spy, huh?"

She looked a sorrowful sight, eyes puffed up and red. "Make Daddy proud. It seemed that when I eventually did close it down, it messed up their other communications, something to do with the relay." She pointed to the mass of wires under the tables. "They had to come and fix it. That's what George was telling me when you came in. We didn't want it to get mixed up with the job he's sent you to do—"

"Hold on—your dad sent me?"

"Didn't you know? He's controlling both operations. Nick, you must believe me, this really is the first time we've done anything like this."

I moved from pissed-off to depressed very quickly. It was just like old times. I sat in the other chair as she sniffled herself back to normality. Aaron came into the room, his eyes darting between the two of us, trying to assess the situation.

She looked up at him, eyes red, wet, and swollen. "I've told him," she said. "I've told him everything."

Aaron looked at me and sighed. "I've always hated this. I told her not to get involved." It was as if he was talking to me about our child.

He turned his attention to Carrie. "George should never have gotten you into this. It isn't worth it for what you want, Carrie. There has to be another way." This was anger, his lips were wet, but it didn't last long. Taking two paces forward, he threw his arms around her, stroking her head when she laid it against his stomach, making soothing sounds, just as I imagined he'd done with Luz and I used to do with Kelly.

I stood up and walked back into the living room, following my own mud trail back toward the porch. The screen door squeaked open and I joined the mosquitoes by the wall light as I threw the pillows onto the floor and started untying the hammock, feeling quite sorry for both of them, and Luz.

I was very clear about what was happening—a total gangfuck. Everything she'd said would have made sense, if it weren't for the Pizza Man. If he had seen Aaron at the locks, or even the Mazda, it made sense why he'd bolted so quickly: if Aaron and Carrie didn't know he was on the ground, then of course he didn't want to be seen by them. I was tempted to tell her, to pump her for more information on him, but no. That would stay in my pocket in case I needed it—especially as there was still the question of his going to Charlie's that I couldn't work out.

I undid the knot at the end attached to the hook in the wall and let it fall, then started on the thick rope wrapped around one of the porch's supports. The other tie fell to the floor, and I left it and stepped off into the mud.

What now?

I opened up the back of the Mazda and saw in the light from the porch that everything had been packed into an old canvas bag. I dragged out the blue towrope, which reeked of gas, and walked back toward the house.

I still hadn't answered the question: What now?

I stepped up onto the porch and peered through the screen into the house. Aaron couldn't be seen but Carrie was still in the director's chair, bent over, arms on her thighs, studying the floor. I watched her for a few moments as she rubbed her hair before dabbing her eyes.

As I bent down to gather up the hammock I realized what I was going to do about it. Nothing. Absolutely nothing. I didn't have the luxury of doing anything other than I'd come here to do: keep Kelly alive.

I had to keep mission-oriented; that was the only thing I had to concentrate on. Forget everything else. My sole focus had to be keeping the Yes Man happy: he was the one who could fuck life up bigtime for both of us, not whatever was going on down here.

I cut away from all extraneous thoughts and mentally confirmed what my whole life should have been about since Sunday. The mission: to kill Michael Choi. The mission: to kill Michael Choi.

With the hammock and tow-rope gathered in my arms I pulled the screen door open just as Aaron tiptoed out of Luz's darkened bedroom and gently closed the door. He put his hands together against the side of his face as he walked toward me.

I kept my voice low. "Listen, I didn't know anything about Carrie, her dad, or any of the other stuff until today. I'm sorry if life is shit, but I've come to do a job and I still need to be taken to do it."

He rubbed his face so hard that the bristles rasped, and drew a long, deep breath. "You know why she's doing this, right?"

I nodded, shrugged, tried to get out of it, and failed. "Something to do with a passport, something like that?"

"You got it. But you know what? I think she would have done it anyway. No matter how much she hates to admit it, she's just like George, takes the Stars and Stripes gig to the max, know what I mean?"

He placed a hand on my shoulder and forced a smile. I nodded, not really having a clue what he was going on about, and not really wanting to explore it further.

There was a pause before he withdrew his hand and held up his wrist to show his watch. "Anything you need?" He was right: it was nearly ten o'clock, time to go.

"There is. I put all of that explosive from the hut in one of your tubs, and I've left it down there."

"You taking it with you?"

I nodded.

He took another of his deep breaths, trying hard not to ask why. It seemed there were other things apart from the move north that Carrie didn't talk to him about.

"Okay, gimme five."

We parted, him to his bedroom and me back to the storeroom. Carrie was still sitting on the director's chair, her elbows on the desk, cradling her head. I left her to it and packed the hammock and other stuff into the bergen.

The screen door squeaked and slammed as Aaron left to collect the device. Remembering that I still needed dry clothes, I went back to the computer room. "Carrie?" There was no reply. "Carrie?"

She slowly lifted her head as I walked into the room, not looking too good, eyes and cheeks red. Things had changed: I felt sorry for her now.

"I need some more clothes." I pulled at my mud-covered sweatshirt. "A complete set of stuff."

It seemed to take her a second to understand what I was saying. "Oh, right." She stood up. "I'll, um . . ." She coughed to clear her throat as she left the room. "Sure."

I rummaged around under the cot and shelves for

more thin plastic blanket wrappers. With several ripped ones in my hands, I picked up the rifle and checked chamber by pulling the bolt up and back slightly to expose the brass case and head of the round. I already knew it was there, but it made me feel better to see it and know that when I fired I wouldn't just hear a dead man's click. Satisfied, I swathed the muzzle and working parts in plastic again, completing the seal with tape before checking that the muzzle protection was still intact.

Carrie reappeared with a thick brown cotton shirt and matching canvas pants. She never seemed to provide socks or underwear; maybe Aaron didn't use them. They went into the protective plastic in the bergen, which I then closed down with the other two mosquito nets on top.

She watched as I checked my leg. The bandage was covered with mud but that didn't matter; the important thing was that there was no sign of leakage.

I gave my pants a good squirt of deet before tucking them into my very smelly socks, then doused them as well. Once I'd finished the front I got to work on my forearms, my hands, all around my neck and my head, even getting it into my hair. I wanted to be armor-plated with the stuff, and I'd go on replenishing it all the time I was on the ground. I carried on squirting it over my clothing and rubbing it in. Anywhere that wasn't covered in mud got the treatment. I threw her one of the bottles as she stood, zombie-like. "Do my back, will you?"

It seemed to snap her out of her trance. She started rubbing it roughly into my sweatshirt. "I'm taking you."

"What?"

"It's my job, I'll take you. I'm the one who wants the passport."

I nodded. I didn't want to get involved and talk more about it. We had done enough of that. All I wanted now was the lift.

The rubbing stopped. "We ought to be going."

The half-used bottle appeared over my shoulder. "But first I want to tuck my child in."

She walked out, and I packed all the deet bottles in the top flap and started to wrap the weapon in the blanket for protection, not too sure if I was looking forward to the ride or not.

28

The atmosphere was strained as Carrie and I shook around in the cab, following the beam as it bounced off the jungle around us. The wet foliage shone as if it had been coated with varnish.

For several miles her eyes had been fixed on the section of track carved out by the lights, trying to negotiate the ruts that rocked us rhythmically from side to side. I let my head wobble but kept a hand on the rifle between my knees to protect the zero.

We eventually emerged from the forest and passed through the valley of dead trees. At last she cleared her throat. "After all that we have said to each other . . . this doesn't need to change things, Nick."

"Yeah, well, we all make mistakes."

"No, Nick, it wasn't a mistake, I need you to believe that. What you said means something. I'll never abuse that trust."

"Is that why you told your dad I had a fever?"

"Like I said, no one ever need know. I don't lie, Nick."

"Thanks."

"Am I forgiven?" She glanced at me to check that

she really was, before her eyes darted back to the track as we tilted left.

"Can't your dad just give Luz a passport? Surely he can sort that out?"

"Sure he can, I know that. But he knows I'm desperate. I've never gotten anything from him for free. I always had to earn it first. It was only going to be for locating the relay board. Then it got worse, some food and stores, a few gallons of premium. They didn't want to go to Chepo in case they got recognized, I suppose. . . . Then you came along."

I sat and watched her as her eyes concentrated on the driving but her mind was elsewhere.

"Aaron was right. He told me that once it started it'd never stop, he'd keep using me. You know what? Maybe he's right, but as soon as the passport comes we'll be out of here."

"You'll go to your mother's? Boston?"

"She's got a house in Marblehead, on the coast. I have a job waiting at MIT and Luz is set for school."

"What's the score with your dad? I can't work out if you hate him, love him, or what."

"I can't either. Then, sometimes, I even get a little jealous of the attention he gives Luz, and at others I think he only does it to keep an eye on me."

Still concentrating on the road, it seemed it was her turn to open up. "I never knew who he really was, what he really did. He just went away, came back sometimes with something he'd pick up for me last minute, normally something totally unsuitable. Then he left again as soon as I'd gotten used to his being around. Mom just waited till I'd gone to college and she left, too. He's a cold man, but still my father."

I tapped the muzzle. "He gave you this."

She turned for a second and a fleeting smile came to her lips.

"His way of saying he loves you, maybe?"

"Maybe, but maybe it was only because he forgot to pack it when leaving the Zone after his tour."

"Aaron said you're very much like him—something about stars and stripes?"

She laughed: this was obviously well-trodden ground.

"Aaron only thinks that because, for once, I agree with George on what's gone wrong in this country. Aaron's too stubborn to see it, that's why he wants to stay. He's hoping for a brighter future but it ain't coming on its own. The Zone as he remembers it has gone. We, America, let that happen. It's disgusting."

"You guys could come back if the canal was threatened. Isn't there a clause in the treaty, something in the small print?"

"Oh, yeah, sure—like the Russians are going to invade. I'm not planning my future around it."

"What's the big deal? After all, you guys gave the thing back, didn't you?"

She bristled. "No—Carter did."

We nearly hit the roof as the truck bounced out of a rut deeper than it had looked.

"We built the canal, we built the country. Geographically, it's virtually part of the U.S. coastline, for Christ's sake. People like Lulu died for it—and that peanut-munching inadequate threw it away like a Kleenex." She paused. "Do you really want to know why it's such a big deal?"

I nodded. "Why not?"

"Okay, there are two major problems to address." Her right index finger sprang upward from the bucking steering wheel. "SOUTHCOM's drugs interdiction and eradication capability is now about a third of what it used to be before 'ninety-nine. In short, it's history. People like Charlie and FARC are getting a free run. Unless action is taken, and quickly, we lose the drug war forever. If you think there's a problem now, watch this space." She shook her head in disbelief at her countrymen's folly. "You know what I mean, don't you?"

I did. I'd gotten to know quite a few of the victims these last few months.

"So, the only answer was what Clinton did—throw a billion plus at Plan Colombia, with troops, hardware, all to kick ass down there. You know what Plan Colombia is, right? Of course, stupid, sorry."

The suspension creaked and things rattled under the truck as she fought with the wheel. "Without the Zone, we had no alternative but to project farther south, take the fight to them in their backyard."

I was studying the red glow on the side of her face as she concentrated on the track.

"But it ain't going to work. No way. We're just getting dragged into a long, costly war down there that's going to have little impact on the drug trade."

Her eyes, still fixed on the way ahead, gleamed with conviction. Her father would have been proud of her, I was sure.

"I'm telling you, we're getting pulled into their civil war instead of fighting drugs. Soon it'll spread into Venezuela, Ecuador, and all the rest. This is Vietnam the Sequel. Because we have given away the Zone, we have created a situation where we now need it more than ever. Crazy, no?"

It made sense to me. "Otherwise it'll be like launching the D-Day invasion of France from New York?"

She gave me a smile of approval, between fighting the ruts.

"Panama's going to be needed as a forward operating area from which to project our forces, as well as a buffer to stop the conflict's spreading into Central America. What Clinton has done is a very dangerous alternative, but without the Zone and what it stands for, he had no choice."

We lapsed into silence again as she negotiated the last bit of track and we finally hit the road to Chepo.

"And the most scary, fucked-up thing of all is that China now runs the canal. When we left, it created a power vacuum that China's filling. Can you imagine it? Without one shot being fired, Communist China is in control of one of the United States's most important trade routes, in *our* backyard. Not only that, we actually let the very country that could back FARC in the war take control."

I could see now what Aaron had been going on about. "Come on, it's just a Hong Kong firm who got the contract. They run ports worldwide."

Her jaw tightened as she gritted her teeth. "Oh, yeah? Well, ten percent of it is owned by Beijing—they operate the ports at each end of the canal and some of our old military locations. In effect, we've got Communist China controlling fourteen percent of *all* U.S. trade, Nick—can you believe we let that happen? A country that openly calls the U.S. its number one enemy. Since 1919 they have recognized the importance of the canal."

She shook her head bitterly. "Aaron's right, I do agree with George, even though his politics have always been to the right of Attila the Hun."

I was starting to see her point. I'd never look at Dover docks in quite the same way again.

"Charlie was one of the group instrumental in pushing the Chinese deal. I wonder what his kickback was—freedom to use the docks for business? And you know what? Hardly anyone knows up north—the handover deadline just sort of sneaked up on America. And Clinton? He didn't do a thing."

She didn't seem too keen on Democrat presidents.

"The threat to the U.S. is real, Nick. The hard reality is that we're getting dragged into a South American war because we gave away the canal to China. The Chinese, not us, are now sitting on one of the world's most important trade routes—and they haven't paid a cent for the privilege. It's our bat and ball they're playing with, for Christ's sake."

I started to see pinholes of light penetrating the blackness ahead: we were approaching Chepo. I gave her a long, hard look, trying to figure her out as we rumbled over the gravel, and she kept glancing rapidly over at me, waiting for some kind of response.

"I guess this is where I fit in," I said. "I'm here to stop Charlie handing over a missile guidance system to FARC so they can't use it against U.S. helicopters in Colombia."

"Hey, so you're one of the good guys." She'd started smiling again.

"That's not the way it feels." I hesitated. "Your dad wants me to kill Charlie's son."

She jolted the truck to a halt on the gravel, the engine turning over erratically. I could now see her full face in red shadow. I couldn't make out whether the look in her eyes was shock or disgust. Maybe it was both. It soon became a mixture of confusion and the realization that I had been as economical with the truth as she had.

"I couldn't tell you because of OPSEC." I tried to fight it but couldn't, the lid was still completely off. "And also because I'm ashamed. But I've still got to do it. I'm desperate, just like you." I glanced out at the expanse of muddy, water-filled potholes caught in the headlights. "His name is Michael. Aaron teaches him at the university."

She slumped in her seat. "The locks . . . he told me about—"

"That's right, he's just a few years older than Luz. "

She didn't respond. Her eyes joined mine, facing forward and fixed on the tunnel of light.

"So, now you have the misfortune of knowing all that I know."

Still nothing. It was time for me to shut up and just look out at the illuminated mud and gravel as the truck moved off. Then I turned and watched as she pursed her lips, shook her head, and drove as if she was on autopilot.

29

We'd hardly exchanged another word as we bounced around in the cab for the next couple of hours.

I finished getting the bergen out of the back of the truck and pulled on the leaf sight as far as it would go to check that the battle sights were set at 400.

"Nick?"

I leaned down to her half-open window. Bathed by the red glow of the dash, she was moving the blanket I'd thrown from the weapon, which had landed on the shift.

"Michael is dying in order to save hundreds, maybe thousands of lives. It's the only way I can deal with it. Maybe it'll work for you."

I nodded, concentrating more on protecting the zero than trying to justify myself. Charlie should be taking the heat, not his boy.

"It's certainly going to save one, Nick. One that you love very much, I know. Sometimes we have to do the wrong thing for the right reasons, no?" She held my gaze for another couple of seconds, then glanced down at the shift. I wondered if she was going to look up again, but she chose Drive, and hit the gas.

I stood and watched the red taillights fade into the darkness, then waited the three minutes or so it would take for my night vision to start kicking in. When I could see where I was putting my feet, I tied the gollock around my waist, checked for the hundredth time that the map and docs were still secure in my leg pockets, and felt for the Silva compass that hung around my neck under my T-shirt. Then I shouldered my bergen, heaved the tub on top, and held it in place with a straight arm, my left hand gripping the handle. With the rifle in my right, I moved down to the road junction, then headed west toward the house.

I soon broke out in a sweat under the weight of the load, and could taste the bitterness of deet as it ran into my mouth. Only three and a half hours of darkness remained, by the end of which I needed to be ready at the gate. As soon as it was light enough to see what I was doing, I needed to place the device and find a firing position in the opposite tree line. It was pointless trying to rig it up in darkness; I'd spend more time rectifying my mistakes at first light than if I'd just done it then in the first place.

The plan was so simple that as I pushed on, listening and looking for vehicles, there wasn't much to think about until I got there. My mind was free to roam, but I wasn't going to allow that. It was time for nothing else but the mission.

After a few changes of arm supporting the weight of the tub, I was finally at the gates. Keeping over to the right, in cover, I dumped the tub while I caught my breath. Ground-mounted perimeter lights illuminated the walls, making it look even more like a hotel. When eventually I looked through the railings of the gate, the fountain was still lit, and I could see the glint of light on a number of vehicles parked haphazardly in the drive beyond it. The gold side windows of the Lexus winked back at me.

The house was asleep, no light shining out, apart from the enormous chandelier, which sparkled through a large window that I took to be above the main entrance.

There wasn't going to be any finesse about this device, but it had to be set very precisely. As the vehicle moved through the gates, the force of the shaped charge had to be directed exactly where I wanted it. I would also have to make sure it was well camouflaged with the mozzie net.

I went back and collected the tub, then stumbled along the animal track that ran between the wall and the canopy. The wall ran out after just seven or eight yards, and at that point I moved a few feet back into the trees to wait for first light. There was no need to go farther. Besides, some of Diego's traps might still be set.

Keeping the bergen on my back, I sat on the tub with the weapon across my legs to protect the zero, the plastic protection rustling gently each time I moved. I was just willing the mozzies to try to take a bite out of me now I was 95 percent pure deet, but they seemed to know better.

I changed my mind about keeping the bergen on. It wasn't serving any purpose and, besides, I wanted water from the side pouch. As I took slow sips I unstuck the T-shirt from my itchy chigger rash and gazed enviously at the house with its air-conditioning and refrigerators working overtime.

The occasional animal made a noise in the jungle as the mozzies still circled in holding patterns around me, sounding like kamikaze planes heading for my face before changing course after a sniff of what I had waiting for them.

Once I'd put the water back into the bergen I gave myself another rubdown with the deet, just in case they discovered a gap in the defenses. The tiny bits of leaf and bark on my hands scrubbed against my face and stubble.

I sat, scratched my back, felt the fur on my teeth with my tongue, and wished I'd hit the fire pressel three times when I'd had the chance.

About forty-five boring minutes later I began to see an arc of pale light rising above the tree line. It was going to be a dull one. The birds took their cue to get noisy, and the howler monkeys on the other side of the house woke up the rest of the jungle—as if the crickets ever slept.

I began to make out a low mist lying on the mud of the clearing and, higher up, black and gray cloud cover. It would be good for me if the sky stayed overcast: it meant no chance of sunlight reflecting off the objective lens.

Another ten minutes and light was penetrating the canopy. I could just see my feet. It was time to start rigging the device.

After rechecking the score marks on the sight, and that the battle sights were pulled back to 400, the gear went back on and I moved slowly toward the gate. I dropped the tub and bergen about two yards short of it, laying the weapon on the ground and not against the wall to avoid any chance of its falling.

It didn't take long to find a tree of the right height and structure to take the charge—there were enough of them about. I took the nylon tow-rope out of the top flap pouch of the bergen, tied one end of it to the tub's handle, and gripped the other between my teeth.

The taste of gasoline nearly made me gag while I looked up and worked out how to climb my chosen tree. My calf was throbbing painfully.

It was a noisy ascent but a time comes when you just have to get on with it, and now was the moment, before everybody in the house began to stir. Trapped water fell onto my head and I was drenched again by the time I reached my vantage point.

At last I could just see over the wall toward the house, and to the other tree line to my right, where the bottom couple of feet of the trunks were still shrouded in mist. My firing point was going to be somewhere along that tree line; it was maybe 300 yards away and the tub should be easy enough to find from that distance with the optic. I thought about placing a large leaf or two on top of the wall as a marker to guide me in, but it was too risky. If I could see it, so could anyone driving toward the gate. I had to assume they were tuned in, and that anything unusual would be treated with suspicion. I'd just have to open my eyes and find it once I got into position.

I was still working out how I was going to strap the tub in position when I heard the noise of an engine start up in the driveway. I turned my head to look toward the source. The only things moving were my eyes and the dribble from the sides of my rope-filled mouth.

It was impossible to make out what was happening. There were no lights from any of the vehicles, just the low, gentle sound of an engine turning over.

I had to act. This might be the only chance I got.

I opened my mouth to release the rope, and almost fell as I scrambled down the trunk. Adrenaline surged as I grabbed the weapon and ran back to the end of the wall, frantically tearing at the plastic, trying to check the score marks, feeling for the ready rounds, feeling for my docs.

I dropped onto my right knee, brought the weapon up, and looked through the optic, gulping in deep breaths to oxygenate me for the shot, wiping the deet sweat from my eyes before removing the safety.

An oldish guy moved around in the low light, the tip of a cigarette glowing in his mouth. He was wearing flip-flops, athletic shorts, and a badly ripped dark polo shirt, and was wiping the night's rain and condensation off the sleek black Lexus with a polishing cloth. The engine must be running for the A.C., which meant he was expecting passengers soon.

I sat back on my right foot and braced my left elbow on my left knee, the soft bit just above the elbow joint jammed into the kneecap, butt pulled firmly into the shoulder. Then I checked my field of view into the killing ground.

There was no pain in my leg now, no feeling anywhere as I prepared myself mentally, visualizing the target coming from the front door, heading for either the rear or front of the Lexus.

Condensation formed on the lens.

I kept the weapon in the aim and, with both eyes on the killing ground, rubbed it clear with my right thumb and T-shirt cuff. All the time, taking slow, deep, controlled breaths, I was hoping it was going to kick off, and at the same time hoping that it wouldn't until I was in a better position.

The old guy made his way conscientiously along the Lexus with his cloth. Then the two huge doors at the front of the house opened and I was aiming into a body, the chandelier backlighting him perfectly. The post sight was in the middle of a white, short-sleeved shirt-and-tie, one of the BG, either Robert or

Ross, whichever had gone out for the drinks. He was standing in the door frame, talking on his Nokia and checking progress on the Lexus.

My heart rate soared, then training kicked back in: I controlled my breathing and my pulse started to drop; I blocked out everything around me, closing down into my own little world. Nothing else existed, apart from what I could see through the optic.

The BG disappeared back into the house but the front door was still open. I waited in the aim, hearing—feeling—the pulse in my neck, taking controlled breaths, oxygenating my body. If I felt any emotion, it was only relief that it might soon be over and done with.

There he was. Michael stepped outside, green on blue, carrying a daypack, smiling, talking with Robert and Ross on either side of him. I got the post on him, center of the trunk, got it on his sternum, took first pressure.

Shit . . . A white shirt moved between us.

Keeping the pressure, I followed the group. I got part of his face, still smiling, chatting animatedly. Not good enough, too small a target.

Then someone else, a dark gray suit, blocked my view completely. This wasn't going to work—too late, too many bodies blocking.

They were at the car. *Shit, shit, shit* . . .

I released first pressure, ducked back behind the wall, and ran for the gate while applying Safe. No time to think, just to do. Inside my head I was going apeshit. *Opportunity target! Opportunity target!*

Fuck the off-route mine now, I just wanted an explosion. Still screaming silently at myself, I grabbed the tub.

There was a strange, empty feeling in my stomach, the sort I used to have as a kid running scared from something, wishing my legs could go as fast as my head wanted them to.

Gasping for air, I reached the gate and dropped the tub against the wall, the blue rope still attached, the rest trailing behind.

Opportunity target, opportunity target!

The engine note of the Lexus changed as the car started down the drive toward me. It got louder as I picked up the bergen and sprinted along the edge of the trees by the road.

It was time to hide. I launched myself into the foliage at a point about thirty yards from the gate.

Fuck, too near to the device . . .

I got into a firing position in the mud, using the bergen just like the mound, my breathing all over the place.

The electric whine of the motor opening the gates drowned out the noise of the Lexus as it came nearer and then stopped.

I was too low, I had no muzzle clearance.

I jumped up in a semi-squat, grabbing air, legs apart to steady myself, butt of the rifle in my shoulder as I pulled and twisted to get the fucking stupid safety off.

I could see the wraparound sunglasses of the two white-shirts in front as we all waited for the gates to open, and I knew I was exposed to them. I kept as low as I could, my chest heaving up and down as the Lexus finally started to roll forward.

Just twenty feet to go.

The car stopped so suddenly the rear bucked up on its suspension.

Shit! I stopped breathing and fixed both eyes on the tub. I brought the weapon up to refocus into the optic, and took first pressure.

The engine went high-pitched into reverse and I

saw the blurry whiteness of the tub and the post clear and sharp in the middle of it, then fired.

I dropped the weapon as I hit the floor, screaming to myself as the shock wave surged over me. It felt like I'd been freefalling at 100 m.p.h. and was suddenly stopped by a giant hand in midair, but my insides kept going.

Grabbing the rifle, I reloaded and got to my feet, checking the battle sight. There was no time to watch out for the debris falling from the sky: I had to confirm he was dead.

The car had been pushed back six or seven yards on the pavement. I started toward the dustcloud as shattered masonry and bits of jungle fell back to earth, butt in the shoulder, ears ringing, vision blurred, my whole body shaking. Rubble and twisted ironwork lay where part of the right-hand wall and gates had once stood.

I closed in on the mangled wreck, running in a semi-stoop, and took up a position by the remains of the wall just forward of a smoldering, man-sized crater. Chunks of brick rained down on the car. The once immaculate Lexus now looked like a stock car, smashed, beaten, its side windows missing, the windshield safety glass shattered and buckled.

I took aim with the battle sights through the driver's window. The first round thudded into the bloodstained white-shirt who was slumped but recovering over the steering wheel.

"Two!"

Maintaining the weapon in the shoulder and supported by my left hand, I reloaded and took another shot into the second slumped, bloodstained white-shirt on the passenger side.

"Three!"

With only four I had to remember my rounds fired;

I was crap at it and counting out loud was the only way for me.

Only smaller fragments of leaf and tree floated from the sky now, landing on the vehicle and pavement all around me as I moved in, weapon up, toward the rear door. The angle changed: I saw two slumped bodies covered in shattered glass: one the green T-shirt and blue jeans, the other the dark gray suit. I closed in. The suit was Charlie. I hoped he was alive.

30

The target was more or less collapsed in the footwell, with his dad down on the seat draped over him. Both were badly shaken, but alive. There was some coughing from Charlie and I could see the target moving.

Mustn't hit Charlie . . .

I took another couple of steps to get me right up against the door and rammed the weapon inside with my face through the window gap. The muzzle was no more than two inches from the target's bloody, glass-covered, and confused head.

Bizarrely, the air conditioner was still blowing, and a Spanish voice jabbered on the radio as the target moaned and groaned, pushing his father off him. His eyes were closed; I could see fragments of glass trapped in his eyebrows.

I felt the second pressure on my finger pad, but it was refusing to squeeze further. Something was holding me back.

Fuck, get on with it!

The muzzle followed his head as it moved about,

turning over onto his side. It was now virtually in his ear. I moved it up a little, to the tip.

It wasn't happening, my finger wouldn't move. What the fuck was the matter with me?

COME ON, DO IT! DO IT!

I couldn't, and in that instant I knew why. A stab of fear ripped through my body.

My brain filtered out almost everything, but it let in the shouts; I turned to see partly dressed men starting to pour from the house, carrying weapons.

I withdrew the rifle, reached in the front, and pulled the Nokia off the BG's belt. Then I wrenched open the buckled metal and seized a fistful of suit. I dragged a fucked-up Charlie onto the pavement, virtually running with him to the other side of what was left of the wall. "Move! Move!"

I kicked him to his knees and he fell forward onto his hands. Stepping back out of grab range, I aimed at his head. "Can you hear me?"

The shouts were getting nearer. I kicked him. "The missile guidance system, make sure—"

"What is wrong with you people?" He coughed as blood dribbled from his chin, not lifting his head as he shouted back angrily, without a trace of fear. "It's been delivered—last night! You have the launch control system—you have everything! The Sunburn is complete! What more do you want?"

"Delivered? This is about getting it delivered?"

He looked up at me, staring along the barrel that moved up and down as we both fought for breath.

"Last night! You people use my son to threaten me, demanding it by tomorrow night, you get it and still—" As the blood ran down his neck he saw my confusion. "Don't you people know what each other is doing?"

"Tuesday—the guy in the pink Hawaiian shirt. He was here—has he got it?"

"Of course!"

"Why should I believe you?"

"I don't care what you believe. The deal is done, yet you still threaten my family . . . Remember the condition—no Panamanian targets. Why is it still here? You said it would move straight to Colombia—not use it here. Do you know who I am? Do you know what I can do to you?"

"Fatherrrrr!" Michael had seen us and his eyes widened. "Don't kill him—please don't kill him. Please!"

Charlie yelled something in Spanish, probably telling him to run, then fixed his glare on me once more. There was not a flicker of fear in his eyes. "Well, Englishman, what now? You already have what you came here for."

I took a swing with the rifle butt and got him on the side of the neck. He curled into a ball of pain as I turned and ran along the tree line, back toward the bergen. I grabbed it in my spare hand, looked back, and saw Michael limping toward his dad as people and vehicles converged.

That was the problem. Michael was real people. He was a kid with a life, not one of the shadow people I was used to, the sort of target I'd never thought twice about killing.

I hurled myself into the jungle, crashing through wait-a-while, not caring about sign. I just wanted to get my ass out of here and into the wall of green.

Barbs tore into my skin and my throat was so parched it hurt to take a breath. But none of that mattered: the only thing that did was getting away.

The commotion behind me gradually faded, soaked up by the jungle as I penetrated deeper—but I knew it wouldn't be long before they got organized and came in after me.

There was automatic fire. The follow-up was much quicker than I'd expected: they were firing blindly, hoping to zap me as I ran. That didn't bother me, the trees would take the brunt. The only important thing was whether or not they were tracking me.

I pulled out my compass, checked, and headed east for about twenty yards, toward the loop, taking my time now, trying not to leave upturned leaves or broken cobwebs in my wake. Then I turned north, then west, doubling back on myself but off to the side of my original track. After five or six yards, I stopped, looked around for a thick bush, and wormed my way into it.

Squatting on my bergen, butt in the shoulder, safety off, I fought for breath. If they were tracking, they would pass right to left, seven or eight yards in front as they followed my sign. The rule about being chased in the jungle, learned the hard way by far better soldiers than me, was that when the enemy are coming fast you've got to sidestep and creep away. Don't keep on running, because they'll just keep on following.

Slowly peeling three rounds from one of the ready rounds, I pulled back the bolt. The bearing surfaces glided smoothly over each other as I caught the round it was about to eject, then fed the four rounds slowly and deliberately back into the mag before pushing the bolt home.

I sat, watched, and listened as I got out the blood-smeared cell phone. No matter what was going on down here—stop delivery, guarantee delivery, whatever—I'd failed to do what the Yes Man had sent me here for, and I knew what that meant. I had to make a call.

There was no signal, but I tried the number anyway, just in case, my finger covering the tiny speaker hole that sent out the touch tone. Nothing.

Baby-G said it was 7:03. I played with the phone, found Vibrate, and put it away again.

Shit, shit, shit. The pins and needles were returning. I had the helpless feeling that Carrie had described, that awful emptiness when you think you've lost someone and are trying desperately to find them. *Shit, not here, not now . . .*

A frenzied exchange in Spanish brought me back to the real world. They were close.

There were more shouts from under the canopy—but were they following me? I sat motionless as seconds, and then whole minutes, ticked by.

Nearly seven-fifteen. She'll be getting up soon for school . . .

I had fucked up, I had to accept that. But what was more important now, at this very moment, was getting a signal on the cell phone, and that meant going back uphill toward the house, where I'd seen it used.

There was the odd resonant yell that sounded like a howler monkey, but I saw no one. Then there was movement to my front, the crashing of foliage as they got closer. But they weren't tracking: it sounded like too much of a gangfuck for that. I held my breath, butt in the shoulder, pad on the trigger, as they stopped on my trail.

Sweat dripped off my face as three voices babbled at warp speed, maybe deciding which direction to take. I could hear their M-16s, that plastic, almost toylike sound as they moved them in their hands, or dropped a butt onto the toecap of a boot.

A burst of automatic fire went off in the distance and my three seemed to decide to go back the way they'd come. They'd obviously had enough of this jungle lark.

Anyone tracking me, even if they'd lost my sign

and had had to cast out to find it, would have gone past my position by now. Even with my trying to cut down on sign, a blind man could have followed the highway I'd made if he'd known what he was feeling for.

I got just short of the edge of the tree line, all the time checking the signal bars on the cell phone. Still nothing.

I heard the heavy revs of one of the bulldozers and the squeal of its tracks. Moving forward cautiously, I saw plumes of black diesel smoke billow from the vertical exhaust as it lumbered toward the gate. Beyond it, the front of the house was a frenzy of people. Bodies with weapons shouted at each other in confusion as vehicles moved up and down the road.

I moved back into the wall of green, applied Safe, and started checking up at the canopy as I unraveled the string on the weapon to make a sling. I found a suitable tree about six yards in: it would have a good view of the house, looked easy to climb, and the branches were strong enough to support my weight. I took out the strapping that was going to be my seat, got the bergen on my back, slung the weapon over my shoulder, and started to clamber up as engines revved and people shouted out in the open ground.

When I was about twenty feet up I tried the Nokia again, and this time I got four bars.

Fastening the straps between two strong branches, I hooked the bergen over another next to them, settled into the seat facing the house, then spread one of the mozzie nets over me before closing down the bergen in case I had to buy out.

I was going to be here for a while, until things had quietened down, so the net had to be hung out onto branches so it wasn't clinging to me, and tucked under to cover the straps. I needed to hide my shape, shine, shadow, silhouette, and movement; that wouldn't happen if I didn't spread it out a bit to prevent myself looking like a man in a tree with a mosquito net over him. Finally, cradling the weapon across my legs, I calmed myself down as I hit the keypad.

Not giving him time to think or talk, I got to him in a loud whisper. "It's me—Nick. Don't talk, just listen. . . ."

31

"Josh, just listen. Get her to safety, do it now. I've fucked up big-time. Get her away somewhere safe, she needs to be where no one can get at her. I'll call in a few days, got it? Got it?"

There was a pause.

"Josh?"

"Fuck you! Fuck you! When does this stop? You're playing with a kid's life again. Fuck you!"

The line went dead. He'd hung up. But I knew he'd take this seriously. The last time I'd fucked up and put kids in danger, they'd been his own.

I felt a flood of relief as I removed the battery before the cell phone went back in my pocket. I didn't want to be traced from the signal.

Tasting the bitter deet as sweat ran into my mouth, I watched the commotion outside the house. I wondered if the police would be up here soon, being given my description, but doubted it. Charlie would want to keep something like this under wraps and, anyway, it wasn't as if the explosion would have disturbed the neighborhood; big bangs would have been a daily occurrence as they cleared the jungle to make way for his house.

I leaned over to the bergen, got out the water, and took a few swigs, feeling better about Kelly now. No matter what Josh thought of me, he'd do the right thing for her. It wasn't the answer, just the best short-term solution I had available.

She and I were still in deep shit. I knew I should have called the Yes Man, explained to him what I thought I knew, and waited it out. That was what I should have done, so why hadn't I? Because a voice in my head was telling me something different.

Charlie had said Sunburn. The Yes Man had sent me here to deal with a missile system that was a threat to U.S. helicopters in Colombia. A ground-to-air missile system. That wasn't Sunburn—Sunburn was surface-to-surface. I remembered reading about the U.S. Navy's worry because their antimissile defenses couldn't defeat it. Sunburn was their number-one threat.

I tried to recall details. It had been in *Time* or *Newsweek*, something like that, last year on the TV at Hampstead . . . it was about ten yards long because I'd visualized being able to fit two end to end in a sub-way car.

What else? I wiped the sweat from my forehead.

Think, think . . .

The Pizza Man . . . He had been at the locks on Tuesday. The locks webcam was part of the relay comms from the house. The Pizza Man's team were monitoring drug movements by FARC. He'd also been at Charlie's house and maybe, if Charlie had told me the truth, he had Sunburn.

I suddenly saw what was happening. George was carrying the fight to the enemy: they'd been monitoring drug shipments through the canal, and now it looked as though they were getting proactive, maybe using Sunburn as a threat to FARC that if they used the canal to ship drugs they'd get taken out.

That still didn't answer why I'd been sent here to stop Charlie delivering a ground-to-air system . . .

The noise of rotor blades clattered over the canopy. I recognized at once the heavy bass *wap wap wap wap*—the unique signature of American Hueys, coming in low. The two helicopters shot past, immediately above me. The massive downwash made my tree sway as they flared into the clearing, then, just feet off the ground, crept toward the front of the house. Mud puddles were blown away, and jungle debris was blasted in all directions. The house was now behind a wall of downdraft and heat haze blasting out from the Hueys' exhausts. A yellow and white Jet Ranger followed behind, like a child trying to keep up with its parents.

The scene before me could have come straight from a Vietnam newsreel. Armed men jumped from the skids and doubled toward the house. It could have been the 101st "Air Assault" screaming down for an attack, except these guys were in jeans.

The Jet Ranger swooped down so close to the front of the house it looked as if it was actually going to ring the doorbell, then it backed away and settled on the pavement near the fountain.

The heat haze from its exhaust blurred my view, but I could see Charlie's family begin to stream toward it from the front door.

I sat and watched through the optic as my former target comforted an older Latino woman, still in her nightgown. On her other side was a bloodstained Charlie, his suit ripped, his arms around her. All three were surrounded by anxious, shouting men with weapons, shepherding them forward. As I followed them with the optic, the post was on Michael's chest for what felt like an age.

I looked at his young, bloody face, which showed

only concern for the woman. He belonged to a different world from his father, George, the Pizza Man, and me. I hoped he'd stay that way.

The air was filled with the roar of churning blades as they were bustled inside the aircraft. The two Hueys were already making height. They dipped their noses, and headed toward the city.

The Jet Ranger lifted from the pavement, and headed in the same direction. There was relative quiet for a few seconds, then somebody barked a series of orders at the men on the ground. They started to sort themselves out. Their mission, I guessed, was to look for me. And this time I had the feeling they'd be better organized.

I sat in my perch, wondering what to do next as truck after truck left the house packed with men and M-16 assault rifles, and returned empty. Checking Baby G, I knew I'd have to start moving out of here soon if I was to make maximum use of daylight.

Last light, Friday. That had been my deadline. Why? And why were the Firm involved in all this? They obviously needed Sunburn in place for tomorrow. I had been bullshitted with the ground-to-air story. I didn't need to know what it was really about because, after the London fuck-up, sending me was their last desperate attempt to get their hands on the complete system.

Last light. Sunset.

Oh, fuck. The *Ocaso* . . .

They were going to hit the cruise liner, real people, thousands of them. It wasn't a drug thing at all . . . why?

Fuck it, why didn't matter. What mattered was that it didn't happen.

But where was I going? What was I going to do with what I thought I knew? Contact the Panamanians? What would they do? Cancel the ship? So what? That would be just another short-term solution. If they couldn't find Sunburn in time, the Pizza Man could just fire the fucking thing at the next ship that came along. Not good enough. I needed an answer.

Go to the U.S. embassy, any embassy? What would they do—report it? Who to? How long would it be before someone picked up the phone to George? And however important he was, there'd be some even more powerful people behind him. There had to be. Even C and the Yes Man were dancing to their tune.

I had to get back to Carrie and Aaron. They were the only two who could help.

Movement outside the house was dwindling: no more vehicles, just one or two bodies walking around, and to the left and out of sight, the sound of a bull-dozer shunting the damaged Lexus off the road.

It was 8:43—time to leave the tree. I unpinned the pants-leg pocket and pulled out the map. I bent my head down so my nose was just six inches from it and the compass on its short cord could rest on its faded surface. It took me thirty seconds to take a bearing, across green, then the white line of the loop road, more green, to the middle of Clayton and the main drag into the city. As to how I got back to the house from there, I'd just play it by ear—anything, just as long as I got back.

Having checked that my map was securely pinned in my pocket, I clambered down with the bergen and weapon, leaving the hiding place to the birds. Once the bergen was on and the string back around the weapon, I headed east toward the loop and Clayton, taking my time, focusing my mind and my vision on the wall of green, butt in the shoulder, safety off, finger straight along the trigger guard, ready to react.

I could have been back in Colombia, looking for DMPs, carefully moving foliage out of the way instead of fighting it, avoiding cobwebs, watching where I stepped to cut noise and sign, stopping, listening, observing before moving into dead ground, checking my bearing, looking in front of me, to my left, to my right, and, just as important, above.

I wanted to travel faster than I was going, desperate to get back to Aaron and Carrie's, but I knew this was the best and safest way to make that happen. They'd no longer be thrashing about or firing blindly, they'd be waiting, spread out, static, for me to bumble into them. Tactical movement in the jungle is so hard. You can never use the easier high ground, never use tracks, never use water features for navigation. The enemy expects you to use them. You've got to stay in the shit, follow a compass bearing, and move slowly. It's worth it: it means you survive.

Sweat laced with deet dripped into my eyes, not just due to the humidity inside this pressure cooker but because of the stress of slow, controlled movement, constantly straining my eyes and ears, and all the time I was thinking: What if they appear to my front? What if they come from the left? What if they fire first and I don't know where the fire is coming from? Contacts in the jungle are so close you can smell their breath.

32

It had taken me two hours to reach the loop, which was a lot quicker than I'd expected.

I dumped the bergen, and unstuck my T-shirt from my back in an attempt to relieve the chigger bites. Then I fingered my wet, greasy hair off my forehead and started moving slowly forward, butt in the shoulder. As I neared the road it was time to apply Safe and get down on the jungle floor. Using elbows and the toes of my Timberlands, I dragged myself to the edge of the canopy. The weapon lay along the right side of my body; I moved it with me, knowing that with the safety firmly on, there was no chance of a negligent discharge.

Last night's rain filled the dips and potholes in the pavement, and the sky was still dull. A motley collection of black, light, and dark gray clouds brooded above me as I looked and listened. If the boys had any sense, they'd have triggers out along the roads, doing a bit of channeling of their own, waiting to see what emerged from the canopy. Even if they did, I had a bearing I had to stick to.

Edging my way forward a little more so that my

head was sticking out from the foliage, I couldn't see anything up the road to the right, apart from the road itself disappearing as it gradually bent left. I turned my head the other way. No more than forty yards away was one of the trucks from the house, a gleaming black Land Cruiser, facing me and parked up on my side of the road. Leaning against the hood was a body with an M-16 in his hands, watching both sides of the bend. He was maybe in his twenties, in jeans, yellow T-shirt, and sneakers, and looking very hot and bored.

My heart pumped. A vehicle was my fast track out of here—but did the body have pals? Were they spaced up and down the road at intervals, or was he on stag, ready to whistle up the rest of the group if he saw anything as they enjoyed a quiet smoke behind the truck?

There was only one way to find out. I inched slowly backward into the tree line, finally getting up onto my hands and knees before crawling to the bergen. Shouldering it, I removed Safe and slowly closed on the truck by paralleling the road, butt in the shoulder, eyes and ears on full power. Each time my foot touched the jungle floor and my weight crushed the leaves, the sound seemed a hundred times louder to me than it really was. Each time a bird took flight I froze in midstride, like a statue.

Twenty painstaking minutes had passed when I was brought to a halt once more. From just on the other side of the wall of green came the sound of his weapon banging against the side of the Land Cruiser. It seemed to be just a little forward and to my right, but no more than about eight yards away.

For a minute or two I stood still and listened. There was no talking, no radio traffic, just the sound of him coughing and spitting onto the pavement.

Then came the noise of metal panels buckling. He was standing on the roof or hood.

I wanted to be in a direct line with the truck, so I moved on a little farther. Then, like a DVD in extreme slow motion, I lowered myself to my knees and applied Safe, the barely audible metallic click sounding in my head as if I'd banged two hammers together. Finally I laid down the weapon and took off my bergen one strap at a time, continually looking in the direction of the truck, knowing that if I moved forward just two yards I would be in plain sight of my new best pal and his M-16.

Once the bergen was on the ground I rested the rifle against it with the barrel sticking up in the air to make it easier to find. Forget the zero, I didn't need it now. Then, very slowly and deliberately, I extracted my gollock. The blade sounded as if it was running along a grinding stone instead of just gliding past the alloy lip of the canvas sheath.

Down onto my stomach once more and with the gollock in my right hand, I edged carefully forward on my toes and elbows, trying to control my erratic breathing as I wiped the deet very slowly out of my eyes.

I neared the edge of the tree line at a point about five yards short of the truck. I could see the nearest front wheel, its chromed alloys stained with mud at the center of a lot of wet, shiny tire.

I edged forward a little more, so slowly it would have made a sloth look like Carl Lewis. Another couple of yards and the bottom of the door sills and the front panel came into view—but in the gap between them and the grass, I saw no legs. Maybe he was sitting inside, maybe, as the buckling sound had suggested, he was standing on the roof. My eyes strained at the tops of their sockets as I tried to look up. I heard the coughing up of phlegm and spitting; he was definitely outside, definitely up there somewhere.

I counted off sixty seconds before moving again. He was going to hear me soon. I didn't even want to swallow: I was so close I could have reached out and touched the wheel.

I still couldn't see him, but he was above me, sitting on the hood, and his heels had started to bang rhythmically against the panel farthest away from me. He must be facing the road.

I knew what I needed to do, but I had to psyche myself to do it. It's never easy to take on somebody like this. Up there was virgin ground, and when I got onto it, I had to react quickly to whatever I found. What if there was another guy in the truck, lying asleep? What if he had heard me and was just waiting for me to pop up?

For the next thirty seconds I revved myself up as mozzies hovered around my face. I checked I was holding the gollock correctly with a good firm grip, and that the blade was facing the right way. I took one last deep breath and sprang to my feet.

He was sitting on the opposite panel with his back to me, weapon on the hood to his left. He heard me, but it was too late to turn. I was already leaping toward him, my thighs striking the edge of the hood, my feet in the air. My right hand swung around and jammed the gollock across his neck; with my left I grabbed the blunt edge of the blade and pulled tight, trying to drag his head onto my chest.

The M-16 scraped over the bodywork as he moved back with me over the panel, my bodyweight starting to pull us both to the ground as his legs kicked and his body twisted. His hands came up to grab my wrists, trying to pull the gollock away, and there was a scream. I squeezed his head against my chest and committed to falling backward off the truck. The air exploded out of me as my back hit the ground and he landed on top of me, and we both cried out with pain.

His hands were around the gollock and he writhed like a madman, kicking out in all directions, banging against the wheel and panel. I opened my legs and wrapped them around his waist, forcing my feet between his legs, then flexed my hips in the air and thrust out my chest, trying to stretch him as I pushed the gollock against his neck. I worked my head down to his left ear. "Ssssh!"

I could feel the gollock in the folds of his skin. The blade must have penetrated his neck a little; I felt warm blood on my hands. I shushed him again and he finally seemed to get the message.

Keeping my hips thrust out, I bent him over me in an arc. He stopped moving, apart from his chest, which heaved up and down. I could still feel his hands against mine as he gripped the blade, but he wasn't struggling anymore. I kept on shushing into his ear.

He didn't say or do anything as I forced him over to the right, pulling back on the blade, murmuring, "Come on, over you go, over you go," not knowing if he could even understand me. Soon my chest was on his head, pressing his face into the leaf litter, and I was able to look behind me for his M-16. It wasn't far away; I got my foot into the sling and pulled it within reach. The safety catch was on, which was good: it meant the weapon was made ready, that there was a round in the chamber, because you can't apply Safe on these things otherwise. I could hardly use it to threaten him if he knew it wasn't ready to fire.

There was snorting from his nostrils as they filled

up with mucus from shock, and the movement of his chest made me feel I was on a trampoline. I still had one of my legs wrapped around him and could feel the weight of his hips on my knee in the mud. The important thing was that apart from his breathing he was motionless—exactly as I would have been in this situation because, like him, I'd be wanting to come out of it alive.

I untangled my leg while keeping the pressure on his neck with the gollock, and the moment I was free I used my left hand to grab the M-16. Then, still keeping the blade against his neck, I slowly got up, shushing gently until I was hovering over him and could take away the blade.

He knew exactly what was happening and did the right thing by keeping absolutely still, his face wincing with pain as the blade ran along his neck. It wasn't cut that much, and they weren't deep gashes. Once free, I jumped back and got the M-16 on him with just my left hand.

I spoke gently. "Hello."

His eyes locked on mine, full of fear. I put the gollock to my lips and gave him another shush, nodding for him to get to his feet. He complied very slowly, keeping his hands up even when I began to steer him into the jungle, back in the direction of my gear. There wasn't really enough time to be doing this because more of his crew might arrive at any minute, but I needed to retrieve Carrie's rifle.

We reached the bergen site and I got him to lie facedown while I hurriedly shouldered the Mosin Nagant and sheathed the gollock. I pulled back the cocking piece on the M-16 just to make sure there was a round in the chamber, and that both of us hadn't fucked up.

He stared at me, straining his eyes to his extreme

left. He was panicking, thinking he had a date with a 5.56mm round at any moment.

I smiled. "Speak English?"

There was a nervous shaking of his head as I moved a few paces toward him. *"Como esta?"*

He nodded shakily as I got the bergen on. *"Bien, bien."*

I put my thumb up and gave him a smile. "Good, good." I wanted to bring him down a bit. People who think they have nothing to lose can be unpredictable—but if he thought he was going to live, he'd do as he was told.

I wasn't really sure what to do with this boy. I didn't want to kill him because it might turn noisy, and there wasn't any time to try to tie him up properly. I didn't want to take him with me, but there wasn't any choice. I couldn't just let him run wild—not this close to the house, anyway. I jerked my head. *"Vamos, vamos."*

He got to his feet and I pointed toward the Land Cruiser with the M-16. *"Camion, vamos, camion."* It wasn't exactly fluent, but he caught my drift and we moved.

At the truck it was simply a matter of shoving the bergen and rifle into the back, then maneuvering him into the passenger footwell with the M-16 muzzle twisted into his shirt and lying across my lap. The safety catch was on automatic, and my right index finger was on the trigger. He got the message that any movement on his part would be suicide.

The key was in the ignition. I turned it and selected Drive, and we were moving. The Land Cruiser was shiny and new, still with its showroom smell, and it gave me a strange sense of security. As we headed for Clayton and the city, I looked down at my passenger and smiled. *"No problema."*

I knew there wouldn't be any problems from him. I'd just seen a wedding band on his finger and knew what he would be thinking about.

The rain was coming early today by the look of the multiple shades of gray, so low now that they were shrouding the rugged, green peaks in the far distance. It wouldn't be long before the sky opened big-time.

What was I to do with my new pal? I couldn't take him through the toll. I might be in a lot of trouble there as it was, if it was now being watched.

We passed one of the Clayton playgrounds between the married quarters and I stopped, got out, and opened his door. He stared down the barrel of the beckoning M-16.

"Run. Run."

He looked at me, confused, as he climbed out, so I kicked him on and waved my arm. "Run!" He started legging it past the swings as I got back into the driver's seat and headed for the main drag. By the time he found a phone and made contact, I'd be in the city and well out of the area. I was certainly safe from the air: nothing was going to be flying when the skies opened. I checked the clouds once more, just to make sure.

I also checked the fuel: just under full. I had no idea if that was enough, but it didn't matter, I had cash.

The M-16 was shoved between the door and seat as I hit the main drag and headed for the tollbooth.

33

The 4x4 pitched and rolled along a waterlogged jungle track, launching walls of water and mud in all directions. I was just glad to be doing it with windows closed and air-conditioning humming. Maybe ten more minutes until I reached the clearing and the house.

The rain had started as soon as I hit El Chorrillo, slowing everything down. By the time I joined the Pan Am Highway, it was dropping from the sky like Niagara Falls, and had carried on like that for the next hour. After that, the cloud had stayed really low and threatening all the way to Chepo. I stopped off at the store the old Indian had been sitting outside two days before, and bought a couple of Pepsis and a package of little sponge cakes. When those were gone I dug around in the bergen for the sesame bars and water.

There was no drama on the next bit of road apart from the mud and the water. I gave a bit of thought to having to ditch the truck later on, but the main preoccupation was getting back to the house and persuading those two to help me. Maybe there was a way that

Carrie could get George to stop it. Maybe they knew how to themselves. Maybe if I ripped the dish off the roof . . . Maybe, maybe.

Bouncing along the track, I came into the clearing to see that the cloud had lifted. But there was no sun yet, and no one to be seen. Both their trucks were parked outside the house, and the generator was chugging as I passed the tubs, hitting the horn as it seemed to be the thing to do around here.

As I got nearer the house I saw Carrie come to the screen door and stare out.

I parked the Land Cruiser and climbed out into the humid air. She opened the screen door for me as I stepped onto the porch, clearly trying to work out the Land Cruiser.

I waited until the hinges stopped squeaking. "I'll explain that later. . . . There's been a fuckup—Charlie's already handed over the guidance system . . . last night . . . There's more."

My muddy boots clumped on the porch boards as I passed her and entered the living room. I wanted them both together before they got the news. The fans were blasting away and Aaron was sitting in an armchair facing me, leaning over a mug of coffee on the table.

"Nick." His little finger was dipping aimlessly into the black fluid and letting it drip onto the wood.

I acknowledged him as the screen squeaked and slammed, Carrie staying behind me by the door.

He kept his voice low as he rubbed the side of his forehead, twisting in the chair to check that the computer-room door was closed. "Michael dead? She told me all about it when she got back." He turned back and took a messy, nervous swig from the mug.

"No, he's alive."

"Oh, thank God, thank God." Slumping back in the chair, he held the brew on his thigh, wiping his beard dry with an open palm.

Carrie was still behind me by the door. She, too, let out a sigh of relief. "We've been so worried. My father stood you down last night, missed us by an hour. He said you weren't needed anymore and went totally crazy at Aaron when he found out you'd already gone."

I turned to her, almost whispering, "Oh, he's crazy all right." I slowed down so that there would be no mistake. "I think your dad's planning a missile attack on a cruise liner, the *Ocaso*, tomorrow. It's going to happen once it's in the Miraflores. If he succeeds, a lot of people, thousands, are going to die."

Her hand shot to her mouth. "What? But you're here to stop . . . No, no, no, my father wouldn't—"

"George isn't pressing any buttons." I pointed toward the fridge. "But *he* is, the one with the scar on his stomach. You know, the beach babies, your favorite picture." They both followed my finger. "I saw him at the Miraflores, running as soon as he saw Aaron and the Mazda. He was also at Charlie's, at his house, on Tuesday, and then here last night. He stayed in the truck, he didn't want to be seen. . . . Charlie just told me that he was the one who took delivery. . . ."

"Oh, God. Milton . . ." She leaned against the wall, holding her neck with her hands. "Milton was one of the Iran-Contra procurement guys in the eighties. They sold the weapons to Iran for the Lebanon hostages, then used the money to buy other—weapons—for—the—Contr— Oh, shit."

Her hands fell to her sides, the tears starting to well up. "That's his job, Nick, that's what he does."

"Well, he has just procured himself an antiship

missile and I think he's going to use it tomorrow on the *Ocaso*."

"No, he couldn't, you must be wrong," she stammered. "My father would never let that happen to Americans, for Christ's sake."

"Yes, he would." Aaron had something to say. "The DeConcini Reservation. Think on it, Carrie, think on it."

His eyes were locked on hers, and he spoke with bitter calm, trying hard to keep his voice down. "George and those guys . . . they are going to take down that ship so the U.S. has just cause to come back. And you know what? He's made us part of it— my God, we're part of it. I knew something like this would happen, I told you there was more to this . . ."

Carrie slid down to the floor, maybe realizing at long last what her dad had really been up to all his life.

I turned to the rasp of beard bristles being slowly rubbed.

Aaron spoke. "She gets into the locks at ten tomorrow morning—my God, what are we going to do?"

But the question hadn't been addressed at me. His eyes were still fixed on her. "Why'd he get you involved, huh? Maybe you wanted more than a passport. Maybe you wanted a reason for your get-back-to-Boston ticket, huh?"

"I didn't . . . and I didn't know, Aaron. Please believe me, I didn't know."

He paused. I could hear breath traveling in and out of his hairy nostrils as he tried to keep calm, before flicking his eyes at me. "You, Nick, have you been used too?" He pointed behind me. "Just like her?"

"It's the story of my life," I said. "Carrie, you will have to talk to George—beg him, threaten him."

I turned, but Carrie ignored me. She just stared submissively at her husband.

Aaron's voice was still low but now laced with heavy sarcasm as he met her stare. "Why should he stop? Hell, he thinks it's a neat idea. So neat he gave his daughter some of the action as a surprise." His eyes became enraged as he forced his mug onto the tabletop and leaned forward. "So that means everybody's happy—Uncle Sam comes back and saves the day, the money guys, the military, the right-wingers, they all get the Zone back. And, hey, if it goes wrong, other guys take the heat." He pointed at Carrie, his eyes burning into her once more. "That's you, and me, and Luz. It's one fuck of a passport out."

I opened my mouth to speak, but Aaron wasn't done.

"Our child will be getting letters from her mother on Alcatraz letterhead, and that's if we're lucky. That's if they don't execute you. It's out of control. How will we live with ourselves after this?"

Aaron held up his left hand, displaying his wedding ring. "We're a team, remember? I told you this was wrong. I told you he was lying, I told you he was using you." He slumped back into the chair, wiping his eyes with straight fingers and rubbing his beard in distress as he checked out the computer-room door once more.

I turned. Carrie was looking down, tears rolling down her cheeks too.

"I'm contacting him again tonight. . . . It wasn't supposed to be like this."

That was a start.

"Good. If I close down the relay board now will you still be able to make contact?"

She was opening her mouth, but if words came out I didn't hear them. From above us came an unmistakable and ponderous *wap wap wap wap wap*.

We all looked up. The noise was suddenly so loud it was as if the roof weren't there at all.

Both of them rushed toward the computer-room door. "Luz, Luz!"

I moved to the screen door. I checked back to see them barge into the other room. Shit, it was still on—"The webcam, close down the camera!"

I pressed my nose against the screen. I wanted the M-16 in the Land Cruiser, but it wasn't going to happen. The two dark blue helis were hovering above the house now, having already disgorged their payload. Pairs of jeans carrying M-16s were closing in on the porch. Michael must have made the connection with Aaron from the meeting at the locks.

I ducked back into the room out of sight, just as the other two came running in with a frightened Luz.

The heli noise was overwhelming. One of them must have been hovering just inches from the roof; the bookshelf was shaking so much that books were tumbling onto the floor.

The scene beyond the screen was a maelstrom of flying twigs, foliage, and mud as men bobbed about, cautiously approaching the porch and pointing weapons.

Aaron's face was stone, glaring over Luz's head as they knelt on either side of her, curled up in the armchair, her eyes shut tight in fear. Both of them cuddled and tried to reassure her.

From behind them came shouts in Spanish from the storeroom.

I could see bodies now on the porch.

It was all over. I dropped to my knees and threw my arms up in surrender, yelling at Aaron and Carrie, fighting against the rotor blades to be heard, "Just be still! Be still, it'll be all right!"

I was lying, I didn't have a clue what was going to happen. But you've got to accept that when you're in the shit you're in the shit. There is nothing you can do but take deep breaths, keep calm, and hope. I thought of my failure, and what that meant, as the pins and needles returned to my legs. This was not a good day out.

Men spilled into the room from the back of the building at the same instant as the screen door burst open. There was crazed shouting between them as they tried to make sure they didn't shoot each other. I kept my head down in submission and could feel the movement in the floorboards as they stamped about. Out of the corner of my eye, I saw the flicker as the image on the screen of the PC refreshed itself. *Shit!*

I chanced a look up and saw the expressions of relief on their faces that they hadn't encountered any resistance. Over their civilian clothes, they were all wearing black nylon chest harnesses for their spare mags. Four of them surrounded Aaron and Carrie, still crouched around the armchair comforting Luz. She was giving out high-pitched, hysterical screams, terrified by the frantically pointed weapons just inches from her face.

I stayed on my knees, not looking at anyone in particular, just making sure I looked scared—which I was. But at least there was one positive; I knew we were being kept alive for some reason, otherwise we'd have been shot on sight. All the weapons that I could see were on Automatic.

I kept still, looked down, took deep breaths, trying to keep myself calm and my head free—but it wasn't happening too well.

When people get excited and scared with weapons in their hands anything can happen—especially as I could see, now that I was viewing them close up and not through an optic sight, that some of these people were only just getting used to having facial hair. It only takes one jumpy young man to fire, then everyone joins in out of fright and confusion.

Boots and sneakers rushed past as loud instructions came from commanders trying to make themselves heard over the continuous thumping of the rotor blades. Radios blasted out incomprehensible mush that even they couldn't hear properly.

The sole of someone's boot kicked me between the shoulder blades to get me down on the floor. I went with it, flat onto my stomach, hands out to break my fall and save my face; then, showing compliance, I quickly placed them on the back of my head. I was roughly searched and lost everything out of my pockets, which made me feel naked and depressed.

The shiny Nokia went into someone's pocket as the helis' noise subsided, and shouts filled the vacuum, mixed with the din of corrugated iron getting banged and the storeroom being ransacked. I bet anything nice and shiny in there was falling straight off the shelves and into their pockets as well.

The clatter of rotors slowed gradually and there was the high-pitched whine of the turbos as both engines closed down.

Carrie and Aaron's comforting sounds to Luz dropped with the noise level as rapid Spanish radio traffic echoed from the storeroom. Everybody else was much quieter in the house now; maybe it had just been the noise of the helis whipping them into a frenzy.

But then came the sound of lighter rotors. My stomach churned and I knew that an already bad day was about to get a whole lot worse. Maybe the reason we hadn't been killed on sight was that Charlie wanted to see to it in person.

34

As the Jet Ranger's rotor blades cut out, I heard the barking of orders and bodies started rushing from the room. Three remained covering us, two nervous young guys, maybe their first time out, and one older, in his early thirties.

Outside on the porch I could hear a lot of warp speed jabbering. The boys were probably swapping stories about how particularly good they were during the attack. I kept my head turned to the left.

The family were still huddled around the armchair. Carrie was nearest to me as they cuddled and stroked Luz's head. Aaron's eyes burned into her. It was hard to read his expression: it looked to me like pure anger, but then he reached out and stroked her face.

Calmer and more controlled Spanish came from the rear of the house, sounding more cultured than the guys with weapons yammering. I tilted my head very slightly and screwed my eyes to the top of their sockets to see what was happening.

Charlie, dressed in a navy tracksuit and white sneakers, had three or four others buzzing around him like presidential aides as he strode into the room.

He walked toward me, looking as if he had need of nothing, not even oxygen. I felt scared.

There was nothing I could do physically about things at the moment. If I saw the chance to get away I would grab it, but right now I just had to look away from him and wait. Whatever happened, I knew it was likely to be painful.

They came toward me, talking quietly to each other as he was called by one of the bodies still in the computer room, and then there was the squeak of rubber-soled sneakers on floorboards as the group promptly turned and headed back from where they'd just come.

I glanced up and saw them hunched around the PC as the screen flickered and slowly rolled down the image of the lock as it was refreshed. One was pointing at the picture, talking as if he was giving Charlie a multimedia presentation. The others nodded and agreed.

I turned my eyes to the armchair. Aaron and Carrie were looking anxiously over Luz's head at the group. Aaron turned and stared back at his wife, his eyes swiveling in their sockets as he leaned to kiss a sobbing Luz's hair. The guys were still mumbling on the porch behind me.

I watched as one of the crew broke away from the PC and came back into the living area. He'd had a change of gear since I stole his Land Cruiser, and now boasted a clean, shiny black tracksuit. His neck was covered with a gauze dressing, held in place by surgical tape, and there was a big smile on his face as he sauntered toward me.

I lowered my eyes, clenched my teeth, and tensed up.

He crouched down and cocked his head so we could have eye-to-eye.

"Como esta, amigo?" His prominent Adam's apple bobbed up and down under the blood-spotted gauze.

I nodded. *"Bien, bien."*

He gave the thumbs-up with a smile. *"Sí,* good, good."

I kept my body tensed but still nothing happened. He was joking. I couldn't help but smile back as he got to his feet and returned to the crew at the PC, then addressed a few remarks to Charlie, probably telling him I was indeed the same man—and maybe confirming to him that I was the only one on the ground earlier.

Charlie seemed very cool about things, not even turning to look at me. Instead he smiled and pinched both cheeks of the Land Cruiser guy as he handed over the plastic bag carrying my docs. Charlie then went back and muttered to some more of his aides by the screen.

My Land Cruiser friend pulled out my roll of dollars from the bag, before leaving via the storeroom. Seconds later, one of the Hueys sparked up, turbos whining. Some of the boys were being lifted out.

The heli took off, thundering over the roof, as the staff meeting came to an end. They streamed back into the living area, Charlie in the lead, my bag of docs in his hand. He made a beeline toward me. I did my best to bury my face in my shoulder.

His mud-stained sneakers stopped a foot or two away from my eyes, shoes so new they didn't even have creases in the nylon yet. I concentrated on my shoulder as he crouched down with a crack of his knees and grabbed my hair. I just went with it: what was the point of resisting?

Our eyes met. His were dark brown and bloodshot, no doubt due to the force of the explosion. His skin was peppered with scabbed-up pockmarks from the shattered glass, and the side of his neck was dressed like that of the guy from the Land Cruiser. But for all that, he didn't look angry, just in command.

He stared at me, his expression impenetrable. I could smell his cologne and hear his steel watchstrap jangle as he grabbed my chin with his spare hand.

The palm was soft, and well-manicured fingers pressed into my cheeks. There still was no anger in his eyes, no hint of any emotion whatsoever.

"Why are you people so stupid? All I wanted was some assurance the device wouldn't be used inside Panama. Then you could have had the launch control system. Some form of assurance, that's all." He threw my docs to the floor. "Instead, I have my family threatened . . ."

I let the weight of my head rest in his hands, my eyelids drooping as he shook me about some more.

"So I comply and take the rest of your money, you then assure me everything is fine, just business. But still you try to kill my family. Do you know who I am? What I can do to you, all of you people?"

He held me, looking at me, his eyes giving nothing.

"You are going to use Sunburn against a ship in the Miraflores—that's the target, isn't it?" He shook me again. "Why you are doing it, I don't care. But it will bring the U.S. back—that I care about a great deal."

As my face moved from side to side I caught glimpses of my passport and wallet, discarded in their plastic on the floor by the bookshelves, and both Aaron and Carrie, still covering Luz on the armchair, their faces red and set with fear.

Charlie brought his mouth to my ear and whispered, "I want to know where the missile is, and when the attack will take place. If not, well, some of my people here are only a few years older than that one in the chair and, like all young men, eager to display their manhood. . . . That's fair, isn't it? You set the rules—children are now fair game, aren't they?"

He kept my head in his hands, waiting for my reply. I looked into his eyes and they told me what I needed to know: that none of us was going to leave here alive, no matter what we said or did.

It was Aaron who broke the silence, with a scoff: "He's just the hired help." His voice was strong and authoritative. "He was sent here to make you hand over the guidance system, that's all. He doesn't know a thing. None of us knows where Sunburn is, but I can get on line at eight-thirty tonight and find out. I'll do it—just let these three go."

I studied Charlie's face as he stared at Aaron. It was a good try on Aaron's part, but a bit naive.

Carrie went ballistic. "No, no—what are you doing?" She begged Charlie, still hovering above me. "Please, he—"

Aaron cut in at once. "Shut up. I've had enough, it's got to end. It's got to stop—now!"

Charlie released my head and I let it fall to the floorboards, the right side of my face taking the hit. He wasn't too keen to have my hair grease on his hands and bent down to wipe it on my shirt before walking over to the coffee table.

Aaron followed him with his eyes. "Eight-thirty—I can't do anything until then. That's when I can make contact and find out—eight-thirty. Just let them go." He stroked Luz's hair.

Charlie muttered instructions to the people around him as he walked toward the kitchen area, not acknowledging me as he passed.

Aaron and Carrie obviously understood what was going on and started to rise with Luz as two guards crossed the floor. Carrie still tried to talk sense into

Aaron. "What are you doing? You know he'll just—"

He was tough with her. "Shut up! Just shut up!" He kissed her on the lips. "I love you. Stay strong." Then he bent down and kissed Luz, before the guards dragged him toward the computer room. "Remember, Nick," he laughed, "once a Viking, always a Viking. Some things never change."

He disappeared, jabbering some kind of explanation or apology in Spanish to the men who pulled at his arms.

The screen door squeaked open behind me and commands were shouted at the boys on the porch. The other two had already been herded into Luz's bedroom, and the door was closed.

Charlie had been inspecting the coffeepot and now checked the mugs. He obviously decided the blend was crap, or the mugs weren't clean enough, so he came back toward me and hunkered down once more, bending his head to connect his eyes with mine.

"Sunday—London—you were there?"

My gaze remained locked on his. It was like two kids playing stare as I kept my mouth firmly shut.

He shrugged. "It doesn't matter, not now. What does is the Sunburn—I want it back. Do you know how much you have paid for it?"

I had to blink now, but I remained locked on. Fuck him, we were all dead anyway.

"Twelve million United States dollars. I'm thinking of reselling it—good business, I think." He stood, to the cracking of knees once again. He paused and took a breath. "It seems the war down south will escalate quite soon. I should imagine FARC would very much appreciate the opportunity to buy Sunburn, to prepare, let's say, for when the Americans send a carrier fleet to support its troops." He smiled. "After all, the

Russians designed the missile with just one target in mind: the American aircraft carrier."

I was pushed toward Luz's bedroom and opened the door to see both of them lying on the bed in a huddle. Carrie was stroking Luz's hair; she looked up in terror as the door creaked open, her expression only changing when she saw it was me.

The door slammed shut. I moved over to the bed and sat down beside them with my finger to my lips. "We've got to get out of here before these kids get organized."

She looked down at her daughter, kissed her head, and spoke in whispers. "What's he doing? He knows nothing. George won't say a—"

"I don't know, sssh . . ."

I was only just beginning to understand what Aaron was doing, but I wasn't going to tell her.

I got up and went to the window, which was protected by a wire-mesh screen on the outside. The windows, side-hinged types that opened inward, were caked with faded, flaking cream paint. The hinges had long since lost their coat, with luck through use. The screen was held in place by wooden pegs that swiveled on screws.

I looked out and studied the tree line two hundred yards away as Luz sparked up behind me. "Is Dad coming?"

Carrie soothed her. "For sure, baby, soon."

The ground outside was littered with freshly broken terracotta tiles from the roof. There was intermittent chat and the odd laugh coming from the porch to my left.

I inspected the window, my mind still very much on Aaron. He wasn't as naive as I'd thought. "Once a Viking, always a Viking." They slash, they burn, they pillage. They never change. He'd told me that. He'd come to the same conclusion as I had. No way was Charlie letting us out of here alive.

I was expecting some resistance from the windows, but they gave quite easily and opened toward me with just one pull. Immediately closing them again, I went over to the bed. "Here's what we're going to do. We're going to get out through the window and get ourselves into the trees."

Luz had been looking at her mother but her head jerked toward me. Tears streaked her face. "What about Dad?"

"I'll come back for him later. There's no time for this. We've got to go right now."

Luz looked up at her mother and silently implored her.

"We can't," Carrie said. "We can't leave him. What will happen when they find us gone? If we stay put and don't antagonize anyone, we'll be all right. We don't know anything, why should they harm us?"

The whine of the turbos on the Jet Ranger started up and the rotors were soon turning. I waited until they reached full revs before putting my mouth to Carrie's ear.

"Aaron knows we're all dead whatever happens—even if George does tell him the location. You understand? We all die."

The heli took off as her head fell onto Luz's. I followed to keep contact with her ear. "He's buying me time to save you two. We must go now, for Luz's sake, and for Aaron's. It's what he wants."

Her shoulders heaved with sadness as she hugged her daughter.

"Mom?"

The tears were infectious. Both of them were sobbing now into each other's hair as the noise of the Jet Ranger disappeared over the canopy.

35

There was still more than an hour to go till last light but I had made my decision. We had to get out of here as soon as we physically could.

Mumbling and laughter still drifted from the front of the house, as if to remind me of the risk we'd be taking. If somebody was on watch at the edge of the porch, we'd be in full view for the entire two hundred yards. It would take us at least ninety seconds to make that distance over muddy ground, and that's a very long time for an M-16 to have you in its sights.

But who knew what the next hour held? The three of us could be split up and moved to separate rooms, killed, or even put into the remaining Huey and flown out. We had no control over that, and by waiting we could end up squandering the chance Aaron had given us.

As I looked through the glass and screen, it was easy enough to confirm our route—right toward the dead ground, then into the tree line. We'd be moving at an angle away from the front of the house and the porch, but there'd come a point where we cleared the corner at the back and were in the Huey's line of sight. Would there still be people aboard? Maybe the pilot carrying out his checks? There was no right or wrong about the decision to go now. These things are not a science: if we died, I'd have been wrong; if we lived, I'd have been right.

Once absorbed by the wall of green we'd be relatively safe; we'd just have to contend with a night out on the jungle floor, then spend the next day moving through the canopy toward the dead valley, navigating by paralleling the track. We'd cross the tree graveyard at night, hiding under the dead wood in the day, until we made Chepo. From there, who knew? I'd worry about that then. As for Aaron, I doubted that he'd last much past eight-thirty.

Carrie and Luz were still comforting each other on the bed. I went over to them and, with Britney on the wall overseeing events, whispered, "We're going to go for the trees."

Luz looked at her mother for reassurance.

"The thing to remember is that we must spread out when we're running, okay? That way it's harder to be seen."

Carrie looked up from her child and frowned. She knew that wasn't the reason. She knew a single burst from an M-16 could kill all three of us, and if we were spread out, we'd be that much harder to hit.

Luz tugged at her mother's arm. "What about Daddy?"

I could see Carrie fighting back the tears and I put my hand on her shoulder. "I'll come back for him, Luz, don't worry. He wanted me to get you two into the jungle first. He wants to know you're safe."

She nodded reluctantly, and we heard more mumblings from the porch and boots on the other side of the door. Going immediately was the right thing to do.

"If we get split up," I said quietly, "I want you two to carry on into the trees without me, then make your way toward the far right corner and wait for me there." To Luz I added, "Don't come out if anyone calls for you, even if it's your dad—it'll just be a trick. Just my voice, okay? Once you're safe, I'll come back for him."

I'd cross that bridge when I came to it, but for now a lie was necessary to keep them quiet so I could get on with what he was sacrificing himself for.

"Ready?"

Both heads nodded. I looked at Luz. "Me first, then you, all right?"

I moved back to the window and out of whisper range. Carrie followed, looking out to the tree line, listening to the laughter out front.

"They're outside, on the porch, Nick, isn't it—"

"No time, not interested."

"But how are we going to get to the trees without—"

"Just get her ready."

She was right. How were we going to make it? I didn't know. All I did know was that there wasn't any time for fancy plans, even if I could think of one. We just had to get on with it. We were dead anyway, so anything else was a bonus.

Pulling open the windows let the sounds of crickets and the boys on the porch trickle into the room. I thought of the Beirut hostage who could have escaped within the first few days of capture when a bathroom window was left open. But he didn't take the chance, didn't seize the moment. He had to live with his regret for the next three years.

My mind went into auto-drive, just getting on with the job. Fuck 'em, fuck the noise outside, fuck the Huey. I was almost wanting them to see us.

The wooden pegs squeaked as I swiveled them to

release the window screen. It rattled in its frame as I pushed it free. I froze, waiting for the murmuring on the porch to change into shouts. It didn't happen. I pushed again and this time the screen came away. Slowly and carefully, I lowered it toward the ground. Boots banged about on the decking and the front door slammed as I felt the screen touch the mud and broken tiles.

I clambered out feet first. My Timberlands squelched into the mud and I moved the screen to one side before beckoning Luz, not even bothering to check the noises. I'd know if they saw me. Better to concentrate on what I was doing rather than worry about something I had no control over.

Her mother helped her, even though she didn't need it, and I guided her down beside me into the mud. Using one hand to hold her against the wall, I held out the other for Carrie as the boys on the porch appreciated a punch line and one of the rocking chairs was scraped across the wood.

Carrie was soon beside me. I got her to stand next to Luz against the wall, and pointed to the tree line to our right. I gave them the thumbs-up but got no reply so, taking a deep breath, I took off. They knew what to do.

Within just a few strides the mud had slowed our run into not much more than a fast walk. Instinct made all three of us hunch low in an attempt to make ourselves smaller. I pushed them ahead of me and kept motioning to them to spread out, but it wasn't working. Luz ran close to her mother, and it wasn't long before they were actually holding hands, breathing hard five or six yards ahead.

It was difficult going and I fell twice, sliding as if on ice, but we'd covered the first hundred yards.

The heli came into view to our right, parked just

short of the dead ground. There didn't seem to be anyone in or around it, or any sort of movement at the rear of the house. We pushed on.

There were maybe thirty yards to go when I heard the first reports. Not big, inaccurate brass, but single, aimed shots.

"Run!" I yelled. "Keep going!"

An enormous flock of little multicolored birds lifted from the canopy. "Keep going, keep going!" I didn't look behind us; it wouldn't have helped.

Carrie, still gripping her daughter's hand, was focused on the tree line, half dragging Luz along as she shrieked with terror.

The rounds cracked behind us as they went supersonic. My mind was trying to beat them by going at a million miles an hour, but my feet were only taking me at ten.

With maybe twenty yards of open ground left, the rounds finally started to zero in on us. The cracks were accompanied by thuds as they slammed into the mud ahead and to the side of us, until all I could hear was an almost rhythmic *crack thump, crack thump, crack thump* as they opened up big-time. "Keep going, keep going!"

Carrie and Luz lunged into the jungle, still slightly ahead and to my right. "Go right, go right!"

Almost at once, I heard a scream. It was a strangulated half gasp, half howl of pain, just yards into the foliage.

More rounds ripped into the jungle, some with a high-pitched *ziiinnng* as they ricocheted off the trees. I dropped to my hands and knees, gasping for breath. "Luz! Call to me—where are you? Where are you?"

"Mommy, Mommy, Mommy!"

Ziiinnng-ziiinnng . . .

"Luz! Lie down! Keep down! Keep down!"

The single shots now become bursts as I started crawling. The M-16s were firing into the entry points in an effort to hose us down; we needed to move offline to the right, downhill into dead ground. Leaves give cover from view but not fire, dead ground does.

"I'm coming, keep down, lie down!"

Some of them were long bursts, the rounds going high as the weapon barrels kicked up, but some were short, the tuned-in guys aiming three and five rounds at a time as I heard a truck revving up to join in the frenzy.

I covered six or seven yards through the foliage until I found them. Carrie was on her back, panting, eyes wide open, tear-filled and big as saucers, her cargo pants bloodstained on the right thigh, with what looked like bone pushing at the material. Her injured leg appeared shorter than the other, and the foot was lying flat with the toes pointing outward. A round must have hit her in the femur. Luz was hovering over her, not knowing what to do, just staring open-mouthed at her mother's bloodstains.

The rounds had died down for now as the shouts and engine noise got louder.

I grabbed Carrie by the arms and, shuffling on my ass, started to drag her through the leaf litter in the direction of our emergency RV, the corner of the tree line, and into the dead ground. Luz followed on her hands and knees, sobbing loudly.

"Shut up! They'll hear you!"

We only managed five or six yards. Carrie cried out uncontrollably as her injured leg got jarred and twisted; she covered her face with her hands in an effort to keep quiet. At least the noise meant she was breathing and could feel pain, both good signs, but the two of them were making such a racket that it was only a matter of time before we were heard.

I jumped up, grabbed Carrie's wrist, and heaved her over my shoulder in a fireman's lift. She screamed as her damaged leg swung free before I held it in place. I pushed through the vegetation with long, exaggerated strides, trying to keep the leg stable with one hand and keeping a tight grip on Luz with the other, sometimes by her hair, sometimes by her clothing, sometimes around her neck, whatever it took to keep us moving together.

The BUBs (basha-up beetles) now sparked up as frenzied shouts and the high revs of the engine came from behind us. Short bursts from M-16s randomly stitched the area. They were at the entry points.

We crashed our way through some more wait-a-while and Carrie's leg got snagged. She screamed and I half turned, pulled it free, knowing there was a chance that the broken ends of her femur could act like scissors, cutting into muscle, nerves, tendons, ligaments—or, worst of all, sever the femoral artery. She'd be history in minutes if that happened. But what else could I do?

We crashed on, and began a gentle descent. I guessed we were about level with the heli in the clearing to my right. I could still hear people hosing the place down behind us, but the jungle was soaking up a lot of it and we seemed to be out of the initial danger area.

The BUBs reminded me I'd have to stop soon and fix up Carrie. I needed that last precious light.

I pushed toward the tree line until I could see the beginning of the open ground, then dragged Luz back with me so we were just behind the wall of green. At last I was able to lay Carrie down, making sure as I did so that her feet were pointing at the tree line.

The M-16s only fired sporadically now, up on the

higher ground, though there was still a lot of vehicle noise and shouting up and down the tree line. I didn't care: if there were any dramas we'd just drag farther back in. The priority now was fixing her up.

Carrie lay on her back taking short, sharp breaths, her face contorted. I joined in with her pattern of breathing as I tried to get my breath back. Luz was bent over her on her knees. I gently straightened her. "You've got to help your mother and me. I need you to kneel there, behind me. If anyone comes you just turn around and give me a tap—not a shout, just a tap, okay? Will you do that?"

Luz looked at her mom, then back at me.

"That's good—this is really important." I positioned her behind me, facing the tree line, then turned to Carrie. No way were we going to be walking out of here, but that wasn't my major concern: fixing her up was.

She fought the pain through gritted teeth. There was blood. Her femoral artery wasn't cut or quarts of the stuff would have been pouring out over her leg, but if she kept leaking like this she would eventually go into shock and die. The bleeding had to be stopped and the fracture immobilized.

Not even bothering to explain what I was up to, I got down at her feet and started to work with my teeth at the frayed hem of her cargo pants. I made a tear, gripped both sides of it, and ripped the material upward. As the injury was exposed I saw that she hadn't been shot. She must have fallen badly and overstressed the femur: the bone was sticking out of what looked like a rack of raw, blood-soaked beef. But at least there was muscle there to contract, it hadn't been shot away.

I tried to sound upbeat. "It's not so bad."

There was no reply, just very rapid breathing.

With military casualties in the field I had always found it better to lighten the tone, not feed their worries. But this felt different: I wanted to reassure her, to make her feel okay. "It looks a lot messier than it is. I'll make sure it doesn't get worse, then get you to a doctor. It'll be fine."

With her head tilted back she seemed to be looking up at the canopy. Her face was fixed in a terrible grimace, eyes screwed tight.

I cleared some leaf litter that had stuck to the sweat on her forehead and whispered into her ear, "Really, it's not that bad . . . it's a clean break. You haven't lost that much blood, but I've got to fix it so the bone doesn't move about and cause any more damage. It's going to hurt more while I fix it up—you know that, don't you?"

I caught sight of Luz, who was still in position on her knees, looking back at us. I gave her the thumbs-up, but all I got in return was a fleeting, tear-stained half-smile.

Carrie's chest heaved up and down as she sucked in air, quietly screaming to herself as she took the pain.

"Carrie, I need you to help me, will you do that, will you help me? I want you to hold on to the tree behind you when I say, okay?"

Forcing the words out haltingly through the tears, she sobbed, "Get on with it."

There was a burst of fire farther up the tree line Luz flinched and looked back. I held up both my hands and mouthed to her, "It's okay, it's okay."

The firing stopped and Luz turned back to her task. The BUBs echoed about us in the fading light as I gently eased Carrie's inch-wide webbing belt through the loops of her cargo pants and put it down by her feet. Then I took off my sweatshirt knowing I was sentencing myself to being one big mozzie banquet.

I ripped a sleeve away from its stitching. Carrie's eyes were closed, her lips quivering, as I started pulling on the large waxy leaves that drooped down about us. "In a minute, I'm going to move your good leg next to your bad one. I'll do it as carefully as I can."

Rolling up the leaves into big cigar shapes, I gently packed them all the way down between her legs, to act as padding between the good leg and the bad. I carried on as the odd Spanish shout penetrated the canopy, then picked up her good leg. "Here we go, here we go." She was breathing as rapidly as if she was giving birth. I brought it gently over toward her injured one, just as the first splatter of rain hit the canopy. I didn't know whether to laugh or cry.

Luz moved back to me on her knees. "It's raining, what do we do?"

I shrugged. "Get wet."

Carrie's features twisted again in agony. As rain tumbled onto her face she held out her hand for Luz to grasp, and mother and daughter whispered to each other. I needed Luz on stag. I signaled that I wanted her to move, and she shuffled back to her post.

I pushed the sleeve through the mud below Carrie's knees and laid it out flat, then frantically ripped the rest of the now soaking-wet sweatshirt into strips to improvise bandages.

"Nick, the ship . . ."

"The ship has to wait."

I carried on ripping and tearing as the rain notched itself up to monsoon strength. I couldn't even hear the BUBs anymore, or the people in the open ground—if they were still there.

I leaned over her, right up to her ear. "I need you to

bring your hands back and grab hold of the tree behind you."

There was a deep rumble of thunder directly above us as I guided her hands around the thin trunk, debating whether or not to explain what I was going to do with her next.

"Grip hard and don't let go, no matter what."

I decided against it; she was in enough pain without anticipating more.

I crawled back down to her feet and fed the belt under both her ankles, digging into the mud so I didn't move her damaged leg any more than I had to. Then, kneeling in front of her, I gently picked up the foot of the injured leg between my hands, the right supporting her heel and the other on her toes.

Her whole body tensed.

"It's going to be okay, just keep hold of that tree. Ready?"

Slowly but firmly, I pulled her foot toward me. I rotated it as gently as I could, stretching the injured leg out straight to stop the taut muscles from displacing the bone any more and, I hoped, bring some relief from the pain. It wasn't easy, there was a lot of thigh muscle to pull against. Every movement must have felt like a stab from a red hot knife. She gritted her teeth and for a long time didn't make a sound, then finally it all became too much. She screamed as her body jerked, but didn't release her grip as the exposed bone started to retract from the open wound.

Rain fell in torrents and more thunder rumbled across the darkening sky as I continued with the traction. She screamed again and her body convulsed as I sat down, pulling her leg with all my weight.

"Nearly there, Carrie, nearly there . . ."

Luz came running over and joined in the sobs. It was understandable, but I didn't need it. I hissed at her, "Shut up!" There was no other way that I could think of, but it just made her worse. She whimpered again, and this time I just let her get on with it. My hands were busy and I couldn't cover her mouth. I couldn't let go because the muscle contraction would pull it back in again and cause more damage.

I started to feed the canvas belt over Carrie's ankles with my left hand, and then over her sandaled feet in a figure eight. "Keep your good leg straight, Carrie, keep it straight!" Then I pulled back on the ends of the belt to keep everything in place, tying a knot with the belt still under tension to keep her feet together.

Carrie had been jerking like an epileptic, but still held on to the tree and, more importantly, kept her good leg straight. "It's okay, okay. It's done."

As I sat up Luz fell on top of her mother. I tried to get her off. "Let her breathe." But they weren't having any of it, clutching each other tight.

It was getting so dark I could hardly see beyond the two of them now, and the fracture still had to be immobilized so it couldn't do any more damage. I gently folded over the sweatshirt sleeve lying under her knees and tied the ends together with the knot on the side of her good knee. Large lumps of bright green leaf protruded between her legs now that they were getting strapped together.

I placed strips of sweatshirt firmly and carefully over the wound. I fed the material under her knees and then worked it up before tying off on the side of the good leg. I wanted to immobilize the fracture, and put pressure on the wound to stem the blood loss.

Rain cascaded down, blurring my vision as it ran into my eyes. I was working virtually by feel as I tied off the other sleeve around her ankles, adding more support to the canvas belt.

I stayed sitting at Carrie's feet, almost shouting to

make myself heard above the rain. "Now you can give me my Scout's first-aid badge."

All I had to do now was make sure that the sweatshirt wasn't tied too tight. I couldn't tell if the blood supply was reaching below the ties; without light I couldn't see if the skin was pink or blue, and finding the pulse was a nightmare. There was really only one option. "If you feel pins and needles, you've got to tell me, okay?"

I got a short, sharp "Yep."

I couldn't even see my hand in front of my face now as I checked Baby-G. The dial illuminated and it was 6:27. Just behind me, I could hear both of them crying, even above the drumming on the vegetation.

I was starting to feel cold. Not too sure where their heads were, I called out into the darkness, "You two must keep physical contact with each other all the time. You must each know where the other is all the time—never let go of each other." I put my hand out and felt wet material: it was Luz's back as she cuddled her mother.

No way were we walking out of here. What the fuck was there to do now? I didn't really know. Well, actually I did, but I was trying to deny it. That was probably what was making me feel cold.

I was kneeling there in the rain when I heard Luz speak up. "Nick?"

I tapped my hand on her back to acknowledge her.

"You going to get Daddy now?"

36

It seemed I had come to that bridge.

"I'll be no more than a couple of hours."

She wasn't wearing a watch, but some kind of timing would be something to cling to.

"Eight-thirty, Nick, eight-thirty . . ." Carrie fought between short, sharp breaths, as if I needed reminding.

"If I'm not back by first light," I said, "you need to get out into the open ground and make yourself known. You'll need taking care of. Once the weather clears they can use the heli to get you to the hospital." Maybe, maybe not: I didn't know what they'd do, but there was no other way if I didn't return.

Going back to the house had been a simple choice to make. Carrie needed medical attention. I needed a vehicle to get her to Chepo. I had to go and get one, and that meant getting Aaron out of there too. Stealing a truck in the middle of the night, then picking Carrie up so close to the house was a no-no: it simply wouldn't work. I needed to have control of the house and the people in it first.

I didn't know if it was the physical pain, or the

realization that what I'd just talked about was a contingency plan for if Aaron and I were both dead, but Carrie let out a loud sob. Rain drummed on Luz's back as she knelt over her mother and joined in. I just let them get on with it, not really knowing what else to do while I tried to think through what I'd do once I was at the house—without coming up with much.

I checked Baby-G: 6:32. Less than two hours till Aaron's bluff was called.

I felt my knees sinking into the mud. "I'll see you both soon. In fact, I won't see you, I'll hear you. . . ." I gave a weak laugh.

I drew an imaginary straight line down Carrie's body to her feet. She hadn't shifted position since I'd laid her down, so I knew that that was the way to the tree line. I started crawling, feeling my way over the wet leaf litter, and soon emerged into the open ground.

There was an immediate difference in the ambient noise. The dull pounding of rain into mud took over from the almost tinny noise of its hitting leaves. It was just as dark, however, and because of the dead ground I couldn't see any lights from the house.

I stood up and stretched, then ripped an armful of palm leaves from some trees at the edge and laid them out on the ground at my entry point, throwing mud on top to keep them in place. Then, with the heel of my boot, I scraped deep score marks into the mud for good measure. It didn't matter if Charlie's men found the long straight puddles after first light— by then I'd either have done my job and be away from here, or it would all have gone to rat shit anyway and Carrie and Luz would need finding.

I set off toward the house, conscious that the helicopter would be somewhere to my left. I was tempted to make my way over to it and look for a weapon. But what if the pilot was asleep inside or listening to a Walkman? What if they had somebody on stag? It was unlikely, in the middle of nowhere and with us now lost in the jungle, but still, I couldn't take the chance of a compromise so far from the house. The aim was to get all of us out of here, not go the best of three rounds with someone in a helicopter.

As I crested the high ground, I saw the glimmer of light from the single bulb burning away in the shower area. There was no other lighting, nothing from Luz's bedroom, or Carrie and Aaron's. I certainly couldn't tell if our escape window was still open or not, and I didn't intend getting close enough to that side of the house to find out. Why bother? It was wasting time. I'd go to the side where I knew there was an entry point that would definitely get me in.

I moved back down the slope and, avoiding the helicopter, made my way around to the other side of the house as more thunder rumbled above. Picking my way through the mud, eventually moving up to the left of the house, I crested the high ground again. The shower-area light was now to my right, still trying to penetrate the curtain of rain.

Approaching the tubs, I became aware of the chug of the generator, and at that point got onto my hands and knees and began to crawl. The mud felt warm and lumpy on my bare skin, almost soothing the itchy swellings on my stomach.

The chug was soon drowned out by the rain beating on the lids of the plastic tubs. There were no signs of life from the house, and it wasn't until I drew level with the storeroom that I could just make out a thin sliver of light coming from beneath the door. I kept moving, and eventually saw a dull yellow glow filtering through the screen on the window between the bookshelves, but no movement inside.

There was no need to crawl anymore as I got to the end of the tubs and drew level with the porch and vehicles. Covered in mud, I stood up and moved cautiously toward them.

I headed for the Land Cruiser, now pointing toward the track through the woods, rain hammering on its bodywork. I stood off to the side and could see movement inside the house, though from this distance they wouldn't be able to see me. "Lurking," standing in the shadows and watching, was a skill I'd learned as a young squaddie in Northern Ireland, during long hours on foot patrol in Republican housing projects. We'd watch people eat their dinners, do the ironing, have sex.

Through the haze of rain and screens I could see the fans still spinning by the armchairs, which were empty. Three guys were sitting at the kitchen table, all dark-skinned and dark-haired, one with a beard. Weapons lay on the floor. Two of the guys wore chest harnesses. All of them were smoking, and seemed to be having a sober conversation. They were probably trying to make up the story of how we'd managed to get away.

There was no sign of Aaron.

I checked Baby-G as I blew out the water that ran down my face and into my mouth. Less than ninety minutes to go before they discovered he knew jack shit.

I moved off to the right so I could get an angle through the front entrance and see the bedroom doors. Both were closed. He was either in one of them, or inside the computer room; I'd find that out soon, but the priority was to check if the Mosin Nagant or M-16 were still in the Land Cruiser. There had been no light, no movement or steamed-up windows in any of the three trucks. It was safe to approach.

I wiped the water from the side windows and checked inside. No sign of either weapon or gollock, not that I could see much in the dark. It was a long shot, but I'd have been making a basic error if I hadn't checked.

I went to the rear of the truck and slowly but firmly pressed the release button and opened the glass top section of the rear gate six inches, just enough for the interior lights to come on, then bent down and scanned the luggage area. No weapons, no bergen, no gollock. I pushed the section back down until it hit the first click and killed the lights.

I moved toward the storeroom to take a look through the gap under the door. As I passed the bookshelf window, too far from it for the weak light to illuminate me, I saw that all three were still sitting at the table.

The tin roof above me was getting pummeled bigtime as I moved in toward the side of the house and stepped up on the concrete foundations of the extension. The noise drowned anything it might have been useful to hear.

Moving back out into the rain and around the water barrel, I could now see the light seeping from under the storeroom door. I got back on the concrete and down on my hands and knees, shook my head to get off as much water as I could so it wouldn't run into my eyes, then shoved my right eye against the gap.

I saw Aaron at once, sitting in one of the director's chairs under the glare of the computer-room fluorescent lighting. A man, maybe mid forties, in a green shirt and with no chest harness or weapon visible, was sitting next to him in the other canvas chair, in the act of offering him a cigarette, which he took.

Beyond them, sitting at Luz's computer and with his back to me, was a younger man, in blue, with long hair tied in a ponytail like Aaron's, except his was still black. I guessed by the primary colors darting about the screen and the frenzied movement of the mouse that he was playing a game. An M-16 was resting against the table beside him.

I looked back at Aaron. His nose was bloodied and his eyes swollen, and the right one had blood leaking from it. But he was smiling at the green guy, maybe feeling happy with himself that he'd gotten us away. I was glad he didn't know what had happened since.

By now the cigarette had been lit and he took long, grateful drags. Green Guy got up and said something to Blue, who didn't bother to turn from the game, just raising his free hand instead as Green Guy went into the living room to join the other three.

Right, so there were at least five of them, and there might be more in the bedrooms. What now?

I lay on the concrete and watched the inactivity for a few minutes as Aaron enjoyed his cigarette, taking it from his mouth, examining it between his thumb and forefinger, exhaling through his nose. I was trying to come up with something that would get me Aaron and one of those weapons.

Taking the final drag, he turned in his chair to look at Blue playing Luz's game, then he ground the butt into the concrete.

Shit! What's he up to?

I leaped back and scrambled behind the water barrel just as the door burst open and light flooded the area. Aaron launched himself off the concrete into the mud, followed by startled Spanish screams.

As he ran and slithered into the darkness toward

the tubs, there was a long burst of automatic fire from within the storeroom.

I curled up, making myself as small as possible as yells echoed from the living room, together with the sound of feet pounding on floorboards.

Rounds were hitting the tin wall with dull thuds as the weapon burst out of control.

Aaron had already faded into the darkness when Blue got to the door, hollering in panic, and took aim with a short sharp burst.

I heard an anguished gasp, then chilling, drawn-out screams.

His pain was quickly drowned by panicky M-16s opening up through the window between the bookshelves to my right, just blasting away into the night. Their muzzle flashes created arcs of stroboscopic light outside the window, as the mesh screen disintegrated.

Blue was screaming at the top of his voice—probably to cease firing, because that was what happened. Panic and confusion ricocheted between them in rapid, high-pitched Spanish. Someone was with Blue at the door, and they shouted at each other as if they were trading on the stock market. Other voices weighed in from just inside the living area.

I stayed curled up to conceal myself behind the water barrel as Blue moved out into the rain toward Aaron. The rest withdrew inside, still shouting at each other.

I had to act: now was my time. I stepped into the rain after him, keeping to the right of the door to avoid the light, quickly checking through the storeroom for movement. There wasn't any.

Rain fell into my eyes and blurred my vision. Blue's back was just visible in the light spilling from the storeroom, as he advanced on the dark, motionless shape of Aaron on the ground a few yards ahead of him. The M-16 was in his right hand, and the muzzle was trailing down alongside his calf.

I was no more than five paces behind him, and still walking. I didn't want to run and risk slipping. I kept moving, concentrating on the back of his head. He was taller than me. Now nothing else mattered as I entered his zone. He'd sense I was there soon.

I leaped behind him and a bit to his right, jamming my left leg between his, bodychecking him, at the same time grabbing at his face with my left hand, pulling hard, trying to pull him back over me. I wanted his mouth, but felt mostly nose when the warmth of his shout hit my hand. The weapon fell between us as his hands came up to snatch my hand away.

Still pulling hard, I arched him backward, yanking back his head, presenting his throat. I raised my right hand high above my head, palm open, and swung down hard to chop across his throat. I had no idea where it landed, but he dropped like a stunned pig in a slaughterhouse, taking me with him into the mud.

I kicked myself free, scrambling over the top of him until I lay across his chest, feeling the hard alloy of the magazines between us. My right forearm jammed into his throat and I leaned on it with all my weight. He wasn't dead; it hadn't been that good. The chop had gotten the nerves that run on each side of the trachea and messed him up for a while, that was all.

No reaction, no resistance, no last kicks yet. I pressed into him, shaking the rain off as it kept trying to get into my eyes. Looking up, I could see into the storeroom. The others were probably still in the living room, trying to come to terms with the even bigger nightmare they were now facing, waiting for Aaron's body to be dragged back by this dimwit who'd let him escape.

I looked down on him, his eyes closed, no kicking or resistance. I eased off and put my ear to his mouth. No sound of breathing. I double-checked by digging the middle and forefinger of my right hand into his neck to feel the carotid pulse. Nothing.

I rolled off him and felt for Aaron. My hands were soon warm with his blood as I felt up his body for his neck. He, too, was dead. I scrabbled around in the mud for the M-16, then started to remove Blue's chest harness. I rolled him over, unclipping it from his back, then dragged off the neck and shoulder straps. His arms lifted limply in the air as I pulled.

With the harness weighing heavily in one hand and the M-16 in the other, I ran to the back of the house for the cover and light it afforded me, and placed the weapon on the sink. The moths had found shelter out of the rain as well, flitting around the light on the wall between the sink and the shower as I gulped air, knowing I didn't have much time before they came out here to see what was taking their friend so long. Forget the heli. If anyone was still in it now, he was deaf.

Aaron's blood dripped off my hands as I took out a fresh thirty-round mag and pushed my thumb down into it to make sure it was full. For me it was too full with thirty rounds—I took out the top one and pushed down again to check that the spring had a chance to do its job. I pressed the release catch on the right and removed the old magazine, then pushed the fresh one home by sliding it into the rectangular housing, waiting to feel it click home before giving it a shake to make sure it was secure. I cocked the weapon: the sound was barely audible above the rain battering the tin roof.

There was a round already in the chamber and it

flew out into the mud as it got replaced with a new one from the mag; it wasn't necessary to have done it, it just made me feel better to see a round going into the chamber.

I applied Safe, quickly checking the other three mags in the pouches of the nylon harness. If I was in the shit and changing mags I didn't want to slap on a half-empty one. This took precious extra seconds but was always worth the effort.

I put the harness on, straps over my shoulders and neck, the magazine pouches across my chest, and clipped the buckle at the back, continuously grabbing air in an effort to keep my heart rate down, while listening for shouts that would tell me they'd discovered Blue.

My panting slowed and I mentally prepared myself. Pulling a magazine from the harness, I held it in my left hand with the curved shape facing away from me so it was ready to be rammed into the magazine housing if this one became empty. Then I grabbed the stock, wrapping my left hand around the whole bunch.

I thumbed the safety, pushing past the first click—single rounds—and all the way to Automatic, my index finger inside the trigger guard, then moved out into the rain once more, toward the heli to clear the corner in the darkness, and on toward Aaron and Blue. Their bodies were lying as I'd left them, motionless in the mud next to each other as the rain bounced in little pools around them. Looking into the storeroom and beyond, I couldn't see any movement apart from the blurred images on Luz's screen.

There was more thunder but no lightning as I moved forward, butt in the shoulder, weapon up, both eyes open. My breathing calmed down as it became fuck-it time once again.

I stepped up onto the concrete and into the light from the storeroom. I moved inside, avoiding the cot, lifting my feet up high before replacing them to avoid the cans, spilled rice, and other shit strewn across the floor. Eyes forward, weapon up.

I could hear them in the kitchen area and began to smell cigarettes. The talking was heated: today had been one big fuckup for all concerned.

There was movement, a chair scraping, boots walking toward the computer room. I froze, both eyes open but blurred by rain, index finger pad on the trigger, waiting, waiting . . .

I was going to have the upper hand for no more than two seconds. After that, if I didn't get this right, I was history.

The boots appeared. Green Guy. He turned, saw me, his scream cut short as I squeezed. He fell back into the living room.

As if on autopilot I followed him through the doorway, stepping over his body into the smoke-filled room. They were panicking, screaming out at each other, wide-eyed, reaching for their weapons.

I moved off to the left, into the corner, both eyes open, squeezing short sharp bursts, aiming into the mass of movement. The hot empty cases bounced off the wall to the right and then my back before clinking against each other as they hit the floor. I squeezed again . . . nothing.

"Stoppage! Stoppage!" I fell to my knees to present a smaller target.

It was as if my world was in slow motion as I tilted the weapon to the left to present the ejection opening. It had no working parts: they were being held to the rear. Looking inside, there were no rounds in the magazine, no rounds in the chamber. My eyes were now fixed on the threat in front.

I hit the release catch and the empty mag hit my leg on its way to the floor. Two bodies were sprawled, one moving with a weapon, one on his knees trying to get the safety off. I locked on to it. The mist of the gun's propellant was already mixing with the heavy cigarette smoke. The bitterness of cordite clawed at the back of my throat.

I twisted the weapon over to its right and presented the magazine housing. The fresh magazine was still in my left hand; I rammed it into the housing, banged it into position from the mag bottom, and slapped my hand down hard onto the locking lever. The working parts went forward, picking up a round as I got the weapon into the shoulder, brought the barrel to what I was looking at, and fired on my knees.

Another mag and it was all over.

There was silence as I reloaded, apart from the rain hitting the roof and the kettle whistling on the stove. Two of the bodies were on the floor; one was slumped forward over the table, his face distorted with a dead man's sneer.

I remained on my knees, surveying the carnage. The acrid stench of cordite filled my nostrils. Mixed with the cigarette smoke, it looked as if a dry-ice machine was running, covering the bodies, some with their eyes still open, some not. There wasn't much blood on the floor yet, but it would be there as soon as their bodies gave it up.

I looked around. Everybody I had seen was accounted for, but the bedrooms had to be checked.

Getting to my feet, butt in my shoulder, I gave three short bursts through the door to Luz's room, then forced my way in, and then the same with Carrie and Aaron's. Both were clear and Luz's window was now closed.

I turned to the kitchen. The floor was covered in a mixture of mud and blood.

I went over to the stove, kicking my way past empty cans that had been shot or pushed onto the floor, and took the kettle off the burner. I poured myself a mug of tea from a tin of bags on the side. It smelled of berries and I threw in some brown sugar and stirred it as I walked toward the computer room, kicking a weapon out of the way. I dragged the blood-soaked Green Guy away from the door; empty cases chinked together as his body moved them across the floor. I stepped into the computer room and closed the door behind me.

Seated in a director's chair, I slowly sipped the sweet, scalding liquid while picking out two empty cases that had gotten caught between my chest and the harness on their way to the floor. My hands were starting to shake a little, as I silently thanked all those years of skill-at-arms training that had made stoppage drills second nature.

Tilting the mug for the last few drops of the tea, I got to my feet and went to Aaron and Carrie's bedroom. I pulled off the harness and changed into an old black cotton sweatshirt with a faded Adidas logo on the front.

It was time to drag Aaron out of the mud. I put the harness back on, gathered up their purple bedsheet, and went to the Land Cruiser with the M-16. I checked that the keys were still inside, lowered the rear seats ready for Carrie, then climbed into the Mazda and fired it up.

The headlights bounced up and down as I bumped through the mud to Aaron. He was heavy to retrieve, but I finally got him into the back of the Mazda and wrapped him up in the sheet. As I tucked one corner over his face, I thanked him quietly.

Closing the tailgate, I left the truck where it was, then dragged Blue and hid him among the tubs before walking back to the house. I turned off the living-room lights and closed the door before kicking Blue's empty cases under the desk and storeroom shelving. Luz didn't need to see any of that: she had seen enough already today. I knew what happened to kids when they were exposed to that shit.

Finally, using a flashlight from the storeroom shelves to light my way, I dragged the cot out into the rain and threw it into the back of the Land Cruiser. It just fit on the opened lower half of the tailgate. Then I headed for the dead ground and the tree line.

37

The wipers pushed away the flood with each stroke, only for it to be instantly replaced, but not before I glimpsed the entry point in the tree line.

The Land Cruiser hit a tree stump and reared up, tilted over to the left, and came back down just as the headlights hit on the palm-leaf markers.

I left the lights and engine running, grabbed the flashlight from the passenger seat, ran around and dragged out the cot. With a firm grip on one of the legs as it trailed behind me, I broke through the tree line.

"Luz! Where are you? Luz! It's me, it's Nick, call to me!"

I shone the flashlight in a broad sweep but it only reflected back at me off the wet leaves. "Luz! It's me, Nick."

"Over here! We're over here! Nick, please, please, Nick!"

I turned to my right and pushed toward her, dragging the cot away from a stand of wait-a-while that wanted to hang on to it. Just a few feet more and the flashlight beam landed on Luz, soaking wet, kneeling by her mother's head, her hair flat and her shoulders shaking. Carrie was lying beneath her, in pain, covered in leaf litter. Seeing Luz's face in the flashlight beam, she raised a hand, trying to remove the hair stuck to her face. "It's okay, baby, everything's okay, we can go back to the house now."

I dragged the cot alongside them, and inspected the job I'd done on her leg. It wasn't as good as it should have been: maybe I didn't deserve that first-aid badge after all. Thunder rumbled and cracked above the canopy.

"Where's Daddy? Is Daddy at the house?"

Luz looked at me from the other side of her mother, squinting into the flashlight beam, her red face wet with rain and tears.

I looked down and busied myself with the dressings, pleased that the weather, distance, and canopy would have soaked up the sounds of automatic gunfire. I didn't know what the hell to say.

"No, he went to get the police. . . ."

Carrie coughed and screwed up her pale face, smothering her child into her chest. She looked at me quizzically over her head. I closed my eyes, put the flashlight on to my face, and shook my head.

Her head fell back and she let out a low cry, her eyes shut tight. Luz's head jumped up and down as her chest convulsed. She tried to steer her mother's thoughts elsewhere, thinking it was only physical pain. "It's okay, Mom, Nick's going to get you back to the house. It's okay."

I'd done as much as I could with the dressings. "Luz, you've got to help me get your mom on the cot, okay?" Moving the flashlight slightly so as not to blind her, I looked at her scared face, nodding slowly as rain coursed down it. "Good. Now get behind your mother's head, and when I say, I want you to lift her from under the armpits. I'll lift her legs at the same time and we'll get her on the cot in one go. Got it?"

I shone the flashlight above Carrie's head as Luz got into a kneeling position behind her mother's head. Carrie was still thinking of Aaron. That pain was far greater than anything her leg was causing. "That's right. Now put your arms under her armpits." Carrie raised herself limply to try to help her daughter.

I jammed the flashlight into the mud. The beam shone up into the canopy and rain splattered onto the front of the lens. On my knees, I slid one arm under the small of her back and the other under her knees. "Okay, Luz, on my count of three—are you ready?"

Thunder reverberated over the canopy.

A small but serious voice answered, "Yes, I'm ready."

I looked at what I could see of Carrie's face. "You know this is going to hurt, don't you?"

She nodded, her eyes closed, taking sharp breaths.

"One, two, three—up, up, up."

Her scream filled the night. Luz was startled. Carrie had gone down harder than I'd have wanted, but at least that phase was over. As soon as she landed she started breathing quickly and deeply through gritted teeth as Luz tried to comfort her. "It's okay, Mom, it's okay . . . sssssssh."

I pulled the flashlight from the mud and placed it on the cot next to Carrie's good leg so that it shone upward, creating horror-movie shadows on their faces. "The hard parts are done."

"It's okay, Mom. Hear that? The hard parts are done."

"Luz, grab your end, just lift it a little and I'll lift this end, okay?"

She jumped to her feet and stood as if to attention, then bent her knees to grip the aluminum handles.

"Ready? One, two, three, up, up, up."

The cot lifted about six inches and I immediately started crashing backward through the vegetation in the direction Carrie's feet were pointing. More thunder rumbled, swamping Carrie's sobs. Luz still thought it was just pain. "We'll see Daddy soon. It's okay, Mom."

Carrie couldn't hold back and cried out into the storm.

I kept checking behind me and soon made out the lights of the Land Cruiser penetrating the foliage. Just a few paces later we were out in the open.

The rain was relentless as we lifted Carrie into the back of the vehicle, like a patient into an ambulance, her legs protruding onto the tailgate. "You need to stay with your mother and hold on to her in case we hit a bump, okay?"

There was going to be no problem with that. Carrie pulled her child down and mourned covertly into her wet hair.

As I drove very slowly toward the rear of the house, the headlights cut through the rain and bounced back off the shiny skin and Plexiglas windows of the Huey. Its rotors drooped as if depressed by the weather.

Carrie was still getting soothing messages from Luz as we pulled up by the storeroom door. It took longer than I'd expected to get her inside, kicking cans out of the way, not worrying now that there was no one to alert. We waddled with the cot into the brightly lit computer room. She was in a bad way, with soaked, bloodstained clothes, pruned skin, glued hair, red eyes, and covered from head to toe in leaf litter.

As we lowered her to the floor near the two PCs, I looked to Luz. "You need to go and turn the fans off."

She looked a bit confused but did it anyway. The fans would make the moisture evaporate quicker, producing a chilling effect. Carrie was in enough danger from shock as it was.

As soon as Luz left us, Carrie pulled me down to her, whispering at me, "You sure he's dead, you sure? I need to know . . . please?"

Luz made her way back to us as I looked her straight in the eye and nodded. There was no dramatic reaction: she just let go of me and stared up at the slowing fans.

There was still nothing I could do to help her with her grief, but I could do something about her physical injuries. "Stay with your mother, she needs you."

The medical suitcase was still on the shelf, though it had been opened and some of the contents scattered. I collected everything together and threw it back in the case, then knelt at the side of the cot and searched through to see what I could use. She'd lost blood, but I couldn't find a drip kit or fluids.

"Luz? Is this the only medical kit you have?"

She nodded, holding hands with her mother, squeezing her fingers tight. I guessed they would have depended on a heli coming in to get them in the event of serious illness or accident. That wasn't going to happen tonight, not with this downpour—but at least it was keeping Charlie at bay. As long as it kept raining so hard he wouldn't be able to fly back to find out why contact had been broken.

I found the dihydrocodeine under the shelves. The label might have said one tablet when required, but she was getting three, plus the aspirin I was pushing from its foil. Without needing to be asked, Luz announced she was going to fetch some Evian. Carrie swallowed eagerly, desperate for anything to deaden what she was feeling. With this batch swallowed it wouldn't be long before she was dancing with the fairies, but for now she was studying the wall clock. "Nick, tomorrow, ten o'clock . . ." She turned to me, her expression pleading.

"First things first."

I ripped the crunchy wrapper from a cloth bandage and started to replace the belt and bits of sweatshirt in a figure eight around her feet. She had to be stabilized. As soon as that was done, we needed to be out of this house before the weather improved and Charlie fired up his helis. Even if the rain stopped when we were halfway to Chepo, the Hueys would catch up to us en route.

"The clinic in Chepo, where is it?"

"It's not really a clinic, it's the Peace Corps folks and—"

"Have they got an Emergency Room?"

"Sort of."

I pressed the soles of her feet and her toes and watched the imprint remain for a second or two until her blood returned.

"Two thousand people, Nick. You've got to talk to George, you must do something. If only for Aar—"

Luz returned with the water and helped her mother with the bottle.

I didn't disturb the dressings over the wound site, or the foliage packed between her legs, but just gradually worked my way up her legs with the four-inch bandages. I wanted to get her looking like an Egyptian mummy from her feet up to her hips. Carrie just lay there, staring vacantly at the now stationary fans.

I got Luz to hold her mother's legs up a little so I could feed the bandage under them. Carrie cried out, but it had to be done. She managed to calm herself, and looked directly into my eyes. "Talk to George, you'll speak his language. He won't listen to me, never has . . ."

Luz was on her knees, holding her mom's hand once more. "What's happening, Mom? Is Grandpa coming to help?"

Carrie stared at me, mumbling to Luz, "What's the time, baby?"

"Twenty after eight."

Carrie squeezed her hand.

"What's wrong, Mom? I want Daddy. What's wrong?"

"We're late . . . We've gotta get Grandpa . . . He'll be worrying . . . Talk to him, Nick. Please, you've got to . . ."

"Where's Daddy? I want Daddy." She was getting hysterical as Carrie held her hand tight. "Soon, baby, not yet . . . Get Grandpa . . ." Then she turned her head away from her daughter and her voice was suddenly much quieter. "Nick has to go and do something for us first—and himself. I don't mind waiting, Chepo isn't that far." She stared at me for a few moments with half-closed, glazed eyes, then rested her head back on the cot, mouth open. But there wasn't any noise. Her big, wet, swollen eyes looked at me and begged silently.

Luz got up and went over to her PC. "We'll see Daddy soon, right?"

Carrie couldn't tilt her head far enough back to see her. "Get Grandpa."

"No, not yet," I said. "Get a search engine—Google, something like that."

Both of them looked at me as if I was mad. My eyes darted between them. "Just do it, trust me."

Luz was already clicking the keyboard of her PC at the other end of the room when Carrie beckoned me closer.

"What?" I could smell the mud caked in her hair, and heard the sound of the modem handshaking.

She stared at me, her pupils almost fully dilated. "Kelly, the Yes Guy. You got to do something . . ."

"It's okay, I've taken care of that, for now at least."

She smiled like a drunk.

"I got it, Nick—I got Google."

I walked over and took her place on the chair, and typed in "Sunburn missile."

It threw up a couple of thousand results, but even the first I clicked on made grim reading. The Russian-designed and -built 3M82 Moskit sea-skimming missile (NATO code-named SS-N-22 "Sunburn") was now also in the hands of the Chinese. The line drawing showed a normal, rocket-shaped missile, quite skinny, with fins at the bottom and smaller ones midway up its ten meters. It could be launched from a ship or from a trailerlike platform that looked like something from *The Jetsons*.

There was a defense analyst's review:

> The Sunburn antiship missile is perhaps the most lethal in the world. The Sunburn combines a Mach 2.5 speed with a very low-level flight pattern that uses violent end maneuvers to throw off defenses. After detecting the Sunburn, the U.S. Navy Phalanx point defense system may have only 2.5 seconds to calculate a fire solution before impact—when it lifts up and heads straight down into the target's deck with the devastating impact of a 750 lb. warhead. With a range of 90 miles, Sunburn . . .

Devastating wasn't the word. After the initial explosion, which would melt everyone in the immediate vicinity, everything caught in the blast would become a secondary missile, to the point of steel drinks tray decapitating people at supersonic speed.

That was all I needed to know.

I moved off the chair and walked toward the other two. "Luz, you can get your grandad now."

38

I knelt down beside Carrie. "The banjo you were talking about, is it a river? Is that why they have a boat?"

The drugs were kicking in. "Banjo?"

"No, no—where they came from last night, remember? Is it a river?"

She nodded, fighting hard to listen. "Oh, the Bayano? East of here, not far."

"Do you know where they are exactly?"

"No, but . . . but . . ."

She motioned me with her head to bend down closer. When she spoke, her voice was shaking and trying to fight back the tears. "Aaron next door?"

I shook my head. "The Mazda."

She coughed and started to cry very gently. I didn't know what to say: my head was empty.

"Grandpa! Grandpa! You gotta help . . . There were these men, Mom's hurt and Daddy's gone for the police!" She was getting herself into a frenzy. I moved over to her. "Go and help your mom, go on."

I found myself facing George's head and shoulders in the six-by-six-inch box in the center of the screen. It was still a bit jittery and fuzzy around the edges, just like last night, but I could clearly see his dark suit and tie over a white shirt. I plugged in the headset and put it over my ears so nothing could be heard over the tinny internal speaker. Luz had been protected so far from all this shit: there was no need for that to change. "Who are you?" His tone was slow and controlled over the crackles.

"Nick. A face to the name at last, eh?"

"What's my daughter's condition?" His all-American square-jawed face didn't betray a trace of emotion.

"A fractured femur but she's going to be okay. You need to fix something up for her at Chepo. Get her picked up from the Peace Corps. I'll—"

"No. Take them both to the embassy. Where is Aaron?" If he was concerned, he wasn't sounding it.

I looked behind me and saw Luz, close to Carrie but within earshot. I turned back and muttered, "Dead."

My eyes were on the screen, but there was no change of expression in his face—nor in his voice. "I repeat, take them to the embassy, I'll arrange everything else."

I shook my head slowly, looking into the screen as he stared back impassively. I kept my voice low. "I know what's happening, George. So does Choi. You can't let the *Ocaso* take the hit. You know how many people will be there? People like Carrie, Luz—real people. You have to stop it."

His features didn't move a millimeter until he took a breath. "Listen up, boy, don't get yourself involved in something you don't understand. Just do exactly what I said. Take my daughter and Luz to the embassy, and do it right now."

He hadn't denied it. He hadn't asked, "What's the *Ocaso*?"

I needed to finish my piece. "Get it stopped George, or I'm reaching out to anyone who will lis ten. Call it off and I'm silent for life. Simple."

"Can't do that, boy." He leaned forward as if he wanted to get closer to intimidate me. His face took up a lot of screen. "Reach out all you want, no one will be listening. Just too many people involved, too many agendas. You're getting into ground that you wouldn't be capable of understanding."

He moved back, his shirt and tie returning to the screen. "Listen up good, I'll tell you what's simple. Just take them to the embassy and wait there. I'll even get you paid off, if it helps." He paused, to ensure I was really going to get the message. "If not? Take my word for it, the future won't look bright. Now just get with the program, take them to the embassy, and don't get dragged into something that's so big it'll frighten you."

I listened, knowing that as soon as I was through those embassy gates I'd be history. I knew too much and wasn't one of the family.

"Remember, boy, many agendas. You wouldn't be sure who you'd be talking to."

I shook my head and pulled off the headset, looking around at Carrie with a shrug of exasperation.

"Let me speak to him, Nick."

"No point. He's hearing, not listening."

"Two thousand people, Nick, two thousand people . . ."

I went over to them both and grabbed one end of the cot with both hands. "Luz, we need blankets and water for your mom. Just pile them up in the storeroom for the journey."

I pulled the cot back so Carrie was within reach of the headset, and placed it over her head, repositioning the mike so it was near her mouth. Above us, George's face still dominated the screen as he waited for my answer.

"Hi, it's me."

The face on the screen was impassive, but I saw the lips move.

"I'll live . . . all those people won't if you don't do something to call it off."

George's mouth worked for several seconds, but his expression remained set. He was arguing, rationalizing, probably commanding. The one thing he still wasn't doing was listening.

"Just once, just for once in my life . . . I've never asked you for anything. Even the passport wasn't a gift, it came with conditions. You have to stop it. Stop it now . . ."

I looked at George, and his cold, unyielding face as he spoke. It was now Carrie's turn to listen. She slowly pulled the headset from her face, her eyes swollen with tears, and let it drop onto her chest.

"Disconnect it . . . get him out of here . . . It's over . . . Comms are closed."

I left them to it as George had already cut the comms himself. The box had closed down. That was because he'd be moving on to the missile crew using the relay.

Looking up at the ceiling, I followed the black wires from the dishes, down behind the plywood boards, and out under the tables, looking like a plate of spaghetti as they jumbled themselves up with white wires and fought with each other on their way to feed the machines.

Sliding under the desk, I started to pull out anything that was attached to anything else as I shouted at Carrie. "Where's the relay board? Do you know where the relay is?"

I got a weak reply. "The blue box. It's near where you are somewhere."

Luz came back into the room and went to her mother.

Under the mass of wiring, books, and stationery I found a dark blue and badly scratched alloy box, just over a foot square and four inches thick. There were three coaxial cables attached, two in, one out. I pulled out all three.

There was mumbling behind me. I turned just in time to see Luz heading for the living-room door. "Stop! Stay where you are! Don't move!" I jumped to my feet and moved over and grabbed her. "Where are you going?"

"Just to get some clothes. I'm sorry . . ." She looked over to her mother for support. I let go so she could be at her mother's side, and as I turned to follow her I noticed a small pool of blood that had started to seep under the door. I ran into the storeroom and grabbed the first thing I could find for the job, a half-empty fifty-pound plastic bag of rice that had been kicked over. I lugged it back and placed it like a sandbag against the bottom of the door. "You can't go in here—it's dangerous, there could be a fire. The oil lamps fell when the helicopters came, it's everywhere. I'll get your stuff for you in a second."

Getting back under the table, I ripped out every wire that was attached to anything, then listened to make sure it was still raining.

"I'll get the clothes for you now, Luz, just stay here, okay?"

I nearly gagged when I opened the door and stepped over the rice bag. The smell of cordite had gone, replaced by death, a smell like a bad day in a butcher's shop. Once the door was closed I turned on the light. The four bodies lay among the splintered wood and smashed glass, their blood in thick, congealed pools on the floorboards.

I tried to avoid stepping in anything as I went and got a spare set of clothes for Luz and a sweatshirt for

Carrie. Opening the door, I threw them out into the computer room. "Get changed, help your mother. I'll stay in here."

Positioning my feet to avoid the blood, I started to pull a chest harness from under Green Guy. It must have been dragged from the table as he collapsed, and was dripping with blood. That didn't matter, what did was the mags inside.

I started to wrench off the other harnesses. They too, were soaking, and some of the mags had been hit by rounds. The nylon had split open, exposing twisted metal and bits of brass.

Hefting three harnesses, all filled with fresh mags, I rescued my docs that had been scattered on the floor and collected two hundred and twelve blood stained dollars from the five bodies. Feeling less naked, I secured them in my leg pocket before checking the bookshelf for mapping of Chepo and the Bayano.

I found what I was looking for, and she was right, it was to the east of Chepo.

There was no time to ponder, we had to leave. The weather might clear at any minute. If the Peace Corps couldn't do anything for her, they could at least get her to the city.

I ran through onto the porch, and out into the wonderful heli-repelling rain. As soon as I got to the Land Cruiser I dumped the gear in the footwell, then jammed the M-16 down between the passenger seat and the door before I closed it. I didn't know why, I just didn't want Luz seeing it.

I went around to the other side and checked the fuel. I had about half a tank. I grabbed the flashlight and headed for the Mazda. When I lifted the squeaking tailgate, the light beam fell on the now blood stained bedsheet covering Aaron. I could also see the gas cans secured at the rear and jumped in beside him, my boots slipping in a pool of his blood. The sickly, sweet smell was as bad as it was in the house. I rested my hand on his stomach to steady myself, and discovered he was still soft. I dragged out one of the heavy containers and slammed the tailgate shut.

I unscrewed the Land Cruiser's fuel cap and pulled back the nozzle of the fuel can. The pressure inside was released with a hiss. I hurriedly poured the fuel into the tank, splashing it down the side of the truck, drenching my hands.

As soon as the fuel can was empty I closed the cap and threw the metal container into the footwell on top of the harnesses. I thought I might be needing it later.

39

Having made sure that mud had replaced Aaron's blood on my Timberlands, I walked back toward the glare of the computer room and checked that the rice bag was still doing its job.

Carrie was smoking, and as I got closer I didn't need a sniffer dog to tell me what. Luz was sitting on the floor beside the cot, stroking her mother's brow and watching the smoke ooze from her nostrils. If she disapproved, she wasn't showing it.

Carrie's flooded eyes stared up in a daze at the motionless fan as her daughter carried on gently massaging her sweating forehead. I squatted at her feet and gave them another pinch. The blood flow was still there.

As I stood up my gaze switched to Luz. "Your mom tell you where it was?" The question about the giggle-weed was irrelevant and I didn't know why I'd asked it—just something to say, I supposed. Her head didn't move but her eyes swiveled up at me. "As if . . . but it's okay, today."

Carrie tried to let out a bit of a laugh, but it sounded more like coughing.

I bent down and retrieved one of the cloth bandages from the floor and put it into my pocket. "Time to go."

She gave a nod as Carrie took another deep drag of the joint.

"Come on, then, let's get your mother out of here."

We both had our hands on the cot, Luz at the feet end, facing me.

"Ready? One, two, three. Up, up, up."

I steered us while she shuffled backward, plowing through the littered storeroom floor. We squelched through the mud and slid Carrie once more into the back of the truck, head first. I sent Luz back into the storeroom for the blankets and Evian while I used the bandage to secure the cot legs at the head end to anchorage points to stop its sliding around on the journey. Carrie turned her head toward me, sounding drowsy on her cocktail of dihydrocodeine, aspirin, and giggleweed.

"Nick, Nick . . ."

I was busy tying off in the dull interior lighting.

"What am I going to do now?"

I knew what she was getting at, but this wasn't the time. "You're going to Chepo and then you'll both be in Boston before you know it."

"No, no. Aaron—what am I going to do?"

I was reprieved by Luz returning with water and an armful of blanket, which she helped me arrange over Carrie.

I jumped off the tailgate back into the mud and went around and climbed into the driver's seat. "Luz, you've got to keep an eye on your mother—make sure she doesn't slide about too much, okay?"

She nodded earnestly, kneeling over her as I started up and turned the Land Cruiser in a wide arc before heading onto the track. The main beams swept over the Mazda. Carrie eventually saw it in the red glow of our taillights as we crept past.

"Stop, stop, Nick—stop . . ."

I put my foot gently on the brake and turned in my seat. Her head was up, neck straining to look out of the gap at the rear. Luz moved to support her. "What's up, Mom? What's wrong?"

Carrie just kept on staring at the Mazda as she answered her daughter. "It's okay, baby—I was just thinking about something. Later." She pulled Luz close and gave her a hug.

I waited for a while as the rain fell, more gently now, and the engine turned over. "Okay to go?"

"Yes," she said. "We're done here."

The journey to Chepo was slow and difficult as I tried to avoid as many potholes and ruts as I could. I really wished there had been time to look for another gollock. Going back into the jungle without one reminded me too much of Tuesday.

By the time we came out into the dead valley the rain had eased a bit further and the wipers were just on intermittent. I looked up over the wheel, knowing I wouldn't be able to see, but hoping all the same that the cloud cover was still low. If not, there'd be a heli or two revving up soon.

Once we hit the road, which looked more like a river in places, we were making no more than about five miles an hour. My nostrils were hit by the smell of cannabis again, and glancing around, I saw Luz kneeling by her mother with the joint just an inch from Carrie's lips, trying hard to get it back into her mouth between jolts. I fished in my pocket for the dihydrocodeine. "Here, give your mother another of these with some water. Show the doctors or whoever the bottle. She's had four in total and an aspirin. Got that?"

Eventually the fortified police station came into view and I called for directions. "Where's the clinic? Which way do I go?"

Luz was the one on top of this now: her mother was well and truly gone. "It's kinda behind the store."

That I did know. We passed the restaurant and the jaguar wasn't even curious as we drove on into the dark side of town.

I flicked my wrist to have a check of Baby-G. It was just before midnight. Only ten hours in which to do what I had to do.

I took a right just before the cinder-block store. "Luz, this the right way? Am I okay?"

"Yep—it's just up here, see?"

Her hand passed my face from behind and pointed. About three buildings down was another cinder-block structure with a tin roof and the circular Peace Corps sign—stars and stripes, only instead of the stars a dove or two. I really couldn't see in this light.

I pulled up outside and Luz jumped out of the back. I could tell it wasn't a medical clinic at all: there was a painted wooden plaque below more doves which read, "American Peace Corps Community Environmental Education Project."

Luz was already banging on the front door as I looked back at Carrie and spoke. "We're here, Carrie, we're here."

I got no response. She was definitely waltzing with the pixies, but at least the pain was subdued.

The door-banging got a result. As I climbed out of the Land Cruiser, heading for the tailgate, a woman in her mid-twenties with long brown sleepy hair appeared on the threshold, wearing a tracksuit. Her eyes darted about rapidly as she took in the scene.

"What's wrong, Luz?"

Luz launched into a frenzied explanation as I got into the rear and undid the security bandage. "We're here, Carrie," I said.

She murmured to herself as the young woman came to the rear, now wide awake. "Carrie, it's Janet—can you hear me? It's Janet, can you hear me?"

There was no time for hellos. "Got trauma care? It's an open fractured femur, left leg."

Janet held out her arms and began to ease the cot out of the truck. I grabbed the other end and between us we lugged Carrie inside.

The office was barely furnished, just a couple of desks, cork boards, a phone, and a wall clock. What I'd seen so far was doing nothing to make me feel happier about their level of expertise. "Can you treat her? If you can't, you need to get her into the city."

The woman looked at me as if I was crazy.

More people were emerging sleepily from the rear of the building, three men in different shades of disarray, and a rush of American voices. "What's happened, Carrie? Where's Aaron? Ohmigod, you okay, Luz?"

I stood back as events took over. A trauma pack appeared and a bag of fluid and a giving set were pulled out and prepared. It was hardly a well-rehearsed scene from *ER*, but they knew exactly what they were doing. I looked at Luz, sitting on the floor holding her mother's hand once more as Janet read the dihydrocodeine label on the bottle.

According to the wall clock it was 12:27—nine and a half hours to go. I left them to it for a while and went back to the truck. Once in the driver's seat I hit the cab light, wanting to save the flashlight because I might need it later, and unfolded the map to get my bearings on the Bayano. It came from the massive

Lago Bayano to the east of Chepo, maybe twenty miles away, and snaked toward the Bay of Panama on the edge of the Pacific. The river's mouth was in line of sight of the entrance to the canal and, a little farther in, the Miraflores. If this was the river they were on, they had to be at the mouth. Sunburn couldn't negotiate high ground: it was designed for the sea. The range to the canal was about thirty miles. Sunburn's range was ninety. It made sense so far.

I studied the map, wondering if Charlie was doing the same before getting out there to look for it. He didn't know what I did so he'd be scanning the sixty to seventy miles of jungle shoreline that fell within Sunburn's range and could be used as a launch point. That was a lot of jungle to sift through in less than ten hours. I hoped it would mean the difference between my destroying it and his repossessing it so he could hand it straight over to FARC.

The map indicated that the only place to launch from was the east bank as the river joined the sea. The west bank also had a peninsula, but it didn't project far enough out to clear the coastline. It had to be the east, the left-hand side as I went down the river. It had to be, and there was only one way to find out.

The Bayano's nearest reachable point was four miles south, according to the map, via a dry-weather, loose-surface road. There, the river was about two hundred yards wide. It then wound south, downstream to the coast for about six miles. In reality it would be more, because of the river's bends and turns. By the time it hit the coastline it was over a mile across.

That was it, that was all I knew. But fuck it, I had to work with the information I had and just get on with it.

I went to the rear of the truck and closed the tailgate, then got back behind the wheel, fired the engine, and moved off.

I bumbled about the dark sleepy town, trying to head south using the Silva compass still around my neck. The map was the same 1980s 1:50,000 scale I'd had for Charlie's house, and Chepo had grown a bit since then.

It was only then that I realized I hadn't said anything to Carrie and Luz. Carrie wouldn't have heard but, still, it would have been nice to say good-bye.

After downing two bottles of Evian during an hour of the dry-weather track, now just a mixture of mud and gravel, I saw a river in the tunnel of light carved out immediately ahead of me. Stopping, I checked the map and distance once more, then jumped out of the truck with the flashlight and picked my way down the muddy bank. The crickets were loud, but the movement of water was louder.

The river wasn't a raging torrent surging with a massive rush, even after these rains: it was wide enough to accommodate all the water coming from the tributaries that fed it with a constant flow. It was certainly moving in the right direction, from my right to my left, heading south toward the Pacific—although so would every other bit of water this side of the country so near to the sea.

Running along the bank, I checked for a boat, anything that would get me downstream quickly. There wasn't even a jetty—no ground sign, nothing, just mud, rough grass, and the odd scabby-looking tree.

I scrambled up the bank, got into the truck, and checked the map and mileometer once more. This river had to be the one I wanted: there was nothing else around here big enough to get mixed up with.

I drove back up the track toward Chepo, checking each side of me for somewhere to hide the Land Cruiser, but even after two miles the ground picked out by the headlights still looked completely bare. I finally parked up on the side of the road, dragged out the dried-out chest harnesses, the M-16, and the fuel can, then tabbed back toward the river with the gear dangling off me like a badly packed Cub Scout.

40

I seemed to have spent my whole life sitting against a tree in the mud, listening to a million crickets disturbing the night. I wasn't under the canopy this time, but down by the Bayano as it rumbled past me out there in the dark. The mozzies weren't out in such force here, but enough had found me to bring up a few more lumps on my neck to replace the ones that had just started going down. I ran my tongue around my mouth: my teeth felt more than furry now, it was as if they had sheepskin coats on. I thought about what I was doing here. Why couldn't I smarten up? Why hadn't I just killed Michael and been done with it in the first place?

With only half an hour to push before first light and a move to the target, I knew I was bullshitting myself. I knew I would have done this regardless. It wasn't just the fact that so many people—real people—were at risk: it was that maybe, just for once, I was doing the right thing. I might even end up feeling a little proud of myself.

Pulling my knees up and resting my elbows or

them to support my head, I started to rub my stubbly, sweaty face on my forearms. I could hear the weak but rapid *wap wap wap* of a Huey somewhere out there in the darkness. I couldn't see any navigation lights, but could tell it was only one aircraft. Maybe Charlie had been back to the house. After what he'd found waiting for him there, he'd be out looking, but I had no control over that. Anyway, for the time being he'd be having those aircraft search the coastline for Sunburn rather than us three.

Invisible birds started their morning songs as a bright yellow arc of sunlight prepared to break the skyline and yield up a hot morning. I'd already repacked my docs and map in the two layers of plastic bags, tying each one off with a knot. I checked the Velcro flaps on the individual mag pouches of the harnesses to ensure that they weren't going to fall out during the next phase. Finally, I made sure all my clothing was loose, with nothing tucked in that might catch water and weigh me down.

I undid the plastic clips for the back straps of the harnesses and fed the ends through the handle of the fuel can before refastening them. I did the same with the neck straps, through the carrying handle of the M-16. I'd learned from my own experiences, and from others, that more soldiers get killed negotiating rivers than ever die in contacts under the canopy. That was why everything was attached to the empty fuel can and not to me, and why I hadn't moved until first light.

I dragged the whole bunch down to the edge of the tepid, rusty-brown water. It felt good as I waded in up to my thighs, then ducked my head in to take the sweat off my face. Refreshed, I heaped the three harnesses and weapon on top of the floating fuel can, which wanted to go with the current. It was stronger than it had looked from the bank, and freshly dislodged foliage, green and leafy, sped past as the fuel can bobbed in front of me, now more than half submerged with the weight of its load. I pushed on into gradually deepening water, forearms over the weapon and harnesses, until eventually my feet began to lose touch with the riverbed. I let myself go with the flow, kicking off from the mud like a child with a swimming float. The stream carried me with it, but I kept contact with the bottom to keep some control, alternately kicking and going with the current as if I was doing a moonwalk.

The loggers had been here and both sides of the river looked like a First World War battlefield, a wasteland of mud and tufted grass, just the odd dead tree left standing.

Because of the river's meandering route I had no idea how long it was going to take to get to the mouth, not that there was much I could do about it: I was committed.

After about half an hour, with the sun low but clearly in view, the jungle began to sprout up on either side of me, and as the foliage got denser it cut out more and more light. The sun wasn't yet high enough to penetrate the gap the river created in the canopy, so above me was just brilliant blue sky. Apart from the noise of the moving water, there was only the odd screech from more invisible birds up in the canopy.

I kicked along, keeping near the left bank, always having contact with the bottom as the river got wider. The opposite bank gradually got farther away, looking as if it were another country now. The jungle gave way to mangrove swamp, making the place look like a dinosaur's backyard.

The river soon widened to well over a mile. As I rounded a particularly wide, gentle bend, I could see the Pacific Ocean lying just half a mile farther down-

stream. In the far distance I could see two container
ships, their funnels spewing smoke as the sun bounced
off the calm, flat surface of the sea. A lush green island
sat out there three, maybe four miles away.

I kept on going, keeping my eyes peeled for anything that would help me locate Sunburn.

The current was slowing and I moved downstream
another five hundred yards. Then, maybe two hundred yards from the river mouth, approaching me to
my left, was a small, open-decked fishing boat that
had been dragged up onto the bank and left to rot; its
rear had collapsed altogether, leaving a skeleton of
gray, rotting wood. As I got closer I could see there
was a clearing beyond the boat in which stood a small
wooden hut in a similar state of decay.

I floated past, my eyes scanning the area. There
had been movement, fresh movement. I could clearly
see the dark underside of some large ferns just up
from the bank, and some of the two-foot-tall grass
growing around the boat was interlaced where it had
been walked through. Only tiny details, but enough.
This had to be it, it had to be. There was no other reason for it to be here. But I couldn't see any sign in the
mud leading from the bank.

I carried on for another fifty yards, with the ocean
in front of me now, until the canopy took over and
the boat disappeared. I touched bottom and slowly
guided the fuel can ashore.

Dragging the gear into the canopy, I got on my
knees and unbuckled the harnesses and M-16. The
weapon wouldn't need any preparation: a brief dip in
a river wasn't going to stop its working.

I donned the first chest harness and adjusted the
straps so that it hung lower than it should have, virtually around my waist. Then I put on the second, a bit
above the first, adjusting it so it was at the bottom of

my rib cage, and the third one higher still. I rechecked that all the mags were stored facing the correct way, so that as I pulled them out with my left hand the curve of the magazine would be facing away from me, ready to be slapped straight into the weapon. Finally, after rechecking chamber on the M-16, I sat on the fuel can for a minute or two longer, mentally adjusting and tuning myself in to the new environment. The coolness of the water on my clothes began to lose out to humid heat once more as I checked Baby-G. It was 7:19, and here I was, Rambo'd up, bitten half to death, my leg held together by a soggy bandage, and no plan except to use all my mags.

This would be my "go, no-go" point. Once I moved from here there would be no turning back unless I fucked up totally and was running for my life. I looked down and watched the drips from the harnesses hit the mud, making little moon craters, not wanting to check my docs in my map pocket just in case the knots hadn't worked. This was wasting time, I was as ready as I was ever going to be, so just get on with it. . . .

Wiping my hair back with my fingers, I stood up, jumped up and down to check for rattles and that everything was secure. Then I removed the safety catch, pushing past single rounds, all the way to Automatic.

I moved toward the hut, pausing every few paces, listening for warnings from the birds and other jungle life, butt in my shoulder, trigger finger against the guard, ready to shoot and scoot with a full mag to scare, confuse, and, with luck, kill while I broke contact.

The ground was a lot wetter and muddier here because we were at sea level. I wanted to get a move on but also had to take my time; I had to check the area around the hut, because it would be my only escape route. If the shit hit the fan it would be a case of straight down to the river, pick up the fuel can jump in and go for it, down to the sea. After that, well—whatever.

Like a cautious bird rooting for food among the leaf litter, I squelched forward four paces per bound, my Timberlands heavy with mud, lifting my feet up high to clear the crap and mangrove vines on the jungle floor as I concentrated on the sun-bleached wooden hut ahead.

I stopped just short of the clearing, went slowly onto my knees in the mud and protective foliage, looked and listened. The only man-made sound around here was the water dripping from my clothes and chest harnesses onto the leaf litter.

The track leading into the canopy had been used recently, and something had been pulled along it that cut a groove through the mud and leaves. On either side of that groove were footprints that disappeared with the track into the trees. I hadn't seen any sign in the mud as I floated past, because it had been covered with dead leaves and maybe even had water poured over it to wash away the sign. Past the bank, though, the sign was clear to see: stones pressed into the mud by boots, crushed leaves, broken cobwebs. I got up and started to parallel the track.

Within twenty paces I came across the Gemini, with a Yamaha 50 on the back. It had been dragged up the track and pulled off to the right, blocking my way. The craft was empty apart from a couple of fuel bladders and some fallen leaves. I was tempted to wreck it, but what was the point? I might be needing it myself soon, and destroying it would take time as well as alert them to my presence.

I moved on, and could still see masses of ground

sign heading in both directions as the narrow track meandered around the trees. Still paralleling the track to my left, I started to move deeper into the canopy, using it as my guide.

Sweat trickled down my face as the sun rose and lit the gas under the pressure cooker. A heart-monitor bird was up in the canopy somewhere, and the crickets just never stopped. Soon the sun was trying to penetrate the canopy, shafts of bright light cutting down to the jungle floor at a forty-five-degree angle. My cargo pants had a life of their own, the weight of the wet, caked-on mud making them swing against my legs after each pace.

I patrolled on, stopping, listening, trying to keep up speed but at the same time not compromise myself by making too much noise. I continued checking left, right, and above me, all the time thinking: What if? and always coming up with the same answer: Shoot and scoot, get into cover, and work out how to box around and keep moving to the target. Only when I knew I was fucked would I try to head back to the fuel can.

There was a metallic clang in the trees.

I froze, straining an ear.

For several seconds all I could hear was my own breath through my nose, then the clang rang out again. It came from straight ahead and just slightly off to my left.

Applying the safety catch with my right thumb, I went down slowly onto my knees, then onto my stomach. It was time to move slower than a sloth, but Baby-G reminded me it was 9:06.

I inched forward on my elbows and toes, with the weapon to my right, exactly as I had done when I attacked the Land Cruiser, except that this time I was having to lift my body higher than I'd have wanted to stop the chest harnesses from dragging in the mud.

I was panting: the crawl was hard work. I put out my hands, put pressure on my elbows, and pushed myself forward with the tips of my toes, sinking into the mud. Moving through the under-growth six inches at a time, I could feel the gloop finding its way up my neck and forearms. I stopped, lifted my head from the jungle floor, looked and listened for more activity but still only heard my own breath, sounding a hundred times louder than I wanted it to. Every soft crunch of wet leaves beneath me sounded like the popping of bubble wrap.

I was constantly looking for alarm trips—wires, pressure pads, infrared beams, or maybe even string and tin cans. I didn't know what to expect.

A mud-covered Baby-G now told me it was 9:21. I made myself feel better about the time by thinking that at least I might finally be on target.

Mosquitoes materialized from nowhere, whirring and whining around my head. They landed on my face and must have known that I couldn't do anything about it.

There was noise, and I froze. Another clunk of metal on metal—then a faint, fast murmur above the noise of the crickets. I closed my eyes, leaned my ear toward the source, opened my mouth to cut out internal noises, and concentrated.

The inflection in the voices wasn't Spanish. I strained to listen, but just couldn't work it out. They seemed to be talking at warp speed, accompanied now by the rhythmic thud of full fuel cans.

It was 9:29.

I had to get closer and not worry about the noise, not worry about the people making it. I needed to see what was happening so I could work out what I had to do within the next twenty minutes.

41

I lifted my chest from the mud and slithered forward. Very soon I began to make out a small clearing beyond the wall of green. Sunlight penetrated the canopy in thick shafts, dazzling me as it bounced off the wet ground and perimeter foliage.

Movement.

The black-shirted guy who'd been on the porch crossed left to right in the clearing before disappearing as quickly as he'd arrived, carrying two black garbage bags, half full and shiny in the sunlight. He wore a U.S. Army webbing belt with two mag pouches hanging down from it.

I took some slow, deep breaths to reoxygenate myself. The thud of my pulse kicked in my neck.

I made another two slow advances, not bothering to lift my head to look forward through the foliage. I'd know soon enough if they'd seen me.

The voices came again from my right, a lot clearer, and faster, but still in control. I could understand them now, sort of . . . They were Eastern European, maybe Bosnians. The flophouse had been full of them.

The small cleared area in the trees was about the size of half a tennis court. I couldn't see anything, but heard the unmistakable hiss of fuel under pressure being released in the vicinity of the voices.

One more slow, deliberate bound and now I heard the fuel splash. Not daring even to rub my lips together to wipe off the mud, I strained my eyes to the top of their sockets, my mouth open. I felt dribble run down from the corners.

Black Shirt was to my right, maybe six, seven yards away, standing with the little fat guy who'd been with him that night. He was still wearing the same checked shirt. The fuel cans were being emptied over the assembled contents of their camp: camouflage netting, American Army cots, a generator turned on its side, plastic garbage bags full and tied. All were piled into a heap. It was nearly time to leave, so they were destroying any evidence linking them to the site.

I remained perfectly still, my throat dry and sore as I tried to listen to the two Bosnians above the din of crickets and bird calls. Their voices still came from my right, but we were separated by foliage.

Holding my breath, straining my muscles to keep total control of them to cut down on noise, I edged forward another few inches, my eyes glued to the two at the garbage dump just a few yards away as the last of the fuel was poured and the cans thrown on top. I was so close I could smell the fumes.

As the area to my right opened up a bit I saw the backs of the two Bosnians, dressed in green fatigue tops and jeans, bathed in a shaft of sunlight. They were bent over a fold-down table, one twisting the hair on his beard as they both studied two screens inside a green metal console. There were two integrated keyboards below each screen. That had to be the guidance system; I'd wondered what it looked like. To the right of it was an opened laptop, but the sunlight was too bright for me to make out what was on any of the screens. Beside them on the ground were five civilian backpacks, two M-16s with mags on, and another fuel can—probably to deal with the electronic equipment after the launch.

I wanted to check the time but Baby-G was covered in mud. I couldn't risk movement so close on target. I watched the two Bosnians talk and point at the console screens, then look over at the laptop as one hit the keyboard. Beyond them I could see cables running down from the rear of the console and into the jungle. The Sunburn had to be at the river's mouth. As I'd have expected, the guidance system was separated from the missile itself. They wouldn't have wanted to be right on top of shed loads of rocket fuel when it went off. There was no generator noise, so I guessed the power supply must be part of the missile platform.

The Bosnians were still babbling as the fifth member came out of the canopy from behind the console. He, too, was dressed in a green fatigue top, but had black baggy pants, an M-16 over his shoulder and belt kit. He lit a cigarette with a Zippo and watched the Bosnians hovering over the screens. Sucking in deeply on his nicotine hit, he used his free hand to wave the bottom of his shirt to circulate some air around his torso. Even if I hadn't recognized his face, I would have known that pizza scar anywhere.

The two fuel pourers moved away from the garbage dump as Black Shirt lit up as well. They were totally uninterested in what was going on at the table just behind them and mumbled to each other as they checked the time.

All of a sudden the Bosnians began to jabber and

their voices went up an octave as Pizza Man sucked on his filter and bent in toward the screens.

Stuff was happening. There must be only minutes left. I had to make my move.

Taking a deep breath, I pushed up onto my knees, my mud-caked thumb shifting the safety to Auto as the weapon came into the shoulder. I squeezed with both eyes open, short, sharp bursts into the mud by the dump. There was a rapid *thud, thud, thud, thud* as the rounds penetrated the first layer of mud and slammed into the harder ground.

Unintelligible screams mixed with the sound of rounds on auto as the Bosnians panicked and the other two went for their weapons. The fifth just seemed to vanish.

My shoulder rocked back with another short burst as I held the weapon tight to stop the muzzle rising. I didn't want to hit the Bosnians: if they could fly the thing, they could stop it. The sounds of automatic gunfire and panic echoed around the canopy and a cloud of cordite hung in front of me, held by the foliage. The mag emptied as I kept on squeezing. The working parts stayed to the rear.

I got to my feet and moved position before they reacted to where the fire had come from. I ran to the right, toward the table, using the cover, the mud heavy on my clothes, pressing the magazine-release catch with my forefinger, shaking the weapon, trying to remove the mud-clogged mag.

I felt the mag hit my thigh as I fumbled at the lower harness and pulled out a fresh one. I smacked it on and hit the release catch. The working parts screamed forward as long bursts of automatic fire came from my left, from the clearing.

I dropped instinctively. Mud splattered my face and the air was forced out of my lungs. Gasping for breath, I crawled like a madman, pushing to the edge of the clearing. If they saw me they would fire where I'd dropped for cover.

I was in time to see the Bosnians disappearing down the track, their terrified voices filling the gaps between bursts of gunfire. I also saw Pizza Man, the other side of the clearing, in cover, shouting at them to come back.

"It's just one man, one weapon! Get back!"

It wasn't happening; the other two were following the Bosnians, firing long bursts into the jungle.

"Fucking assholes!"

Weapon in the shoulder, he took single shots at them. Fuck that, I wanted them alive.

Flicking safety to single rounds, I gulped in air, closed my left eye, and took aim center mass of what little I could see of him, stopped breathing, and fired. He dropped like a stone, disappearing into the foliage without a sound.

The other two were still firing into shadows as they moved down the track.

A cordite mist hung about the clearing as I let off another magazine at them. Steam oozed out of the cooling vents on the mud-covered stock and around my left hand. *Shit, shit, shit* . . . I wanted to create noise, I wanted to create confusion, I wanted to get everyone sparked up, not lose them in the jungle. But I wasn't going to chase them. It was pointless, there wasn't enough time.

I changed mags and crossed the clearing toward Pizza Man, weapon in the shoulder, moving fast but cautiously. The others might still come back, and I still couldn't see him.

He was alive, panting for breath and holding his chest, eyes open but helpless. Blood flowed gently between his fingers.

I tossed his weapon to one side and kicked him. "Close it down! Close it down!"

He just lay there, no reaction.

I grabbed his forearm and dragged him into the clearing, and it was then that I saw the exit wound gaping in his back.

His eyes were shut tight, taking the pain of the round and movement. I dropped his arm as he mumbled, almost smiling, "We're coming back, asshole . . ."

I leaned over him, butt in the shoulder, and thrust the muzzle into his face. "Stop it! Fucking stop it!"

He just smiled beneath the pressure of the metal stuck in his skin. The weapon moved as he coughed up blood over the end of the barrel. "Or what?" He coughed up some more.

He was right. I kicked him out of frustration as I ran to the table, checking the track for the others, checking Baby-G.

Just three minutes to go.

The left-hand VDU was full of Russian symbols, the other was a radar screen with a hazy green background peppered with white dots as its sweeping arm moved clockwise.

The laptop displayed the webcam image of the locks. A cable led from it, along the ground and up a tree, where a small satellite dish was clamped to a branch.

I looked back at the laptop. I could see the band playing, girls dancing, and crowds in the seats and more standing against the barriers. The *Ocaso* was in pride of place on the screen. Passengers thronged the decks, clutching cameras and video cameras.

Scrambling around to the back of the table, I fell to my knees and started pulling out the mass of wires and thick cables that led from the back of the console and out toward the sea. Some were just slotted in, some had a bracket over them, some were screwed into their outlets.

I tried desperately to disconnect them two at a time, almost hyperventilating in frustration as my wet, muddy hands slid about the plastic and metal. I fretted like a child in a blind panic, yelling at myself, "Come on! Come on! Come on!"

I looked over at the dump, wishing I had a gollock. But even if I found one and started slashing cables, chances were I'd electrocute myself. I couldn't tell which were transmission and which were power.

Curled up in pain, Pizza Man was watching me, his shirt soaked with blood and covered with mud and leaf litter.

Fighting another connection, I spun the laptop around just as the image started to refresh from the top.

A high-pitched whine started within the canopy, winding up like a Harrier jump jet before takeoff.

Within seconds the noise surrounded me.

Four cables to go. The more I tried to pull or unscrew them, the more I lost it.

I gave one big tug in frustration and despair. The console slid off the table and landed in the mud. The high-pitched whine became a roar as the rocket engines kicked in.

In almost the same instant there was a deafening, rumbling boom, and the ground began to shake under my feet. I stayed on my knees, looking up into the canopy as its inhabitants took off in a panic.

I didn't see vapor, I didn't see anything, I just felt the sickening rumble as the missile left its platform and surged out of the jungle. The treetops shook and debris rained down around me.

I didn't know what to feel as I released my grip on

the cables and looked over at the laptop, mesmerized, catching the last glimpse of the ship as the image faded.

I could hear Pizza Man, still curled up in the leaf litter like a child, panting, trying to get oxygen. When I looked at him, he was smiling. I was sure he was trying to laugh.

The screen was blank and there was nothing I could do but wait, wondering if I'd be able to hear the explosion, or if the sound would get swallowed up by the jungle and distance.

My chest heaved up and down as I tried to take deep breaths, swallowing hard, trying to relieve my dry throat, just waiting for the screen to refresh—or stay blank forever as the camera would surely be taken out as well.

I was right: he was laughing, enjoying the moment. The first strip at the top started to show and I could hardly contain the terrible feeling of expectation.

Slowly, lazily, the image unfolded and I braced myself for the scene of carnage, trying to convince myself that the camera's being intact was a good sign, then thinking I didn't know how far the camera was from the locks, so maybe not.

The picture refreshed itself. The ship was intact, everything was intact. The dancing girls were throwing their batons in the air and passengers were waving at the crowd on shore. What the fuck had happened? It should have made it there by now: it traveled at two and a half times the speed of sound.

I didn't trust what I was seeing. Maybe it was the image that had been captured just before the explosion, and I was going to wait for the next cycle.

I'd never felt so exhausted, and all other thoughts had left my mind. I didn't even care about a possible threat from the other four, though if they'd had any sense they'd already be dragging the Gemini into the water.

The smell of sulfur hit me as the exhaust seeped through the jungle, creating a low, smoky mist around the area and making it look like God lived here as the vapor was exposed to the brilliant shafts of light.

Pizza Man made gurgling sounds, coughing up more blood.

The top of the image began to unfold and this time I saw smoke. I knew it. I jumped to my feet and hovered over the laptop. Sweat dropped off my nose and chin and onto the screen. My sweatshirt pulled down on me with the weight of mud as I gulped in air to calm my heart rate.

Still the only thing I could see was smoke as the picture rolled on down.

It hadn't worked.

I sat back in the mud, more exhausted than I'd ever been in my life.

Then, as the image filled the screen, I saw that the ship was still there.

The smoke was coming from its funnels. The crowds were still cheering.

The sounds of the jungle returned. Birds screeched above me as they settled back in their roosts. I sat there, almost bonding with the mud, as the seconds ticked by. And then, starting as quiet as a whisper but increasing very rapidly, came the distinctive *wap wap wap* of much bigger birds.

The sound got louder and then came the rapid rattle of rotors as a Huey zoomed straight over me. Its dark blue underbelly flashed across the treetops, and I could hear others circling as its downwash shook the canopy and vegetation rained down about me.

Time to switch on.

I jumped to my feet and grabbed a fuel can, dousing the console, making sure fuel poured into the cooling vents at the back, then I did the same to the laptop. I picked up two knapsacks and threw them over a shoulder, hoping that whatever made them weigh so much was stuff I could use in the jungle.

Finally grabbing the weapon, I moved to Pizza Man, manhandling him over onto his back. There was no resistance. His legs started to tremble as he looked at me with a satisfied smile. The small entry wound high in his chest oozed blood each time he took a breath.

"It didn't work," I shouted. "It didn't make contact, you fucked up."

He didn't believe me and hung on to the smile, eyes closed, coughing more blood. I reached into his pocket and pulled out the Zippo.

The heli had returned and was over by the river, flying low and slow. Others were now closer. There were long, sustained bursts of automatic fire. They had found the escaping Gemini.

I knew he could hear me. "That's Charlie's people. They'll be here soon."

His eyes flickered open and he fought to keep the smile through the pain.

"Believe me, you fucked up, it didn't work. Let's hope they keep you alive for Charlie. I bet you two have a lot to talk about."

In truth, I didn't have a clue what they'd do. I just wanted to kill that smile.

"I hear he had his own brother-in-law crucified. Just think what he's going to do to you . . ."

As I heard heli noise almost directly overhead I ran over to the console and flicked the lighter. The fuel ignited instantly. They mustn't fall into Charlie's hands; then all he would need was another missile and he would be back in business.

I turned and ran from the flames. Passing Pizza Man, I couldn't resist giving him a taste of the kind of kicking I'd gotten back in Kennington.

He did the same as I had, just curled up and took it. I heard shouts from the track. Charlie's boys were here.

I flicked the Zippo again and tossed it onto the dump.

As the roar of the Hueys became almost deafening, I shouldered the knapsacks, picked up the weapon, and ran into the jungle as fast as the mud on my boots would let me.

42

Pulling down the visor to shade me from the sun, I watched through the dirty windshield as passenger after passenger, laden with oversized suitcases, was dropped off outside Departures. I felt a twinge of pain in my calf and adjusted myself in the seat to stretch my damaged leg as the roar of jet engines followed an aircraft into the clear blue sky.

There had been enough antisurveillance drills en route to the airport to throw off Superman, but still I sank into the seat and watched the vehicles that came and went, trying to remember if I had seen any of them or their drivers earlier.

The dash digital said it was nearly three o'clock, so I turned the ignition key to power up the radio, scanning the AM channels for news even before the antenna had fully risen. A stern American female voice was soon informing me that there were unconfirmed reports that FARC were behind the failed missile attack, which appeared to have been aimed at shipping in the Panama Canal. It was sort of old news now and low down in the running order, but it seemed that after it launched, fishermen saw the missile fly out of control before falling into the bay less than half a mile from the shore. The U.S. had already reestablished a presence in the republic as they were now trying to fish out the missile and set up defenses to stop any such further terrorist attacks.

The polished voice continued, "With approximately twelve thousand armed combatants, FARC is Colombia's oldest, largest, most capable and best equipped insurgency. It was originally the military wing of the Colombian Communist Party, and is organized along military lines. FARC has been anti-U.S. since its inception in 1964. President Clinton said today that Plan Colombia, the one point three billion—"

I flicked it back onto the FM Christian channel and hit the off switch before cutting the ignition again. The antenna retracted with a quiet electric buzz. It was the first bit of news I'd heard about the incident. I had done my best to avoid all media these past six days, but hadn't been able to resist any longer the temptation to find out what had happened.

The injury still hurt. Pulling up one leg of my cheap and baggy jeans, I inspected the clean dressing on my calf and had a little scratch at the skin above and below it as a jet thundered just above the parking garage on finals.

It had taken three long, wet, and hot days to walk out of the jungle, clean myself up, and hitch a ride into Panama City. The knapsacks had contained no food, so it was back to jungle survival skills and digging out roots on the move. But at least I could lie on the knapsacks and keep out of the mud, and although they didn't fit very well, the spare clothes helped keep the mozzies off my head and hands at night.

Once I'd reached the city, I dried out in the sun th two hundred odd dollars I'd lifted from the guys i the house and the blood flaked off them like thin scabs. I bought clothes and the dirtiest room in the old quarter that didn't care as long as I paid cash.

Up until Tuesday, four days ago, my credit card still hadn't been canceled, so it looked as if things were still okay with the Yes Man. After I'd cleaned myself up, I went into a bank and took out the max I could on it, $12,150, at some rip-off exchange rate, before using my ticket to Miami. From there I took a train to Baltimore, Maryland. It had taken two days on four trains, never buying a ticket for more than a hundred dollars so as not to arouse suspicion. After all, who pays cash for any journey costing hundreds? Only people who don't want a record of their movements, people like me. That's why the purchase of airline tickets for cash is always registered. I hadn't minded the Yes Man knowing I was out of Panama as he tracked me to Miami, but that was all I'd wanted him to know.

But now, three days later, who knew? Sundance and Sneakers might already be sightseeing in Washington, even phoning that half-sister to tell her that once they'd finished off some business they'd come to New York for a visit.

I heard the door handle open and Josh was at the window of his black, double-cabbed Dodge gas-guzzler. One hand pulled open the driver's door, the other cradled a Starbucks and a can of Coke.

I took the coffee as he climbed into the driver's seat and muttered, "Thanks," as I placed the paper cup in the center console holder. My fingernails and prints were still ingrained with jungle dirt; they looked like I'd been washing my hands in grease. It would take a few more days yet to wash out after my vacation from hygiene.

Josh's eyes stayed on the entrance to the long-term multi-story parking garage, on the other side of our short-term one. A line of vehicles was waiting to take a ticket and for the barrier to raise. "Still thirty minutes to kill until we're due," he said. "We'll drink them here."

I nodded, and pulled back on the pull tab as he tested the hot brew. Anything he said was okay by me today. He had picked me up at the station, driven me about for the last two hours, and had listened to what I was proposing. And now here we were, at Baltimore International Airport, where I should have arrived from Charles de Gaulle in the first place, and he had even bought me a Coke.

He still looked the same, shiny brown bald head, still hitting the weights, gold-rimmed glasses that somehow made him look more menacing than intellectual. From my side I couldn't see the torn-sponge scar on his face.

The Starbucks was still a bit too hot for him so he nursed it in his hands. After a while he turned toward me. I knew he hated me: he couldn't hide it from his face, or the way he talked to me. I would have felt the same, in his shoes.

"There'll be rules," he said. "You hear what I'm saying?"

Another jet came down over the truck and he shouted over the roar as he pointed every other word at me.

"You are first going to sort out this shit you've got us all in, man. I don't care what it's about or what you have to do—just finish it. Then, and only then, you call me. Only then we talk. We don't deserve this shit. It's a grim deal, man."

I nodded. He was right.

"Then, only when that's done, this is how it's going to be—like a divorced couple, a couple that do the right thing by their kids. You fuck that up, you fuc yourself up. It's the only way it's going to work. You hearing me? It's the last chance you're ever getting."

I nodded, feeling relieved.

We sat there and drank, both of us checking the vehicles that were trying to find a space.

"How's the Christian thing going?"

"Why?"

"You're swearing a lot nowadays . . ."

"What the fuck do you expect? Hey, don't worry about my faith, I'll see you if you ever get there."

That put an end to that conversation. We sat for another ten minutes, watching vehicles and listening to the aircraft. Josh gave occasional sighs as he thought about what he had agreed to. He was certainly not happy, but I knew he would do it anyway, because it was the right thing. He finished the Starbucks and put the cup into the console holder.

"That recycled paper?"

He looked at me as if I were crazy. "What? What's with you?"

"Recycled, the cup. A lot of trees are used making those things."

"How many?"

"I don't know—a lot."

He picked up the cup. "The sleeve says sixty percent post-consumer recycled fiber—feel better now, O spirit of the fucking woods?"

The cup went back into the holder. "Meanwhile, uptown . . . they're here."

We drove out of the garage and followed signs for long-term, eventually turning into the multi-story. I bent down into the footwell as if I'd dropped something as we approached the barrier and ticket machine. The last thing Josh needed was a picture of us together at this time.

I could see plenty of empty spaces but we drove

straight up the ramps to the second-to-last floor. The top floor was probably uncovered, and open to observation. This was the next best floor: there wouldn't be many vehicles coming up this far, and those that did would be easier to check out. I had to hand it to Josh, the guy was thorough.

We pulled into a space and Josh nodded at a metallic green Voyager with a mass of cartoon-character baby sunscreens pulled down, effectively blacking out the rear. The plates said "Maine—the Vacation State."

"Five minutes, got it? This is dangerous, she's my sister, for God's sake."

I nodded and reached for the handle.

"Just remember, man, she missed you last week. You screwed up big-time."

I got out and as I approached the Voyager the front window powered down to reveal a woman in her mid-thirties, black and beautiful, with relaxed hair pulled back in a bun. She gave an anxious half-smile and indicated for me to go around to the sliding door as she got out.

"I appreciate this."

There was no answer from her as she went over to Josh's truck and climbed in next to him.

I felt some apprehension at seeing Kelly. I hadn't done so for just over a month now. I slid the door across. She was strapped into the rear seat, staring at me, a little confused, maybe a little wary, as I got inside to conceal us both.

It's incredible how much children seem to change if you don't see them every day. Kelly's hair was cut much shorter than when I'd last seen her, and it made her look about five years older. Her eyes and nose seemed more defined somehow, and her mouth a bit larger, like a young Julia Roberts. She was going to be the spitting image of her mother.

I put on my smiley face, moving baby toys out of the way to sit down in the row in front of her. "Hello, how are you?" Nothing exuberant, nothing over the top as I sat between two strapped-in baby seats and looked back at her. The reality of it was, I just wanted to throw my arms around her and give her the world's biggest hug, but didn't dare risk it. She might not want me to; maybe it felt strange and new to her as well.

Something the size of a jumbo jet was taxiing upwind of us. I could hardly hear myself think and stuck my finger in my ear and made a funny face. At least I got a smile from her.

Josh's sister had left the engine turning over, and I could feel the air-conditioning working overtime as I pulled myself over the backrest and kissed her cheek. There wasn't any coldness in her reaction, but nothing in the way of exhilaration either. I understood: why get excited, only to be let down?

"It's great to see you. How are you?"

"Fine . . . what are those lumps on your face?"

"I got stung by some wasps. Anyway, what are you up to?"

"I'm on a vacation with Monica—are you going to stay with us? You said you were coming to see me last week."

"I know, I know, it's just that . . . Kelly, I . . . Listen, I'm sorry for not doing all the things I said I would with you. You know, call, come visit when I said I would. I always wanted to do those things, it was just, well, stuff, you know."

She nodded as if she knew. I was glad one of us did.

"And now I've mucked it up again and have to go away for a while today . . . but I really wanted to see you, even if it was only for a few minutes."

There was a roar that almost made the Voyager shake as the jumbo thundered down the runway and lifted into the sky. I waited, frustrated that I couldn't say what I wanted to until the noise died.

"Look, maybe I was jealous of Josh when you started to live with him, but now I know it's the right thing, the best thing. You need to be with his gang, having fun, going to Monica's for a vacation. So what I've worked out with Josh is, once I come back from sorting some stuff out, I'll be able to do things—you know, coming to see you, calling, going on vacation. I want to do all those things with you, because I miss you so much and think about you all the time. But it has to be like this now, you have to live with Josh. That make sense?"

She just looked and nodded as I carried on, barely taking a breath. "But just now I've got to make sure I finish stuff so that I can do those things with you. That okay?"

"We will go on vacation? You said we would one day."

"Absolutely. It might not be immediately, though. After you get back from Monica's you'll be going to a teacher for a while, and I have to sort out . . . well . . ."

"Stuff?"

We smiled. "That's right. Stuff."

Monica opened her door with a wide smile for Kelly. "We gotta go, honey."

Kelly looked at me with an expression that I couldn't read, and for one terrible moment I thought she was going to cry. "Can I talk with Dr. Hughes?"

Concern must have been written all over my face. "Why? Why's that?"

Her face conjured up an enormous grin. "Well, my dad just divorced my other dad. I got issues."

Even Monica laughed. "You been watching too much Ricki Lake, honey!"

She closed the door on a smiling Kelly and Monica drove out.

Josh spoke through his window as I walked back, watching his sister leave. "You'll get the transportation for the train station outside Arrivals."

I nodded and turned toward the elevator with a small wave, but he wanted to say more. "Look, man, maybe you ain't quite the dwarf I thought you were. But you still gotta sort your shit out, then we get to sort our shit. You gotta get a grip on your life, man, get some religion, anything."

I nodded as he drove out, two vehicles behind the Voyager, and leaned against a concrete support as another aircraft thundered overhead on final approach.

She was fucked up enough and the way I acted made it worse. But I was no longer going to sign her over to Josh and walk away. That was the easy way out. She not only needed but deserved two parents, even if they were divorced. I hoped that my being there, if only a little, was better than not at all. Besides, I wanted to be there.

So that was the plan. Once I had sorted out the "stuff," I'd come back here and we'd do it correctly. Sort out visitation rights, and a system that gave Kelly what she needed, structure to her life and the knowledge that the people around her were there for her.

However, the "stuff" wasn't going to be easy. Two obstacles had to be overcome if I wanted to stop me, Kelly, and even Josh and his family, from being targets—now and forever.

George and the Yes Man.

The long-term solution to this problem had to be through George. He'd be able to call off the dogs. And the way to contact him would be through Carrie. How I was going to do this I hadn't a clue, because George was going to be severely pissed off. That was a whole new world that I hadn't even started to work out yet.

First I needed to get to Marblehead, and the two trains I was taking would get me there by six tomorrow morning. It shouldn't be hard to find Carrie, or her mother. The place wasn't that big.

As for the short-term problem of the Yes Man, he had to be dealt with quickly, just in case Sundance and Sneakers were already on their way. I still had the security blanket, which I'd tell George about, and Kelly was safe. The Left Luggage ticket was valid for three months and hidden behind one of the pay phones at Waterloo. I would have to go and get it before then and put it somewhere else.

No way was I going to call him yet, though. The call would be traced. I'd do that tomorrow, when the train got me into Boston South. Or maybe I'd call once I got into Union Station in Washington, before getting the connection north.

Then I thought, Why bother going back to the U.K. at all? What was there waiting for me apart from the sports bag?

I started to fantasize and thought that maybe, if I played my cards right, George could even fix me up with a U.S. passport. After all, I had stopped the system getting into FARC's hands and maybe sticking out of the top of an aircraft carrier. I'd say that was pretty Stars and Stripes.

I pushed away from the concrete and reached the lift as the doors opened and a couple pushed out a luggage cart carrying far too many suitcases.

Who knows? Maybe while I was sorting stuff out, Carrie would let me sleep on her mother's couch.

ATRIA BOOKS
PROUDLY PRESENTS

Liberation Day

ANDY McNAB

Coming soon in hardcover
from Atria Books

Turn the page for a preview of
Liberation Day. . . .

1

TUESDAY, NOVEMBER 6, 2001, 23:16 hrs.

The submarine had broken surface ten minutes earlier, and its deck was still slippery
beneath my feet. Dull red flashlight glow
glistened on the black steel a few yards ahead
of me as five of the boat's crew feverishly
prepared the Zodiac inflatable. As soon as
they'd finished, it would be carrying me and
my two team members across five miles of
Mediterranean and onto the North African
coast.

One of the crew broke away and said something to Lotfi, who'd been standing next to me by the hatch. I didn't understand that much Arabic, but Lotfi translated. "They are finished, Nick—we are ready to float off."

The three of us moved forward, swapped places with the submariners, and stepped over the sides of the Zodiac onto the antislip decking. Lotfi was steering and took position to the right of the Yamaha 75 outboard. We bunched up near him, on each side of the engine. We wore black ski hats and gloves, and a "dry bag"—a Gore-Tex suit—over our clothes with elastic wrists and neck to protect us from the cold water. Our gear had been stowed in large zip-lock waterproof bags and lashed to the deck along with the fuel bladders.

I looked behind me. The crew had already disappeared and the hatch was closed. We'd been warned by the captain that he wasn't going to hang around, not when we were inside the territorial waters of one of the most ruthless regimes on earth. And he was willing to take even fewer risks on the pickup, especially if things had gone to rat shit while we were ashore. No way did he want the Algerians capturing his boat and crew. The Egyptian navy couldn't afford to lose so much as a row-boat from their desperately dilapidated fleet, and he didn't want his crew to lose their eyes or balls, or any of the other pieces the Algerians liked to remove from people who had pissed them off.

"Brace for float-off." Lotfi had done this before.

I could already feel the submarine moving beneath us. We were soon surrounded by bubbles as it blew its tanks. Lotfi slotted the Yamaha into place and fired it up to get us under way. But the sea was heaving tonight with a big swell, and no sooner had our hull made contact with the water than a wave lifted the bow and exposed it to the wind. The Zodiac started to rear up. The two of us threw our weight forward and the bow slapped down again, but with such momentum that I lost my balance and fell onto my ass on the side of the boat, which bounced me backward. Before I knew what was happening, I'd been thrown over the side.

The only part of me uncovered was my face, but the cold took my breath away as I downed a good throatful of salt water. This might be the Mediterranean, but it felt like the North Atlantic.

As I came to the surface and bobbed in the swell, I discovered that my dry bag had a leak in the neck seal. Seawater seeped into my cheap sweatshirt and cotton pants.

"You okay, Nick?" The shout came from Lotfi.

"Couldn't be better," I grunted, breathing hard as the other two hauled me back aboard. "Got a leak in the bag."

There was a mumble of Arabic between the two of them, and an adolescent snigger or two. Fair: I would have found it funny too.

I shivered as I wrung out my hat and gloves, but even wet wool keeps its heat-retaining qualities and I knew I was going to need all the help I could get on this part of the trip.

Lotfi fought to keep the boat upright as his pal and I leaned on the front—or bow, as Lotfi was constantly reminding me—to keep it down. He finally got the craft under control and we were soon plowing through the crests, my eyes stinging as the salt spray hit my face with the force of gravel. As waves lifted us and the outboard screamed in protest as the propeller left the water, I could see lights on the coast and could just make out the glow of Oran, Algeria's second largest city. But we were steering clear of its busy port, where the Spanish ferries to'd and fro'd; we were heading about ten miles east, to make landfall at a point between the city and a place called Cap Ferrat. One look at the map during the briefing in Alexandria had made it clear the French had left their mark here big-time. The coastline was peppered with Cap this, Plage that, Port the other.

Cap Ferrat itself was easy to recognize. Its lighthouse flashed every few seconds in the darkness to the left of the glow from Oran. We were heading for a small spit of land that housed some of the intermittent clusters of light we were starting to make out quite well now as we got closer to the coastline.

As the bow crashed through the water I moved to the rear of the boat to minimize the effects of the spray and wind, pissed off that I was wet and cold before I'd even started this job. Lotfi was on the other side of the outboard. I looked across as he checked his GPS (Global Positioning System) and adjusted the throttle to keep us on the right bearing.

The brine burned my eyes, but this was a whole lot better than the sub we'd just left. It had been built in the 1960s and the air conditioning was fading. After being cooped up in diesel fumes for three days, waiting for the right moment to make this hit, I'd been gagging to be out in the fresh air, even air this fresh. I comforted myself with the thought that the next time I inhaled diesel I'd be chugging along ninety yards below the Mediterranean, back to Alexandria, drinking steaming cups of sweet black tea and celebrating the end of my very last job.

The lights got closer and the coastline took on a bit more shape. Lotfi didn't need the GPS anymore and it went into the rubber bow bag. We were maybe four hundred yards off shore and I could start to make out the target area. The higher, rocky ground was flooded with light, and in the blackness below it, I could just about make out the cliff, and the beach Lotfi had assured us was good enough to land on.

We moved forward more slowly now, the engine just ticking over to keep the noise down. When we were about a hundred yards from the beach, Lotfi cut the fuel and tilted the outboard until it locked horizontal once more. The boat lost momentum and began to wallow in the swell. He'd already started to connect one of the full fuel bladders in preparation for our exfiltration. We couldn't afford to fiddle around if the shit hit the fan and we had to make a run for it.

His teeth flashed white as he gave us a huge grin. "Now we paddle."

It was obvious from the way they constantly ragged on each other that Lotfi and the one whose name I still couldn't pronounce—Hubba-Hubba, something like that—had worked together before.

Hubba-Hubba was still at the bow and dug his wooden paddle into the swell. We closed in on the beach. The sky was perfectly clear and star-filled, and suddenly there wasn't a breath of wind. All I could hear was the gentle slap of the paddles pushing through the water, joined now and then by the scrape of boots on the wooden flooring as one or other of us shifted position. At least the paddling had gotten me warm.

Lotfi never stopped checking ahead, to make sure we were going to hit the beach exactly where he wanted, and the Arabic for "right" I did know: *"Il al yameen, yameen."*

The two of them were Egyptian, and that was about as much as I wanted to know—not that it had turned out that way. Like me, they were deniable operators; in fact, everyone and everything about this job was deniable. If we were compromised, the U.S. would deny the Egyptians were false-flagging this job for them, and I guessed that was just the price Egypt had to pay for being the second biggest recipient of U.S. aid apart from Israel, to the tune of about two billion dollars a year. There's no such thing as a free falafel.

Egypt, in its turn, would deny these two, and as for me, the Egyptians probably didn't even know I was there. I didn't care; I had no cover documents, so if I was captured I was going to get screwed regardless. The only bits of paper I'd been issued were four thousand U.S. dollar bills, in tens and fifties, with which to try to buy my way out of the country if I got into shit, and keep if they weren't needed. It was much better than working for the Brits.

We kept paddling toward the clusters of light. The wetness down my back and under my arms was now warm, but still uncomfortable. I looked up at the other two and we nodded mutual encouragement. They were both good guys and both had the same haircut—shiny, jet black buzz cuts with a left-hand parting—and very neat mustaches. I was hoping they were winners who just looked like losers. No one would give them a second look in the street. They were both in their mid-thirties, not tall, not small, both clear-skinned and married, with enough kids between them to start up a soccer team.

"Four-four-two," Lotfi had said smiling. "I will supply the back four and goalkeeper, Hubba-Hubba the midfield and two strikers." I'd discovered he was a Manchester United fan, and knew more than I did about the English Premier League, which wasn't difficult. The only thing I knew about soccer was that, like Lotfi, more than seventy-five percent of Manchester United's fans didn't even live in the U.K.

They weren't supposed to talk about anything except the job during the planning and preparation phase, in a deserted mining camp just a few hours outside Alexandria, but they couldn't help themselves. We'd sit around the fire after carrying out yet another rehearsal of the attack, and they'd jabber on about their time in Europe or when they'd gone on vacation to the States.

Lotfi had shown himself to be a highly skilled and professional operator as well as a devout Muslim, so I was pleased that this job had gotten the okay before Ramadan—and also that it was happening in advance of one of the worst storms ever predicted in this part of the world, which the meteorologists had forecast was going to hit Algeria within the next twelve hours. Lotfi had always been confident we'd be able to get in-country ahead of the weather and before he stopped work for Ramadan, for the simple reason that God was with us. He prayed enough, giving God detailed updates several times a day.

We weren't going to leave it all to Him, though. Hubba-Hubba wore a necklace that he said was warding off the evil eye, whatever that was. It was a small, blue-beaded hand with a blue eye in the center of the palm, which hung around his neck on a length of cord. I guessed it used to be a badge, because it still had a small safety-pin stuck on the back. As far as the boys were concerned, I had a four-man team with me tonight. I just wished the other two were more help with the paddling.

The job itself was quite simple. We were here to kill a forty-eight-year-old Algerian citizen, Adel Kader Zeralda, father of eight and owner of a chain of 7-Eleven-type supermarkets and a domestic fuel company, all based in and around Oran. We were heading for his vacation home, where, so the int (intelligence) said, he did all his business entertaining. It seemed he stayed here quite a lot while his wife looked after the family in Oran; he obviously took his corporate hospitality very seriously indeed.

The satellite photographs we'd been looking at showed a rather unattractive place, mainly because the house was right beside his fuel depot and the parking lot for his delivery trucks. The building was irregularly shaped, like the house that Jack built, with bits and pieces sticking out all over the place and surrounded by a high wall to keep prying eyes from seeing the number of East European whores he got shipped in for a bit of Arabian delight.

Why he needed to die, and anyone else in the house had to be kept alive, I really didn't have a clue. George hadn't told me before I left Boston, and I doubted I would ever find out. Besides, I'd fucked up enough in my time to know when just to get the game-plan in place, do the job, and not ask too many questions. It was a reasonable bet that with over three hundred and fifty Algerian al-Qaeda extremists operating around the globe, Zeralda was up to his neck in it, but I wasn't going to lie awake worrying about that. Algeria had been caught up in a virtual civil war with Islamic fundamentalist groups for more than a decade now, and over a hundred thousand lives had been lost—which seemed strange to me, considering Algeria was an Islamic country.

Maybe Zeralda posed some other threat to the West's interests. Who cared? All I cared about was keeping totally focused on the job, so with luck I'd get out alive and back to the States to pick up my citizenship. George had rigged it for me; all I had to do in exchange was this one job. Kill Zeralda, and I was finished with this line of work for good. I'd be back on the submarine by first light, a freshly minted U.S. citizen, heading home to Boston and a glittering future.

It felt quite strange going into a friendly country undercover, but at this very moment, the president of Algeria was in Washington, D.C., and Mr. Bush didn't want to spoil his trip. Given the seven-hour time difference, Bouteflika and his wife were probably getting ready for a night of Tex Mex with Mr. and Mrs. B. He was in the States because he wanted the Americans to see Algeria as their North African ally in this new war against terrorism. But I was sure that political support wasn't the only item on the agenda. Algeria also wanted to be seen as an important source of hydrocarbons to the West. Not just oil, but gas: they had vast reserves of it.

Only fifty or so yards to go now, and the depot was plainly visible above us, bathed in yellow light from the fence line, where arc lights on poles blazed into the compound. We knew from Lotfi's recce (reconnaissance) that the two huge tanks to the left of the compound were full of kerosene 28, a domestic heating fuel.

On the other side of the compound, still within the fence line and about thirty yards from the tanks, was a line of maybe a dozen tankers, all likely to be fully laden, ready for delivery in the morning. Along the spit, to the right of the compound as I looked at it, were the outer walls of Zeralda's vacation house, silhouetted by the light of the depot.

2

The view of the target area slowly disappeared as we neared the beach and moved
into shadow. Sand rasped against rubber as
we hit bottom. The three of us jumped out,
each grabbing a rope handle and dragging the
Zodiac up the beach. Water sloshed about
inside my dry bag and sneakers.

When Lotfi signaled that we were far
enough from the waterline, we pulled and
pushed the boat so that it faced in the right
direction for a quick getaway, then started to
unlash our gear using the ambient light from
the high ground.

A car zoomed along the road above us, about two hundred yards away on the far side of the peninsula. I checked the traser on my left wrist; instead of luminous paint, it used a gas that was constantly giving off enough light to see the watch face. It was twenty-four minutes past midnight; the driver could afford to put his foot down on a deserted stretch of coast.

I unzipped my bergen from the protective rubber bag in which it had been cocooned and pulled it out onto the sand. The backpacks were cheap and nasty counterfeit Berghaus jobs, made in Indonesia and sold to Lotfi in a Cairo bazaar, but they gave us vital extra protection: if their contents got wet we'd be out of business.

The other two did the same to theirs, and we knelt in the shadows, each checking our own gear. In my case this meant making sure that the fuse wire and homemade OBIs (oil-burning incendiaries) hadn't been damaged, or worse still gotten waterlogged. The OBIs were basically four one-foot square Tupperware boxes with a soft steel liner, into the bottom of which I'd drilled a number of holes. Each device contained a mix of sodium chlorate, iron powder and asbestos, which would have been hard to find in Europe these days, but was available in Egypt by the truckload. The ingredients were mixed together in two-pound batches and pressed into the Tupperware.

All four OBIs were going to be linked together in a long daisy chain by three-foot lengths of fuse wire. Light enough to float on top of oil, they would burn fiercely until, cumulatively, they generated enough heat to ignite the fuel. How long that would take depended on the fuel. With gasoline it would be almost instantaneous—the fuse wire would do the trick. But the combustion point of heavier fuels can be very high. Even diesel's boiling point is higher than that of water, so it takes a lot of heat to get it ignited.

But first we had to get to the fuel. All fuel tanks are designed with outer perimeter "bungs," walls or dykes whose height and thickness depend on the amount of fuel that will have to be contained in the event of a rupture. The ones that we were going to breach were surrounded by a double-thick wall of concrete building blocks, just over three feet in height and about four yards away from the tanks.

Lotfi and Hubba-Hubba had been rehearsing their tasks so often they would have been able to do them blindfolded—which, in fact, we had done some of the time during rehearsals. Training blindfolded gives you confidence if you have to carry out a job in the dark, such as dealing with a weapon stoppage, but it also makes you quicker and more effective even when you can see.

The attack theory was simple. Lotfi was

going to start by cutting out a section of the wall, three blocks wide and two down, facing toward the target house. Hubba-Hubba had turned out to be quite an expert with explosives. He would place his two frame charges, one on each tank, on the side facing the sea and opposite where I was going to lay out and prepare my four OBIs.

As the frame charges cut a two-foot-square hole in each tank, the fuel would spew out and be contained in the bung. The ignited OBIs would float on top of the spillage, burning in sequence along the daisy chain, so that we had constant heat and constant flame, which would eventually ignite the lake of fuel beneath them. We knew that the kerosene 28 fuel oil rising in the bung would ignite when the second of the four OBIs ignited, which should happen as the fuel level reached just less than halfway up the bung wall. But we wanted to do more than just ignite the fuel within the bung: we wanted fire everywhere.

The burning fuel would disgorge through the cut-out section in the wall and out onto the ground like lava from a volcano. The ground sloped, toward the target house. As soon as Lotfi had shown me the sketch maps from his recce, I'd seen that we could cut the house off from the road with a barrier of flame. I hoped I was right; two hundred policemen lived in barracks just three miles along the road to Oran, and if they were called to the scene we didn't want to become their new best friends.

Just as importantly, we could make what happened tonight look like a local job—an attack from one of the many fundamentalist groups that had waged war on each other here for years. That was why we'd had to make sure the equipment was homemade, why all our weapons were of Russian manufacture, and our clothing of local origin. The traser might not be regular Islamic fundamentalist issue, but if anyone got close enough to me to notice my watch, then I really was in the shit, so what did it matter? In less than two hours from now, Zeralda would be dead, and the finger of blame would be pointing at Algeria's very own Islamic extremists, who were still making this the world's most dangerous vacation spot.

They didn't like anyone unless he was one of their own. We hoped that our attack would be blamed on the GIA, the Armed Islamic Group. They were probably the cruelest and most screwed-up bunch I'd ever come across. These guys had been trained and battle-hardened in places like Afghanistan, where they'd fought with the mujahadeen against the Russians. After that, they'd fought in Chechnya, and then in Bosnia and anywhere else they felt Muslims were getting fucked over. Now they were back in Algeria—and this time it was personal. They wanted an Islamic state with the Qur'an as its constitution, and they wanted it today. In the eyes of these people, even OBL (Osama Bin Laden) was a wimp. In 1994, in a grim precursor of attacks to come, GIA hijacked an Air France plane in Algiers, intending to crash it in the middle of Paris. It would have worked if it hadn't been for French antiterrorist forces attacking the plane as it refueled, killing them all.

Unlike me, all the equipment in my bergen was dry. I peeled off my dry bag, and immediately felt colder as the air started to attack my wet clothes. Too bad, there was nothing I could do about it. I checked chamber on my Russian Makharov pistol, pulling back the topslide just a fraction and making sure, for maybe the fourth and last time on this job, that the round was just exposed as it sat in the chamber ready to be fired. I glanced to the side to see the other two doing the same. I let the topslide return until it was home tight before applying safe with my thumb, then thrust the pistol into the internal holster that I'd tucked into the front of my pants.

Lotfi was in a good mood. "Your gun wet too?"

I nodded slowly at his joke and whispered back, as I shouldered my bergen, "Pistol, it's a pistol or weapon. Never, ever a gun."

He smiled back and didn't reply. He didn't

have to: he'd known it would get me riled.

I made my final check: my two mags were still correctly placed in the double mag holder on my left hip. They were facing up in the thick bands of black elastic that held them onto my belt, with the rounds facing forward. That way I would pull down on a mag to release it and they would be facing the right way to slam into the pistol.

Everyone was now poised to go, but Lotfi still checked—"Ready?"—like a tour guide at the airport with a group trip, making everyone show their passports for the tenth time. We all nodded, and he led the way up to the high ground. I fell in just behind him.